THE VACCINE

HASSAN RIAZ

Hill Taper Books

ISBN-13: 978-0-9907063-3-5

First Edition

Cover design by: Keith Klein

Hill Taper Books
Los Angeles, CA

Printed in the United States of America

For Nicole

PROLOGUE—4 WEEKS PRIOR

Don't blink, don't move, Angela Payton told herself. *The data are real.*

She was in Building Pasteur, on the north part of Riogenrix's campus, in a compact building, one of two lower-level biosafety labs directly opposite each other. Pasteur contained two separate wings in each laboratory. She was in the C wing, running biomarker data on the first group of Phase 2 clinical subjects. She was wearing a disposable Tyvek lab suit. There used to be three others like her, one lead biomarker research associate for each wing of Pasteur. Now there was one associate covering all four wings. She was the one person. It was 9:30 p.m. Her world was shifting.

She waited for her mind to mellow as she walked to the fume hoods against the far walls to look at the enzyme assay diagrams again. The diagrams consisted of two sheets of laminated papers. For the ninth time today—she'd been keeping count—she checked her work against the protocols she herself had helped develop.

One—add one hundred micrograms of the NB450 controls into the coated microwells.

Two—incubate for thirty minutes.

Three—wash the microwells.

1

Four—add one hundred micrograms of stop solution.

Five—read the absorbance results at four hundred nanometers with the microplate reader.

She returned to the buffer station and sat down in her rotating metal stool, the same one she'd been sitting in for most of the day. She was sure she was doing the work correctly. She had a master degree in microbiology and immunology and had been the lead biomarker research associate at Riogenrix for the past four years. She was experienced. Yet, she remained unsure. She attributed the uncertainty to two reasons. First, she was tired. Second, she was distracted. And third—no, there was no third reason, she told herself.

She reminded herself anybody would be tired running enzyme assays all day and into the evening within the restrictive confines of Building Pasteur. She'd been here for nine hours today and eighty-nine hours over the past seven. She'd been skipping lunch and packing a peanut butter sandwich in a cooler bag, not getting around to eating it until the biomedical waste team showed up at 10 p.m. and her day actually ended.

So reason number one: She was tired.

Which brought her to reason number two. The second reason for her uncertainty was because she was distracted. Actually, she was petrified. She was concerned about her fiancé, Gerald, who was home at their apartment. She was more than concerned. She was more worried today than she'd ever been in her life about anything. He'd been bedridden for seven days now, holed up in the main bedroom of their two-bedroom apartment in the Gaslamp District of downtown San Diego. She'd been trying to care for him and keep her distance from him at the same time. In the few hours every night when she was home, she slept on the couch in the main room, wearing one of the pan-sensitive, fitted FN99 respirator masks she'd taken from Building Lister, the storage depot. She slept with the mask on, or at least tried, because the past two nights, she'd awaken with her mask thrown onto the floor. The FN99s were difficult enough to wear while awake, borderline stifling, almost suffocating. Her body at sleep clearly thought the same. The first night she'd awaken without the mask, she'd panicked. She'd hunted around the floor, searching for it. She'd found it wedged against the coffee table, and had rushed to put it back on. Last night, she hadn't bothered to hunt for it. There was no point anymore.

Even with the FN99, she'd probably gotten it. Without the FN99, she almost certainly had.

This morning, he'd looked worse—if looking worse was even possible. He'd started coughing in fits again. His skin had changed, becoming grayer and cold. His skin had been so hot for eight days, she'd decided the fever and flushing were good signs because it meant he hadn't succumbed yet. She'd convinced herself that his body was fighting. Today, though, his skin had been different. It felt sweaty and cold, and she was sure that the change was a harbinger of bad things to come. When she tried to feed him, he seized, shaking in a different way than he did when the nighttime chills and sweats overtook him. The seizure hadn't been long, no more than ten or twelve seconds, but it was a new, ominous finding.

Yes, she was distracted. In fact, she was amazed she could focus on the enzyme assays at all.

She didn't try to lie to herself anymore. Even without a formal diagnosis, Gerald had it. They hadn't tried to get a formal diagnosis, because the diagnosis didn't make anyone better. Nothing worked against it. So reason number three was this: Since he had it, she had it too.

But she wasn't ready to accept reason number three yet. Yes, she had body aches and a headache, but she wasn't feverish or coughing. As she sat in the swivel stool, she tried to convince herself that she was simply sleep-deprived. If she was sick, she would know, because she passed the infrareds daily, and her temperatures were still within acceptable ranges. She told herself she wasn't sick. Nonetheless, she'd made sure to keep her distance from others at Riogenrix, which hadn't been hard, because there weren't too many of them left here. She kept to her lab while they kept to their corners.

Or so she tried to convince herself.

Even if something had come up on the thermals, she wasn't sure that Bill, the head of security, would've noticed anyway.

He was spread thin. They all were. And their numbers were dropping by the month, as the company succumbed to the financial pressures of remaining independent in an era of big boy consolidation.

Gerald had it and she had it as well.

Three days for the prodrome.

Seven days of symptoms.

Three days of symptom abatement, as if she'd actually turned the corner.

Then sudden multi-organ system failure from the inevitable cytokine storm.

The rest was obvious. Maybe she was deteriorating already.

Yes, she was sure the data were real. If she wasn't sure, she wouldn't be doing what she was about to. She got up from the stool and went to her workstation in the corner of the laboratory. A compact external hard drive was on the desk. The man in the white lab coat had given it to her twelve weeks ago. At the time, she'd never thought she would use it. She hadn't wanted the seventy-five thousand dollars he'd been offering. But now she could use the money. She connected the hard drive to her workstation. The computer hummed as it copied the Phase 2 data from the mainframe servers.

As the data copied, she left the lab. She walked across the empty hall to the break room, where there was a small staff refrigerator. She removed her insulated lunch bag and went outside. The night was windy but quiet. Bill would be home on a Sunday night, only monitoring campus if the alarms went off. But the alarms weren't going to go off. She had full access to the storage depot. As she walked across campus to Building Lister, she tried to talk herself out of what she was about to do. She was a person of science and the science was clear—there was no way to treat it once you had it. But she didn't convince herself, didn't turn around, didn't take the out she was providing for herself. She understood that despite being a person of science, she needed to feel as if she were doing something to save her fiancé. The Russians were offering experimental treatments. Of course, these treatments were tens of thousands of dollars and ninety-nine percent likely to be quackery and if she would've been asked a month ago about the treatments, she would've asserted without hesitation that these "cures" were intended to rip off the hopeful and unscientific. Now, though, circumstances were different.

When she reached Building Lister, she stood outside the secured door, waiting for the facial recognition camera above it to register her. When it did, the system beeped, prompting her to punch her access code into the keypad to the right of the handle. She entered her access code. The door to Lister clicked, and she opened it. Once inside, she walked across the small building to the temperature-controlled storage fridge. Inside of the fridge, there were eight prefilled single-dose syringes with needles. She took three syringes.

One was for her. In case it wasn't too late.

One was for her fiancé. In case it really, really wasn't too late.

And one was for the man in the white lab coat.

She placed the three syringes into her insulated lunch bag, pushing them under her uneaten sandwich.

Yes, the data were real.

She was sure of it.

PART 1

The astronauts came at night.

Sofia had seen them three nights in a row. They watched the house from the street while she watched them from her bedroom. She knew she needed to tell her daddy about them but he'd been coming home late. She didn't want to tell Mommy about them, though, because Mommy was already worried. She didn't want to stress Mommy more.

Sofia was at the window in her room on the second floor. Her house was on a corner and her window was angled towards the street. The night clock had a twelve and a two and a seven and an a.m. She knew right now was late for her, but she also knew 12:27 a.m. was the right time for the astronauts.

Sofia was eight years old. She used to like people. She used to be social. She didn't remember all of the details anymore, but she used to like talking to adults and kids, hearing their stories and jokes and telling them hers. She used to like playing hide and seek and tag and other games that needed people. She especially liked talking and playing with Uncle Richard, who always had a new story or joke for her and who had the best house for hide and seek. Uncle Richard used to have them over to his big house near the ocean all of the time. The details were hard to remember, but she knew they were like best friends. She knew because she had pictures of her and Uncle Richard on her tablet building pretend cities with blocks and making pretend food with Play-Doh and even looking at real bugs under a microscope.

She used to have neighbors, Mrs. Brennan and Baby Tommy. Mrs. Brennan had been her mommy's friend. She was almost Uncle Richard's age. Baby Tommy was her grandson, whom she babysat a lot. Mrs. Brennan used to live two houses down. Sofia used to visit Mrs. Brennan and Baby Tommy at their house and Mrs. Brennan and Baby Tommy used to visit Sofia in her house. Sofia had pictures of them on her tablet as well. Sofia liked how Mrs. Brennan used to sit on the floor with her and paint her nails. She liked how Baby Tommy followed her around the house. She didn't have a lot of photos of them, but she had enough to remember.

She didn't see Uncle Richard or Mrs. Brennan or Baby Tommy anymore. She knew Mrs. Brennan and Baby Tommy were never coming over again. They were dead. The virus had gotten them. But Uncle Richard was still alive. He was old, but he was alive, and she was waiting to see him again. He still called her, but she hadn't seen him in person in a long time. Her daddy had told her she would see him again when the virus went away. Mommy said Daddy wasn't telling the truth because the virus was never going away. She knew she would see Uncle Richard again, because Daddy was working on a shot so that people didn't get the virus anymore. She knew Daddy would find the shot.

She didn't remember all of the details anymore, but she liked people.

But she didn't like school. Her mommy taught her at the dining table every day. Sofia was shaky with her reading and spelling and completely lost on her math. Her mommy used to do flashcards with her but recently Mommy had been too tired to force Sofia to sit down at the kitchen table and rattle off the 4+4's and 4+5's and 4+6's and everything else while Mommy checked the answers, so recently Mommy just put out the workbooks and told Sofia to get to it. Sofia tried to get to it but most of the numbers didn't make sense. She didn't know why the numbers were supposed to be a certain way unless she counted them all off on her fingers and doing that was so exhausting. Mostly, she just pushed her pencil around the workbook, filled out boxes, and wrote down numbers knowing most of the time her mother wasn't even going to check the answers anyway.

Sofia knew the astronauts weren't really astronauts. She knew about real astronauts. Her daddy used to take her to the space museum back when he used to take her places. She just called them astronauts because of the way they looked and because it was less scary to call them astronauts. Astronauts went to the moon and outer space. These astronauts didn't go to outer space and they didn't have spaceships. She knew that the astronauts were wearing protection suits for the virus. They dressed how her daddy had dressed in the pictures he'd shown her of himself before he'd been a daddy, back when he had been in school, back when Uncle Richard had been his teacher. She knew that the astronauts had something to do with Daddy's work even though she knew they didn't work with Daddy. She also knew she needed to tell Daddy about them. She was waiting for him to get home, so she could tell him.

So she sat at the window and kept an eye on the astronauts. She did this until she couldn't keep her head up anymore. When she couldn't keep her head up anymore, she still tried to watch them by propping her head on her hands and her hands on the windowsill. She watched the astronauts until she couldn't keep her eyes open at all. Sleep overtook her, just like it always did for any eight-year-old. She fell asleep with her head on her folded arms and her arms on the windowsill while the astronauts watched the house from outside.

Dr. Harrison Boyd couldn't enjoy today the way he'd been envisioning. It was early May in San Diego. The winter had been rainy and cold, but the spring was blue skies and puffy clouds, at least for now. He lived in Mira Mesa, an inland community of San Diego, ten miles from the coast. Right now, he was headed to Riogenrix's small campus in Poway, an unincorporated part of the county ten miles further east. He was driving an older, blue Honda Accord, the same one he'd bought when he'd found out Jasmine had been pregnant with Sofia. He was driving down an open Sorrento Valley Boulevard. There was no traffic. There never was anymore and hadn't been for five years.

He thought about Sofia as he drove. He was worried about her. He knew that Jasmine had been slipping away from him for some time but he hadn't recognized until today that the same was happening with his daughter. When he'd checked in on Sofia this morning, he'd found her asleep at the bedroom window. He touched her shoulder to wake her up, and when she didn't wake up, he put an arm under her legs and another around her back, and lifted her out of the chair and into her bed. She stirred as he pulled the covers over her.

"Be safe, Daddy."

"I always am, baby girl. Why were you at the window?"

"Waiting for you, Daddy. I need to talk about astronauts."

She'd fallen back asleep as he'd tucked the blanket under her chin. He figured that she'd been dreaming—or at least thinking—about the past. He'd taken her to NASA's Jet Propulsion Laboratory in Pasadena once and she'd loved the rovers and space suits and had talked about the moon for months. He'd never been able to take her back. He figured she'd been dreaming—like all of them—about better times.

When he arrived on campus, he got out of his car to unlock the front security gate. For the past week, he'd been getting out of the vehicle to unlock it, because for the past week they'd had no security team. Bill Greenblatt had died from nMAQ25. He had gotten the infection from a supermarket in El Cajon. Or at least that's what the Department of Health had told Selene, his chief administrator. His death had been quick—too quick, in his opinion, even for the novel menglavirus strain 25. His demise had occurred over a couple of days instead of a couple of weeks. The quick deterioration had made Harrison wonder if Bill had had other medical conditions that had hastened his worsening. But Department of Health had been clear in assigning Bill's death to menglavirus only.

9

Bill was the second Riogenrix death caused by nMAQ25 over the past few weeks. Angela, their lead biomarker research associate, had died one week before Bill, although her demise had been more typical, occurring over several days. Harrison had felt pain with both of their losses—it still stung. Both had been long-term contributors and each had been crucial to the success that Riogenrix was about to achieve. Riogenrix was a small vaccine developer. Their vaccine work was built on the backs of everyone on campus, no matter their role.

As he unlocked the gate, he reminded himself that he needed to address the issue of security with Selene. He eyed the cameras above the gate. He wasn't sure if Selene was watching him, but figured she wasn't. She had too much to do already—they all did. Harrison saw the empty gate as his failing, not Selene's. She'd been telling him for days to sit in on the interviews for a new head of security, but he'd been too busy with V-202 to deal with the daily grind of administration. He promised himself that after today's approval to begin Phase 3 trials, he would focus more on the nuts and bolts of running a company. He would try to be less tunnel-visioned and more focused on the company as a whole. He got back into the Honda, drove through the gate, and got back out of his car to close the gate again. Finally, he returned to his car to drive onto campus.

As he drove onto campus, he allowed his thoughts to turn towards V-202 in full, like they always did. He parked near Selene's Wrangler, outside of Building Jenner. Campus's geographical footprint was intentionally compact. Harrison hadn't had a hand in designing the campus but considered it perfectly designed anyway. Dr. Richard Hahn, his mentor and partner and the founder of Riogenrix, had designed the campus, using his lifelong experience in the vaccine industry to decide what Riogenrix did and didn't need. The campus was set three miles away from the residential ranches of Poway with the easternmost part of campus abutting the low-rise Iron Mountain. Excluding the vacant security hut, campus contained eight buildings, all together no more than 15,000 square-feet set close together on two acres.

Despite his worries about Sofia and Jasmine, Harrison was excited about the future. He was forty-three years old. He'd been at Riogenrix for ten years and working on V-202 for five. He understood the vast implications of his work. In the afternoon, he had a phone call scheduled with the FDA to advance Riogenrix's clinical trials to Phase 3. When the FDA had approved Riogenrix's Phase 2 studies three months ago, they'd done so the same way they'd done for one hundred and twenty-four other companies and institutions. They'd been shooting in the dark and throwing stuff against the wall. The FDA hadn't really expected Riogenrix to come up with a working vaccine to stop the spread of nMAQ25. And why should they have? Richard, the face of Riogenrix, was no longer active in Riogenrix's daily operations and research. The much bigger players, who had hundreds and thousands of researchers, had all come up empty, one after the other, week after week, none of them getting far enough into Phase 2 to legitimately advance into Phase 3. The only firm currently in Phase 3 studies anywhere in the world was CanFlo, a Chinese firm that represented China's Academy of Military Medical Sciences' Institute of Biotechnology. They'd entered Phase 3 studies eight weeks ago, but had yet to release data for peer review. The global medical community generally conceded that CanFlo's vaccine wasn't very effective at all. CanFlo was more about global posturing than medicine. Out of hundreds of firms spread across the world, Harrison knew Riogenrix was the only one who'd developed a viable vaccine.

Harrison expected the FDA to grant accelerated vaccine emergency authorization in the immediate future for V-202. First, the FDA would approve Phase 3 trials with a big funding push from the National Institutes of Health to administer the vaccine to thirty thousand test subjects. The funding was going to be important. For now, the licensing revenues from Riogenrix's BOOSTers were sustaining their operations but it wouldn't be enough to keep research and development going through Phase 3. Furthermore, they were burning through the three smaller NIH grants they'd received for their work on the nMAQ25 vaccine. Once the FDA confirmed the vaccine worked in the Phase 3 trials—and they *would* confirm because it *did* work—the FDA could begin immediate inoculations within the US and coordinate with other countries throughout the world to do the same, similar to what the FDA had done with Ebola almost twenty years ago. Emergency use protocol would be right around the corner, maybe only months away, not only for the US, but for the entire world.

Riogenrix was not only going to be the first firm to successfully develop a vaccine for nMAQ25 but it was also going to be the first firm to build any vaccine on mRNA technology. When Harrison explained his work to non-scientists—which admittedly, had never been often and nowadays was pretty much never—he started with DNA. People knew DNA as the blueprint for the body. If the DNA was the body's blueprint, the mRNA was the actual lumber used for building. If the blueprint required a stud wall in the kitchen, mRNA was the actual two-by-four cut to specification. Developing vaccines with mRNA yielded significant benefits over other vaccine development technologies—or at least it was supposed to. mRNA was supposed to be faster, more scalable, and less expensive to develop.

Harrison had first been exposed to mRNA vaccine technology during his third year of medical school. He'd been a medical student at Johns Hopkins University in Baltimore, Maryland, when Dr. Richard Hahn—then at the Salk Institute here in San Diego —had opened applications to medical students for rotations through his lab. Harrison had been following Dr. Richard Hahn's career from a distance, so when the opportunity to apply for a six-week rotation popped up, he jumped on it. A few months later, he'd followed up the six-week rotation with a full research year. If he'd had any uncertainty before the research year that he wanted to carve out a career in mRNA vaccine research, he'd had none afterwards.

Of course, mRNA hadn't actually been easy. It hadn't been faster or more scalable. Every day and every project had been a struggle, slow moving and prone to stops. Even so, today would be the culmination of years of methodical work at Riogenrix.

The emergency authorization was going to come right when he needed it most, not just professionally, but personally. On a daily basis, Harrison had three different internal alarms signaling him to leave campus and get home. The first was at 8:00 p.m. This was the time when Riogenrix's office cleaning crew arrived on campus. The cleaning crew was made up of two people, a husband and wife team with whom Riogenrix had contracted since its earliest days. The husband and wife donned basic protective gear and cleaned the administrative offices: emptying wastebaskets, sweeping floors, and disinfecting door handles. They came every evening, Monday through Friday. But they didn't go into the labs.

The second internal alarm was at 10:00 p.m. By 10:00, the husband and wife team had left campus and the second contracted cleaning crew arrived. The second cleaning crew was not a husband and wife team. It was a specialized firm that dealt with biomedical and laboratory waste, a large and established company that had contracts with hospitals, research labs, and biotechnology companies. They kept records of waste removed, wore basic biosafety suits, and helped keep the labs running. They came every evening, including Saturday and Sunday, because for Harrison, research never had a day off.

The third internal alarm was at midnight. At midnight, the lights and air ventilation systems shifted over from the electrical grid to Riogenrix's universal power supply. The shift was done every day of the week, every week of the year. The purpose of the switch was to make sure the universal power supply was functional. If power from the grid failed—and it'd been failing with more regularity every month the nMAQ25 crisis progressed—the universal power supply served as a backup battery. The universal power supply test lasted exactly six minutes. By 12:07 a.m., campus was back on the grid.

When the husband and wife cleaning team showed up, Harrison knew it was 8:00 p.m. He needed to leave campus if he wanted to get home at 8:30. If he got home at 8:30, Jasmine and Sofia were awake. He could read or play a game with Sofia and try to spend time with Jasmine. He could eat the dinner that Jasmine made and she herself had just eaten. If he left campus when the husband and wife team showed up, he was doing okay for his family. If he left when the biomedical waste team showed up, he got home at 10:30 p.m. He would've missed dinner already, but Sofia would still be awake—barely, but she'd be awake. He could give her a kiss, tell her a story, be present in her life that day. At least he showed up. But he'd been leaving Riogenrix when the universal power supply switched on. He hadn't been participating or even just showing up.

Despite all of his struggles trying to participate in Sofia's daily life, the sacrifices he'd made would be worth it. Vaccine development, especially as a small firm in competition with the big guys, was a commitment to technique, trial and error, and lifelong learning. Deep down, he knew that if Sofia was a newborn in his arms again, he would do the exact same thing he'd already done. He would devote himself to Riogenrix all over again in order to achieve the biggest vaccine breakthrough in decades —or maybe even ever. Riogenrix's BOOSTers had been a major contribution to vaccine technology, but they'd been based on Richard's work. V-202, though, was his baby.

Next year, once the world was vaccinated under emergency use protocol, he would be able to take Sofia to the park and movies again. He would take her back to the Jet Propulsion Laboratory. He would have a real existence to spend with her, not just one confined to their house. The world was going to need seven billion doses of V-202, but they would get them, and all the lives placed on pause would resume.

He walked the short distance to the entrance of Building Jenner, the administrative building. He waited for the facial recognition cameras—equipped to recognize persons with masks on —above the double doors to register him. He heard the click, and entered his access code into the keypad. After today's conference call with the FDA, he planned to scale back his time on campus in order to spend more time with his family. He would leave no later than when the husband and wife cleaning team showed up. He would be a better husband and father. He knew there were no clinical trials in family life. After today's Phase 3 approval, he would rededicate himself to Jasmine and Sofia.

It was noon and Jasmine was still coaxing Sofia through the same lessons of the past two weeks. Sofia had woken up later than usual. They'd been at it for only an hour and getting nowhere. Even with the ten-minute break Jasmine had just given her, Sofia wasn't focusing. She wasn't trying. She wasn't learning. Jasmine was trying, though. She was teaching the best she could in a situation that wasn't the best it could be. They sat on opposite sides of the dining table. Sofia had her second-grade lesson book open in front of her, one sharpened pencil resting on the open page and one in her hand, and a short stack of wide ruled paper. Today was math. Every day was math, but today was only math. Jasmine had needed a break from the reading that wasn't happening and the phonetics that Sofia refused to grasp. Sofia had her head on the table and pencil in her hand. She was doodling numbers but wasn't trying to do more than guess at the answers. For Sofia, 14 + 11 was 88.

"Do you want to try again, honey?" Jasmine said, trying to keep her voice level.

Sofia kept her head on the table but wrote another '8' so now 14 + 11 was 888.

Jasmine wondered if there even was a point. Was Sofia ever going to need to know anything other than how to wash her hands, put on a mask, and watch a tablet? If there was a point, she couldn't find it, at least not in the current situation in which they found themselves. Jasmine was trying, and she was tired of trying. She was tired of preparing for the day when all of her work with Sofia was supposed to mean something, when every day Jasmine was beginning to understand it wasn't going to mean anything at all. Sofia was never going to learn a damn thing in this house and it didn't matter anyway because Sofia would never need to do anything in life other than watch videos on her tablet. Sofia knew how to plop and watch. In this way, Jasmine had done well.

"Please try," Jasmine said.

Sofia started to draw yet another '8'. 14 + 11 was on its way to being eight thousand 8888.

Just like Sofia was never going to learn her math, Jasmine was never going back to work. She'd barely worked anyway, only eighteen months before she'd gotten pregnant and left the small firm doing customs and trade law for the San Diego Port. She'd been happy working and happy when she'd gotten pregnant and thought that she would get back to work no later than two years after Sofia was born. She'd never returned to work. In so many ways, motherhood about feeling anxious all of the time. It was duty and worry and occasional reward. Even now, almost ten years removed from her first and only gig as an attorney-at-law, she felt guilty about leaving Sofia to return back to work, even though she hadn't left her yet, because there was no work to which to go back.

At times, when she imagined going back, she tried to convince herself she wasn't leaving Sofia but resuming a career. She told herself she should have no guilt. She tried hard to believe what she told herself. No, she wasn't leaving Sofia, virus or not. She was her mother and she was accessible any time. If Sofia fell down and split her lip, she was a phone call away. She would make sure she took her daughter to the pediatrician and didn't rely on the nanny or Harrison to take her. Even at work, she would be Sofia's mother. So, no, she hadn't been wanting to leave Sofia. She'd been wanting to resume a career. A worthwhile career that'd helped keep the country churning. A career that she'd genuinely enjoyed before she'd left, one in which she'd excelled in making things happen, keeping the ports moving, keeping the firm's clients happy. She told herself that she should never feel guilty because guilt was for people who committed crimes. Resuming her career wasn't a crime. There was nothing criminal about an attorney going back to work. Nothing.

She'd given up trying to convince herself a long time ago, sometime around the second year of menglavirus. Yes, she felt guilty. There was no logic to her guilt, but guilt was a feeling, and she felt guilty.

Now five years into menglavirus, she'd doubled down on her guilt. She had a new source of unease. She was failing Sofia. She was Sofia's everything now—her mother and playmate and teacher. She'd found it impossible to be adept at all of them at once. She felt as if she was competent at none of them, because nowadays, in order to be a mother, she needed to be more than just a nourisher and disciplinarian. She needed to teach Sofia her letters and numbers and how to read and how to write and how to do math and then test her reading comprehension and real-world problem solving.

If Sofia's workbook wanted to be relevant, it needed to ask questions like, "If there are 29 infected people and 6 of them die and 4 of them recover, how many actively infected people do you have left?"

Trick question. The answer was 23, because no one ever recovered from menglavirus.

Jasmine felt herself going out of her mind more every day. Her marriage with Harrison only worsened her mental state. When she'd been a kid, she'd played lacrosse. Her parents had enrolled her. She hadn't been good at it, but she'd played because she'd been on the team. She hadn't enjoyed lacrosse much but the other girls on her team had. They were good, quick with hands and feet, strong throwers and fast runners. No thanks to her, the team got to the playoffs, and then, no thanks to her, the team won the championship. She didn't play much, only the required participation minutes. Yet she got a trophy just like everyone else on the team. She'd participated, so she'd won as well.

She just wanted Harrison to participate. If Harrison simply showed up, he would get a trophy. She could hold onto him. He could be on the team. He just needed to put in the minimum.

Thirty-two-minute games.

Each player gets twelve minutes whether she wants them or not, whether she's contributing to the team's wins or not.

Harrison wasn't putting in the minimum.

Not even twelve minutes.

Jasmine sighed. She'd had enough. "Let's go out," she said to Sofia. Her daughter watched her with her head still on the table, looking at her the same way she looked at Harrison when he told her a knock-knock joke. Sofia was waiting for the punchline.

Knock-knock.

Who's there?

Let's go out.

Let's go out where?

Let's go more out of our minds.

"Let's go out," Jasmine said again, and this time she stood up. Sofia watched her and stayed in her seat with the mismarked second grade math notebook in front of her. Jasmine added, "Let's go outside."

"Outside where?"

"Let's go to the park."

Now Sofia paid attention. She stopped rolling the pencil and picked it up and held the eraser to her chin, like she usually did when she was thinking and which she hadn't done at all this afternoon. "What do you mean?" Sofia said.

"Let's go to the park."

"The park isn't open."

"It isn't closed either. You can't close a park. A park doesn't have doors."

"It's open?"

"Yes."

"Are you sure?"

"Yes."

"If it's open, why haven't we been going?"

"We couldn't go."

"Because of the virus?"

"Yes."

"What about the virus now?"

"The virus isn't in the park."

"It isn't in the park?" Sofia said, and Jasmine heard the suspicious incredulity in her daughter's voice. Jasmine got the sense that Sofia observed her as much as she observed Sofia. Her daughter didn't believe her, of course, and Jasmine didn't believe herself. The virus was everywhere. And there was no recovering from the virus, no tincture of time, to use one of Harrison's phrases.

"No," Jasmine said.

"We don't have to wear our masks?"

Jasmine was about to tell her they didn't. For a second, just a second, she thought about foregoing the masks, because she wanted to show Sofia, really show her, they were going to live life again. Today was the start. But the moment was fleeting. She couldn't imagine walking out of the house without their fitted masks.

"Yes, we have to wear our masks."

"The ones Daddy brought us?"

"Yes, the ones Daddy brought us."

"Okay, I'll go with you," Sofia said, and Jasmine could see Sofia evaluating her. "If you promise it's safe."

"Let's go," Jasmine said again, one last time.

Sofia put her pencil in the middle of the workbook and closed the workbook.

"Okay, Mommy," Sofia said, and stood up.

Today, Jasmine thought, as she watched her daughter, *is the start of a real life.*

The glass could either be half-full or half-empty.

The neighborhood was half empty.

So was her glass.

Thelma McGraw was about to pour herself another glass of gin when she saw the woman and girl. They were in the park across from her house. The mother was leading the daughter to the closed playground. Thelma was sitting in her recliner, working on her third gin and tonic and ready for her fourth. She forgot about the gin for now and got up and went to the window. She never saw anyone at the park anymore, except maybe a couple of teenagers every few weeks, but even teenagers knew to stay indoors. The park was always empty. Not even half-empty; empty-empty. But now she saw the mother and daughter outside. She thought about calling the police, utilizing the 211 number the state had set up to alert the local county sheriff department that people were breaking with ordinances. But she didn't, and instead she watched them. She'd been a sheriff's deputy back before menglavirus, and she knew law enforcement these days no longer provided services for the people. She couldn't blame them, at least not too much. Not anymore. Money had dried up in the county and municipalities long ago.

She relaxed as she watched them, mesmerized. The daughter was tentatively climbing the jungle gym while the mother stood at the bottom of the spiral slide. There was something beautiful in watching the mother and daughter. She felt optimistic as she watched them. She had fleeting hope, happiness even, because the mother and daughter were young and they had their lives in front of them. They lived with the possibility that they wouldn't die a sterile, undifferentiated death in their home while they waited for life to start.

They had a chance.

No, she wasn't going to call 211. Not on these two.

She watched them and thought of her own daughter and felt equal parts sadness and happiness—sad for her and her own daughter, happy for the mother and the daughter in the park.

As she watched the mother and the daughter, Thelma was glad that she could focus on something other than waiting for her own daughter to call—or rather, not to call. Her entire week was focused on waiting for Naomi to call but never getting what she wanted. Naomi had moved to Las Vegas. Thelma knew the desert wasn't the right place for her. The right place for Naomi was San Diego, close to her. They were the only family they had.

Thelma was fifty-one years old but her body was older. She'd been isolated in her house for the better part of five years. She didn't exercise except for a getting on the stationary bike she kept in Naomi's room—or the room that used to be Naomi's—for fifteen or twenty minutes at a time, although over the past few weeks, she'd stopped the exercising as well. She couldn't even hack the stationary bike anymore. After a few minutes, she became lightheaded. Her life was catching up to her. She knew the fatigue she'd been feeling for the past several days had nothing to do with being cooped up in her house for the past five years. Her legs were swelling more. Her body was changing. It'd been changing ever since the furlough from the department had become a permanent layoff. She'd had problems with alcohol before the layoff but they'd been tame compared to what they were now. Her own mother had died early at the age of forty-nine from alcoholic cardiomyopathy—a weakened, enlarged heart. She'd outlived her mother but knew that her gin-soaked genes were catching up to her. She knew her body was failing and she was headed to where her own mother, another gin aficionado, had gone: a premature grave.

She knew she should see a doctor. But she'd been home for so long now, keeping menglavirus beyond her four walls, she didn't know how she would even try to get to one. She hadn't left the house at all in one thousand four hundred and seven days. She'd kept track. She had an old-fashioned chalkboard in her kitchen and every day since the furlough had started, she'd written two set of numbers on the board. The first was the date and the second was the number of days passed. She'd been angry when the number of days passed had hit one hundred and then two hundred and then three hundred and a full year at three hundred and sixty-five.

Then her anger turned into obsession.

Obsessed with staying shut in and passing her time the way she wanted to pass her time, which was with a glass of gin always at her side.

She had no reason to leave.

One thousand four hundred and seventy-plus days and not counting anymore.

She and Naomi had never gotten along. When menglavirus had choked San Diego, it'd been a good reason for Naomi to go.

Fewer people, Naomi had said.

Hotter summers, Naomi had said.

Less crime, Naomi had said.

Farther away from you, Naomi hadn't said. She hadn't needed to say it. They'd both known. Naomi had been only been eighteen when she'd left.

In the case of Naomi, distance hadn't made the heart grow fonder. It hadn't made her more forgiving.

Thelma had been married a lot. She knew the marriages had a lot to do with the strain in her relationship with Naomi. Meanwhile, her work caused the rest of the tension. When Thelma had been younger, she'd needed men, but they'd never needed her as much as they'd said they had, because they'd always found other women. Husband one through husband three. All of them. Maybe the problem had been she'd married men like herself, men who were hardnosed, unyielding, and liked to drink.

Whatever the reasons had been, she didn't have to think about them anymore.

But she still thought about Naomi.

She still called her every Tuesday night at 8:05 p.m. Whenever her chalkboard said 'Tuesday' and her clock above the television said 8:05, she called her daughter. She chose Tuesday because it seemed like the right day to reconnect. Tuesday wasn't Monday. She wouldn't appear so eager. It was past the weekend, so Thelma wouldn't seem intrusive. Tuesday was early enough in the week to give Naomi time to sit down and chat with her for five minutes—or at least early enough in the week for Naomi to decide to call her back before another seven days passed.

She'd been making the phone calls for two years now.

For two years, Naomi hadn't answered or responded to Thelma's voicemails.

Today was Monday.

She was waiting for Tuesday.

One more day.

As she watched the mother and the daughter at the park, she felt oddly optimistic. She had a feeling this was the week Naomi would call her back or maybe even pick up the phone in the first place.

As she and Sofia walked back to the house, Jasmine felt relief. The anxiety faded and she felt relief.

The park was two blocks away, small and local, intended for the immediate neighborhood. It had a jungle gym with a slide, a pair of swings, and a small knoll of grass. Flimsy caution tape was wrapped around the perimeter. When they'd arrived, they'd stood on the sidewalk, outside the tape. Sofia had looked up at her, waiting for Jasmine's final approval. Jasmine nodded, and Sofia walked under the caution tape, and jogged to the jungle gym. Jasmine ducked under the tape as well. She stood just inside and watched her daughter. She watched even though she felt antsy and wrong and knew they should leave the park before something bad—really bad—happened to them, but found she couldn't bring herself to leave, because for the first time in months she felt more than just *mommy, mommy, mommy*. So they stayed. She stood just inside the tape and watched her daughter. She'd felt anxiety every minute, but they'd stayed.

Now that they'd left the park, she felt relief. They were fine. Sofia had done well. Jasmine realized she could do the park every day. Seeing Sofia as a kid again, physically active and in her element, had been uplifting. She'd made the right decision in getting Sofia out of the house. They'd had their filtering FN99 masks. They would be okay.

But as she and Sofia walked the second of two blocks back to the house, Jasmine's anxiety crept back in. She tried to ignore it but couldn't. In fact, she felt something more than anxiety.

She felt dread, the anticipation of something bad about to happen, if it hadn't already. She didn't know if the anxiety was her own conditioning or something more ominous. Either way, she felt as if somebody had been to their house while they'd been away. She looked down Brayton St., and saw the same emptiness, the same rundown houses, the same few cars in driveways. She didn't see anything different.

But the neighborhood felt different.

She didn't know exactly why she felt trepidation other than her gut. Harrison always talked about gut—or instinct, as he called it—as an amalgamation of the entirety of a person's experiences. Her gut was telling her that there was something wrong on the block. There was something wrong at the house.

As they approached the driveway, Sofia stayed in front of her by a step. Jasmine reached out and placed her hand on Sofia's shoulder to slow her down. Sofia didn't turn or stop. She was energized, rejuvenated by their first outing to a place other than a rations facility for years. Sofia's one step ahead became two and then three as they turned into their driveway. When Sofia ran for the front door, Jasmine felt panicky.

"Stop!"

Sofia stopped and turned around. "Mommy?"

Jasmine had shouted. She found that she'd alarmed not only Sofia but herself in doing so.

"Mommy?" Sofia said again.

"Wait for me, baby."

Jasmine tried to regain calm in her voice and stride and purposefully slowed down her walk. Sofia did wait, just at the edge of the walkway leading to the entrance of the two-story house. Jasmine put her hand on her shoulder. "I just wanted to be a team, honey."

Sofia nodded, but she didn't walk forward any additional steps. Now Sofia hung back, like she had when they'd first left the house and headed to the park. Jasmine took the lead again and again Sofia was left to follow.

When Jasmine turned the corner of the walkway towards the

front entrance, she saw the envelope on the entry door. She saw the plain white face without any writing on it, no return address or stamp. The envelope was taped to the door with yellow duct tape.

The trepidation that had started when she'd gotten closer to her house now became legitimate fear and she didn't know why because it was just an envelope.

Except, she did know.

It was an envelope on her door. Taped to her door. Not in the mailbox. Which meant that someone had placed it there. But they hadn't had visitors in years.

Jasmine stopped walking up the entryway. She had a notion that she should turn and hold Sofia's hand and they should run and they should not go back into the house. This was her gut reaction.

Except she didn't know why her gut was telling her this. She glanced around the outside of the house again and then the street. There was no one there—no one here. She took a few steps backwards towards the driveway so that she could see up and down the street as well but again saw no one and nothing out of place. Yet, she felt anxiety. Something was wrong.

"What's wrong, Mommy?"

"Nothing, dear."

Sofia was standing back from the door but now she too was looking at the plain white envelope affixed to it. "We have mail, Mommy."

"Don't touch it." Jasmine had almost shouted again. Sofia stepped further back from the door. Jasmine checked her cell phone. They had video cameras along the front corners of the house and in the doorbell. She pulled up the camera feeds. They'd left an hour ago to the park. She scrolled back through the hour and watched the videos.

It didn't take long for her to find the person who'd attached the envelope to their door. Ten minutes after they'd left, a man in a long, white lab coat walked into the frame from camera 02 from the south portion of the house. She watched him stop at the wildflowers at the front of the yard, snap one off with his fingers, and palm it. She watched him ascend the paved driveway and walk past where she and Sofia were standing now and plant himself at the beige front door. On the doorbell camera, she saw him place the letter against the door. He had something cylindrical in his other hand but Jasmine couldn't distinguish it. Then he turned and left, retracing his steps back down the driveway and past camera 02 and out of view.

Jasmine couldn't pinpoint exactly what about the man felt threatening, but she felt threatened. She felt invaded. He'd come to her house. He could've been anything, an auto insurance broker or a solicitor for a charity, but she knew that he wasn't. He'd been wearing a white coat, as if he'd come from a hospital. Yet the white lab coat wasn't scary in and of itself. It was odd, but not scary.

"Are we going in, Mommy?"

"Wait."

"What are you watching?"

"The cameras."

"Can I see?"

"Not now."

"Why not?"

Jasmine felt the goodwill that the park had brought to their relationship fading. "Not yet."

"Why not? Can I see the video? Who left the letter?"

Jasmine, as she'd been doing more and more, gave in. The easiest path of parenting was that of least resistance. It was the most defeated of paths and she felt defeated again. She wanted Sofia to stop bugging her, be calm for a minute. She wondered if showing Sofia the video would scare her, but decided she was past that consideration. Plus, the cameras only showed a man in a white lab coat. He wasn't doing anything that should alarm an eight-year-old. She showed Sofia the camera feeds. Sofia watched, and tilted her head in study. After only a couple of seconds of watching the video, Sofia verbalized what Jasmine had found threatening about the man but hadn't been able to pinpoint herself.

"The man isn't wearing a mask, Mommy."

No, he wasn't.

Harrison was in the conference room of Building Jenner. He was on the conference call with the FDA, trying to make sense of not only what the FDA was stating directly, but the implications of what they weren't stating, which was that Riogenrix as an ongoing independent vaccine development company was dead.

"The data are equivocal. We need clarity before we can authorize Phase 3 trials," said the voice on the phone.

Equivocal? Clarity? He could understand the FDA wanted more clarity but the data weren't equivocal. The results were right and the analyses had been done correctly. There already was complete clarity.

"As far as I am aware, we are the only group anywhere in the private or public spheres to obtain results consistent with active immunity," Harrison said. "We are the only research group or company to get the same results in vivo and in vitro."

In addition to the FDA, the NIH and the Joint Congressional Committee on nMAQ25 Emerging Therapeutics were also on the call. Dr. Yuri Golosh was representing the FDA, Dr. Mostafa Abdou was representing the NIH, and Senator Scott Spaulding was representing Congress. For Harrison, having Congress on what should've been simply an FDA phone call was a first. Prior meetings with the FDA had strictly been with the FDA. They'd been, relatively speaking, droll affairs, focused on the minutiae of vaccinology and clinical trial results. Although the NIH had consulted on vaccine trials, they'd never been directly involved in therapeutic approval processes, at least not as far as Harrison knew. For sure, Congress never had. And it was Congress—Senator Scott Spaulding—who seemed to be throwing up the most resistance to V-202.

Prior meetings with the FDA also had been more uplifting

than today's. Harrison had come into the meeting with un-muted excitement about Riogenrix's role in ending the mengla-virus era, but with each minute of the conference call that passed, he was becoming unusually discouraged. He wasn't a person who became discouraged. He appreciated the slow march of progress when it came to medicine. However, the phone call so far had been full of roadblocks. Today's meeting had started off questionably and continued to deteriorate.

"There are concerns about the study's scale," Dr. Golosh said. "To be sure, therapeutic application A5650—or V-202 as it is in-ternally called by your company—has shown interesting but far from definitive results. Your studies have been small. The FDA has difficulty drawing the same conclusions from the submitted data that you do. Even if we placed the equivocalness of the re-sults aside, the FDA has real concerns about Riogenrix's ability to shepherd the results from the opening gate to the finish line."

"I don't pretend that Riogenrix has the necessary scale to manufacture seven billion doses," Harrison said, "but our appli-cation was clear in that we aimed to use the Salk Doctrine going forward into Phase 3 and beyond. We see—" He paused. He'd always spoken just like everyone else in medicine, saying 'we' and 'us' all the time, but now he wanted to be clear that V-202 was personal. It'd taken a dedicated staff who'd given all of their effort all the time to get V-202 off of the ground, and he owed it to everyone in the company to fight for the vaccine. Of course, he owed it to himself as well. "*I* see V-202 through the use of the Salk Doctrine as our pathway forward within our global society. I think strongly that V-202 is the solution for novel menglavirus we all have been working towards for five years."

"We're aware of the Salk Doctrine protocol for which you've petitioned and we've taken into account the limitations of your application even with this doctrine," Dr. Golosh said. "And again, we're not enamored with the results. The FDA has limited re-sources—even now—and we need to back the most probable winners."

"It's not a horse race," Harrison said.

There was silence and then Senator Spaulding came over the line.

"Listen, Dr. Boyd," the senator said, "let me be frank with you —the American government doesn't want to fuck this up. Ultimately, when we get a vaccine approved, we're going to deliver it to three hundred and sixty million Americans. We don't want the cure to be worse than the disease. We need to be sure. You don't have a track record. You're a tough bet to make."

Harrison was sure about V-202, but unsure about everything else, wondering why the FDA worked this way these days, dominated by political committees and interferences. He wondered if this had always been how the FDA operated. He wondered how Richard had survived so long in research when there were bureaucratic impediments to good work. Within the FDA, the science always had a political bent, but it'd always been procedural rather than evidence-based. Companies with closer relations to the FDA got approvals for their therapeutics more quickly, but even so, the smaller firms with real results eventually got their seat at the table. The process might be slower, but there was always a finish line.

Now the FDA was telling him there wasn't going to be a finish line at all.

"What do you want me to do with V-202?" Harrison said.

"You can continue working on it, if you wish," Dr. Golosh said. "Get better results and come back to us. Resubmit a new application. You can continue your work on V-202. But if I were you, I would look elsewhere. Messenger RNA isn't promising. It's never been promising outside of the booster space. Try a different technique and let mRNA die the death it has been wanting to die for a decade."

When he'd woken up this morning, Harrison had never believed that the FDA would tell him to abandon V-202, let alone the entire body of work around which Riogenrix had been built. He tried to collect himself. He noticed Dr. Abdou from the NIH was being quiet. Harrison could tell Dr. Abdou was restraining himself, as if he had a contrary opinion. Mostafa Abdou, MD, was a veteran of the NIH. Richard and Dr. Abdou were longstanding colleagues. In fact, Dr. Abdou had been instrumental in securing NIH funding for V-202's development. Harrison didn't understand his reticence now.

"mRNA has shown incredible promise," Harrison said.

"We can't save the American people on promise," Dr. Golosh said. "We allowed mRNA technology for a proposed menglavirus vaccine because we were allowing everything. We are still allowing everything. Menglavirus is bad, and has been bad, and we appreciate your efforts, but we are going to look elsewhere for Phase 3 trials."

"What are your thoughts, Dr. Abdou?" Harrison said, making a last-ditch plea for reason. Surely, Dr. Abdou didn't share the unfounded, ridiculous opinions of the FDA.

There was quiet on the conference call. Dr. Abdou cleared his throat and said, "There's potential here, Harrison, but the FDA is looking for wide scale deployment. The NIH won't be funding any more mRNA research with Riogenrix. But this does not preclude you from working on your own. If you have any significant breakthroughs, we can always talk again."

Harrison was stunned. There was no science in the NIH either. He didn't know what else to say but he also didn't want to end the call. He hoped he could convince the FDA to give Riogenrix the genuine chance they deserved. The bottom line on V-202 was the data were real and the vaccine worked and tens and hundreds of millions of lives could be saved in a matter of months.

"How about this?" the senator said. "Maybe once we get a real vaccine into Phase 3 trials, we can come back to you for your booster things. I'm sure we'll come back to you to license that."

Real vaccine.

And with that, the conference call was effectively over. The FDA signed off and the senator signed off and after a moment of lingering, the NIH signed off.

He sat, shocked, at the empty conference table for longer than he should have. He still had the phone receiver in his hand

and finally he hung it up. He knew he needed to update Selene but couldn't get past his shock. She, like he, had been expecting good news—anyone who'd seen the data on V-202 would. He debated staying in the conference room for the rest of the afternoon to put his thoughts together. Finally, he determined he could delay no more. As the de facto head of the company, he needed to be honest with her. He left the conference room and walked slowly to Selene's office down the hall. She was at her desk. Behind her was a large monitor showing rotating feeds from the campus's security cameras. She was focused on the computer while writing notes on a legal pad.

"Bad news," he said, standing just inside her door but not stepping all of the way into her office. He'd always had a formal relationship with her. "We don't have the results the FDA needs for us to move forward with V-202." He tried to sound cheerful and optimistic but knew he looked and sounded like neither. "We'll keep trying on Phase 2 for now but we may have to look to alternatives."

She put down her pen. "The FDA denied V-202?"

"Yes."

"It has to be a mistake, Harrison."

"It is. But we work in a regulated industry and the regulators have the final word."

"What next?"

"We trudge onwards."

He didn't say anything else. He didn't say they wouldn't be here for much longer because the money from the NIH which had funded a large part of their clinical work on V-202 was going to dry up. Without passage into Phase 3, there would be no more money for them, even though all the big companies were still getting grant funds. Steptech Therapeutics, Richard's old company, had gotten another billion-dollar grant just last week for the testing, production, and delivery of another nMAQ25 vaccine—its third—which was getting more middling Phase 2 results than the prior two. The few million that Riogenrix obtained in NIH grants here and there to keep their vaccine development afloat wouldn't be coming in any longer. For a while, Riogenrix would be able to support their clinical testing on the licensing revenues from BOOSTers, but Harrison and Selene both knew these revenues were not enough to do any new vaccine development.

"I can talk to Richard," Selene said.

Harrison knew what Selene was thinking. Richard could bankroll them like he'd done in the past. But Harrison couldn't stomach the idea of having Richard put more of his money into the company. He'd already spent enough. More importantly, Harrison couldn't stomach the idea of going to his mentor to ask for more money to cover his own failings.

The student has surpassed the teacher, Richard had commented with pride after Harrison had fine-tuned the BOOSTers before menglavirus. Richard had partly been joking in his usual jovial manner, but he had also been serious. But, clearly, the student hadn't surpassed the teacher. Harrison would talk to Richard about the science and regulatory issues, but he wouldn't ask Richard to pour more money into Riogenrix.

"I'll talk to him," Harrison said.

"We'll be okay, Harrison," Selene said, and Harrison was thankful to her that she didn't ask him anything additional about Riogenrix's future, because he didn't want to verbalize what he was thinking—Riogenrix's time as an independent company was likely at an end. The mRNA BOOSTers were worth good money, especially after the current set of licensing agreements expired. Riogenrix would have bidders from the big guys to absorb them as a subsidiary. Harrison knew the big guys would promise to allow Riogenrix to assert their independence and continue their research but eventually the bureaucracies of the big companies would wipe them out. The best-case scenario at this point for Riogenrix was that one day, Riogenrix would be a cog in a larger company like Steptech.

He texted Richard to let him know he would be stopping by La Jolla. Richard had entrusted the company to him over the past five years but he'd let it fall apart. He wanted to tell Richard in person that V-202 was not going to be moving forward.

Jasmine thought about calling the police, but wondered what they would say to her. The police rarely came out anymore. The neighborhood's deterioration was testament to their absence. Their own block was in better shape than the rest of the neighborhood, but every week it was getting more run down.

What's wrong, ma'am?

A man left an envelope on my door.

Is that it?

And he didn't have a mask.

"Come with me," she said to Sofia, and they walked side-by-side back to the driveway and inspected the streets again. They walked along the sides of the house so Jasmine could check them as well. Whoever the man without a mask had been, he wasn't here now. They returned to the front entrance. Jasmine opened the door and the alarm beeped and she deactivated it from her phone. She told Sofia to stay back in the living room while she checked the house. Sofia didn't stay back though, stepping on Jasmine's heels as Jasmine went to check the kitchen. Jasmine wanted to turn around and tell Sofia again to stay put, but she held herself in check. They walked through the first and second stories together. The house was empty and undisturbed. When they got back downstairs, Sofia went to the couch and watched her tablet, seemingly done with the day's excitement.

Jasmine thought again about calling the police and decided she should at least try. So she called the station on Mira Mesa Blvd. She didn't get anybody on the phone for several minutes and when she did get a desk officer on the line, she got nowhere with him. He told her the police weren't investigating suspicious persons, even those who weren't wearing masks, as it wasn't a high priority. She could hear the air quotes in his voice around *suspicious*. He said the person she'd seen on her cameras was probably only mentally unsound anyway as everyone wore masks these days, even the bad guys, and she should stay inside like everyone else anyway. He used those exact words, *bad guys*, and she wondered what kind of policeman was on the other line and whether he had any real-life experience at all. When she told him about the letter the stranger had affixed to the door, the officer sighed and told her to read it and let them know if there was anything clearly threatening, and then he told her again the police weren't investigating non-urgent threats and she should just stay indoors like everyone else.

"Check it and call us back if needed," he said, and hung up.

Jasmine put away her phone. She was on her own. She eyed Sofia, who was still on the couch, transfixed by the videos on her tablet. Jasmine let her be. She had new preoccupations.

For the rest of the afternoon, Jasmine tried to ignore the envelope. She tried to forget it existed. She gave Sofia a snack, a grilled cheese sandwich, which was pretty much all Sofia ate these days. Sofia picked at the grilled cheese while she sat on the couch with her tablet. Jasmine went back to the kitchen to start on dinner, hoping to clear her mind. She put a small chicken nearing its 'sell by' date to roast. Every ten or fifteen minutes, she left the kitchen to check on Sofia. Sofia didn't budge.

After checking on Sofia a few times, Jasmine walked to the front door, hoping she appeared nonchalant, just in case Sofia was watching her. She removed the envelope from the door with a pair of disposable nitrile gloves and took the letter to the kitchen. Sofia didn't look up from the tablet. Jasmine placed a piece of aluminum foil on the counter and opened the letter on the foil. There was a single sheet of paper inside. When she unfolded the sheet, a business card dropped out. She picked it up. The card was plain white and almost bare. On the front, there were two lines—only two lines. The first line was a name, GREGORY MILLER, and the second line was a title, CONSULTANT. The two lines were centered in the middle of the card. There was nothing else on the front of the card, no company name or contact information, no phone number or email address. But on the back there *was* a phone number, written in messy script with blue ink.

She took a closer look at the letter. It had no date, salutation, or signature. It wasn't addressed to her but was clearly intended for her. It had three lines, all centered in the middle of the page and printed in plain font with all caps.

DID YOU KNOW YOUR HUSBAND HAS A
WORKING VACCINE FOR MENGLAVIRUS?

DID HE OFFER IT TO YOU?

DID HE OFFER IT TO YOUR DAUGHTER?

She reread the letter multiple times. It was simple but didn't make sense to her. The letter stated Harrison had discovered a vaccine for menglavirus, which, as far she knew, he hadn't. Or at least, he hadn't mentioned anything to her. She would have thought discovering a vaccine for the virus that had shut down the world would've been worth telling her about. She knew he was *working* on a vaccine—he had been for five years now—and had gotten into Phase 2 clinical trials, but so had a hundred other firms within the US. According to Harrison, Riogenrix's march to a vaccine was slow. For months, he'd spoken very little of his work. She knew his reticence was partly due to their deteriorated relationship but she had also assumed there'd been nothing to report. She'd never considered the possibility he would actually get a working vaccine.

Now, she had questions.

Did her husband have a vaccine for menglavirus? Had Riogenrix succeeded? And if he did have a vaccine, why had he not told her? And more importantly, why had he not given the vaccine to their daughter? To her? Had he given it to himself but not them? Or had he given it to the man without a mask? And was that why he wasn't wearing a mask?

She didn't know. But she would have to find out.

She looked at the phone number on the back of the card and wondered what the man without a mask wanted. She thought the white coat he'd been wearing made a little more sense if he was a physician, but she still didn't know why Harrison would've kept such a monumental achievement from her if the letter were true. She folded the letter back into thirds. She wondered what she should do with it, whether she should hold onto or get rid of it, and if she held onto it, whether she should hide it from Harrison. She decided to leave it where it was. She put the letter back in the envelope, wrapped the aluminum foil around it, and left the entire thing on the kitchen counter. Harrison was never home anyway, so he wouldn't notice.

She went back to the living room to check on Sofia. She hadn't budged. Jasmine watched her. Right now, Jasmine had no inclination to call the number on the back of the business card, but she needed to figure out what the letter meant and why she'd received it—not only for her sake but for her daughter's.

Dr. Richard Hahn waited for Harrison to leave before getting on the phone. It was 11:20 p.m. He left one message for Dr. Mostafa Abdou and was tempted to call back in another attempt to connect but restrained himself. Mostafa wasn't answering and wouldn't answer no matter how many times he called. Maryland, where Mostafa lived and worked, was three hours ahead of California. He figured Mostafa was sleeping, prepping for another involved day at work. Mostafa was a busy man. Richard once had been a busy man as well.

Richard lived in La Jolla, a quick drive down the cliffs from the Salk Institute. He lived in the Paulson House, an architectural gem of San Diego. The house was carved into the cliff with a direct view of the ocean, which these days, made the house way above what he could afford if he needed to rely only on his earnings from Riogenrix. He'd bought the house fifteen years ago, right after he'd left Steptech, back when he could afford a house like this. But the Steptech days were gone. Intentionally gone.

Harrison had left Richard's house a few minutes ago. They'd

sat across from each other, twenty feet apart, each of them with masks on. Harrison had been adamant on swapping out Richard's old N95s for FN99s from Riogenrix. Of course, Richard had declined. Richard never left his house. He didn't need them. He and Harrison had spent hours talking with each other about the FDA rejection. Richard had felt as blindsided as Harrison. Furthermore, he'd felt betrayed. Mostafa was an old friend and colleague. They were as old as friends and colleagues got. Mostafa not only had provided the FDA with the gentle push to coax Harrison's vaccine applications along through Phase 1 and 2 but also had directed NIH funding their way for the corresponding clinical trials. As Harrison told it, Mostafa had been as adamant as anyone on the FDA conference call when Riogenrix's Phase 3 trials were not approved. Richard didn't understand. Mostafa wasn't a person who got swayed by agency politics. Richard couldn't shake the feeling there was more going on with the FDA's Phase 3 denial than bad science and ignored research.

Richard sat in his living room by himself, like he did all of the time these days. The room had large blocks of floor-to-ceiling windows that overlooked the cliffs below and the ocean beyond. In this part of La Jolla, the beach was rocky and waves were violent. The cliff was more for hiking—careful, vigorous hiking—than it was for enjoying the sun and sand. The house had three stories, the living arrangement opposite to what was typical out on La Jolla's flats. As was usual for houses on La Jolla's cliffs, the bulk of the living space—living room, kitchen, main bedroom, den—were on the top floor. Entry was via the top floor as well. The middle floor had bedrooms and guest space. The bottom floor had his home lab, the one he'd retrofitted into the house when he'd first bought it.

It was the time of night when he felt most despondent, regardless of what had happened today. He was by himself. He was seventy-eight and a bachelor, never married and had no kids. When he'd been younger and in his prime, he'd thought of a wife and children only peripherally, as something that would be nice to have, but wasn't necessary for him to be happy, because his sense of self-worth came from his work. He'd never been lonely until menglavirus. The virus had caused him to hole up in his house to protect his health.

Regarding his health, he had sarcoidosis, a lung disease that made breathing difficult. The deterioration in his health had been gradual but progressive. The shortness of breath and fatigue that characterized sarcoidosis was always getting worse. He'd been diagnosed in his forties but had only required the occasional inhaler at first. But when he turned sixty-five, sarcoid had flared. By the time he started work on the BOOSTers at Riogenrix, he'd been placed on powerful pills with tons of side effects to fight the damage in his lungs. He'd needed oxygen at times. Thankfully, when he'd needed to slow down on the BOOSTers developments, Harrison had come aboard Riogenrix, and had adeptly picked up his slack. Even during those days of worsening disease, when he'd had to limit his time at Riogenrix, he'd never felt alone. He'd had work and friends, and had been thankful the two had overlapped. Harrison's daughter—Sofia, his goddaughter—had become the granddaughter he would never have. Despite his varying health, he hadn't needed anything more in his life. He'd had all of the accomplishment, love, and money a person could have.

Now, with each passing day of menglavirus, he wondered if he'd made the wrong choices in life. Due to menglavirus, he didn't see Sofia anymore. He didn't see Harrison except briefly every few weeks to talk about work. He saw Selene even less. He had no wife, no children, no family, other than the one he'd amassed in almost five decades of medical research, and this family wasn't really *his* family. They had their own families. He'd never found a woman who'd been willing to play second fiddle to his work. Now, as he spent the final stretch of his life alone, he wished he hadn't made playing second fiddle a stipulation. He wished he'd prioritized a relationship. He was glad that Harrison hadn't made the same mistake he had.

At times over the past several weeks, Richard wondered if he should ask Harrison for a dose of the vaccine for himself.

This was after Harrison had started to receive the data demonstrating that the vaccine was efficacious. This way, he could gain immunity, leave the house, resume his life at Riogenrix. Of course, Richard had never asked. The thoughts had been fleeting and fantastical. He knew good research depended on objectivity. If Harrison had given him a vaccine dose, Harrison's objectivity in assessing its efficacy would've been impaired. Richard was proud not only of Harrison's research, but also the way he'd embraced Riogenrix's mission statement: Riogenrix developed and dispensed meaningful mRNA vaccine technologies to improve life for everyone. The key word in the mission statement was *everyone*. Richard was willing to wait like everyone else, even if menglavirus was finishing what age and ailing health had started. Waiting was the only way to show whether or not the vaccine actually worked.

Life these days happened in long stretches of nothingness. In the early days of menglavirus, Richard had thought he could contribute to Riogenrix by working from home in the basement lab. As such, he'd vigorously upgraded it, converting it from a basic home laboratory in which he could tinker for fun to a legitimate biosafety facility. But after a few weeks of trying to keep with up with Harrison's work, he'd realized mRNA vaccine technology had passed him by. He truly was an old man who had difficulty learning new processes.

He watched the darkness beyond the cliff. In the daytime, he saw blue-gray skies and white waves and heard seals and gulls. But at night, he saw nothing but blankness and heard only the turbulence of the water below as waves rolled and crashed. As he sat by himself, he told himself he was not going to let Harrison down. Despite Richard's middling relevance over the past five years, Harrison had come to him for guidance. He might be an old man, but he could still be valuable.

When Harrison arrived home close to midnight, the kitchen

smelled like roasted chicken. He checked the fridge and saw the leftovers, but wasn't hungry. Instead, he poured himself a glass of apple juice for dinner. He was home earlier than the past several days, but not early enough to participate. Remembering that morning, he went upstairs to Sofia's room to check in on her. Again, he found her asleep at the windowsill. He wondered for how many days she'd been sleeping at the window, waiting up for him. He tried to take solace in the fact that he wouldn't be home late anymore because he had no more V-202 to occupy him at work but found little comfort in the realization. He didn't like being at home because he'd failed. He wanted to be at home because he'd succeeded. As Sofia slept at the window, Harrison put his arms under her legs and back and lifted her up in the same way he'd done this morning. He laid her in her bed and pulled the covers up.

"You're home, Daddy," she said, partly awake. "Be careful, please," she said, before falling asleep again.

He felt crushed all over again, the last few years of barely being home stinging even more now that he had nothing to show for it other than a daughter whom he'd harmed. He'd always tried to convince himself that Sofia had adjusted well to menglavirus, but he knew he'd been deceiving himself. He wondered how much Sofia knew about the virus or how much she remembered about a different life when there had been no nMAQ25. When she was three, she'd had difficulty appreciating the sudden changes they'd placed on her with the onset of menglavirus, including the paradoxical admonishment that seemed to sum up their new life: Wear a mask when you go outside but don't go outside anyway.

When the changes had started, he'd been direct in telling Sofia there was a germ outside that could cause people to get very sick. She'd been sick before, of course, like all kids had, with infections like gastroenteritis and bronchiolitis, and she remembered enough about getting sick to know she didn't want to get sick again. The first few days of the virus were easy. She could appreciate the fact she should stay home to stay healthy. She'd been three years old, and had heard the word 'menglavirus', but had understood 'Jenga pirates,' so for her, nMAQ25 had something to do with the blocks with which Mommy and Daddy played and mean pirates who were outside on the streets causing trouble. But by the third or fourth week, she didn't want to stay inside anymore. She didn't understand why the park to where he had taken her so many times was now off limits. She didn't understand why she couldn't take her balance bike outside and ride. She didn't know why she wasn't going over to Uncle Richard's house anymore or why Mrs. Brennan and Baby Tommy didn't visit her at her house anymore. She didn't understand why she was stuck at home or why she was suddenly isolated from everyone and everything she'd previously loved. It hadn't been in her genetics or social programming to be homebound—or that of any three-year-old. Of course, over time, she'd understood. 'Jenga pirates' became 'menglavirus'. Now, she knew, of course— the virus.

He kissed her on the forehead and was about to leave her room when he felt as if someone were watching them. He listened. He heard nothing but stillness. He looked around the bedroom. He saw nothing he didn't expect to find: toys arranged against one wall, a small desk, a half-full hamper. He went to the window and pulled the blinds up. He looked outside and saw nothing but yard and part of the street. He wondered if when the blinds were up in the daytime, people on the street could see her. He'd lived here for ten years but had never paid attention to the angle into Sofia's window from the street. He craned his neck. He didn't see anybody.

Maybe the activity he'd felt was the raccoons and skunks who had always been a part of the neighborhood but had doubled in population during menglavirus. As people had stayed home, the neighborhood critters had prospered. The house had overgrown shrubbery surrounding it that he was supposed to have gotten rid of a long time ago. If he was honest with himself, he wasn't sure he liked the critter effect of the menglavirus era. He disliked the raccoons for their aggressiveness and the skunks for their odors. The screams of the raccoons at night always sounded like they were murdering each other and the smells from the skunks woke him up. He listened and sniffed now. He didn't hear the screams of the raccoons or smell the pungent odor of the skunks.

Nonetheless, he returned downstairs. He got mothballs and critter spray out of the utility closet near the entrance of the house and stepped outside to toss the mothballs into the shrubbery and spray the perimeter of the yard. As he walked around the house, he watched the streets. The houses were quiet and streets were empty. Yet, he felt activity. He waited and watched some more. He still saw nothing. No movements, no shudders. Then he did. He saw bright eyes. And two raccoons darted across the street. He shook his head and let out a sigh of exasperated relief. He was tired, all of the adrenaline from the past several weeks that had kept him going depleted now. There was no one here but the critters. He finished spraying and went back inside.

When he got upstairs, he checked on Sofia again. She was still asleep in her bed. He went to the main bedroom, hoping Jasmine would be asleep too, like she usually was when he got home. Thankfully, she was. He didn't want to argue tonight. All he wanted to do right now was close his eyes and forget the whole day.

For a moment, Gregory Miller wondered if Harrison Boyd would come to him. He waited on the south end of the street, several houses down, seated in a van and watching the house. He reached for a canister. He'd sent the security contractors home an hour ago, but he had his weapon of choice, so he wasn't worried.

Harrison didn't come towards the van.

Gregory was slightly disappointed. He wouldn't have minded getting the next few days of waiting over tonight. Action over diplomacy. Straight to the source.

The senator was delusional if he thought Harrison was just going to hand over the vaccine.

Harrison Boyd turned around and went back inside the house.

Gregory put the canister back down.

PART 2

J asmine waited for Harrison in the kitchen. She'd been asleep when Harrison had come home last night and he'd been asleep when she'd woken up this morning. She'd deliberately woken up early. She wanted to talk to him. Harrison usually brewed two cups of coffee for them in the morning, but today she brewed the coffee, only a single cup for herself. She sat at the counter and waited for him to come down. While she waited, she sipped at the coffee. It was barely tolerable, but so was life with Harrison these days. She couldn't remember the last time he'd slept in or woken up late. Certainly, it'd been before he'd started at Riogenrix. Finally, she heard the subfloor shifting upstairs as he got out of bed. She recognized the specific way the house felt different when he moved through it and wondered if the day were coming when they wouldn't be sharing a house anymore.

He looked weary when he entered the kitchen. She didn't wait for him to settle in or explain why he'd woken up late today for the first time in years. "Do you have a menglavirus vaccine?" she said.

He went to the coffee pot. He saw that it was empty, but didn't flinch. "It depends. What do you mean by 'vaccine'?"

"Do you have a vaccine that prevents menglavirus?"

"I thought I did. I guess I don't."

She hadn't expected the answer to be easy with Harrison. The answers were never easy. He always felt a need to demonstrate

44

the complexity in his work. "Now what do *you* mean?"

"We started Phase 2 trials three months ago with the mRNA vaccine we've been developing for the past five years. Yesterday, the FDA said it doesn't work. They're not on board. They denied our Phase 3 application."

"But do you have a vaccine?"

"Yes."

"Does it really work?"

"I think it does, yes."

"For how long have you known it's worked?"

"Always."

She composed herself and rephrased. "For how long have you had *results* that it worked?

"For a few weeks."

"How many?"

He looked at the ceiling. He was thinking. She recognized his countenance. He was remembering back, calculating. She'd seen this look on his face—the lifted brow and head tilted upwards—thousands of times in their fourteen years together. It was a look she'd found endearing when they'd been dating, a look which signified to her that she'd found the right man to marry: a man who thought, a man who remembered events and dates and details. But, of course, she'd found the look less endearing during marriage, particularly the past five years. Before it'd been a look about them and their plans—we can move here, we can plan this, we can aim for that—but now it was a look only about him, a look about the work that consumed him. Or when it was a look about her, it was now a look of silent disapproval. You didn't get to the reading lesson? You didn't make Sofia do the flashcards? You let her finish early?

But now it was about him and she felt strangely placated that she'd turned the tables on him. She knew later she would feel disappointment in herself for forcing him to talk if he didn't want, but she needed to know.

"Thirty days," he said. "We got the first batch of antibody results thirty days ago."

"And you didn't tell me?" she said.

He looked perplexed. She knew the gist of what he was going to say to her before he said it—she didn't care to hear about his work at Riogenrix. But he was wrong. She *did* care. She *had* cared. She cared a lot. In the beginning, she'd felt as if she'd been a part of Riogenrix in the way spouses' lives were intertwined. When she'd landed her job doing trade and port law, she'd felt as if her accomplishment were his as well. They'd dated when they'd been in professional school, going through their professional educations together. They'd started with no careers together. He'd been part of the reason for her success. And in the beginning, he'd voiced the same about her. She'd been with him when he'd applied to residencies and gone through the Match. She'd been with him when he'd been a resident. She'd been with him when he'd decided to forego a career as a clinician to expand on the scientist part of his physician-scientist training by joining Richard's startup.

Sure enough, he said, "You don't believe in my work."

She felt the crux of her questions fading into oblivion as they veered towards the ongoing conflicts of their marriage. No, she did believe in his work. But he didn't want to share his work, not in a way that didn't acknowledge his genius. He wanted to tell her about his work not to educate her but to show off his own brilliance. *What, you don't know about multiplexing mRNA product profile? Wait, you don't remember everything I already told you about ORFs for target antigens?* When she'd been working, she could've done the same, used all of the legal jargon only she would've understood, but she'd always tried to include rather than isolate him from her career. She'd always wanted to *share* her work. In order to share her work with Harrison she was okay with simplifying it. Her own position in their relationship wasn't dependent on being better than the other.

She didn't allow herself to get sidetracked down the same path and argue the same defense. She stayed on what mattered. "Do you have a vaccine?" she said again, just wanting a simple answer: *Yes, I have one,* or *No, I don't.* They'd been together long enough for him to know what she needed. She waited to see if he would participate in allowing her a simple response. She didn't need to know all of the science, all of the setbacks and accomplishments. Did he have a vaccine? And was he going to tell her?

"Yes," he said.

She knew he wanted to say something else, knew he wanted to say everything, why he didn't really have a vaccine or why he might potentially have one, but didn't. For once, he'd given her what she needed, the simple insight into his work.

She thought about the man without the mask and the letter he'd left. She thought about the way he'd worn a lab coat. She thought about the almost empty business card and the messy, scribbled number on the back. "Are you going to give the vaccine to us?" she said.

"No," he said. At first, it seemed like he was going to leave his response at that, but she saw him leaning back and looking up and knew that there was more he was going to say, more he was going to explain, more condescension he needed to drop on her.

She spoke first to cut him off and framed him with the questions that only needed a 'yes' or 'no.' If he wanted to act like the smartest man in the room, she would act like an attorney who only needed to know the answer. "You don't want to vaccinate your daughter? Our daughter?"

"I do, but—"

"But what?"

"I can't."

"Why?"

"It's not approved. The FDA hasn't allowed its use as a preventive agent."

"Does it work, though?"

"Yes."

"Why won't the FDA approve it?"

He shook his head and she knew the question wasn't simple and he wouldn't make the answer simple. She didn't have to appreciate all his research to understand this point, but again, she just wanted something to hold onto, something straightforward, something he could tell her that made her think she mattered.

"I don't really know," he said.

The answer wasn't what she expected. He always knew. She'd expected a longwinded explanation. For a moment, she felt tenderness for her husband. She felt the fatigue he felt, the disappointments he'd never let get him down before but were getting him down now. She saw what he saw—the opportunity to make good on a decade of Riogenrix's work fading away.

She softened, and reached for his hand as he stood across from her at the kitchen counter. "Does the vaccine work, honey?" she said.

"Yes."

"It works? It stops people from getting menglavirus?"

"Yes."

"Do you *think* it does or do you *know* it does."

"We're only in Phase 2 trials. Or we *were* only in Phase 2 trials. But we produced sky-high antibodies. It works. I know it does."

"It works *in vitro*, honey, but does that mean it works *in vivo*? It works in a lab, but does it work in people?" Again, she was gentle, and she knew what to ask, because she hadn't been a dummy all these years. She'd learned much more than he'd given her credit for.

"Yes. We had no infections in any of our Phase 2 test subjects. Out of three hundred people who were inoculated with our vaccine in Phase 2, none of them got menglavirus."

He said nothing else, and in that moment, she believed him, even if the FDA didn't. The vaccine worked.

She asked him what she should've asked him months ago, but never thought to ask, because she'd never believed he had a therapeutic.

"Have you given yourself the vaccine?"

"No. I wear the masks every day, Jasmine. I have not given myself the vaccine."

Her tenderness faded. She could tell he was disappointed she even asked him such a question. He was an ethical man. He wouldn't give himself the vaccine until others also could receive it. He was acting indignant, as if she were an idiot for even asking. But she would continue with the line of questioning until she knew what she needed.

"Have you given anybody the vaccine outside of Phase 2?"

"No, only the test subjects. And the clinical trials themselves are double-blinded. I don't know who the subjects are until the study is over."

"You haven't given the vaccine to anybody else? Not even Richard? Not even to Selene?"

"No. I haven't given the vaccine to anybody, Jasmine. I'm not going to say it again."

She knew where the conversation was headed, towards another argument they'd never finished which had nothing to do with the vaccine. She didn't want to go back to old arguments. She wanted to talk about the future.

"Since the vaccine works, are you going to give the vaccine to Sofia? Are you going to give it to me?"

"Like I said, administration is double-blinded. It means—"

"Yeah, I know what that means," she said, interrupting him. She knew what double-blinded meant. None of the researchers knew who got the vaccine or a placebo and none of the subjects knew if they'd gotten the vaccine. There was the vaccine and there was the injectable placebo and no one knew who'd gotten which one until the data were crunched and the study was unblinded. "I'm not asking if you're going to enroll us in a study. You already said there is no more study. I'm asking if you're going to give us the vaccine you developed. Since it works, are you going to give it to us?"

He paused, choosing his words. "If I give it to you, I won't have the objectivity to assess its efficacy. I'll be biased."

There it was. He'd said there would be no Phase 3, but still he was holding out hope that there would be. He wasn't willing to affect Phase 3 in case they started it up after all. Either way, she was tired of hearing 'no.'

"We went out yesterday," she said. "We went to the park."

"What park?"

"We went to the park down the street. Sofia enjoyed it. I enjoyed it. We've been cooped up in this house for five years. She's never been in a real school, for God's sake. She's never had any kind of normal childhood."

"You went to the park yesterday? Jasmine, the park isn't safe."

"You go out every day."

"I don't go 'out.' I go to work. I come back. And at work, we have strict infection control protocols. At the park, you don't know who sneaks there and you don't know who might've had it. It's ferociously airborne."

She hated how she had mixed feelings for him, tenderness and love one moment and anger and resentment the other. She didn't understand how she couldn't feel conflicted. Her feelings towards him were a consequence of their convoluted interactions.

"You can make the park safe for us," she said. "If the vaccine works, give it to us."

He didn't answer. And she didn't try to coax him to give one, because she knew he wouldn't give her the answer she and Sofia needed. So she left her cup of coffee on the counter, and she left him, and she left the kitchen.

And she went upstairs to check on Sofia.

Mostafa was coming up on Montgomery Avenue in his Mercedes sedan when the name he'd been avoiding popped up on the center console screen of his car. He was headed to the NIH campus. He'd received three calls and three voicemails from Richard overnight and was now receiving the fourth. It was late morning in Maryland, which meant it was early in California, especially so for Richard these days. Mostafa knew why he was receiving the calls and wondered if Richard had slept at all last night or if he'd woken up early this morning specifically to call him. Mostafa himself had barely slept. He usually slept so well, no problems, no stressors. But he'd known for several days that the FDA was not going to approve Riogenrix's menglavirus vaccine. Yesterday's conference call only had been the ugly confirmation.

The FDA rejection had been contrary to Mostafa's prior fifty years in medicine. He was causing harm and knew he was causing harm. A week ago, he'd been ecstatic when he'd analyzed the Phase 2 data from Riogenrix's application. He'd been ecstatic not only for his old friend, but for the results, because the results were what mattered for the world, and the results were outstanding. The world needed a way to resume life. Riogenrix had found the way to do so in their vaccine. Richard's company had gotten to where they all needed to get. Mostafa even forwarded the data to Col. Burt Johnson, the commander at USAMRIID-West, the person who was going to be leading the US Army's charge in the expedited distribution of a working menglavirus vaccine not only within the US but to the rest of the world. But then he'd gotten the call over the weekend from the senator saying the FDA wasn't going to accept the application for Phase 3 for reasons related to national security. After that, the white Chevy Suburban started following him around.

When Mostafa looked back on his life, he'd accomplished everything he'd wanted. He'd been at the forefront of research for the entirety of his medical career, establishing national policies to save lives and advancing vaccine development into the next generation. He was seventy-eight years old and had been in medical research in one form or another for almost fifty years, starting as a medical student in Johns Hopkins University, when he'd found and fallen in love with medical research. He'd known from the first week of dishing pipettes and petri dishes that immunology research had been for him.

He wasn't the only one who'd known.

Richard had known as well. They'd been in the same Johns Hopkins class. Although they'd had a competitive rivalry on test scores, class rankings, and clinical evaluations, they'd been good friends, classmates who could rely on each other to navigate the vagaries of medical school. They were two young men who came together for cadaver dissections and pathology slide reviews in their academic years and then helped each other with tips on how best to deal with attending physicians during the clinical years. They'd both stacked up as many clinical research rotations as they could. They shared cheap food recommendations from around campus that filled them up—the huge lump crab cake sandwiches from Madeleine's and the loaded-to-the-brim burritos from Pronto's—while simultaneously going easy on their limited medical student wallets. They even had crushes on the same classmate for a time, although neither one had actually drawn her interest or been brave enough to actually ask her out. Even after medical school, they'd stayed around Johns Hopkins for residencies in internal medicine, each of them proud to be part of the training program that once had been the country's first. They were academic brothers.

Thereafter, Richard had gone to University of Washington on the west coast for an immunology fellowship, telling Mostafa he wanted to step out of Johns Hopkins' shadow in order to make a name for himself away from the prestige of the university that over the years had become synonymous with the term *physician-scientist*. Mostafa had stayed back at Johns Hopkins for his own immunology fellowship. He'd been hurt to see his friend leave but also relieved. He knew the attending physicians and researchers at Johns Hopkins had started to view the two of them as the same person. Wherever Mostafa was, Richard was there too. Two men with the same educations, training, and aspirations. Two men aiming for the same lives in research. When Richard had headed to the west coast, Mostafa had been relieved to know he could finally make a name for himself away from the constant comparisons to Richard Hahn.

Of course, Richard's career had taken a more commercial turn than Mostafa's. Richard had stayed on the west coast after fellowship to join forces with Dr. Jason Carr on a vaccine and therapeutics venture in Seattle, while Mostafa had accepted his dream position as a staff researcher at the National Institutes of Health. While Mostafa was initially relieved when Richard went to the west coast, he became disappointed with Richard for staying out there for commercial pursuits. He'd expected bigger things from Richard than hunting down patents. Nevertheless, he allowed his friend to pursue his own goals and tried not to be too judgmental about the commercial path Richard had chosen.

At times, Mostafa wondered what his own life would've been like if he'd gone a more commercial route like Richard, but these moments of uncertainty were usually brief, because he had accomplished so much in his career. Even if he didn't have as much money as Richard, he had earned more than enough—an excellent amount, really—for doing something he loved. However, there were times when he saw the commercial success Richard had had with Steptech and wondered what he'd missed out on. The second-guessing had been greatest ten years ago when Richard had invited Mostafa to spend the week with him in La Jolla shortly after Richard had started his new venture in San Diego. Mostafa had been impressed with the modern house on the cliffs. When he'd seen the onsite lab facilities nestled into the ground floor, he wondered why he'd decided to spend his life in public service rather than private industry. He left San Diego feeling upset with his own life decisions, almost unaccomplished. After San Diego, it took him weeks to get out of his funk. He'd finally gotten away from the self-pity by rededicating himself not only to his work at the NIH but to his wife and daughter. For all Richard had achieved, Mostafa knew he could never live in a big house on the cliffs of La Jolla by himself, with only his work to support him. As he'd gone back into spearheading research projects, distributing funds to the next generation of researchers, and living the same life he'd always lived with his family, he'd realized his self-pity had been juvenile. Each of his classmates at Johns Hopkins had carved out their own paths through medicine and he was happy with the path he'd carved out for himself.

He checked the rearview mirror to see if the white SUV was behind him. Officially, the men were supposed to be providing him security, since he was the lead contact at the NIH for the menglavirus vaccine, but Mostafa knew the senator's men were monitoring him, keeping tabs on his location and doings. He knew the men were plugged into his electronic communications and phone calls as well. The senator knew where he was, what he was doing, and with whom he was speaking, which was why he didn't answer Richard's phone call now and hadn't answered any of the three prior ones overnight.

Last night, he'd woken up his wife and asked her about the old days together, how they'd both devoted themselves to medicine and family. His wife had been confused at first about the sudden reminiscing as she had a full day of clinic scheduled for today, but she'd played along. She must've felt the earnestness in Mostafa's tone. Even though she too recently had become a septuagenarian, she was busier than ever as a private practice clinician. He'd reminisced with her until dawn broke. She hadn't known, but he'd been saying goodbye to her.

He let Richard's call go to voicemail and hoped Richard wouldn't leave another one. He drove hesitantly as he entered campus, waiting for Richard to call again. For now, Richard didn't, but Mostafa knew he eventually would. Richard wondered how much longer he could ignore him. When a few minutes had passed and he was sure Richard wasn't going to call back, he called his daughter instead. She also was a physician, an internist like his wife who also worked in private practice. He wanted to make sure he said goodbye to her too, because he knew he would eventually pick up one of Richard's calls. He'd devoted himself to medicine. He didn't have a choice but to pick up and tell the truth.

When Harrison pulled up to the security gates of Riogenrix in his old Honda three hours later than he ever had in the ten years of working there, a black Cadillac Escalade was already parked in front of the gates. A bulky man in a polo shirt, khaki pants, and fitted mask stood outside of the large SUV, at the front of the vehicle, and another man in a polo shirt and fitted mask was sitting in the driver's seat. Harrison positioned the car so he could peer inside the tinted rear windows. He couldn't see through the darkened glass but knew someone was inside the back.

He brought his sedan to a standstill opposite the SUV. As he put the Honda in park, his first reaction was to assume a major catastrophe had occurred at Riogenrix, along the lines of a biosafety containment leak. He began to worry about the staff on campus and the neighboring community. He immediately started thinking about how he would cooperate to contain the leak that might've occurred.

The tinted passenger window in the Escalade rolled down. A man with slicked-back graying hair and a fitted FN99 mask pushed his head through the window. He was wearing aviator sunglasses and a white dress shirt open at the collar. He appeared to be about the same age as Harrison. "I hope I didn't startle you by being here," he said.

"Have we had a safety leak?" Harrison said, saying without delay exactly what he feared.

"Have we, Dr. Boyd? I hope not."

Harrison didn't know the man but the man clearly knew him. The man looked familiar though. The voice was also familiar. He didn't know how much of his inability to recognize the man in the Cadillac had to do with the mask the man wore or how much it had to do with his own fragility this morning. He was emotionally drained. The despondency he'd felt after the FDA phone call yesterday had only intensified—first, after finding Sofia in front of the window again last night, and second, by the quick deterioration in his relationship with Jasmine that had been all too evident this morning. Even though he'd gotten up later than usual this morning—he no longer saw the point in adhering to the strict schedule he maintained—he'd slept only a couple of fitful hours. If his life were only his own, he probably could've found the energy to trudge onwards with V-202, give the Phase 3 application another shot, but after seeing Sofia sleeping at the window and waking up to a marriage at the breaking point, he understood he'd sacrificed his family for nothing, because V-202 had become nothing. The realization was casting a despondency over him he'd never felt before.

"Have we met?" Harrison said.

"Not in person, doctor, but we did speak yesterday. I'm sorry for the unannounced visit. I'm Senator Scott Spaulding."

It took Harrison a moment to recognize the name, but even then, he wasn't sure. "You're Senator Scott Spaulding from the Congressional Committee on Menglavirus Prevention and Treatment? You're Senator Scott Spaulding from the FDA conference call?"

"Yes, doctor, I am."

Harrison felt his despondency butt up against confusion. Harrison had no idea why the senator in charge of the US efforts for menglavirus vaccine development was at Riogenrix's front gate. Scott Spaulding, the Chair of the Congressional Committee on Menglavirus Therapeutics, should've been in his home state of Nevada with his constituency or at least in D.C. briefing the White House and managing his own presidential campaign, but he wasn't, and instead, he was in San Diego. He clearly wasn't in San Diego just to visit, because he wasn't even in the touristy parts of San Diego, the fancier parts of La Jolla and Del Mar, where visitors went—or at least used to go. He was in Poway, far enough inland from coastal San Diego to be regarded as the Sahara Desert. For whatever reason, the senator was at the Riogenrix campus.

"How can I help you, senator?"

"I'm sorry to just drop in, doctor, but I wanted to catch you in person. I'm here to learn more about your research. More about your vaccine. V-202 is what you call it, right? I'm here to learn more about V-202. I'm here to learn more about you."

Harrison's confusion doubled. The senator had been clear yesterday in his support of the FDA's decision to deny their Phase 3 application. Harrison wasn't sure about anything anymore.

"You denied V-202's Phase 3 application, senator. I don't know why you would want to learn more about it."

Denied, Harrison thought to himself. The word truly stung.

"Understood. Nevertheless, our phone call from yesterday—the conference call, that is—was so formal I don't think I really got a good sense of who you are and the work you're doing. I like to meet a man and shake his hand and look him in the eye in order to get to know him and his work. I like the old-fashioned ways, when men met face-to-face. I'm a people person. The conference calls and video calls don't provide the same satisfaction for me as a face-to-face visit does. Of course, I can't shake your hand today, doctor, but I sure can look you face-to-face. We can look each other in the eye. I can see the man whom the FDA denied, and you can see the man who supported the denial."

"Here I am," Harrison said, knowing he was being glib, but not caring. "With all due respect, senator, I'm not sure why you're at Riogenrix. Poway isn't much of a tourist area, not before menglavirus and definitely not now. Why are you at my company?"

"I want to see if perhaps I made a mistake with the denial of your Phase 3 application," the senator said.

Harrison felt even more confused. He wondered if he'd heard correctly. Harrison waited for his mental fog to clear. His goal today had been to start the process to wind down V-202, and in so doing, he expected Riogenrix to cease development and testing operations as well, in anticipation of getting the company ready for whatever was next, which was likely going to be a sale. The BOOSTers patents were worth good money. The big guys would make offers, and if Selene was on board with her shares, he would be on board with his as well, because he already knew Richard would defer to them, having been clear that he'd had his career already.

The senator watched Harrison. So did the senator's security team. Harrison knew members of Congress had security detail from the Capitol Police but he also knew these men weren't part of that group. They were security contractors, former military men who'd fought for profit overseas during the War on Terror era but were now making their living stateside by protecting politicians and corporate executives. Menglavirus had been good for the contracted security business.

"You made the largest mistake of the modern age in denying our Phase 3 application," Harrison said.

The senator chuckled. His laugh was one of those laughs he'd seen—heard, actually—time-to-time from people like politicians and venture capitalists. It was a laugh which maybe once had started off as genuine, but now was just a reflex, something they could use to convey a relaxed conviviality. However, in the case of the senator, Harrison got the distinct impression the laugh was less about friendliness and more about authority.

Understandably, Harrison felt tangled, and now he felt angry too. He didn't know why the senator was here, and he didn't want to know. He only wanted to get into his office and speak to Selene. He wanted to let her start the process of shutting down the V-202 trials. He wanted to move on from V-202 and focus on his wife and his daughter. He'd given himself to Riogenrix and now it was time to give himself to his family before there was no more family to which to give.

"I want to make sure we made the right decision, doctor," the senator said. "Menglavirus is a horrible, horrible thing. Horrendous. It is clearly the most pressing concern I've ever faced while serving the public good. I want to see what we've rejected here. I want to make sure we haven't made any mistakes." He paused, and smiled, and chuckled again, the same manufactured laugh as before. "Why don't you tell me more about V-202? Why don't you show me around your campus here, doctor?"

Over the ten years Harrison had been at Riogenrix, he'd stayed away from politics. He had neither met with very many politicians nor gone to many political functions. Richard always had been the people person of the company. At times, Richard had lamented their intentional lack of political savviness, wondering if it would detract from their research over time, but ultimately, he and Harrison had been likeminded in believing the research results spoke for themselves. Even so, Harrison knew now they should've had a lobbying presence within Congress and the FDA. Clearly, results didn't speak for themselves. They should've adhered to the political mores of research development in the US.

"What do you say, doctor? Are you ready to give me a tour of your facilities?"

Harrison felt tired, not only from yesterday and today, but from twelve weeks of Phase 2 trials and five years of V-202 development. He wondered how perceptive he was being, whether he should acquiesce to the senator's requests. But as he thought about a new life for V-202, he realized he wasn't ready to concede after all. "Let's go," he said, and reached for the padlock on the front security gates to unlatch it. The senator's security team got back into the Escalade. Harrison stood aside to let the senator drive onto campus. As the Escalade rolled by Harrison, the senator stuck his head out of the window. "What happened to your security, doctor?"

"Here I am," Harrison said.

The senator raised his eyebrows.

"Our head of security died a week ago," Harrison said. "We're looking—we *were* looking—to hire new lead security."

"You'll have to expedite the hiring, doctor, especially if we can get your menglavirus vaccine moving forward after all."

The senator rolled up his window and the Escalade plowed through the entrance.

Harrison got back into his sedan. He was truly perplexed. He didn't know if he'd understood correctly—the senator had just inferred V-202 was going to get approval for Phase 3 after all. He put the Honda into drive and drove through the gates. The senator hadn't waited for Harrison. As Harrison got out of his car again to close the gate, he got the distinct impression the senator didn't really want a tour. Harrison found he didn't know how to feel about the senator, whether he should be optimistic he might be able to revive V-202 after all, or suspicious there was a greater game being played.

Jasmine let Sofia sleep in again. She thought about awaking her, but decided instead to lie in bed with her daughter. Jasmine appreciated the quiet. It gave her time to think. For a moment, she felt as if the world was okay. So long as she stayed in bed with her daughter, she felt no anxiety. She felt as if she could protect her. She remembered how she used to sleep in Sofia's room when Sofia was a newborn. Jasmine had set up a futon so she could be close to her daughter all of the time. For months, she'd slept next to Sofia's bassinet and then her crib. Jasmine had felt unsure and tired all of the time as a new mother, but now she felt proud of those days. She'd gotten through them and Sofia had prospered. She'd given her daughter what she'd needed until her daughter hadn't needed Jasmine at her side all the time.

She'd always tried to protect her daughter. In Sofia's infancy, this had included making sure the linen sheets in Sofia's crib had been properly tucked away and the baths in her baby tub had always been no hotter than a hundred degrees Fahrenheit, and then as a toddler this had included putting covers on the outlets and moving all the knives in the kitchen well out of sight into the top cabinets. She'd stayed on top of Sofia's safety from day one. She'd always made sure to keep Sofia as safe as possible, because physical safety always had been a straightforward part of Sofia's existence. Before menglavirus, protecting Sofia had been easy. Now she had to worry about so much more.

After menglavirus, it'd been so hard, almost impossible, to protect Sofia because there'd been no way she could keep Sofia physically safe without keeping her inside the house all of the time. If she never left the house, she couldn't get sick. She couldn't end up like Mrs. Brennan or Tommy, who'd gotten menglavirus. She'd followed the same game plan millions of mothers were following in the country and hundreds of millions of mothers were following across the world. But as she'd kept Sofia physically safe, she'd put Sofia mentally at risk and she'd put her own mental health at harm as well. Yesterday, she'd taken Sofia to the park to heal the both of them.

Do as I say, not as I do.

In trying to keep Sofia physically safe, she'd been making both of them less mentally sound every day.

The park had been her attempt at delivering a vaccine for their mental health.

Their fates were intertwined. If Jasmine wasn't feeling right, there was no way she could keep Sofia feeling right.

And truth be told, those first few minutes yesterday at the park had been scary but exhilarating. She'd felt liberated.

But now there *was* a vaccine.

Harrison had admitted as much and he believed the vaccine worked. He believed it was *efficacious*, as Harrison would say, and she knew what efficacious meant both in theory and practice, because even though Harrison thought she didn't take an interest in his work, she had always taken an interest in all of him.

The vaccine existed. It was efficacious. It worked.

She felt betrayed. She wondered if her feelings towards Harrison were justified or if she was overreacting.

Besides, as she'd learned over the years, she had to protect Sofia on her own. She had her pistol upstairs, the one Harrison had pooh-poohed when she'd gotten it at the start of menglavirus. If the world broke down more than it already had, she could protect Sofia physically.

But she had no way to protect Sofia from the inside. She had no way to protect Sofia from the mental deterioration that had resulted from avoiding the virus.

Again, she wondered now if the man without the mask had been vaccinated himself. She wondered if that was the reason he'd worn no mask.

She lay next to Sofia in Sofia's bed in Sofia's room and didn't get out of the bed until almost midday. She let Sofia sleep and returned downstairs. In the kitchen, she saw Harrison had made another small pot of coffee, including a cup for her. She felt her heart tearing, but didn't go to the coffee, as if it were the virus itself, as if pouring herself a cup would ruin her attempt to live a new life for her and her daughter without the constant disappointments of having Harrison as her husband and Sofia's father. Instead, she went to the fridge and poured herself a glass of water. Today would be the day she stopped drinking Harrison's coffee.

She took the glass of water to the counter. The letter from the man without a mask was still there. Just as she'd predicted, Harrison hadn't touched it. She watched the envelope, as if it were an object to be viewed, like Sofia's tablet. She opened the envelope again, removed the business card, and called the number on the back. The number didn't ring. The call went straight to voicemail. She checked the card and called the number again. Again, it went to voicemail. She hesitated, thought about leaving a message, but had no idea what she would say: *Hey there, this is the woman who received your letter and instead of me telling my husband about the letter or even destroying it myself, I'm calling you.* No, she wouldn't say anything.

She hung up and didn't call back.

She felt shame and wondered if this is what it felt like to cheat. She wanted to erase what she'd done. She couldn't remember if a person whose phone was off got a missed call notification. She hoped they didn't. She left her phone on the counter and went upstairs to wake Sofia. She'd let Sofia sleep long enough. Another day awaited them.

Mostafa was walking across NIH campus from Building 32 to Building 41 when he received what he knew was the first of the next batch of phone calls from Richard. After three calls this morning from Richard, there'd been silence, but now the calls were starting up again. Mostafa was thinking of the conversation he knew was inevitable. He shortened his steps and slowed down. He knew he couldn't put off answering the phone anymore. He wouldn't.

The day had brightened into a warm Maryland afternoon. He didn't usually eat lunch other than a few pieces of fruit and a handful of nuts but he liked to maintain at least a thirty-minute afternoon break to walk around campus and keep his mind fresh before making one final push into the evening. He'd found as he'd gotten older that he needed these moments of downtime to get his thoughts organized. His mind still worked, but it needed more prodding and maintenance. He usually traversed one of the outdoor paths the NIH had set up a few years before menglavirus to promote healthy habits. Today, he found himself walking in the opposite direction of his usual path, towards his vehicle, as if he'd known already that Richard would be calling again. And of course, he'd known.

His car was in Lot 41, one of few on-campus parking lots. He had a dedicated spot, a benefit of having been with the NIH for almost forty years. He joked to the younger researchers at NIH that not having to walk in and off of campus twice a day to get to his vehicle was reason enough to stick around NIH until his last breath. Instead of continuing onwards to Building 41 as he usually did, he turned towards Lot 41. Mostafa knew that he couldn't ignore his old friend anymore, because to ignore Richard was to ignore the improprieties that were happening at the FDA at the hands of the senator. In turn, ignoring the improprieties meant ignoring nMAQ25 and its horrible, ongoing burden on the global population. He was close enough to the research—hell, he'd funded NIH grants to over one hundred and fifty-seven different US-based companies and research institutions over the past five years and another fifteen to internationals—to know the FDA was considering Phase 3 applications from far inferior investigational agents than that of Richard's company. Mostafa knew none of these other agents were ever going to deliver legitimate vaccines with legitimate in vivo results, but the FDA was throwing Hail Mary's. Richard's vaccine, though, wasn't a Hail Mary. It was a solid, no-nonsense run right down the middle—a bulldozer cutting through the failures of all of those Hail Mary's.

It was something clearly headed to the end zone. But the FDA wasn't playing that game. The senator wasn't playing that game. As he stood outside of his car in the parking lot, he answered the phone.

"How are you, friend?" he said.

"What the hell, Mostafa?"

"Don't ask me, Richard. Ask the FDA."

"I am asking you, Mostafa. The NIH and FDA are walking side-by-side these days. There is no difference. What happened with our vaccine?"

"I don't really know, Richard."

"Come on, man."

"Hold on, Richard."

Mostafa held the phone against his chest to mute it as he got into his car. Once inside, he looked around the parking lot. He didn't see any white Suburban SUVs, but he never did on campus. The SUVs were always waiting for him outside the entrance gates. He started the car and transferred the phone to hands-free. As he looked at the sign in front of him denoting his dedicated parking spot, he knew he'd been telling the truth when he'd told junior researchers the parking spot was reason enough to stick around NIH until his last breath. For him, it was recognition apropos.

"I don't know, Richard," he said. He'd been rehearsing this conversation all day, thinking about how he could reveal what he needed to reveal without revealing it. He'd been a medical researcher his entire career. He would talk about the research. Even so, his voice wavered. "I know what I think of the data."

"What do you think, Mostafa?"

"It was good. Great, really. Excellent."

"So why didn't we go to Phase 3? Millions of people are dying in the world every month, Mostafa."

"I know all of this, Richard. Trust me, I know."

"What happened?"

"There are a lot more players involved in the menglavirus vaccine than there were with the BOOSTers you developed before."

"And?"

"And I'm sure they're probably reviewing everything I'm saying to you as well."

"What does that even mean, Mostafa?"

"Nothing, I guess."

"You're seventy-eight, Mostafa. We both are. We've devoted our lives to medicine. Be clear with me."

And here was their relationship coming forth. The crisscrosses, camaraderie, and rivalries. Here were five decades of medicine and four decades of being involved in medical research. He'd known Richard would keep calling and digging because that's exactly what he would've done.

"I know how old I am," he said.

"So?"

"So what?"

"Tell me why the FDA doesn't want to advance us to Phase 3."

Yes, he was seventy-eight years old. Seventy-eight wasn't a bad age to die—although he clearly wasn't ready to die. He thought he had many years, maybe even a decade, of being productive still. But if he had to die, seventy-eight wasn't a terrible age. He was no different than anyone else in the world in that he wanted to live forever. However, he knew he never would, and as such, he'd never tried. He'd never focused on how to stay young. He'd been as responsible for NIH's development of vaccines with private industry over the past four decades as anyone. He was content with his career.

Medicine was one of those fields where the old dogs didn't die. Doctors spent decades learning a specialty, and even then, they never knew it all. They reached a point of mastery, where they knew what they were doing, but they never reached a point where they knew *everything*. They never knew enough to call it quits.

"Your vaccine works, Richard," Mostafa said. "I don't know how you created one of the most important vaccines in the modern microbiology era, but you pulled it off—and you pulled it off with mRNA no less. Your vaccine works. The numbers were good. Excellent, in fact. It was completely legitimate. A game changer. No matter what analyses—developmental and statistical—the NIH threw at it, your vaccine held up to scrutiny."

Mostafa waited for Richard to respond. He expected a barrage of anger and disappointment from his colleague and friend. After all, Mostafa was angry and disappointed in himself and he could only understand Richard feeling the same. He waited for the berating.

Instead, Richard was quiet. He seemed to be collecting his thoughts. Finally, he asked, "What's happening, Mostafa?"

Now it was Mostafa's turn to collect his thoughts. From here onwards, there was no turning back, no undoing what he was going to do or unsaying what he was going to say. Again, he thought—he knew—he had several more good years to give to the NIH, and he thought—he *definitely* knew—he had even more good years to give to his family.

"It's not normal—it's not typical—to have politicians sit in on a vaccine trial—" He trailed off, not knowing if he needed to say more or if Richard understood.

"But?"

He breathed. Richard was going to get it all out of him.

"They've been sitting in on all of the vaccine trials. None of the trials of any of the investigational vaccines the FDA has approved for Phase 1 and Phase 2 have been promising enough to interfere much in the process. But once they saw your data, they took control of the FDA. They understood they had a vaccine that worked."

"So, who gave the order to the FDA to cripple the application? Who gave the order to stop us from getting into Phase 3?"

"The Chair of the Congressional Committee on Menglavirus Vaccines and Therapeutics."

"Who is that?"

"Senator Scott Spaulding."

"The guy from television?"

"Yes."

"Why would he do that? Why would the Committee allow him to stifle our vaccine? Why would anyone allow this?"

"He wants to control its distribution. He doesn't want the vaccine distributed to countries that aren't friendly with the United States. The senator views control of the vaccine as the key to the country's reemergence on the international stage. Or so he says." He didn't say more. He didn't think he needed to say more. Anyone who'd followed the news over the past five years would understand.

"That's the equivalent to murder, Mostafa. We're physicians and scientists. We don't decide who deserves a therapeutic and who doesn't. For us, everyone deserves a therapeutic. We can't deny a vaccine that would save a billion lives just because diplomacy between us and China has broken down over a goddamned virus."

"I know and agree. Senator Spaulding doesn't agree, though."

"What about the White House? What about the administration?"

"Doesn't matter. Eight years are almost up for this administration. Spaulding will be the White House soon."

"What's next, Mostafa?"

From here onwards, there absolutely would be no going back. Again, Mostafa thought about his wife and daughter and the years he could still spend with them. Then he thought of the tens of millions of lives Richard's vaccine could save and the commitment to public good on which Mostafa had built his career. "The senator has formed his own team. He's going to get your vaccine, either through cooperation or force. Probably through force."

"He won't get it through cooperation. Not if he's going to withhold it from billions of people."

"I know, Richard. Trust me, I know."

Mostafa told Richard everything he knew. Both men went quiet. Mostafa had been sitting in his car with the engine running as he spoke but now he backed his Mercedes out of his parking space. He eased it onto the campus roadway. He didn't speak and neither did Richard. Mostafa had no doubt both of them understood the implications of the conversation they'd just had.

After several seconds of quiet, Richard spoke again. "I forgot to ask you how you're doing, Mostafa. I forgot to ask how you've been, old friend. How is Elizabeth doing? And your daughter? We haven't spoken in a while, Mostafa. Too long probably. I know we're not the stalwarts anymore—or at least I'm not—but we had good careers, you especially. You shepherded dozens of vaccines from conception to production. You've done excellent work, Mostafa, although you don't need me to tell you what you already know. You not only moved forward vaccine development and distribution, but you did well by your family. I've always admired you, Mostafa. Thank you, old friend, for always being by my side."

Mostafa understood what was happening. He felt a profound appreciation for Richard's words. They'd spent a life both together and then apart in medicine, as colleagues and sometimes rivals, but had remained friends throughout.

"I'm excellent, Richard. How are you, buddy?"

"I'm also excellent, Mostafa."

"We'll talk again, Richard," Mostafa said, although he knew—and he was sure that Richard knew as well—that they wouldn't.

They said their goodbyes and hung up. Mostafa's hands had been tensed on the steering wheel for the entirety of the call. He removed his hands from it, shook them, and waited for the muscles to relax. When they did, he placed them back on the steering wheel and pulled the Mercedes off the campus roadway onto the main street. He headed south. He wasn't sure where he was going. He was just driving, heading down a route he'd taken thousands of times over his almost four decades at the NIH.

He drove for several minutes, driving on reflex rather than intention. As he drove, he saw Fred's Steakhouse on the left. It was a multigenerational icon out here, having existed in some form or another since the 1950s. He'd gone to Fred's so many times over the years, spending at least a hundred evenings in the private room, listening or giving lectures to other physicians who were attending meetings at the NIH or Johns Hopkins or USAMRIID. Starting as a medical student, he'd gone to Fred's whenever he could snag an invitation from the physician lecturers, and as he progressed in his career at the NIH, he'd become an expert lecturer himself. The restaurant had been shuttered for five years now and he could tell by the silence surrounding the place that no one had stepped inside for years. Or at least, no one who'd been legitimate. The outside was boarded up with plywood and covered in graffiti. He knew he would never see the steakhouse again, not as a lecturer discussing breakthroughs in vaccine technologies, not as a researcher sharing ideas and stories with colleagues, and not as a passerby, but he hoped there would be a new generation of lecturers and students filling the space.

He got to George Washington Parkway before he saw the white Suburban behind him. He drove for a quarter-mile. When nothing happened, he wondered if—maybe, just maybe—the Suburban wasn't for him after all. He eyed the 14th Street Bridge as it came up and put on his signal before easing into the left lane.

The Suburban flashed its high beams and honked, telling Mostafa to pull over. He considered gunning it, putting the Mercedes through its paces, but knew the effort would be futile. He wasn't a stunt driver—he wouldn't be able to get away. He slowed down his vehicle and pulled over to the side. The SUV pulled up behind him. Clearly, he'd been right from the start—they'd come for him. He'd spoken to Richard and so they'd come for him. The only thing he hadn't mentioned to Richard had been the gain of function issue. He figured if Richard succeeded in getting his vaccine out to the public, to the world, the gain of function work would be irrelevant. The vaccine was the key.

A bearded man wearing wrap-around sunglasses was driving the Suburban. He stayed inside. But the back door on the passenger's side of the SUV opened and a man in a biosafety pressure suit got out. The man had an aerosolized can in his hand. Mostafa knew that after five years of not getting menglavirus, it was finally coming for him.

He looked towards the roadway, wondering if anyone would stop. No one did. He figured that if he were a layperson and saw an individual in a white biosafety positive pressure suit on the roadway, he wouldn't have stopped either. He probably would've sped up.

Seventy-eight wasn't a bad age to die and it wasn't a good age to die. For him, it was simply the age at which he *would* die.

The longer the tour of Riogenrix's campus went, the more discouraged Harrison became. The senator seemed to be humoring him, barely paying attention. Harrison took the senator first to Building Jenner, where he did in silico modeling and analyzed the reams of data pouring in from V-202. From Jenner, he took the senator to the Pasteur Labs, where the senator asked no questions whatsoever. Harrison felt as if he was giving himself a tour rather than the senator. The entire time, one of the senator's security contractors trailed them, standing outside the rooms while they went in. As the tour progressed, Harrison found himself talking less and less as he realized V-202 wasn't going to be saved after all. The senator truly seemed to be here to conduct a final check on the application denial. He didn't seem eager to reopen V-202.

But when they got to the eastern end of campus, where Building Petri, Building Lister, and Building Koch were situated, the senator perked up. Again, Harrison got the eerie sense that the senator was already familiar with the Riogenrix campus. As Harrison led them towards Building Petri, where the bulk of their higher-level biosafety research was conducted, the senator turned in the direction of Lister instead.

"What about there?" he said, pointing.

"Lister is a storage depot," Harrison said. "No active research gets conducted in Lister."

"Let's take a look anyway, doctor."

On the few tours Harrison had given to different agencies over the years, visitors had been interested in the clinical spaces. The labs were shiny and fun. But no one ever had asked to tour Lister—the storage depot. Harrison ignored his own hesitation at the oddness of the request. Again, he held onto the hope the senator might revive V-202. So instead of leading the senator to the lab spaces, Harrison began walking towards the storage depot. Harrison noticed the senator became more animated as they approached Lister. He also noticed that the security contractor who'd been trailing them throughout the tour broke off and went back to the Escalade.

Lister had the typical security measures implemented by Riogenrix: facial recognition camera, badge reader, keypad. As they neared Lister, the senator slowed his pace, as if he'd realized he'd been walking faster than his guide. Harrison approached the camera and waited for the first click, swiped his badge, waited for the second click, and finally entered his access code into the keypad. The door clicked for a third time and Harrison held it open for the senator as they went inside. Harrison glanced back towards the walkway to locate the security contractor who'd broken off from them but couldn't see him anywhere.

Harrison didn't know what to show the senator in Lister. Lister was an amalgam of Riogenrix. It contained laboratory equipment such as centrifuges and hood vents that hadn't yet been placed into service and those retired from service; a small administrative space consisting of a workstation for monitoring equipment inventories; and refrigerated storage facilities. Lister supported the work elsewhere on campus but wasn't the place where the work was conducted. Mostly, they kept equipment and biomedical reagents here. Harrison didn't come to Lister often. In fact, he couldn't really remember the last time he'd been here, even though he was supposed to be keeping tabs on Lister as much as he was supposed to keep tabs on the laboratory spaces. Again, he chastised himself for not taking better care of the administrative aspects of running Riogenrix. But then he saw the senator eyeing the refrigerated storage unit and Harrison remembered what else they stored here besides refrigerated reagents, refrigerated controls, and refrigerated growth media. They stored working vaccines.

Riogenrix was a research and development organization rather than a manufacturing facility. They developed mRNA vaccines but did not manufacture them. Vaccine manufacturing was a business unto itself with its own set of competencies. After Riogenrix had developed BOOSTers, they'd licensed the technology to the large vaccine firms, who then manufactured their own vaccines in their own production facilities. If Harrison did end up getting approval for V-202, Riogenrix would contract with the same large vaccine firms to produce the boosted V-202 vaccine in the quantity of billions of doses. Vaccine manufacturing had its own challenges, from the seemingly simple, such as securing enough glass vials and rubber stoppers for billions of manufactured doses, to the clearly complex, such as producing unadulterated product.

However, Riogenrix did manufacture small amounts of V-202 on its own. At this stage of development, none of the large players wanted to produce V-202, since there was no financial benefit to them for producing batches of eight single-dose-syringes with needles, which was the batch size that Riogenrix used in its Phase 2 studies. Riogenrix's in-house V-202 vaccine production happened in Pasteur on a small scale. They maintained the eight doses in a custom-made, CDC-compliant refrigeration unit that was able to maintain an exact temperature to the tenth of a degree.

The senator moved towards the refrigerated unit now. "What do you know about USAMRIID, doctor?" he said, pronouncing USAMRIID as *you-sam-rid*, as he stood in front of the vaccines.

Harrison was familiar with the United States Army Medical Research Institute of Infectious Diseases as the nation's— and probably the world's—most strenuous biosafety laboratory. USAMRIID was where the US Army studied and developed biodefense systems. It was where the bulk of the army's work on

Ebola vaccines had been conducted two decades ago. It was where the army continued to study anthrax, botulism, plague, and hundreds of other well-known and sparsely-known dangerous pathogens, including novel menglavirus strain 25.

Currently, two laboratories in the world were responsible for the bulk of the aero-virology knowledge base as related to the virus's in vitro spread and replication. The first was the Chinese Army's virology lab in Shanghai. Although the Chinese government had been slow to acknowledge the virus as an infectious aerosolized threat in the beginning stages of nMAQ25's spread, they'd eventually dedicated themselves to understanding it. The world's first good virology data had come out of China. However, since then, the bulk of the medical community's understanding of nMAQ25 had come out of USAMRIID. In many ways, the two laboratories—and two countries—were engaged in a race to label the other as inadequate. As a physician-scientist, Harrison had never played the blame game to which many politicians had been inclined. Viruses were evolutionary remnants of DNA and RNA replication. They'd always existed and always would. Although it was important to know from a virology standpoint from where a virus originated and how it became pathogenic, there was no utility in assigning blame for natural phenomena that had been affecting humans in one form or another for millennia.

"I'm familiar and unfamiliar at the same time, just the same as all civilian researchers." Harrison said.

"We have a new USAMRIID facility in Nevada, called West. It's been up and running for several weeks and it's where we are now conducting the bulk of our next-generation research on menglavirus. USAMRIID-West is off the books, but I'd like to take you there. I would like to take your vaccine there and I would like our top virologists to take apart your vaccine under your guidance and put it back together under your guidance. The FDA tells me there's real promise in your vaccine even if it's not quite ready for Phase 3. Give us a few months at USAMRIID-West and we'll get whatever imperfections in your vaccine sorted out—with your guidance, of course. We'll work with you to get your vaccine ready for expedited Phase 3 studies."

Harrison was confused. First and foremost, he didn't understand how the FDA could say V-202 didn't work. Even a day later, he couldn't understand. In fact, now, he understood even less. Even a medical student could analyze the data and see its legitimacy. Even a research fellow could review the developmental work and see it was a breakthrough. The FDA should've been ecstatic there was a preventive treatment for menglavirus already developed that only needed further testing before ridding the world of its most horrible pathogen. Harrison didn't understand why the FDA had rejected V-202 outright if they'd seen promise in it as the senator had said.

"You didn't indicate yesterday that the vaccine was promising. In fact, you stated the opposite. You said it was a waste of time and money for the American public."

"You have to understand, doctor, menglavirus is more than just a public health threat. It's a homeland security concern. Riogenrix is a small company, much smaller than any of the other companies and institutions who have submitted vaccine candidates to the FDA thus far. We weren't confident that Riogenrix possessed a sophisticated enough vaccine security system. In other words, we weren't confident some of the state actors— I don't think I need to mention which ones—weren't listening in on your calls and tapping your data and monitoring your servers. We didn't want to give the state actors any leads, both for your own safety and that of the American public. After today, I don't think you can blame us, doctor. You don't even have a security guard. The reality is your vaccine needs very little work, but your vaccine development program needs a lot of work. We need to finish your vaccine development within the secure confines of West."

Harrison wavered between anger and hope. He was angry the senator said V-202 still needed developmental work when it didn't, but he was also hopeful the vaccine would see the light of day after all. The senator was throwing him a lifesaver but he'd also been the one who'd sunk his vaccine. He tried to let go of the anger and hold onto the hope. After all, the senator was correct in recognizing some of Riogenrix's shortfalls on the security side. Harrison had been lax on the administration.

"What's the next step?" Harrison said.

"You come with me. We go to Nevada today. Right now. You bring the vaccine and you bring your knowledge."

"Now?" Harrison said, thinking about his family. He thought of Sofia at the window yesterday morning and again last night—both of which seemed like ages ago now. He thought of Jasmine and the confrontation they'd had over her being kept in the dark on the work he'd been doing at Riogenrix. "I can't go anywhere today, senator. Riogenrix is right here. I stay here."

"Nevada is a short flight away. It's early, doctor. We'll have you back as soon as we can. You can come back tonight. When you're ready to come back to San Diego, you give the word. I only ask you to hear my pitch."

Harrison considered what the senator had said. He'd never been to USAMRIID in Maryland although he'd always wanted to go. He'd never received an invitation. Richard, though, had received multiple invites over his career, including an extended stint as a guest lecturer. Richard had mentioned to Harrison the three days he's spent there as a guest lecturer during his Salk days had been amongst the highlights of his professional career. He'd also mentioned to Harrison he knew it was only a matter of time before Harrison was invited as well. Harrison guessed the invitation was happening now. Sure, Harrison wasn't going as a lecturer, but he also wasn't going to have to go for three days. He also wasn't going to have to go to Maryland. The senator was right—Nevada was only a little more than an hour's flight away.

"What can I share with my wife?" he said.

"You can share the truth—the country needs you. Just don't tell her about USAMRIID-West. We're not ready to let the world know about West yet. Give her a call now, if you need."

Harrison pulled out his cell phone. He thought about what to tell Jasmine before realizing he had no cell reception. He remembered Riogenrix's biosafety storage facilities were built with multiple layers of concrete block units, the same as the labs. Cellular coverage didn't permeate here. He wondered if the senator had known there was no cellular coverage in Lister, but pushed the thought out of his mind. He decided he would call Jasmine as soon as he landed in Nevada, once he had a clearer idea of when he would be home. Either way, he fully intended to be home tonight. He put the phone away.

"I'll go to USAMRIID-West in Nevada with you," Harrison said, "but we have to plan to have me back in San Diego tonight." He started towards the door but the senator didn't budge.

"Aren't you forgetting something, doctor?" the senator said.

Harrison tensed. "What am I forgetting?" he said. Now, he knew what the senator was going to say, but hoped he was wrong.

He wasn't wrong.

"You need to bring the vaccines," the senator said. "Bring two of them. We need them for development."

Again, Harrison debated going with the senator. He knew there was more happening with the senator than what he was sharing. However, Harrison couldn't let go of V-202. If the senator was offering a way to get V-202 approved and distributed, Harrison would proceed, albeit with caution.

He turned around and went to the refrigerated unit. He fished his keys out of his pocket and removed the padlock. He immediately located five prefilled syringes in the back of the fridge. He knew there were supposed to be eight prefilled syringes in stock at all times, though. After all, he'd established the protocols. He looked for the other three syringes that should've been in the unit but couldn't find them. He wondered if perhaps the additional three syringes were interspersed with reagent and control solutions, but told himself now wasn't the time to worry about them. He grabbed two syringes, deciding he could call Selene later to go through the refrigerated unit to truly confirm whether three doses were missing or only misplaced. As he pulled two syringes, he reminded himself not only did he need a new head of security for Riogenrix, but also a new lead research associate. The company was barely staying afloat and it showed in the company's protocols.

A binder was tethered to the fridge. He opened it and signed out two of the vaccines. Despite how computerized medical research and vaccine development had become, he'd never gotten around to changing the old-fashioned system of signing in and signing out vaccine doses for the clinical trials. These were the controls that Richard had established and Harrison had never updated. Again, he promised himself he would spend more time on the administrative aspects of running a company that Richard once had been so adept at managing. Based on today's encounter with the senator, Riogenrix might survive after all.

When Harrison and the senator returned outside, the security contractor who'd left them earlier was standing on the walkway with a small cooler in his hand. When Harrison saw the cooler, he understood the senator always had expected to leave with the vaccine. Harrison wondered if the senator had been intent on leaving with the vaccine even if Harrison had refused the senator's offers, but again he pushed the troublesome thought out of his mind. He reminded himself V-202 had new legs. Phase 3 and a compassionate use protocol were truly just around the corner. The security contractor opened the cooler and Harrison placed the two syringes inside.

Harrison was about to walk past the contractor to the SUV, but the contractor didn't budge. He outstretched his hand.

"We need your cell phone, doctor," the senator said, speaking for the contractor. "USAMRIID-West remains off the books. We need to make sure no one is tracking you. We don't want the state actors to know West exists."

Again, Harrison ignored the voice of concern that was pushing through his head. He told himself to focus on V-202. He withdrew his cell phone, but before handing it over to the contractor, he texted Jasmine, figuring a text was easier than a call in explaining to her why he was going to be home late.

I have a new meeting today, he messaged. *I'll be home late but will keep you updated.* He paused, and added, *I love you and I love Sofia...I am sorry for keeping you in the dark.*

He handed the phone over to the contractor, who showed it to the senator. The senator nodded and the contractor turned it off. Harrison wondered if the contractor was going to do anything with his phone other than turn it off, such as insert it into a shielded container, but he didn't. Instead, the contractor slipped it into the side pocket of his khaki pants.

The other security contractor had brought the senator's Escalade to the roadway adjacent to the walkway. The driver got out of the vehicle to open the rear doors for Harrison and the senator. As Harrison got into the SUV, he told himself to ignore the concerns percolating in his head. He told himself not to worry, because V-202 was alive again.

If Richard Hahn was the heart of Riogenrix and Harrison Boyd had become its brains, Selene Ramirez was its arms and legs, hands and feet. She was the person who kept Riogenrix moving forward through a thicket of regulatory and business concerns and everyday barriers. Research at Riogenrix involved the same aspects involved in all institutions, whether they were private institutions like Riogenrix, grant-based labs like the Salk Institute, or government-funded organizations like the NIH. Research involved compliance, payroll, and human resources. It involved the minutiae of making sure the systems stayed on all of the time and ensuring they had the right workstations and mainframes needed to crunch data and proffer mRNA solutions and run office email as well. Although she almost never stepped into the labs, she was Riogenrix's problem solver. She kept the lights on and the staff paid and the company running.

For the past week, she'd been the security guard as well. She'd set up three monitors in her office to keep an eye on the video feeds. Most of the time—pretty much all of the time—there was nothing to watch, so she didn't spend a lot of her day watching the feeds. She had too much else to do. But this morning, she'd been watching the feeds. Harrison hadn't shown up this morning at his usual time. She was keeping an eye on the cameras to know when he arrived. News of the V-202 Phase 3 application denial had spread quickly through the vaccine industry. She'd received phone calls and emails already from investment banks wanting to "discuss the future of Riogenrix." She'd even received an email from the acquisition arm of Steptech, Richard's old company—and her old company as well. She wanted to discuss with Harrison how Riogenrix was going to proceed. She was strongly inclined to continue on with Riogenrix as an independent company, but knew that because Harrison drove Riogenrix's research, the decision to continue on or sell would be his.

She saw the black Cadillac Escalade at the gates, noticed the exempt plates, and waited for the SUV to either call the number for her office in order to ask for passage onto campus —she'd posted a sign with her extension on the gate—or simply turn around and leave. It did neither. She watched the monitors and Harrison showed up several minutes later. She watched as Harrison got out of his sedan and approached the SUV. She watched them speak. As they spoke, she zoomed in on the person in the backseat of the Escalade. She recognized him almost immediately. He was Senator Spaulding. He was one of the more vocal Congress members, rotating his way through all of the television news shows, setting himself up for a presidential run, although everyone knew he was trailing the other candidates. He'd also been on yesterday's conference call with the FDA. She'd never cared for him, even before yesterday. He had the slickness that was bred from being in politics for an entire lifetime. She had a saying—never trust a politician with slicked back hair. She didn't trust his slicked back anything. Clearly, the senator had been waiting for Harrison.

She became increasingly concerned by what happened next. Selene stopped responding to the flood of emails pouring in from investment banks and leveraged buyout firms. She watched as Harrison led the senator from building to building and finally to Lister. She found it odd that Harrison was showing the senator the storage depot, because no actual research work occurred there. Before menglavirus, when Richard had still been on site every day, he'd given tours of the campus to colleagues and government agencies like NIH and DARPA, but had never included the storage building. Nonetheless, Harrison took the senator to Lister. She watched as the burly man in khaki pants broke off and returned with a cooler. She watched and waited as Harrison and the senator went inside the building. When they returned outside several minutes later, she watched Harrison hand over two separate objects. Then she watched as Harrison and the senator got into the SUV. The Escalade left campus and Harrison left along with it.

As she watched, she considered calling Harrison throughout, but didn't. Her relationship with Harrison was different than her relationship with Richard. Whereas she'd worked with Richard for the entirety of her professional career, becoming not just colleagues but close friends, she had a much more formal relationship with Harrison. Selene was fifty-two. She'd started as Richard's assistant and now was Riogenrix's chief administrator. In her personal life, she was a widow. Her husband had died fifteen years ago in a climbing accident in Utah. This had been during the tail end of her and Richard's stints at Steptech.

When she'd met Michael, he'd already been an experienced climber, a retired semi-professional, meaning he'd once been too good to be called an amateur, but hadn't made enough money at climbing rocks to quit his career as a medical device representative. She'd always hated and loved his passion for rock climbing. She loved that he was good at it but hated the worry that accompanied it. When they met, he tried to get her into rock climbing, but she didn't have the desire to scale cliffs with ropes. He adapted, and they went on hikes instead of climbs. Washington State, where they were living, had abundant hiking opportunities, and they made regular weekend jaunts to the best trails. Even so, he never stopped being a climber. He still went on two large climbing trips a year with his friends, most of whom also were retired semi-professionals. He died while simultaneously rappelling down the cliff with another climber. They'd needed to get down the cliff face quickly as the weather took a turn for the worst. The rope had become unbalanced and Michael had fallen.

The work that she and Richard had done immediately after Michael's death had been instrumental in getting her to continue living her life when all she'd wanted to do was stop doing anything. She'd never remarried, because she'd never truly recovered from her husband's death. She'd never hiked again, either. She'd been happy to leave Seattle with Richard for San Diego to start a new life. She'd tried dating for a while when she arrived in California, but she'd realized the pain from her loss hindered her ability to get close to anyone else. These days, Selene wasn't close with anyone other than Richard. She and Harrison were friendly in the way that people who'd worked together for a decade were, but they weren't personal friends. They didn't have conflict with each other but they didn't have the same closeness she had with Richard. Harrison was more reserved, never interested in delving into the personal lives of those who worked with him. Her relationship with Harrison always had been overly professional, even awkward at times. So she didn't call Harrison until he got into the SUV. By the time she did, the call went straight to voicemail.

She wasn't sure what was happening.

She logged into the server for the security cameras in order to watch the feeds again. Her uncertainty intensified. On the second viewing, she concluded that Harrison first had handed V-202 vaccines to the burly guy in the polo shirt. Then he'd handed over his phone.

She was definitely worried. Harrison seemed to have gone with the senator willingly, but she had a feeling the willingness didn't matter. She wished they'd installed security cameras in the storage depot itself. She also wished their cameras had sound. Richard had provided for the installation of video cameras when he'd designed the Riogenrix campus. This had been a decade ago, before the BOOSTers had come through. At the time, sound hadn't been a standard feature but only a part of the much more expensive cameras. The cameras they'd installed weren't cheap, at least not at the time. They'd been expensive, but they'd been much less expensive than those with sound capabilities. Such was life within Riogenrix. They worked on small company budgets and did what they could.

She considered how to proceed. She could call San Diego Police and report what had just happened with the senator and Harrison, although, again, she wasn't sure *what* had just happened. She only knew something not right had occurred. She reached for her cell phone and entered 911 on the keypad. But she didn't press the call button. She had a dawning realization. Calling the police would be a mistake because she knew what Harrison always had known. The vaccine really worked. V-202 worked.

She shivered. She understood the implications of what this meant for a small company like Riogenrix. Their tiny, scrappy firm in San Diego had accomplished what none of the huge conglomerates and well-funded transnational outfits had.

They'd found a way to stop menglavirus.

Stop the death.

They'd found a way to start life anew again in this country and every other country in the world. And people—important people, powerful people like the senator—were getting involved in what Riogenrix had set out to do and achieved. She didn't call the police. Even if she knew what to say to them, the senator was bigger than the police.

So she did what she hadn't done in a while. She decided to call the person with whom she'd spent almost three decades solving problems—first at Steptech, then the Salk Institute, and finally at Riogenrix, until the problems of health, age, and menglavirus had sidelined him—because now they had a problem they needed to solve. She called Richard Hahn, not as a friend this time checking in to see how he was doing during menglavirus, but as a colleague who would need to work with her again to figure out what the hell had just happened.

Even though it was past noon, Jasmine gave Sofia a real breakfast of French toast, not the Fruit Loops Sofia tried to eat every day. When Sofia went to the couch to get her tablet, Jasmine gently took her hand and led her to the dining room table, where they sat for lessons. They started off well enough—not well, but well enough—compared to what the lessons had been for the past several weeks. The math worked today. But then the afternoon came. The afternoons always were the hardest—for her and Sofia. In the afternoons, focus melted away. Today was turning out to be no different as the progress of the morning faded. She didn't blame Sofia—not today, not before—for the daily work with her that seemed like hair pulling, the slow progress towards nothing, the backwards stumbling, the few illusory steps forward. Earlier, they'd been swimming. Now they were treading water again. She felt herself failing Sofia.

"We'll go to the park when we're done," Jasmine said, providing the incentive she thought Sofia needed—and she needed—to keep going.

Like the day prior, Sofia eyed Jasmine. But unlike the day prior, there was no doubt in Sofia's glance. Jasmine wasn't trying to bribe her daughter, she told herself. She was only trying to give her normalcy, the small rewards children needed to keep moving forward.

For the next forty-five minutes, they did better. Sofia did better. Jasmine did too.

After they finished math, they ate lunch, and although Jasmine still had difficulty getting Sofia to entertain anything other than a grilled cheese sandwich, at least they ate lunch together. Jasmine made herself a chicken sandwich from the leftovers from the prior night.

They read after lunch, and, again, Sofia showed the effort Jasmine had found lacking for the entirety of what was supposed to be Sofia's second year of elementary school lessons. When

Jasmine felt Sofia slipping again, she placed her hand on Sofia's workbook and gently closed it.

"You did well," she said. "Let's go."

Today, Sofia didn't question if or where they were going. She knew.

They walked to the park. The day was chilly and overcast but still pleasant. A breeze was starting up. If Jasmine had more days like today, she would've liked San Diego more. If menglavirus hadn't happened, she might've been happier here. She was happy now, though. Momentarily okay. She was headed to the park for the second day in a row with her daughter. It felt good not to worry about Sofia's lessons, about how she was falling behind on reading and math, how she was disinterested in learning anything from Jasmine at the dining table. It felt good not to think about Harrison and his absence and his bizarre actions with his vaccine. It felt good not to think about the letter on her door and how she'd called the number on the back of the business card this morning. It felt good to be with her daughter. It felt good to be outside.

There was no one at the park other than Jasmine and Sofia, the same way it'd been only them for the entirety of menglavirus, or really, for their eight years together as mother and daughter. Sofia played on the jungle gym while Jasmine watched. Eventually, Sofia grew restless climbing ladders and going down slides by herself. Sofia asked Jasmine to join her on the jungle gym. Jasmine did, following her daughter in climbing the stairs and fitting herself down the narrow slide. When Jasmine found herself testing her luck one too many times by hurtling herself down the children's slide, she told Sofia that they should head to the swings instead. Sofia was excited at the suggestion. They went to the swings at the other end of the park, where Sofia climbed onto one of them with help from Jasmine. Jasmine pushed her daughter. She tried to get Sofia to swing on her own, teach her how to kick out and lean back. It took several minutes, but Sofia learned. Finally, when she was kicking out with confidence and ferocity, she said, "Can you swing with me,

Mommy?"

Jasmine shook her head. "I'll watch you, honey."

"You can swing with me, Mommy. There are enough swings for both of us."

There were two swings, of course, just enough for the both of them. She'd always chided Harrison for not participating. She told herself to participate. She sat on the swing beside her daughter. It was rusty and creaked but held her weight. She swung her legs in front of her. "Higher, Mommy," Sofia said, and Jasmine swung again and got higher and Sofia laughed.

As she swung beside her daughter, Jasmine felt happy that Sofia finally knew how to swing. She tried not to dwell on the fact Sofia hadn't learned until she was eight years old. Sofia didn't have a bike and didn't know how to bike but Jasmine told herself this would be next for Sofia. She would try to give her as much of a normal childhood as she could, despite menglavirus. She was happy to have been the parent to have taught Sofia how to swing and would be happy to be the parent to teach Sofia how to ride a bike. Swinging and riding a bike were tangible actions from which Jasmine could see tangible benefits right away. Knowing how to swing for an eight-year-old was essential. It wasn't like the lessons, the reading and writing and math that never got good enough fast enough.

Jasmine had her phone in her back pocket and it slipped out as she swung. She felt it sliding away from her but she didn't care. She felt freer with each kick of the legs and let the phone fall.

Richard was confused. From his conversation with Mostafa, he knew Senator Scott Spaulding on the Congressional Committee of Menglavirus Vaccines and Therapeutics had been responsible for denying Harrison's Phase 3 application in order to control the vaccine himself, but he couldn't put the rest of the pieces together. Mostafa had told Richard the senator would stop at nothing to get total control of the vaccine. Even so, Richard couldn't figure out the senator's intentions. He couldn't understand how the senator could put billions of lives at risk for whatever personal gains he was seeking—even a presidency.

He trusted Mostafa and Mostafa trusted him. Richard knew Mostafa had placed himself in danger by relaying the senator's actions to him and he hoped he could repay his old friend at some point by finishing the vaccine's development and getting it manufactured and distributed. He didn't want to think about the repercussions of what his friend had done. Mostafa had known the dangers of telling him. He'd also known the outcome of not telling, which is why he'd spoken to him. Mostafa had devoted himself to a career serving the public good as a physician-scientist at NIH. Meanwhile, Richard had spent the bulk of his career pursuing commercial success, or at least he had while he'd been at Steptech. Riogenrix was his opportunity to atone. He would atone with Harrison's vaccine. He would do right by his old friend by getting the vaccine out to the public.

After getting off the phone with Mostafa, Richard called Harrison twice and sent him a barrage of text messages. The calls went to voicemail and the messages were listed as undelivered. Richard knew reception in the Riogenrix labs was weak at best because of the multiple layers of concrete block units that made up the walls. He hoped Harrison was working but couldn't convince himself this was the case. He got the sense that Harrison was in trouble.

He was about to call Selene when she called him. They spoke all of the time, but he had a sense today's call was different than their usual checking-in conversations.

"Are you okay, Selene?" he said. "What happened?"

"I'm fine. I'm not calling about myself."

"Are you calling about Harrison?"

"Yes."

"What happened to him? I've left voicemails and sent text messages but haven't heard back from him."

"I don't know."

"Is he on campus?"

"He was."

"He was?"

"He's not anymore. He left. He left with the senator, the one on television, the one who heads up Congress' vaccine committee."

"Senator Scott Spaulding? He left with him?"

"Yes."

"The senator was on campus?"

"Yes."

"Do you know where they went?"

"No idea, Richard."

"No matter what happens, tell security not to let anyone else on campus."

Selene was silent.

"Selene?"

"I am security."

"What do you mean, Selene?"

"Exactly what I said."

"You are security?"

"Yes."

Richard didn't understand but didn't have time to wait for an explanation. "If you are security, then *you* don't let anyone else on campus. I need all of the modeling and development data for Harrison's vaccine..." He trailed off. He could never remember Riogenrix's internal name for Harrison's vaccine. He couldn't remember quite a few things anymore. "What do we call Harris' vaccine?"

"V-202," Selene said. He felt the gentleness in Selene's voice and he wondered what he would do if something happened to her—or Harrison.

"Yes, V-202," he said. "I need all of the modeling and development data for V-202."

"Everything is on the servers."

"Then I'll need the servers. I'll see you in an hour."

"You're coming here?"

"Yes."

Again, there was silence. "Do you think that's a good idea, Richard?"

Now *he* was quiet.

"Richard?"

"I know it's a good idea," he said, and finished the call, telling her he would be there soon.

He went to the garage. Despite being boarded up in his La Jolla home for the past five years, he'd made sure to maintain a schedule to keep him as mentally sharp as possible. He woke daily at 9 a.m.—two hours later than he'd gotten up while actively working at Riogenrix but still on the right side of noon—in order to start a day of nothingness. He shaved every day. He got dressed in slacks and loafers. As part of his schedule, he went to the garage twice a week—Tuesdays and Fridays—to take his vehicles—a six-year-old Lexus sedan and a vintage Range Rover—for a drive around the block, thereby keeping the batteries working and oil circulating. Today was Tuesday. He was due for a drive anyway. He told himself he was going to be due for a drive on Friday as well and to make sure he kept up the schedule. He needed to secure Harrison's vaccine. Since the vaccine worked, he needed to get the vaccine out to the people.

Richard put on his old, expired N95 respirator mask. As he prepared to leave the house, he knew the world had changed permanently. Even with a vaccine, there would be a permanent difference in the way people interacted with each other. The suspicion and mistrust of each other and of the institutions that were supposed to serve and protect them wouldn't go away with a vaccine. After five years, what had once been a new behavior was now old. Even with Harrison's vaccine, novel airborne viruses were here to stay. The world was too vast and populated not to have another disaster. He doubted whether he would ever see another virus disaster himself since he was an old man and wouldn't live long enough, but he knew the newest generations inevitably would.

Despite his health conditions, he left the house. He headed to the Riogenrix campus for the first time in five years.

Thelma McGraw saw them again, for the second day in a row, although later in the day today than yesterday. Again, she felt optimism at seeing the mother and daughter together. She even felt happy. They went to the swings and she watched the mother coax the daughter through the technique of getting airborne. As she watched them, she felt hope for herself and her own daughter as well. She only had a few more hours until she called Naomi. She felt this would be the week Naomi picked up. As she watched the mother and daughter, she drank her gin and felt a renewed hopefulness. Yes—today, Naomi would be waiting for her phone call.

But then she saw the man at the edge of the park and her optimism faded. She felt dread instead. She saw the daughter on the swings and she saw the mother on the swings with her and she saw the man watching them from a distance. The man was tall and he looked like he was in his early forties and from a distance he looked well built. But Thelma didn't notice the man because of what he looked like. Instead, she noticed the man because of what he was—and wasn't—wearing. He was wearing what looked to be a doctor's white coat. And he wasn't wearing a mask. For five years, everyone had been wearing filtering masks. Even if they hadn't in the beginning, they certainly were now. But he wasn't wearing one.

She also noticed him because he was watching the mother and daughter.

The park was immediately in front of her and she had a clear view of the playground. The man was further up the street, out of view of the mother and the daughter, but Thelma could see him. From a distance, she studied his face, trying to remember him if she needed to describe him later on to whatever law enforcement decided whatever had happened was serious enough to come around. He had his arms folded across his chest and was leaning against a wall that abutted a municipal electricity transformer. She had a horrible feeling about him. She knew the mother couldn't see him but she knew he could see the mother and she knew he was watching the mother and the daughter. He had his body turned towards the park and he had his phone out but wasn't talking or texting on it. He was holding it in his hand and rotating it with a nonchalance that seemed to indicate he belonged. He didn't belong, though, not in the tranquility of the park, not amongst the mother and the daughter. He wasn't only an outsider, but he was an intruder. She knew he didn't belong.

For a second, she wondered if he was one of those few people who'd been purported to have immunity to the virus, one of the people who'd been purported to have a genetic variation that made the virus unable to infect them. She was pretty sure the alleged immunity had been disproven a long time ago, but still she wondered. Or maybe he was only a physician out for a walk on a cloudy day after a long stint in the hospital.

Except, deep down, she knew he wasn't. She didn't need to wonder if he had false immunity. She didn't care about him. She cared about the mother and daughter.

Every night, she slept with her pistol. It was a compact 9 millimeter, the same one she'd used while working. She kept it in the top drawer of her nightstand. Back in the old days, when Naomi had been young and Thelma had still been part of the department, she'd kept the pistol in a quick access firearm safe with a programmable code. The code had been 5270. The number had had no meaning, not a birthday or an anniversary or a favorite set of numbers. It'd been random, the same number assigned from the factory. Nowadays, there was no more lockbox and no Naomi at home. She kept her pistol in the top drawer of the nightstand. In the earlier days of menglavirus, the pistol had come in useful when the looters, squatters, and debt collectors had come around. She wondered if it was going to come in useful again today.

She watched the man to see if he was going to move on. She hoped he was. She hoped she'd been wrong in thinking he'd been watching the mother and the daughter with ill intent. But he didn't stop rotating the phone in his hand and he didn't stop leaning against the block wall and he didn't stop watching.

She calculated the distances between herself and the park and the man and the park and herself and the man. She was fifty feet away from the park. The man was two hundred and fifty feet away from the mother and daughter. This meant she was close to three hundred feet away from the man. If the man headed towards the playground, she would be able to position herself on the driveway with a clear view to intercept him with a shot. Even if he didn't approach the mother and daughter, she didn't like the way he was observing them. He was up to no good. She wanted to let him know *she* was here too and *he* wasn't supposed to be here. She would stand on the driveway with her pistol so the man could see her. If he made any movements towards the mother and the daughter, she would handle him. She didn't think she would need to fire her weapon. A show of force would likely be good enough.

She needed to get her pistol, of course, and she needed her mask. She needed her mask first. She usually kept it by the entrance. She only had a single FN99. She didn't go outside anymore, but she used the mask when she opened the door for gin and grocery deliveries from the provisions facility. She left the window to go to the console table at the entrance.

She wondered if anybody else was watching the man. She wondered if anybody else cared.

She went to the entryway and put on the mask, fitting it against her cheeks and over the bridge of her nose. She returned to the window to check on the mother and daughter and saw they were still in the playground. The man without the mask was still at the block wall. He had his free hand in the pocket of the white lab coat and seemed to be playing with something in there. She wondered if he had a gun. She rushed towards the bedroom to get her pistol.

She felt hot and sweaty. At first, she thought her discomfort was because of the mask, but then she felt a flutter in her chest and then she felt lightheaded and her worry changed to anxiety and she knew that she wasn't sweating because of the mask. Today wasn't hot at all. In fact, it was cool, and getting cooler. But she was one day older and one day more pickled, and at this age of fifty-one, a single day was significant, and she had a panicky sense today was her day. She knew she wasn't healthy and didn't have unending years in front of her but hadn't thought today was going to be the end.

Her heart fluttered. As it did, she thought not of her own life and the years she'd lived and the years more that maybe she could've lived if she'd been different, but she thought about Naomi, whom she hadn't spoken to for two years now. She thought about the man out there in the park who wasn't wearing a mask, the man who was watching the mother and daughter, the man whom she knew was up to no good, no good at all.

Thelma McGraw didn't die from menglavirus but from a supraventricular tachycardia brought on by worsening alcoholic cardiomyopathy. She died in her house during the fifth year of menglavirus, survived by a daughter three hundred miles away.

They went south to San Diego International Airport. Even now, after having lived in San Diego for over a decade, Harrison was in awe of the airport. The airport abutted downtown, nestled in between high rises and the Pacific Ocean. The first time he'd flown into San Diego had been as a third-year medical student when he'd taken the six-week research rotation with Richard at the Salk Institute. The descent into San Diego International had been unnerving the first time, unlike anything he'd experienced on the east coast. The plane had cut right over downtown's skyscrapers while approaching the ocean with alarming velocity. As the plane had descended—perilously fast, Harrison thought—it had seemed as if it would overshoot the runway and land in the water. Of course, it hadn't, but it seemed as if the balancing act had been unbalanced from the start.

He felt as if right now he was conducting his own landing, trying to bring V-202 down as smoothly as he could despite the imbalance he felt all around him. They were on the 163, headed towards the coast. He was in the back seat with the senator, separated only by an arm's distance. Everyone wore fitted FN99 masks but Harrison felt uncomfortably close to everyone. He watched the contractors to see if they too felt uncomfortable, but they didn't seem to be bothered. He figured, why would they? They were mercenaries, after all.

Harrison and the senator didn't talk. Instead, the senator spent the drive to the airport on the phone, discussing governance issues with an aide. The bulk of the conversation centered on the distribution of foodstuffs to residents through provisions facilities. Harrison found it oddly comforting to hear the senator speak about the more mundane aspects of being in Congress. He felt more relaxed knowing the senator had work to do other than monitor menglavirus vaccines. When the senator was done speaking to his aide, he winked at Harrison, and made another phone call, this time to what seemed to be a spouse or girlfriend or partner. Harrison wasn't sure. He didn't know if the senator was married or single or something in between. He'd never thought to wonder. Until this morning, he'd never imagined he would ever want to know. In fact, until yesterday, when the senator had unexpectedly been on the FDA conference call, Harrison never would've thought he would have spoken to the senator at all.

When they arrived at the airport, the contractors took the Escalade through a private terminal. Homeland Security spoke briefly with the contractor who was driving before waiving them through the gates onto the tarmac where a jet was waiting for them. Harrison had never flown on a private jet before and as he looked at the jet that was just for them, he felt oddly exhilarated. He felt special. Despite the nagging feeling that something about today was unbalanced, he couldn't help but feel accomplishment in being with the senator at the airport on his way to a classified military research lab in Nevada. He felt as if his work over the past decade as a vaccine developer—and the prior decade as a student and resident and staff physician—was paying off. The despondency weighing him down this morning was lifting.

The contractors opened the Escalade's doors and all of them boarded the jet via an air-stair. The plane had four captain chairs, an upholstered bench, and a small table. The senator and Harrison each took a captain chair while the contractors sat at the rear of the plane on the bench. Again, Harrison and the senator didn't speak. The senator was on his phone, reading and replying to emails. Harrison got the odd sense the senator was being deliberately reticent with him, as if he didn't want to say too much—or anything at all—until they were in the air and well on their way to Nevada, as if he didn't want Harrison to change his mind about going with him. They didn't taxi long, just a few minutes. Then they were gone. As the plane ascended, Harrison waited to see if the senator now would speak to him about V-202 or USAMRIID-West but the senator still answered emails and sent text messages. After the plane reached cruising altitude, the senator finally turned to him.

"What do you know about GOF, doctor?"

Harrison was caught off guard. He hadn't been expecting the question, so for a moment, he didn't know anything about GOF. He wondered if the senator had misspoken or if he'd heard wrong. But the senator didn't seem to have misspoken. He was waiting for Harrison to answer. The senator really *had* asked him about GOF. Undoubtedly, Harrison knew a lot more about GOF than the senator, but still he wasn't an expert. His own research didn't involve it—it never had. Nonetheless, Harrison found it immediately concerning that the senator had brought up the subject.

"I keep myself generally updated on major work but I don't follow it closely," Harrison said.

"I'd never heard of it until menglavirus."

"It usually isn't a lay concern."

"It is a concern for the Committee."

"What does it have to do with my vaccine?"

"I don't want to spoil anything, doctor. Let's wait until our destination. It's easier to talk when we get to where we're going. Safer too. We can't shield planes because of flight instruments."

The senator leaned back in his swivel and made another phone call.

Harrison turned away. He was concerned. In asking him about gain of function, Harrison wondered if the rumors regarding nMAQ25 were true. He could think of no other reason for the senator to mention it unless they were.

He checked his watch. It was nearing the end of what in the pre-menglavirus days would've been the school day. Jasmine and Sofia would be finishing lessons right around now. The plane ride would be short, an hour and change until touchdown in Nevada. He still felt as if he could get home tonight, but he felt more uneasy than he had before. He was worried about Jasmine and Sofia. The creeping realization that novel menglavirus strain 25 could be related to GOF was troublesome.

Horrendously troublesome.

As they left the park, Jasmine tried to decipher the text message Harrison had sent her while she'd been on the swings. She couldn't. The screen had cracked when the phone had fallen from her back pocket. She considered calling Harrison to find out what he wanted but decided there was no point. He had probably texted her to let her know he would be home late. Ninety-five percent of his text messages were as such. At some point, she would have to send out her phone for repairs. She would be without it for a few days but she didn't care. Being on the swings with her daughter had been worth the cracked phone —and more.

As they rounded the block back towards the house, Jasmine felt Sofia press her hand into her own. Jasmine looked down and she could tell something was wrong.

"The man without a mask is here," Sofia said. "The man who left the letter. The man from the video."

Jasmine slowed down to turn her head to look for the man but Sofia pulled her forward.

"Where? What man?"

"He's following us, Mommy."

Jasmine stopped completely now and turned her entire body towards the park. She saw him. He was wearing the same white coat he'd worn yesterday when he'd placed the letter on their door. He still had no mask. She had no trouble seeing what Sofia had seen. He was the man whom she'd called this morning. She felt more regret than ever over having contacted him. She felt extreme guilt.

"Walk faster," Jasmine said. She tried to sound calm but wasn't. Sofia was right—the man without a mask was following them. He wasn't strolling or enjoying the nonexistent scenery of their deteriorated neighborhood. He was watching and following. He hadn't sped up his pace after they had, but he was trailing them nonetheless.

He doesn't have to speed up, Jasmine thought. *He knows where he's going. He knows where we're going.*

They were returning to the house and he was following them there. They were two blocks from getting home. Again, she wondered if Harrison had vaccinated the man without a mask, if perhaps he was a business associate or even a test subject. She couldn't figure out the craziness in which Harrison might be involved due to the vaccine—or what he was now involving them in. Harrison had found the cure and the cure must matter. Of course, her husband would be quick to point out a vaccine wasn't a cure but a preventive measure, but for her, a vaccine *was* a cure if it stopped the madness of their wash, rinse, and repeat lives. It was a cure if Sofia could go to a real school for the first time in her life and have real playmates and friends. Or at least, that's what she'd thought this morning. Now, she wished the vaccine didn't exist. It wasn't a cure for anything.

"Should we run?" Sofia said.

"Just walk fast. Quickly."

"He doesn't have a mask on."

"I know, honey. I know."

"Should we call Daddy?"

"Not now."

"Daddy will know what to do."

"No, he won't."

"He will. I need to tell him something."

She wanted to stop walking and turn to her daughter and crouch until she was eye to eye with Sofia and say, *Daddy isn't here. It's just Mommy. It's just you and I. Daddy won't know a damn thing about what to do.*

But she didn't. Whatever was happening right now wasn't Sofia's fault. Jasmine resolved not to take her own stresses out on her daughter. They shouldn't have left the house. She shouldn't have called the number on the back of the business card. She continued with her quickened pace. Being a mother was about endurance and restraint, keeping everything inside while you and your child were trapped in the same house day after day without end.

Jasmine didn't care about work and a career at all anymore. She found it difficult to believe she'd once considered customs law important. She only cared that her daughter could be safe while progressing in life. She'd gone to the park—*the park for Christ's sake*—and put herself in danger. Put her daughter in danger. And why? Because she'd wanted her daughter to get better? Or because she'd wanted *herself* to get better?

"Call Daddy," Sofia said.

Instead of strangling her daughter like she felt like doing, she gave up, like she seemed to do a lot these days. Sofia didn't feel safe, and if she could make Sofia feel safer, she would do so. Without slowing her pace, she pulled her phone out of her back pocket, and called Harrison, struggling with the cracked screen but getting it done. As she called, she made sure to be clear she was making a phone call, hoping that when the man behind them saw she had her phone to her ear, he would turn around and leave them alone and go back from where he'd come.

Of course, Harrison didn't pick up. The call went directly to voicemail, like it did half of the time when he was lost in his lab. Most of the time when he was at work—which was almost all of the time—he didn't pick up. Today was nothing new. She pretended he had, though, thinking if the man without a mask saw her talking to someone on the phone, he would be more inclined to leave them alone. She turned and looked at the man to make sure he saw her on the phone. He was still following them. He'd picked up his pace.

She hung up, and said, "We're going to jog home, honey."

"Can we run?"

"Yes, we can run. If we need to run, we can run. But we can jog for now. We can just speed up a little bit more. We can get back home a little bit more quickly."

"And if the man without the mask starts to run, we'll run?"

"Yes, dear. He won't run, though. He's not following us."

As soon Jasmine said the man wasn't following them, she regretted it. These moments of false optimism—outright lies to her daughter—in which she said everything was going to be all right weren't bringing her and Sofia any closer. If anything, it was another of the reasons for the continued distancing. She tried not to dwell on the matter. Right now wasn't the time for her to self-scout her own parenting.

She glanced at the houses to her left and right with drawn shades and shuttered windows. She wondered who was watching and if they would do anything if the man reached them. She didn't think they would. Knowing your neighbors didn't mean anything anymore.

"Let's start, honey," she said. "Let's jog."

And as soon as she started jogging, she decided she wanted to run. She wanted to get Sofia home and she wanted to get Sofia home now.

"Okay, honey," she said. "Let's run."

Sofia started to run and Jasmine ran beside her. They ran down Crane Street, and turned right onto their own block.

When they rounded the corner, Jasmine said, "Can you go faster, honey?" and Sofia did go faster, a lot faster, and Jasmine went faster too. They turned into the driveway of their house and rushed inside. She locked the doors and sent Sofia to the kitchen but Sofia wouldn't leave her side so Jasmine put an arm around her and pulled her close. She steeled herself, and pulled back the window. She watched as the man without the mask neared and then walked in front of their house. He stood on the sidewalk adjacent to the driveway, turned towards them, and walked to the front entrance of the house. Jasmine stepped back and pulled Sofia back with her into the rear of the living room. They stood far away from the door, and waited. She pulled up the cameras on her phone. The image was imprecise because of the broken screen but she could see him standing at the entry. Jasmine thought about her pistol and whether she would be able to get it from upstairs before the man forced his way into the house. She wondered if taking out her pistol would scare Sofia more and decided she would rather have Sofia scared but safe. As she was about to tell Sofia they were going to run upstairs to Mommy and Daddy's bedroom, he knocked. And she froze. She watched the cameras on her phone. Again, the images were tough to decipher. He didn't wait any longer at the door or knock again. He turned and returned to the street. Once he was back on the sidewalk, he watched the house for several more seconds before turning back towards the sidewalk and continuing to walk past the house. She watched the man until he disappeared from the cameras.

They waited several minutes in silence for the man to return. He didn't return. Finally, she sat down and hugged her daughter. She felt Sofia's tiny heart pounding in her chest as she brought her close and embraced her. Jasmine was shaking too as she hugged her daughter. She was never as glad as she was now to be home. She told herself she would never leave this house again.

For the first time in five years, Richard turned his Lexus right onto Riogenrix Way, the small street leading onto campus. Since starting Riogenrix over a decade ago, he'd always felt pride when arriving. The pride wasn't because of campus itself, but because of the work they were doing. He believed in Riogenrix's mission. He'd atoned for his profit-oriented Steptech days—or so at least he'd thought.

But today he didn't feel the usual pride. The front gate was open and the security station was empty. He felt dread, as if he'd arrived on campus too late to make a difference. Harrison had developed a viable vaccine for stopping the unchecked spread of menglavirus but Harrison was gone. Whether by crook or cajole, Harrison was with the senator, the very man who'd stopped Harrison's vaccine from going forward, the very man about whom Mostafa had warned him, the very man who had his own intentions. Richard feared not being able to contact Harrison earlier today meant he would never be able to contact Harrison ever again. He worried that Harrison's vaccine was lost to the world. He worried even more about the troubling possibility that Harrison was lost to *him* as well.

Selene was waiting for him outside of Jenner. He hadn't seen her in person for several months. At the start of menglavirus, she'd visited him at the house, dropping off journals that he usually read, but as menglavirus had stretched onwards, he'd asked her to stop coming. There'd been no point in her bringing him the journals anymore because he'd found it hard to keep up. As he saw her now, he thought she looked older than the last time he'd seen her, but he knew he looked older too.

He parked, struggling to get his vehicle squeezed into a single space. He never would've thought driving would've become so different, but it had. He wasn't the same driver anymore. He knew he wasn't the same person anymore either. He reached across the console to open the passenger door. She stepped in.

"You need a mask, Richard," she said.

"I have a mask."

"It's only an N95. You need a fitted FN99. We can find you one."

"I don't need one, Selene."

"Is your mask even current?"

"It works fine." Despite the recent months during which he hadn't seen her in person and the way they'd both aged during this time, he felt familiar with her. They'd always worked well together, complementary. When he'd left Salk to form Riogenrix, he'd offered Selene ten percent of the new venture. His former business partner at Steptech, Dr. Jason Carr, had scoffed at him for offering her equity, since she wasn't a researcher, but he'd looked at the offer as the right decision. His success had always been dependent on Selene and the work they did together. She'd kept them pointed forward. Now, as he sat with her for the first time in months, he felt as if he'd abandoned Selene as much, if not more, than he'd abandoned Harrison. He wondered if all of the decisions he'd made over the past five years had been wrong. "Do we have the servers ready?" he said.

"Working on it."

"Can you show me what happened?"

"I've checked the cameras. I haven't gone to the buildings yet but I think Harrison gave the senator the vaccines we have on hand."

"Where's our guard? Bill? Billy?"

"Bill Greenblatt. He died."

"Of what?"

She turned towards him but he didn't need her to say anything else for him to know.

"How many vaccines do we usually have on hand?" he said.

"We maintain an in-house inventory of eight. We distribute them for Phase 2. Or at least we did."

"Where should we start?"

"We'll start with the vaccines. We'll start with Lister."

He reversed, and they drove towards the eastern part of

campus. They parked outside of Lister, and Selene led them up the walkway to the building. As he followed her, he knew she'd slowed her pace for him, which both saddened and frustrated him.

Selene approached the entry system for Lister, waiting for the facial recognition camera to identify her. As Selene waited, he asked her to step aside. He wanted to see if the system would still recognize him. It was set up to constantly adapt to facial changes. She moved to her left and he stepped forward. He waited for the click, the signal that the camera had recognized him. The click didn't come. Five years away had been too much. He looked different, of course, and the cameras hadn't adapted to him.

"Let me, Richard."

"I don't have a badge on me anyway," he said, speaking the truth.

Once inside Lister, he walked amongst the equipment, sweeping his hand over the fume hoods and centrifuges. In here, not much had changed. When he'd started the company, he'd designed these buildings in conjunction with the architects and engineers, allocating every square foot for function. Riogenrix's campus was deliberately concentrated, intentioned as a nimble reaction to the bureaucratic behemoth Steptech had become in his final days there. The pride that had eluded him earlier when he'd gotten on campus surfaced now. Even if he didn't belong at the forefront of the vaccine development space anymore, he still felt as if he belonged at Riogenrix. He felt his influence in the simple placement of storage units, inventory workstations, and cabinets, all of which he'd designed for efficiency and productivity. Everything good he'd learned while co-founding and running Steptech, he'd poured into Riogenrix, while also trying to keep out everything bad he'd learned at the same time.

Selene led them to the refrigerated units. She unlocked a large custom unit with three sliding doors that he recognized. He'd ordered the unit ten years ago, spending a good chunk of money on the best engineering and manufacturing available in the US, knowing vaccine development depended on reliable progress. Selene pushed aside reagents as she searched for the vaccine syringes. Finally, she pulled out three prefilled syringes and placed them on the hardtop counter.

"We only have three," she said, wearied distress entering her voice.

Richard shuffled to the binder attached by a chain to the unit. He spent several seconds reviewing the logbook, another system he'd developed a decade ago. For a moment, he felt pride again, but then it disappeared, and he felt disappointment. Manually logging vaccines worked but wasn't standard procedure nowadays. Digital inventory monitoring was. He didn't pretend to be an expert in inventory monitoring but knew he should've been on campus the past five years to shepherd Riogenrix through the systems changes it'd needed. He hadn't brought Harrison on board for administration. He'd brought him aboard because of his scientific brilliance and tenacity. Meanwhile, Selene's expertise was non-clinical. It was general administrative. He'd set up Riogenrix so he himself could guide the company through system controls. He'd failed Selene. He'd failed Harrison. He'd failed the company.

"Harrison signed out two, so we should have five remaining," he said. "We're missing three."

"Let me check," Selene said.

He let Selene double-check the logbook but knew her gesture was superfluous. He knew the controls he'd set up and how to interpret his own work. It was everyone else's work—particularly Harrison's—he had difficulty understanding.

He pointed to several lines. "Angela Payton's name is all over the log. Who is she?"

"She was our senior research associate. She had a lot of duties as we thinned out our personnel, including maintaining our vaccine inventory and signing it out to testing centers for Phase 2 studies."

"I should talk to her."

"You can't."

He waited for the answer he knew was coming. "But?"

"She died two weeks ago from menglavirus."

"Two employees have died from menglavirus over the past month?"

"She didn't contract it here. She got it from her fiancé."

"And Bill Greenblatt?"

"Department of Health said he got it from a grocery store."

"Do we believe them?"

"Maybe not anymore."

He adjusted his mask, wondering about his own exposure. But he reminded himself he could no longer stay home. Riogenrix was the right place for him, no matter how many people had died from menglavirus. He didn't know if he would be able to understand how to reconstruct Harrison's vaccine from his notes on the server but he had no choice but to try. He'd spent his life in vaccine development. Old man or not, he expected himself to figure out his protégé's work.

Even so, he knew Riogenrix couldn't produce the vaccine, at least not at the scale needed. They were a developer and not a manufacturer. Riogenrix needed help. They'd expected the government to help them with production—they'd expected the government to be ecstatic about helping them—but clearly that was not the case. If the government wasn't going to help them produce and distribute the vaccine to seven billion people worldwide, Harrison would find another partner. He knew of one company who had the scale and influence necessary to produce and distribute Harrison's vaccine. He didn't maintain good relations with his former partner at Steptech anymore, but he would have to swallow his pride to get Harrison's menglavirus vaccine distributed to the world.

"How long do you think we have until the servers are ready?" he said.

"We'll have partials in two or three hours. But for full mirrors of the servers, we're going to need most of the night, maybe even part of tomorrow morning."

"I can start with partials. I should be able to figure out some of Harrison's work. For the full mirrors, though, let's create copies. Then let's wipe the onsite servers. From here on out, only we have access to Riogenrix's data."

"Two copies?" she said. Richard knew Selene was thinking the same as he.

"One for me. One for—well, let's see what we can do with the other copy."

He didn't need to verbalize what both of them already knew. If he needed to grovel to Jason Carr, he would grovel. Harrison had worked on a vaccine, and found it, and now Richard would make sure to get it distributed. Harrison's vaccine would be Richard's last hurrah.

"We also shouldn't keep our in-house vaccines here anymore," Selene said. "If we are wiping ourselves clean, we need to *really* wipe ourselves clean."

"Are they temperature sensitive?"

"Yes. But I have a cooler bag that I bring for lunch."

"Where is it?"

"Jenner. In the office."

"Let's get it."

Selene palmed the three remaining syringes and turned towards the door. Richard followed her.

They got back into his Lexus. He paused before starting up the engine, wanting to make sure he expressed himself now in case he couldn't in the future. "Thank you, Selene," he said. "Not just for today, but for the three decades we've worked together." He paused, choosing his words. "We have accomplished so much but we have one more goal to achieve."

As she turned towards him, he again saw an older person than the one he remembered. He was reminded again of how much time had passed for the both of them.

"Of course, Richard," she said. "Just like old times." She turned in her seat to face the front. "Now let's get moving, Richard. We can reminisce later."

He put the car in reverse and they headed back towards Building Jenner.

They landed at a military airstrip in Nevada in the late after-noon. By the flight time, Harrison estimated they were three to four hundred miles north of Las Vegas. All of them—Harrison, the senator, and the two security contractors—got into another Escalade similar to the one they'd taken from Riogenrix to the airport. Like the previous one, the new vehicle also carried ex-empt plates. The contractor in the passenger seat opened the glove compartment and placed Harrison's phone inside of it. The senator put his own phone away as well, tucking it into his pants pocket. He finally seemed as if he wanted to talk.

"We have some time until we reach West, doctor," the sen-ator said. "Tell me about your work. How on earth did you man-age to accomplish what no one else could?"

Harrison didn't speak often about his work to anyone other than Richard. He remembered the argument he and Jasmine had had this morning. He didn't know if his reticence was a function of his personality or if his reluctance to share the details of his work was because he didn't want to simplify it, make it seem as if A always led to B and B always led to C, when in reality, mRNA vaccine research was more like A led to A which led to more A and then maybe it led to B but it probably didn't.

"It's hard to boil down my work to a summary, senator," Har-rison said. "But if I had to condense it, the summary would be that I worked five years on a menglavirus vaccine, the vaccine works, and the FDA—or you, I'm not sure who—denied it."

The senator laughed. "Touché. Humor me."

He tried to talk but found himself not knowing how to reduce mRNA vaccine technology to a soundbite. But he understood more and more as he *tried* to explain V-202 to the senator how he'd kept Jasmine out of his world. As he talked, he discovered the answer to his question about why he'd shut her out of his life at Riogenrix—he'd been reticent with Jasmine because of his own arrogance. There was no other explanation. He'd wanted to show her how complicated his work had been. The best way to do so had been to say nothing to her at all. Now, he understood his failure.

Thankfully, after Harrison gave the senator a brief explanation of V-202's development, the senator stopped asking. The senator went back to his phone. Harrison was glad for the silence, and the afternoon faded as they drove through the pink and purple-skied desert. As evening neared, they arrived at a military installation in northeast Nevada. They idled in a depot outside of manned gates and barbed wire fences. A white Chevy Suburban was already parked in the depot. The Suburban also had exempt plates. Harrison tried to distinguish the driver of the other SUV, but the driver didn't get out of the vehicle. Nonetheless, Harrison understood he too was a security contractor, one of the senator's men. As the two SUVs idled beside each other, Harrison thought that if menglavirus didn't kill them, carbon monoxide would.

"How much longer until we go into USAMRIID?" Harrison said.

"Not long, doctor. I promise you—the wait will be worth it, both professionally and personally."

Harrison looked out the window at the military installation. It was imposing and serious, different even from a distance than anything he'd experienced thus far in his career. He wasn't sure what he was going to find at USAMRIID-West, but he was eager—and worried—to find out. So he settled into his seat. He was willing to wait, whether it took an hour or two or more to get into USAMRIID-West. Despite the knowledge he would be home late tonight, he knew he had to be here.

The house felt different when the sun went down.

After the man without a mask had disappeared from the cameras, Jasmine had gone outside to make sure he'd really left. She scanned the streets, and saw no one. After the ineffectiveness of the last time, she didn't try to call the police. But she did call Harrison. Again, he didn't answer. Again, she wasn't surprised. She sent him a text message. It didn't go through. He'd said this morning he was stepping away from the research labs but of course he hadn't. She pictured him in gloves and masks, behind fume hoods and hunched over tubes and pipettes. She'd taken Sofia's tablet and downloaded onto it the application to view the house's security cameras, wanting a clearer view of the street than what her cracked phone was offering.

Throughout the rest of the afternoon, she found herself repeatedly taking Sofia's tablet from her and checking the cameras before giving the tablet back with as much nonchalance as she could muster. She put on a calm face and tried her best to erase the day from the house. There'd been no more lessons. She'd let Sofia stay on the couch.

Now it was evening. She was by herself. *They* were by themselves.

Again, she thought about her gun. She'd never needed to use her pistol, a Springfield XD, at least not yet. Every month or so, she opened up the lockbox in the primary closet, checked it, and placed it back on the top shelf. Once, Sofia had asked to hold the pistol. She'd been barely four years old, just old enough to ask to do something rather than just doing it. Of course, Jasmine hadn't handed it to her, and of course, she'd instructed her to never seek it out or ask for it again. But Jasmine had felt sadness in that moment, knowing that their lives required a gun. During her five years of ownership, she'd fired the pistol for only one session, back when she'd gotten it, back at the beginning of menglavirus, when the shooting ranges still had been open. It wasn't hard. She wouldn't be able to snipe somebody on the sidewalk, but if somewhere were walking into her front door with malicious intent, she wouldn't miss, not if her daughter's life depended on her. If she had to use it, she would use it.

As evening became night, Jasmine asked Sofia what she wanted to eat. She didn't usually ask. She just made. Of course, she tailored dinner to Sofia's particular tastes—grilled cheeses, plain pasta, prepackaged chicken nuggets—when she wasn't in the mood to push a nutritious meal. Other times, she gave Sofia whatever she'd made for her and Harrison, something more substantial, like the roasted chicken from the other day, even though most of the time Harrison didn't show up and Sofia didn't eat it. Either way, Jasmine knew she'd been remiss with Sofia's meals today. She'd let Sofia sleep in too late, given her breakfast for lunch, skipped lunch for the park, and now was going to give Sofia her second and last meal of the day as dinner. She again felt as if she were drowning, not even one nostril above water. She told herself to wade and breathe.

Sofia didn't answer. She was immersed in her shows on the couch in the living room. For the first time, Jasmine was happy Sofia was watching the tablet, acting normally despite the park and the man without the mask. Jasmine asked again, attempting to show her daughter that she was in control. "Come with me to the kitchen, honey. What do you want for dinner?" She had no intention of letting Sofia out of her sight. Sofia sat down at the kitchen counter while Jasmine went to the fridge and waited for Sofia's response. Jasmine again asked Sofia what she wanted to eat.

"Small chocolate chip pancakes."

Jasmine heard Sofia's answer but wasn't prepared to heed her request. She asked Sofia again what she wanted for dinner.

"I already said, Mommy. I want small chocolate chip pancakes."

Jasmine put her hands on her hips and stared at her daughter. Sofia didn't look up. She was acting as if she asked for small chocolate chip pancakes all of the time, as if they were her specialty and not Harrison's. She hated making pancakes, even the out-of-the-box ones. They never came out right, not the same way Harrison's did, whenever he decided once every few months on a Sunday morning to stay home and make them. They would know in advance Harrison was cooking pancakes when he arrived home Saturday night from whatever he'd been doing at the lab or in the office with a bag of groceries containing the buttermilk he needed for the pancakes—and which Jasmine never needed for anything else. She hated the buttermilk. Harrison would use it once, and then it languished in the fridge for weeks until Jasmine finally poured the chunky, acrid, concoction into the sink. Whenever Harrison arrived home with a bag of groceries on a Saturday night, Sofia knew she was getting chocolate chip silver dollar pancakes in the morning. Harrison's were always fluffy and perfectly browned, whereas Jasmine's were never the right consistency or color. Jasmine could whip up lasagna and a whole roasted turkey and chicken enchiladas in ways that Harrison never could, but no matter what, he always made better pancakes than she. Jasmine used to love the pancakes back when they'd been dating, when they'd known their future was meant to be filled with accomplishment and togetherness. Now she disliked them, not because she didn't like the pancakes, but because they were too much a salve for Sofia. He could spend weeks out of the house while he labored away at Riogenrix but appear suddenly on a Saturday night with a bag of buttermilk, eggs, and chocolate chips, and Sofia melted, as if their relationship was okay, whereas Jasmine worked at her relationship with Sofia day in and day out without break and got nowhere.

Jasmine understood Sofia was asking for her father in asking for pancakes. Harrison wasn't here, though. If Sofia wanted pancakes, she would make them. Tonight was not going to be a nutritious dinner. Tonight was going to be about keeping a nostril above water.

She spent too long making the small, chocolate chip pancakes, substituting milk she had for the buttermilk she didn't. Even then, the silver dollar pancakes were too dense and overcooked. Nonetheless, she placed the small chocolate chip pancakes on two plates and set one plate in front of Sofia and took the other plate for herself. Sofia ate the pancakes—or at least she tried. Jasmine could tell Sofia didn't like them. With Harrison's, she dove in, finishing them off within minutes. Now, she was taking small bites. Fifteen minutes after Jasmine laid the pancakes in front of Sofia, she was still pushing through them.

Finally, Jasmine said, "It's okay, honey. I know they're not the best. I'll make you a grilled cheese. I'll make both of us grilled cheeses."

Jasmine took the two plates of uneaten pancakes to the trash, dumped them, and started on the sandwiches. She wouldn't allow herself to drown.

After they ate the sandwiches, Sofia went to the couch with her tablet and plopped herself down again. Jasmine trailed her. The listlessness that had taken hold of her daughter months ago had gone away and returned, all in the space of a day. She thought about her daughter, wondering if Sofia were treading water or drowning. Having not yet spoken directly about this afternoon, Jasmine knew they needed to discuss what had happened. She'd spent the afternoon and evening pulling up security cameras on Sofia's tablet, acting as if nothing had happened earlier on. Finally, she said, "Do you want to talk about the park?"

"No," Sofia said, not looking up from the tablet.

"Do you want to talk about the man?"

"The man without a mask?"

"Yes."

"No."

"Why?"

Sofia didn't answer and went to the next video. Jasmine waited, and asked again, but Sofia still didn't answer. Jasmine knew she shouldn't dwell if Sofia didn't want to talk so Jasmine stopped asking. Instead, Sofia watched a YouTube video about a kid named Randy opening boxes of toys. Jasmine couldn't stand the channel, not even today. And she was still Sofia's mother, so she said, "Something else, baby."

Sofia didn't answer. She didn't stop watching the videos. The kid opened toys and Sofia watched with intense focus.

Jasmine debated how much she wanted to fight tonight. She decided she didn't. So she sat with her daughter on the couch and watched as well.

She knew the future was her and Sofia.

It wasn't Harrison and it wasn't this boy opening toys and it wasn't this life.

Their future wasn't today.

Over the two weeks since Col. Burt Johnson had assumed the position as Commander of the US Army Medical Research Institute of Infectious Diseases West Division, he'd spent the bulk of his time securing biosafety protocols. He'd come from Maryland, where he'd been in charge of quality control for level four biosafety facilities. He was new here, and the lab was new, established in response to menglavirus, but the protocols were old, time-tested and proven. His goal was to make sure no one at West cut corners. He'd spent his first two weeks here getting all the right controls in place. Now, he was ready to start real work, and get a vaccine out to the American public and the rest of the world. He'd come aboard with clear intent—get rid of menglavirus.

He'd come to medicine circuitously. He'd spent several years on the boots side in Army Infantry, serving in Iraq, before getting commissioned as a second lieutenant through the Health Professions Scholarship Program. After the commission, he completed a residency in surgery at Walter Reed Army Medical Center. Since then, he'd spent his career battling infectious epidemics for the US Army, starting with the Ebola outbreaks in Africa twenty years ago. He was an expert in figuring out the logistics of administering millions of vaccine doses to disparate populations. Now, he was coordinating the army's domestic vaccine response to nMAQ25 via USAMRIID-West, preparing for the day when he had a viable vaccine—which according to an email he'd received last week from Dr. Mostafa Abdou at the NIH was going to be very soon. He thought of himself as a physician more than a soldier these days, but he knew where he came from, and understood that the discipline and problem-solving skills he'd developed as an infantryman had been crucial to his career in military medicine.

He was in his office, a mostly barren room in Building Charlie. He had a laptop with a large screen open on one side of his steel desk and a workstation on the other. He was using the laptop to reply to emails, which, he'd learned, were an unending duty of the commander of USAMRIID-West. He had just received two new emails from the senator and was debating how to handle them. He'd replied to neither yet, but knew he needed to act, otherwise the senator would start with a barrage of secured text messages. Sure enough, as Burt was typing a response to the senator, the text messages flooded his satellite phone. He couldn't help but think about how he and his team were constructing the protocols and procedures for USAMRIID-West with so much care, but for all the redundancy he'd built into the system to keep the country—the world, really—safe, there were always bureaucratic shortcuts undoing their work that threatened them all. If the senator kept insisting on coming by West, the colonel needed to know well in advance, not just a few hours beforehand. Biosafety level four protocols did no good if the senator showed up whenever he wanted.

Burt had had an unpredictable two weeks, which meant he was still figuring out the difference between what he was *supposed* to do at USAMRIID-West and what he *was* doing. He was a doer, accustomed to the grind. Yet, the longer his command had become—admittedly, two weeks was barely a command, but it was a start—the more he'd felt as if his job were to look the other way while others around him did work. The setup was strange, completely opposite that of the original USAMRIID in Maryland, the one with a public presence. There was a civilian hierarchy here in West that didn't extend to the Department of Defense but to Scott Spaulding instead. It was as if West was the senator's individual project rather than an extension of Maryland. There were still parts of campus—Building Delta, in particular— for which Burt didn't even have access codes yet. Yet again, the D.C. bureaucracy wasn't keeping up with the work he needed to get done.

After all, he didn't want what happened in China to happen here. But if laypeople like the senator kept insisting on flaunting their high-level clearances—clearances seemingly higher than his—to gain access to West, something horrendous *was* going to happen. Menglavirus was horrible enough. He didn't need the country overrun not only with nMAQ25 but anthrax and Ebola and filovirus as well.

And now the senator was here again.

He knew it was a mistake giving a non-military, non-medical person such a high level of security clearance. For all the good the US Army did on a daily basis, both domestically and abroad, it was stunted by horrendous breaks in the system like this. He understood, ultimately, the army worked for the American people and the American people had its civilian leadership, but some of the civilian leadership wasn't up to par.

The senator's texts noted he'd arrived at West and he was waiting. Col. Burt Johnson returned a text message in acknowledgement. He felt as if he were working more for the senator than the American people.

At least the senator was finally headed in the right direction. He was bringing Dr. Harrison Boyd with him, the mRNA vaccine researcher, rather than the odd guy in the white lab coat. Burt Johnson was excited to meet the physician-scientist whom Dr. Abdou had mentioned in his emails. Truly, the data Dr. Abdou had forwarded him a week ago were remarkable. Dr. Boyd's vaccine seemed to work. The development seemed to be spot on. He'd always believed mRNA had extreme therapeutic potential and was glad to see the doctor had realized it. The colonel was excited and honored to have the chance to work with the doctor on expediting Phase 3 trials, ramping up for production, and finalizing worldwide distribution channels. For all of the flack the US Army had gotten during menglavirus, here was the reason why they existed in the first place—to support the country. The army had the necessary reach to ensure diverse distribution. Despite the bureaucracies, the country—and the world—would be okay after all.

He got up from his desk and phoned one of the specialists to take a Humvee to the perimeter to pick up the senator. Meanwhile, he stayed back in his office, preparing West for yet another of the senator's arrivals.

Richard Hahn didn't like the way the night was starting. He left the workstation in his basement biosafety lab. He returned to the living room on the top floor, where he'd spent the bulk of the past five years. The La Jolla air was foggy and dense at night, so different than the afternoon. It was if this part of La Jolla became a different planet after the sun went down. He couldn't see anything through the windows. Mentally, he felt the same fogginess in his brain as he saw outside. He couldn't fully understand the steps that Harrison had taken to get the menglavirus vaccine to where it now was.

Selene had turned over a partial mirror of the server. It contained parts of Harrison's vaccine work and his own BOOSTers work. As he'd tried to piece together Harrison's vaccine, he'd found himself struggling to decipher the work. He'd gone back to BOOSTers, finding himself slipping down a rabbit hole as he reviewed the mirror, reading and rereading the developmental steps he and Harrison had taken almost a decade ago to produce the immunity accelerants. Before BOOSTers, vaccine immunity had been a slow process. Typically, the human body needed two or three weeks to mount an adequate immune response after a vaccine inoculation. Before BOOSTers, someone who received a flu or shingles or measles vaccine on the first of the month wouldn't have active immunity until the fifteenth. However, BOOSTers had accelerated the body's immune response, such that someone who'd received a flu or measles vaccine on the first of the month would have partial immunity within hours—minutes, really—and full immunity within one or two days. BOOSTers had been game-changing for vaccine developers. They'd combined it with their traditional vaccines. It'd been the main reason why Richard had left Steptech. He'd wanted to develop BOOSTers away from the commercial licensing constraints of Steptech, the profit-driven company he'd cofounded —and come to despise. In the end, Riogenrix had licensed BOOSTers to all of the major vaccine developers and worldwide governmental organizations for minimal fees, just enough to keep Riogenrix afloat and innovating. They'd left billions of dollars on the table so people throughout the world could benefit from faster, more efficient immunity.

As he went down the rabbit hole of information related to his own BOOSTers—mostly out of frustration from not getting very far with Harrison's menglavirus vaccine—he realized how much of a hand Harrison had in its development. When Richard had left Steptech, he'd developed the framework for BOOSTers, but it'd still needed Harrison's meticulous touch to get all of the details right. Richard had gotten some of the details right on his own when he'd taken up residency at the Salk Institute, but BOOSTers really hadn't come together until he'd started Riogenrix. To be even more specific, BOOSTers hadn't really come together until Harrison had joined Riogenrix. As such, he wasn't surprised he was struggling to get a handle on V-202. What did he expect of himself after being out of the game for so long? Nonetheless, he was bothered by his current ineptitude. Specifically, he wasn't sure he could lead a meaningful discussion about his own company's menglavirus vaccine. Certainly, there would be a discussion with Jason Carr when he turned the vaccine over to him. Jason would come out their discussion realizing Richard had done nothing to develop the vaccine he was brokering. Although he wouldn't say so, Jason would think he'd made the right decision on not trying to get Richard to stay at Steptech fifteen years ago.

Richard knew where he was headed in terms of reconstructing Harrison's vaccine—nowhere. The acknowledgment pained him. Yet allowing menglavirus to continue unfettered pained him more.

He *was* an old man.

He called Harrison again, the fifth phone call of the evening. Again, it went to voicemail. He wondered if he should get in contact with the police or FBI but got the feeling they wouldn't do anything. Video footage from Riogenrix showed Harrison willingly getting into the senator's SUV. There was no kidnapping here, just a turned off or dead phone.

Or so he told himself.

In the early morning, Selene would have the full mirrors of the servers ready. At that point, he would call Jason and strike a deal to turn them over to Steptech. The deal wouldn't be financial, at least not for Riogenrix. They would make no money on the transaction. Rather, Riogenrix would ensure Harrison's vaccine was available to all. Steptech would obtain credit for V-202's development, but Jason would have to agree to distribute the vaccine at cost. If Jason agreed to Richard's terms, Steptech would make no money on V-202, but they would gain incredible prestige throughout the world as being the company that found a way to stop menglavirus. Ultimately, Steptech would become even more profitable because of V-202's halo effect. After Richard conveyed a full mirror to Steptech, Riogenrix would then be an asterisk on the development of V-202. Steptech would take the vaccine the rest of the way to approval and distribution.

Richard hadn't spoken to his old partner yet, but he knew Steptech would agree to the terms if he could get Jason on the line to convince him. Steptech generated all of the money it could ever need, but it'd failed with at least two vaccine efforts in stopping menglavirus. Jason would relish the opportunity to be the company that put an end to the most crippling public health crisis in over a century—maybe even ever.

Richard stood at the floor-to-ceiling windows of the living room. He looked out at the turbulent ocean below him. So long as the vaccine got to the people, he told himself, he would gladly play second fiddle to his old partner of his old company.

An open top Humvee came out from the military installation and pulled into the lot. "They're ready for us," the senator said as he stepped out of the Escalade into the dry Nevada night. Harrison tried to get out of the SUV too, but couldn't. The child locks were set on his side. One of the contractors came around to Harrison's door to open it. As Harrison got out of the vehicle, he tried not to think about why the child locks had been set. Instead, he found himself thinking about Sofia. He'd set the child locks on his Accord years ago and thought they were probably still set. When Sofia had been a toddler, she'd always been pulling on the door handle and even sneaking out of her car seat, thinking it was funny whenever Harrison or Jasmine reacted. Back in those days, whenever Harrison had had time—which he thought in retrospect was often compared to now—he would take Jasmine and Sofia around a San Diego that was still new to all of them. He took them to the beach in Mission and the stores in Carlsbad, the museums in downtown and the zoo in Balboa. In the beginning, he'd been trying to be a real father and husband. He knew he'd stopped being both.

He got into the Humvee with the senator while the contractors stayed back in the idling Escalade. A young man in uniform drove them past the manned gates onto the military installation. At each successive gate, the driver slowed down, but didn't stop, as the guards at the gates waved the Humvee through. They reached a two-lane road and took it east for several more minutes, probably four or five miles. Finally, they went through one more set of manned gates. Once inside, they stopped outside of a quartet of single-story concrete block buildings. Each building was large, twice as big as anything on the Riogenrix campus. Each building was spaced out from the others by several hundred yards. There was no landscaping, only asphalt and desert. The entire area was bathed in floodlights, making it hard for Harrison to make out much more than the general layout.

"We're here, doctor," the senator said.

They got out of the Humvee and another uniformed soldier took them along a fenced walkway to one of the buildings, where an officer with a colonel patch sewn on his uniform was waiting for them. The colonel was wearing sunglasses because of the floodlights. He removed them and used his hand to shield his face from the lights as he approached them. He was wearing a fitted FN99 mask too—like everyone was nowadays. He introduced himself as Col. Burt Johnson, the commander of USAMRIID-West. In turn, the senator introduced Harrison to the colonel.

"This is the man who's discovered a preventive vaccine for menglavirus," the senator said. "This is Dr. Harrison Boyd."

They didn't shake hands but nodded at each other. Harrison got the sense the colonel wasn't happy to see the senator, but was curious to meet him nonetheless. Likewise, Harrison was curious to meet the colonel. Harrison hadn't met so many new people in years. Again—if he allowed himself to ignore the alarms going off in his head—he felt as if he were finally getting recognition in his field.

"Are we ready?" the senator said.

The colonel nodded and handed the senator and Harrison badges. After the senator affixed his to the lapel of his suit and Harrison clipped his to the pocket of his button down shirt, the colonel led them towards a windowless building marked 'C.' Two soldiers manned the short walkway leading to the building. They saluted the colonel as he approached. When they reached the two metal doors on the outside of the building, the colonel swiped his badge at the access point and entered a code on the keypad. Harrison noticed the point of care security into the buildings wasn't very different than what they had at Riogenrix. Of course, the colonel had manned gates at several points surrounding the campus. Nonetheless, Harrison found it interesting that security still came down to an access code.

As they began the show and tell, Harrison felt a begrudging

reluctance from the colonel. At first, Harrison thought the reluctance was directed towards him, but as the show and tell progressed, he understood it was directed towards the senator. If anything, the colonel seemed to be waiting for Harrison's responses, although Harrison had little to give.

First, they took him to a changing room, where he changed out of his clothes, showered, and dressed into medical scrubs. Then they took him to a windowless conference room without any phones, computers, or electronic equipment. Harrison sat at a long stainless steel table and the senator sat beside him as the colonel started the presentation. There were no slides or projectors, just the colonel speaking.

The colonel told him about a new group of native strains of menglavirus identified in the fecal matter of Chinese bats two years before menglavirus came stateside. However, the infectious strains that had hit China and then spread to the rest of the world were not the same native strains identified in the fecal matter of bats. Rather, nMAQ25 was a GOF, or gain of function, experiment gone wrong—a modified version of native menglavirus had accidentally gotten out from China's Institute of Virology. The reason nMAQ25 was so virulent was because it wasn't a naturally evolved virus. It was a virus that had evolved in the lab.

To demonstrate the in vitro source of the knowledge, the colonel then took Harrison—and the senator—to an infection control room, where they put on headsets, white infectious control suits, and positive pressure respirators. From there, they walked to an animal research laboratory containing hundreds of individual bats in hundreds of individual cages. Harrison saw two workers wearing biosafety suits and respirators similar to their own drawing blood samples from the cages.

After walking through the research laboratory, the colonel took them to a decontamination unit where they rinsed off the suits with a prepped sodium hypochlorite solution. Then they changed into new biosafety suits and hooked up new respirators. The colonel led Harrison and the senator to a level four biosafety laboratory. This was the facility where the army was working with the known strains of menglavirus to conduct origin research—along with the army's own version of gain of function. Here, Harrison saw two more lab workers in safety suits and respirators. One of them was huddled over a logbook and the other was working with pipettes under a pressure hood. The lab was clean and uncluttered, exactly the way a high-level infection control lab should be. Harrison noted the workers were following several necessary protocols for preventing the escape of dangerous pathogens: extensive use of negative pressure fume hoods where pathogens were manipulated; logbooks and computers systems for documenting each step of their work; and access to multiple redundant monitoring systems for pressure, temperature, and contamination. Even though Harrison was slightly unnerved to see GOF work on menglavirus being done on US soil—albeit for the purpose of origin research—he was also exhilarated.

The colonel took them to another decontamination unit, where they rinsed and suited again before heading to another animal research laboratory. In the second animal lab, the colonel showed Harrison a wide variety of specimens, including some he'd never seen in person before. The colonel showed him the pangolin and civet, pig and lamb, dog and cat, and dozens of other wild and domestic animals. Then they walked to a third decontamination unit where each of them removed their headsets, suits, and respirators. They showered in private stalls and changed back into their clothes. Finally, the colonel took Harrison and the senator to a different windowless conference room. They sat at another steel table that was smaller than the first. The colonel placed dozens of the army's research documents in front of them. He walked Harrison through reams of genetic data that demonstrated not only did nMAQ25 differ significantly from known menglavirus strains in bats but nMAQ25 didn't even take hold in them. Nor did nMAQ25 take hold in the pangolin, civet, pig, lamb, dog, or cat, which were long considered by most within the medical community to be intermediary hosts. As Harrison looked with a critical eye at the data the colonel gave him, the senator sat impassively with a bored look on his face. Harrison didn't need long to analyze the data in order to accept the colonel's conclusion. The data were strong. The genetic variations that enabled nMAQ25 to cause rapid *human-to-human* transmission were the same variations that made it so the virus could *not* cause *animal-to-human* transmission. The data confirmed it—nMAQ25 wasn't a native strain. It was a genetically modified virus created in a Chinese gain of function laboratory.

Finally, they let him speak. During the show and tell, Harrison had found himself trusting the colonel more. His knowledge was impeccable and Harrison got the sense his character was as well. As much as Harrison felt iffy around the senator, he felt just as confident in the colonel. He noticed the stringency of controls at USAMRIID-West. If nMAQ25 had originated through GOF experiments in a Chinese microbiology laboratory, the virulence of the genetically altered virus was a clear demonstration to all countries of the dangers not only of creating more infectious organisms than those found in nature, but of the need to maintain strict protocols at high level biosafety facilities. He believed the data—nMAQ25 was a GOF disaster.

GOF stood for gain of function, which in turn referred to the tinkering scientists did to native viral DNA and RNA. It involved giving viruses additional functions in vitro—in the lab— so viruses could theoretically become more virulent in vivo—in real life. The theoretical goal in making native viruses stronger and more dangerous in the lab was to study them before they became stronger and more virulent on their own through evolution. GOF was supposed to guide future therapeutics by predicting the future *before* it happened. It was clearly controversial, but the reasoning behind GOF was that viruses mutated on their own all of the time, thereby leading to horrible consequences in the real world, so it was best to mutate them *yourself* to see what the horrible consequences could be in order to get ahead of vaccines and therapeutics.

Even though Harrison found the GOF link to nMAQ25 remarkable, he didn't understand how gain of function related to V-202. He still didn't know why the FDA had rejected Riogenrix's vaccine. When he tried to ask the colonel about it, the senator cut him off. Harrison could tell by the look of concern on the colonel's face that he hadn't known the V-202 application had been denied.

Afterwards, the tour—or meeting, if that was what it was —wrapped up quickly. The senator said Harrison needed to get back to San Diego—and he certainly did—and asked the colonel to lead them back to the Humvee. The colonel did and the Humvee took the senator and Harrison back across the four miles to the manned gates at West's perimeter while the colonel stayed behind. As Harrison looked back in the direction of West while he sat in the back of the Humvee, he wondered how much he should trust the senator and what was happening in Building D, the one he hadn't toured.

They went to bed late, both of them clearly waiting for Harrison but neither of them voicing their obvious thoughts, especially not Jasmine. But Harrison didn't come home and Jasmine didn't bother to call him again just to get another no-answer. When they got upstairs, Jasmine asked Sofia if she wanted to sleep with Mommy in Mommy's bed and Sofia said yes. They got ready for bed in the same bathroom. Afterwards, Jasmine put Sofia in the middle of the bed while she squeezed onto her own side.

"I'm sorry, Mommy." Sofia's speech was slow and sleepy.

"About what, sweetie?"

"I should've told you about the astronauts."

"What do you mean, honey?" Jasmine didn't understand and wasn't even sure she'd heard correctly. "Honey?"

Sofia didn't answer—she'd fallen asleep. Despite the anxiety and terror Jasmine knew eight-year-olds felt these days, she was still a kid and there was always a point where kids just couldn't stay awake anymore. Jasmine lay in bed with her daughter. She knew where her marriage with Harrison was headed, if it wasn't there already. They were getting divorced. Harrison's absence was too great. Jasmine was mentally checking out more by the day. She'd kind of believed him early this morning when he'd said he was winding down his work at Riogenrix because of the FDA denial. She'd kind of believed he would actually be home tonight. Of course, she'd been wrong to believe.

She reached for her phone on the nightstand and pulled up electronic forms for divorce via the San Diego County's Superior Court's website. She and Harrison would undoubtedly need attorneys to represent them, but tonight was a legitimate start. She printed the forms, sending them to the inkjet printer downstairs in the den, a room she'd once used as her own office away from home but now rarely entered as it was too much of a reminder of a life she'd never gotten to live. Except for tomorrow morning when she would retrieve the forms, she had no business being in the den anymore—just like Harrison had no business being married to her anymore.

Jasmine put away her phone, placing it back on the nightstand. She was exhausted through and through. She let herself sink into the king-sized bed she and Harrison usually shared. She fell asleep as she listened to her daughter breathing.

As the Hummer pulled up to the West parking depot, a helicopter was waiting. It was ready for takeoff. The blades were spinning and the door was open. The two security contractors who'd accompanied them from San Diego were at the open helicopter door, ducking below the fast-moving blades. When Harrison saw the helicopter, he thought of Jasmine and Sofia again. He was going to be home much later than he'd thought, well past midnight and much closer to dawn. Clearly, he'd lost track of time. But even if he hadn't, he didn't think it would've mattered.

He'd been on the senator's clock, not his own. He was eager to leave Nevada, get back to San Diego, and return to his own clock. He hoped Sofia hadn't spent another night at the window and Jasmine hadn't waited up for him. He was glad there was a helicopter. He waited for the senator to take the lead in getting out of the Humvee and heading towards it.

But the senator didn't move. "I apologize for keeping you so long," Scott Spaulding said, shouting over the rumble of the Hummer's diesel engine and the *whack-whack-whack* of the chopper. "But I think you'll agree tonight was worth it."

"The colonel seemed surprised to hear the FDA denied V-202's Phase 3 application," Harrison said.

"The colonel is new to West. He's been on site for only a couple of weeks. We're still bringing him up to speed. Don't hold him too responsible yet for not being completely up to date."

"I thought by coming here with you, I would gain clarity as to why you denied V-202's Phase 3 application. I haven't gained any clarity. I'm only more confused. And angry. The origins of nMAQ25—gain of function or otherwise—don't matter in terms of stopping its spread. The FDA needs to get V-202 going forward again. *You* need to get it going forward, senator. I don't care how menglavirus started. I care we have a way to end it."

"Here's the situation, doctor: The US would like to control the vaccine. We would like to take it over from this point forward. We'll bring you aboard USAMRIID-West as a civilian medical director. It'll be a first. You'll get royalties, of course. But we would like to control the vaccine."

"We didn't do V-202 for the money. We want to get the vaccine out to as many people as possible as safely and expediently as possible."

"As do I."

"In which case, why did you deny the Phase 3?"

"Like I previously mentioned, doctor, we're not sure Riogenrix has the ability to usher history's most important vaccine through the security challenges to come. We don't want China or any of the other state actors to know your data is real."

Harrison wondered if it even *mattered* if China got wind of V-202. Riogenrix had every intention of distributing it to *every* country, no matter how politically strained diplomatic relationships were. Countries weren't just their governmental institutions. They contained people. People needed to be done with menglavirus.

"China is welcome to V-202," Harrison said. "Everyone is. We want to work with China on local manufacture of the vaccine. We want to work with every country. We want to end menglavirus."

"We'll discuss China when the time is right."

"What happens if I want to keep V-202 under Riogenrix?"

"We'll still need to work with you to set up security. We'll still have a presence on your campus. Your vaccine is protected technology now. I'll need to protect it."

Harrison noticed the senator's change from *we* to *I*. He got the clear sense the senator was getting involved in V-202 no matter what Harrison decided. He felt exhausted, from tonight and the days prior. He didn't know what to think anymore. He should've been home hours ago and wanted to end the night— get home to Jasmine and Sofia as soon as he could. As late as he'd been working at Riogenrix over the past several weeks, he'd never spent the entire night away.

"I need to get home," Harrison said, suddenly weary. He had no more argument in him.

"Understood. But I'm going to need an answer on your vaccine by the time you land. My team member will drive you back to the airstrip. I'm not going back with you. I have work to do here in Nevada. I'll be taking the helicopter to Vegas. My team member will accompany you back to California. He'll keep you safe until we can get a full security detail for you. Have a safe flight, doctor."

Harrison now understood the helicopter wasn't for him—it was for the senator only. The realization only made Harrison more perturbed. The senator got out of the Humvee, crouched, and ran to the helicopter. The driver from the idling white Suburban—he was wearing the same polo shirt and khaki pants as the other two contractors—was waiting for Harrison at the SUV. Harrison climbed out of the Humvee. The driver had the rear door of the Suburban open for him. Harrison hurried to it. He was tired of the noise coming from everywhere. More tired than he'd ever been. He closed his eyes and fell into an uneasy space between wakefulness and sleep.

By the time Harrison climbed the air-stairs to the senator's private plane an hour later, the chilly night air had become piercingly cold. He sat down in the same swivel chair he'd sat in on the flight out of San Diego as he waited for takeoff. The senator had told him he'd needed an answer on transferring V-202 to the senator's supervision at USAMRIID-West by the time Harrison arrived in San Diego. No matter how he analyzed the situation, he couldn't come to a satisfactory answer as to why he needed to remove Riogenrix from V-202's further development and testing. He understood Riogenrix needed help in the manufacturing and distribution phases of V-202, but the senator could help in these aspects without assuming control of the vaccine itself. There was more at play.

He didn't need to ponder any further or wait until he landed in San Diego to know his answer regarding USAMRIID-West. He was going to hold onto V-202 and enlist the senator's help in manufacture and distribution without dissolving Riogenrix's role in its further development. He understood Riogenrix had security concerns, so he would allow the senator to step in on the security front. But Riogenrix needed to remain in charge of V-202's development. He had no doubt the colonel would be an exceptional partner in distributing V-202 but no matter how much Harrison explained V-202's step-by-step development to a partner, he would never be able to explain the steps yet to come. He worked on intuition. V-202 needed Harrison in order to get across the finish line.

Plus, he didn't like how the senator had emphasized *only* domestic distribution. He disliked the idea that the senator would ration the vaccine to so-called "allies" and hold it from so-called "enemies." He abhorred the idea. Seven billion people needed the vaccine, so seven billion people would get the vaccine. He wouldn't allow V-202 to be weaponized. It wasn't a political therapeutic.

He reflexively reached for his pocket to pull out his phone but it wasn't there. He remembered how he'd handed it over to the senator's men. The contractor from the Suburban was in the other swivel chair. Harrison got the feeling the contractor wasn't protecting him but surveilling instead.

"I need my phone," Harrison said. "I'm ready to call the senator."

"I don't have your phone, sir," said the contractor. He was looking straight ahead. He didn't make eye contact with Harrison.

"Your guys took my phone. The other security member."

"He hasn't provided it to me, sir." He reached into the side pocket of his khaki pants, withdrew a phone that wasn't Harrison's, and handed it over. "But I have this phone for you. It's yours to take. The senator's number is already programmed inside."

Harrison took the phone. He was tired and didn't know how much to believe and how much to push back.

"When do I get my phone back?"

"I'll have it messaged to us as soon as we land in San Diego. I'll get it on a plane. You'll have it by the end of the afternoon."

Harrison watched the contractor, waiting for him to contact the other guy to arrange the messaging. He didn't. Harrison didn't dwell. He called the senator.

"Thanks for your phone call, doctor. That wasn't long. Are we going to be partners in saving the world?"

"Yes," Harrison said, choosing his words, "but as part of Riogenrix. I need to be involved in the fine-tuning of V-202 during Phase 3. And I need Riogenrix to be a part of V-202. I've only ever known Riogenrix and I'll do my best work from my own labs. But I do welcome your help in security, manufacturing, and distribution. So, yes, we will be partners."

The senator was silent for a moment before saying, "Good plan, doctor. We will support you however we can."

"When will you discuss Phase 3 with the FDA?"

"We'll set up security protocols for your company over the next forty-eight hours and by Monday we'll have you in Phase 3 trials."

"Thank you, senator."

"No, doctor, thank you."

As Harrison hung up, he felt less relieved than he should have. Something—a lot of things—about the senator bothered him, even if he couldn't elucidate them. He told himself he was being overly critical. He let the unease pass and tempered his thoughts. He closed his eyes and waited for the plane to take off. He was ready to return to San Diego.

Sofia was awake. She was in Mommy's bed in Mommy and Daddy's room. She'd woken up when Mommy's clock had read 1:05 a.m. At first, she'd thought she'd woken up because she'd heard noises, but then she listened to the quiet night and realized she hadn't heard anything. She'd woken up because she was supposed to keep an eye out for Daddy. She was supposed to tell him about the astronauts. She woke up because she was supposed to be awake. She hadn't stayed awake the past two nights, but now her body had listened to the alarm clock she'd put in her head.

She went to her bedroom, grabbing the tablet from the floor as she left Mommy and Daddy's room. When she got to her own room at the end of the hall, she realized she'd forgotten to make her bed this morning. Mommy had forgotten to tell her to make it as well. Mommy didn't usually forget, but she was always worried. She'd been worried even before the man without a mask and now she was worried even more. She took her tablet to the window and sat in a chair and watched for the astronauts.

As she looked out the window, she watched another video of

Randy opening toys. She put the volume low. There was a button on the screen where she could have the words of what was being said appear and she pushed the button. She tried to read the words and recognized a few of them—*the* and *of* were really easy. The video wasn't that good. He was opening water guns, but if she had a water gun, she wouldn't have anyone to play it with. She'd been watching Jesse open toys since before he'd become famous. Eventually, she got tired of working on the words that were on the screen and she became disinterested in Randy and she felt herself falling asleep again. She tried to keep her eyes open but she felt them closing.

She opened them again when she heard a car coming.

She remembered Mommy had loaded the app for the security cameras to her tablet and she opened the live video, knowing the cameras had night vision. She looked at the camera on the driveway. She didn't see anything. She told herself Daddy would be home soon.

She closed her eyes to rest for a few seconds and when she opened them again the time on the tablet said 1:43 a.m. She blamed herself for falling asleep, but at least she'd woken up again. She looked out the window and saw nothing. She pulled up the cameras on the tablet again. As soon as she did, she wished she hadn't fallen asleep.

She saw the man without the mask. And she saw two astronauts with him. They were on the sidewalk.

She jumped off of her chair and ran down the hallway to Mommy's room with the tablet. She shook Mommy's shoulder. Her mommy was snoring.

"The man without a mask is here."

The snoring stopped. Mommy pushed herself up in bed.

"What?"

"The man from the park is here."

"How do you know?"

Sofia showed Mommy the tablet. As her mommy took the tablet from her, the doorbell rang from downstairs.

Mommy looked up from the tablet, waiting for the doorbell to ring again.

It didn't. Instead, there was a boom and the sound of glass breaking.

"Come with me," Mommy said.

Mommy got out of the bed and she grabbed her arm and pulled her towards the closet. Mommy and Daddy had a big closet, the kind in which she would play hide and seek if she'd had anyone to play with. She watched her mommy reach for the top shelf. She knew her mommy kept a gun in the house and she knew Mommy kept it on the top shelf of her closet so Sofia wouldn't try to play with it. But Sofia never had thought of playing with it. Hide and seek in the closet would've been fun and nice but the gun wasn't anything she was interested in.

Her mommy was opening the box. She was entering codes.

There was a crash downstairs.

And footsteps. A lot of them. Heavy footsteps and fast footsteps, as if the man without a mask and the two astronauts were giants. The footsteps were so much heavier and faster than her Daddy's.

Whenever she heard Daddy's footsteps around the house, she felt calm. She felt happy he was home.

Now she was scared.

Mommy had the gun in her hand. The gun looked mean and serious—a lot bigger than how guns looked in the movies she sometimes watched on her tablet when her mommy wasn't looking.

She wondered if Daddy would come home before the men got upstairs. Even if he did, she didn't know if he could do anything now. She'd waited too long to tell him about the astronauts.

"Stay here behind the clothes, honey."

Sofia knew the clothes weren't going to hide her, but she listened to her mommy, and got down, burying herself behind Daddy's pants.

From behind the pants, she saw her mommy leave the closet. She stayed. She listened. She heard more footsteps, close now. And then she heard the men's voices.

"Just relax, Mrs. Boyd," one of them said, and even though Sofia couldn't see who was talking, she knew it was the man without the mask because the voice was clear. It wasn't muffled like people's voices were when they wore masks—or astronaut suits. "We'll get vaccines for you and your daughter. Just come with us."

"Leave now," her mommy said. Her mommy spoke with force, and Sofia felt a moment of comfort, as if her mommy were truly going to get the man without a mask to leave.

"Nothing bad will happen to you," the man said. "We'll get in touch with your husband. We'll get the vaccine. You'll come back here. Tomorrow morning, you'll be back home. We can get this all done right away."

Sofia heard a gunshot. It was incredibly loud. She felt as if her head were going to break. She put her hands to her ears to cover them, trying to get rid of the sound as it bounced around her brain. Her mother shouted but Sofia couldn't understand what she said right now.

An astronaut appeared in the doorway of the closet, blocking her view from everything. He reached for her daddy's pants and pulled her out from the pile. She yelled and wanted to cry but tried to hold herself together. She tried to be as strong as she could for her mommy. Sofia kicked at the astronaut but he just picked her up and wrapped one of his arms around her shoulders and the other around her legs. She saw the man without the mask lying on the ground. Mommy had shot him. But he wasn't dead. He was moving. He was shaking his head. The other astronaut had her mommy in his arms. He pulled the gun away from her. It fell to the floor and he kicked at it and it slid under the bed. He had a hand over Mommy's mouth and he was trying to tie her hands together with a strip of plastic.

"So difficult," said the man without the mask. "Relax. For your daughter's sake."

But Mommy didn't stop struggling, so neither did Sofia. Sofia tried to withdraw from the astronaut who was holding her. She bit him in the arm, tasting the chemicals of his astronaut suit. She felt the grip around her torso loosen and then she felt herself get dizzy and fall. She knew she hadn't put a hole into the astronaut suit with her bite but at least he'd let go of her. She lunged across the floor towards the bed and pushed herself under it. She saw Mommy's gun under the bed and reached for it. Her finger was almost there. She almost had it. She didn't exactly know what she would do with it when she got it, but she could point it at the men and scare them off, and if they didn't back off, she would shoot them.

Her fingers scraped against the handle. It was warm, almost hot. But she couldn't close her hand around the gun. She felt herself being pulled back. She felt astronaut arms around her again. She felt pressure. And the same plastic ties they'd put around Mommy were being put around her as well.

The man without the mask was standing up again. He was shouting at the two astronauts as the two astronauts dragged them out of Mommy's and Daddy's room towards the stairs. He was rubbing his chest but wasn't bleeding. She knew from You-Tube that he'd been wearing a bulletproof vest—she'd watched a movie that she wasn't supposed to watch about a bank robbery where the robbers wore them too. Then the two astronauts were taking her and Mommy down the stairs. Mommy was shouting and biting, so Sofia did the same thing, but her mommy didn't escape and neither did she.

They dragged her and her mommy through the family room.

They took them through the front door.

They took them outside.

The night was cold, so different than the daytime, when they'd gone to the park.

One of the astronauts opened the van and dragged them inside.

And the neighborhood returned to being as quiet as it always was.

PART 3

Naomi McGraw was in Las Vegas on the balcony of the sixty-first floor of the unfinished Trasium Towers. She was sweating despite the chilly night air. The nightly lows over the past week had been in the high forties and tonight was no different. As she stood high above the darkened strip, she should've been cold, because she was always cold, and had been cold her entire life, but she wasn't cold now. She felt warm and the cold air felt relieving. She watched the dying city below her and wondered if this was one of the changes.

It was early for her but late for everyone else, well past the city's curfew, a so-called travel night for him and a personal night for her, even though in reality, tonight was neither. She was supposed to be sleeping but wasn't and hadn't been sleeping much lately. She was walking the balcony in short, slow steps with her hand over the flat of her stomach, wondering when she would start to show, wondering when she would have to tell him. She linked telling him to showing and partly felt comfort in the idea she could delay the inevitable but she was also angry at herself for always thinking the same way, always delaying everything, always waiting until she had no other options. She was only weeks pregnant, not months, no trimester scans on a truncated calendar awaiting her. She still had time. Plenty of it. Maybe she wasn't even pregnant at all. Maybe the take-home tests were wrong. Everything was wrong these days. The tests could be wrong too.

She'd been late before, but this time felt different. She didn't *look* any different, but this time *felt* different. She'd bought the tests in the morning, lining up with the rest of her provisions facility group at 6:30 a.m., instead of ordering the tests to her room like she did for everything else—mini soda cans, mini cereal boxes, large bottles of flat water. She'd actually left the unfinished casino condominiums, beating back the stares from the contracted security manning the building's exits and entrances. She rarely left the condo—and never left the casino—so she'd taken small, controlled solace in the possibly delusional hope that security would be too shocked to do anything but watch her. She'd been right, for once—they hadn't followed her. The security men on the ground floor watched her exit the elevator, not sure what to do with this new occurrence of her on the empty casino floor, and when she reached the service entrance at the back of the casino, away from the Strip side, she crossed her arms across her chest and thumped her foot on the ground, staring with what she hoped was deathly intensity at the two men manning the door, waiting for them to step aside and speak into their two-way radios to tell central security on the second floor to buzz her out. They did step aside and she was buzzed out. Nobody had followed her.

Of course, they technically didn't need to follow her. They could've just tracked her, not through the GPS on her phone—because she'd left the phone at home—but at least through the cameras they'd installed along the Strip.

They probably had. And if they had, they would've seen she'd gone to the provisions facility. They would've seen her walk the service streets along the side of the casino with long, fast strides, until she'd met up with Las Vegas Boulevard, and then they would've seen her slow her walk and shorten her strides, trying to be more casual, trying to convey to the developing collections of people on the streets who were part of her provisions facility grouping that she was just like them, she was one of them, she belonged here as much as they did, she didn't live in Trasium Towers. They would've seen her standing in line like everybody else, cautiously guarding her own particle mask with her hand, while she waited for the National Guard to confirm her distribution grouping and then finally grant her entry into the provisions facility.

That's all they would've seen. They wouldn't have seen her seeking out the pregnancy tests in aisle eighty-eight. They wouldn't have seen her using cash to purchase them. They wouldn't have seen her asking for a disposable, onetime use plastic bag and carefully placing the pregnancy tests in it.

They wouldn't know for sure until they accessed the security cameras from inside the provisions facility, if they were capable of doing so. She didn't know if they were. She figured they probably did, but also figured such access wasn't an immediate thing, that it would take them some time, a few hours or maybe days. She wanted time—time to figure out how to withdraw from the nightmare. But he was coming, so she didn't have time. She would have to tell him or decide to keep her secret.

Her mother hadn't called. For the first time since Naomi McGraw had left San Diego, Thelma McGraw hadn't called on Tuesday night, which was strange and unsettling, because for the first time in two years, she'd planned to pick up, share the news, get advice. Although her mother had never directly said so, Naomi had always suspected her mother hadn't planned for Naomi, but had accidentally gotten pregnant by a man who'd briefly become her mother's husband, but who was never truly Naomi's father. No, her mother hadn't called for the first time in two years. She wondered at the significance of her mother not calling and figured the universe was trying to tell her something —this decision was hers.

Or maybe she didn't have a decision after all. Maybe she wasn't pregnant. The tests were messed up anyway, she tried to tell herself. The tests used to come from China, until China closed itself off, and then the rest of the world closed China off. Now they came from a place in South Carolina. She knew because she'd checked the box. She'd always been a box checker, a tag reader. She'd always wanted to know where things came from. She'd matched up the address on the box with a search online and found out the tests had come from an old automobile factory. Buy American, right? Before the virus, she'd always tried to buy American, and now she had no choice.

Naomi had been living on the strip for two years in the high-rise condominium he'd set up for her. She'd tried to live on her own in Las Vegas but menglavirus had had different plans. At first, she'd been thankful to him for taking her in, getting her out of a life floating through other people's studio apartments, spare rooms, and converted warehouses. She'd been flattered he'd been interested in her, even if she knew he had a fiancé. She was also relieved to know she would not have to go back to San Diego. He was a powerful man who wanted to see her succeed— or at least that's what she told herself. She'd taken solace in the knowledge his fiancé had been his fiancé for seven years but had never become his wife. Of course, she'd been naïve. He hadn't wanted to see her succeed, because there was nothing to succeed at anymore. Nor had he cut ties with his fiancé. Now, she wasn't thankful to him, because he certainly wasn't letting her live here without cost. Still, Naomi was thankful for something or maybe someone, maybe even God, that she had a place to stay with twenty-four-hour armed security patrolling the perimeters of the always deserted casino. The former cops reminded her of her mother, hardened and cynical, although she didn't appreciate the former military men who worked directly for the father of her baby. They didn't carry pistols in holsters. Instead, they carried automatic rifles in their arms at all times. They unnerved her.

She walked the eleven steps from one end of the balcony to the other, staying in the part that had completed construction. The strip was joyless. No neon, no fountains, no digital bill-boards. The streetlamps were on and there were three roving floodlights operated by the casino but otherwise the street was empty. Soon—later tonight if he stayed true to his texts, and she hoped he didn't—he would be at the condo and she would have to tell him. For now, she could walk the balcony with her child, because up here on the sixty-first floor of Trasium Towers, there was no menglavirus, and for now there was no Senator Scott Spaulding.

Selene headed to La Jolla with the mirrors and vaccines. It was almost three in the morning and damp outside. She'd worked through most of the night on campus to get mirrors of the servers made. Her work there wasn't done—she still needed to erase the servers—but she'd completed the work she'd needed to finish in order for Richard to broker a deal with Jason Carr. She was glad to be leaving campus, given everything she'd learned over the past twelve hours. She had a feeling she would be the only one on campus from here on out.

Richard let her inside his La Jolla house. He'd regained the spark in his voice when he talked, as if being needed again had reenergized him. She handed him the hard drives.

"Any issues?" Richard said.

"None."

"Let's see what we got."

She followed him to a computer workstation in his top floor office. He hooked the hard drives to the back of the workstation. He looked at the screen.

"Good?" she said.

"Good," he said. "Harrison sure wasn't one to fill in the blanks. It needs interpretation, but it's good. I should be able to figure out the details. Thank you, Selene."

"I brought the vaccines too."

"All three of them?"

"Two."

"Two?"

"Three before, but two after," she said. She opened the cooler bag, and removed a prefilled syringe. "You need one, Richard. I'll administer it to you."

"I don't want it."

"You're back in the world, Richard. We need you to stay back in the world. The vaccine works. You need it. You need to shepherd the vaccine to existence. Harrison would want you to get it."

"Harrison and I are the same. He wouldn't want me to mess with the science. He wouldn't want me to take advantage."

"Stop worrying about influencing the data. We are past that stage. Well past it. The data is good. The vaccine works. Now, we need to distribute the vaccine to the public before it's lost forever."

"I'm an old man, Selene. I don't need it. I'll get the vaccine when we *all* get the vaccine. When the whole *world* gets it. No sooner than anyone else. You hold onto them. All of them. All three of them. But I'll hold onto the mirrors."

She didn't try to argue with him. She'd worked with him long enough to know when he would and wouldn't budge. She knew when it came to the vaccine, he wouldn't. She put the prefilled syringe back into the cooler bag with the other two.

"But you should take it," Richard said.

"Take what?"

"The vaccine."

The suggestion surprised her. She was as much a part of Riogenrix as anybody else. She had the same goals as Richard and Harrison, which was to get the vaccine out to everybody. She would wait like them.

"I don't need the vaccine, either," she said. "We'll hold onto all three of them for now, in case we need them for reverse engineering."

Richard nodded but didn't comment. He was already immersed in Harrison's work, diving into the mirrors. She recognized the focus. They were friends, but now was time for work. Today was not a social visit. Richard only had a few of hours—if that—to tinker with the mirrors before Jason Carr would arrive in his Seattle office. She knew Richard wanted a crack at the mirrors before turning them over to his former partner. She wanted the same for him.

"I'll see myself out, Richard."

He didn't try to get her to stay. So she turned, left the top floor office, and walked across the expansive living room to the foyer. She glanced at the darkened, whirling ocean beyond the glass. She felt chilly just looking at it. This time of year—almost year-round in this part of San Diego—the water was cold enough to need a wetsuit. She wanted to linger but didn't. She wasn't sure when she would see Richard again, but hoped today wasn't going to be the last time.

Dr. Jason Carr was on campus and headed into his office—his *building*, really. It was nearing five o'clock in the morning in suburban Seattle. He was an early riser, even now. Especially now. Business was brisk and getting brisker. Despite its menglavirus failures, Steptech had been well positioned to succeed with its portfolio of cardiovascular, neurological, and immunological treatments. People were getting sicker by the day as they stayed home. They needed more medications. Steptech had been able to raise prices one hundred percent on several items. The cardiac injectables had become particularly profitable. Before menglavirus, America had been a pill-taking nation, but now it was a self-injecting nation. The weekly injections were easier for people to remember to take than the daily pills when all the days and hours ran together. Steptech had never been more profitable, which was saying a lot.

Of course, there were concerns on the horizon, particularly as it related to the pipeline. Steptech had invested heavily in several menglavirus vaccines, partnering with the NIH on research and development, but had come up empty twice thus far. They had a third vaccine—referred to internally as DK9—in Phase 2 but the data weren't looking promising. Steptech's own internal parameters mirrored those of the FDA, which required a fifty percent reduction in menglavirus contractions versus the placebo. Three months into Phase 2, they'd gotten only nine percent, which, when run by the statistics teams, was barely statistically significant. Nonetheless, nine percent was better than nothing, and Jason already had confirmation from the FDA that they would approve DK9 for Phase 3 if they could at least get into double digits. Again, something was better than nothing.

As he entered Building H-G2, his security team peeled off to review the rapid menglavirus testing results of the employees. He waited in the clean room, where the security team maintained newspapers from around the world. He went through them while he waited. There was nothing new—no letup in the national or worldwide menglavirus infection rates, no improvement in the mortality rates, no cooling of the hostilities between the US and China. After several minutes, the security team returned, and they took him on the elevator to the fortieth floor, where the executive office was located.

His two executive assistants—early risers by necessity—were waiting for him. As soon as he entered the lobby, one of them started to summarize his phone messages while the other handed him the day's research briefings. There were the usual messages: manufacturing teams wanted to discuss expanding capacity for their cardiac lines; research and development wanted guidance on updated efficacy rates; and the FDA wanted to check in on post-marketing studies for their established medications. He was about to enter his personal office to review the daily research briefs and start on returning phone calls and answering emails when he noticed one of his assistants hesitating. "What else?" he said.

"You've received two messages from Dr. Hahn."

"Richard Hahn? My former partner?"

"Yes. He left two phone numbers. He said if you cannot reach him on his cell, to call the second number. He said he'll definitely answer one or the other."

"What does he want? If he wants to discuss our takeover offer, we have an acquisitions team that handles that."

"He wouldn't say. But he says it was urgent."

"With him, it always is. Always was."

He entered his office and sat down at his desk. He had a setup of three computer monitors. The left monitor was tracking on-going research and development projects within the company, the middle screen was for monitoring industry developments, and the right monitor was for emails. He glanced at the third screen. He had fifty-two emails awaiting him, and these were the ones his assistants had already screened, the ones they'd determined needed his personal attention. If he included the emails already handled by them, he would've needed to up the tally to several hundred.

As he settled into the work day, he considered calling Richard. He figured the call was about the acquisition offer Steptech had made for Richard's company. He'd made the offer as soon as he'd received notice from his contacts in the FDA that his old partner's Phase 3 application for their menglavirus vaccine had been denied. He figured Richard was calling now because he wanted to yell at him with his holy righteousness. Admittedly, Jason had made a low offer.

Jason hadn't spoken to Richard in years, not since the start of menglavirus, when it'd been in vogue to reconnect with everyone you'd ever known to see how they were doing. They'd founded Steptech together almost forty-five years ago here in Seattle—and split twenty-five years later. The quarter-century anniversary of Steptech had prompted a midlife crisis in Richard —or at least that was how Jason had seen Richard's split from the company. Richard had suddenly become outraged at the profit motives in industry, as if he hadn't participated in them for a quarter-century already. He was outraged at the prices Steptech charged for its vaccines and pharmaceuticals and the royalties and licensing fees it charged for its patents and intellectual properties. At the time, Richard had just started in-house work on a new mRNA technology that promised to speed immunity in the vaccine space, cutting host response from weeks to only hours or days. Richard had referred to them as mRNA BOOSTers, short for BiOavailable Organized Step Treatments. Suddenly angry at Steptech's sustained profitability, Richard had wanted to go in a different direction with the BOOSTers. He wanted to give them away, license them for pennies to their industry rivals.

Of course, that hadn't happened. The BOOSTers hadn't progressed, at least not while Richard had been at Steptech, thereby making the arguments about Steptech's corporate mission pointless. But the tension between him and Richard never abated. By their twenty-sixth year in business together, Jason bought out Richard's share of the company at a discounted sum in exchange for relinquishing all claims against Richard's BOOSTers, which Richard was free to take elsewhere to develop.

Jason viewed Richard's new venture at Riogenrix—or not so new anymore, because he'd started it a decade ago—as Richard's attempt to atone for sins that didn't actually exist. Richard was guilty in his own mind and Riogenrix was his own arrogant experiment in righteousness, his attempt to live like a monk after living like a king.

Jason admitted he harbored resentment toward Richard not only for leaving the company, but for taking the BOOSTers away with him. Even though Richard had needed almost another decade to develop the boosters—including a stint at Salk that clearly had been intended to further serve Richard's misguided altruistic needs—they'd become a remarkable scientific achievement. Steptech had funded their initial development, yet received none of the credit for their positioning in the vaccine space. Of course, now the BOOSTers were yesterday's news, well-established and part of every vaccine, new and old, licensed for cheap to every major manufacturer developer in the world—including Steptech. The *new* news was the elusive menglavirus vaccine.

He thought about calling back Richard to see what he wanted to do with Steptech's offer. He couldn't imagine Richard could stay independent anymore. If Richard didn't accept Jason's offer, he would have to accept someone else's. Jason knew it would only be a matter of time before his old partner's health took a turn for the worse, as it would for all of them one day, but sooner for Richard. The sarcoidosis had already started to flare during Richard's final days at Steptech. Jason couldn't imagine the menglavirus era was doing Richard's health any favors.

Even so, Jason was surprised by the instructions Richard had left with his assistant. Richard had said to call his cell, but if the call didn't go through, to call the alternate phone number. From his own experience, Jason knew the reason for a call to a cellular telephone not to go through was because the person receiving the call was in a shielded laboratory. He wondered what Richard was doing, whether he was holding out, playing hard to get, pretending that he still had work left inside of him by holing himself up in a lab.

Now, he had fifty-four emails to address, because his assistants had just placed two more in his inbox. If he had time, he would call during lunch. If not, he would aim for the end of the day, and if not the end of the day, maybe the weekend. He would give Richard his current cell phone number as well when they spoke. He preferred to have his acquisitions team deal with Richard, but he supposed he had to speak to him at some point. Despite the ugliness with which they'd split over a decade ago, they remained colleagues. Richard shouldn't really have to go through his assistants in order to talk to him, although he was kind of glad that at least for now he did. He would call Richard back as a professional courtesy, not because he especially wanted to talk to him.

Gregory Miller was in Chula Vista. He was in rented house number three—the one that didn't contain the wife and daughter or his hired security contractors. The house was barren. There was no furniture, only a sleeping bag in the rundown living room. He'd outfitted the main bathroom with a decontamination unit—of which he had little use anymore—when he'd first taken up residence in the San Diego area well over a month ago. He'd had a full night last night. He was going to have a full day today as well. He'd secured the wife and daughter but had more work to do. Much more.

Gregory wasn't a physician, but he should've been. He was a consultant in the field of competitive research, focused on vaccine technology. In other words, he was a corporate spy. Companies hired him to obtain proprietary information on their competitors. Or at least they used to. Now, he only had one client. The senator had hired him a year ago to hunt down a viable menglavirus vaccine. Initially, he'd been disinterested in working for the senator. Then the senator had told him about the canisters and Gregory had become very interested.

Even though he officially wasn't accepting new clients, Russia recently had reached out to him. He wasn't explicitly working for Russia, but he saw a future with them, one that was much more interesting than the future the senator was providing. If he brought a vaccine to the Russians, they would be able to compensate him in ways the senator couldn't. Russia was on the table. They'd been poking around his work for months. They'd offered him direct developmental involvement in whatever menglavirus vaccine he could deliver to them. Gregory wasn't a physician, but Russia would make him one.

Or at least, Gregory *technically* wasn't a physician. He'd gone to medical school. But he hadn't graduated. He'd left Johns Hopkins six weeks before commencement after Johns Hopkins has screwed him over. He'd deserved to match at Johns Hopkins for his internal medicine residency, but they'd disregarded him. In fact, all of the top internal medicine programs in the country had disregarded him. He'd matched at a second-tier program in the south. He'd decided to leave medical school six weeks before graduation rather than play second fiddle to the bozos in his class who'd matched at better residencies. He was smarter than they. Hell, he was smarter than the attending physicians. He deserved better than what Johns Hopkins had given him. He wore the white coat every day as a reminder to himself of what he'd gone through.

Regarding Harrison Boyd, Gregory had gotten to the Riogenrix researcher first and then he'd gotten to their head of security. He'd had good timing with the researcher. When they'd met for the exchange, he could tell she'd already vaccinated herself. But he could also tell she'd been too late. He could see and hear the death on her, the paleness of her skin and tremor of her voice. He knew she'd gotten it from her fiancé, whom she'd been trying to save in the first place. If Gregory hadn't been in a bio-containment suit when he'd given her the money and the "medicine" from Russia, he would've gotten it too.

After all, vaccines were preventive. They stopped the virus from taking root but didn't stop the virus after it was already in a person's system. Or at least, they weren't supposed to. Once you got menglavirus, you had it, and once you had it, you were dead. If you were one of the five percent of people who were lucky enough not to die, you had compromised lung function for the rest of your up-and-down life. Wheezing, recurrent pneumonias, obstruction, fibrosis—you would die eventually from cardiopulmonary failure.

The Riogenrix researcher had been willing to believe the rumors of a Russian treatment that worked. Of course, Gregory had been willing to feed into her belief by handing over the Russian "treatment." He'd given her the pills and the money and she'd given him the hard drive of Phase 2 data and a single prefilled syringe of the V-202 vaccine. He'd injected himself with the vaccine the minute he'd gotten back to the rented house in Chula Vista, back out of the biocontainment suit, and done with decontamination. Forty-eight hours later, he went after the guard—sans suit. The guard had been a lifer at the company, but as soon as the results from V-202 had started coming in, he'd been the wrong person for the job, not ready for the larger stage upon which Riogenrix was going to play. He certainly hadn't been ready for Gregory. Riogenrix had needed a much more comprehensive level of security. Gregory had gotten to him easily. He'd walked up to him at a provisions facility while the guard had been looking at eggs. Gregory had walked behind him, opened up the canister, and kept an eye on him for the next twenty-four hours to make sure he'd died. Gregory had felt kind of bad about releasing the canister in the dairy section of the provisions facility, but people were getting menglavirus one way or another. It didn't matter if they got the so-called *natural* menglavirus or the *modified* version—they were going to get it and they were going to die. Maybe they lived a couple extra weeks with the natural version of menglavirus, but those two weeks were full of fevers, body aches, delirium, cognitive decline, and multi-organ failure, so Gregory wasn't convinced those two extra weeks mattered.

Of course, Gregory had worn a mask that day in the provisions facility because he hadn't wanted to stand out, even though he hadn't really *needed* to wear anything to protect himself. He'd already gained immunity. Now, he didn't wear a mask at all. He agreed with the researcher. In memoriam, of course. The data were real. He was living proof.

Gregory was looking forward to seeing Harrison again. It'd been a long time since they'd gone through fourth-year internal medicine together at Hopkins. He wasn't surprised Harrison had discovered a menglavirus vaccine. After all, Harrison was in many ways his counterpart, but the docile, kiss-ass version.

He washed his face and removed the crust from his eyelids in the main bathroom. He'd slept a couple of hours overnight, which was all he needed for now. He returned to the living room and ironed his white lab coat on a plywood board he'd set up on the floor in the corner. He put on the coat and went outside to the van. He didn't bother locking the house. He had his security team nearby in case anyone tried to access his home base. Furthermore, he had plenty of canisters on hand. He got into the van and headed north towards Riogenrix. He eyed the horizon. The morning was overcast but darker clouds were coming.

Senator Scott Spaulding replayed the conversation he'd had with the doctor in his head. He had one goal—secure the White House. He knew the election in November would be fiercely contested but he had a plan and no matter what the doctor said, he was going to execute his plan. The polls showed the public didn't warm to him as much as the other candidate but he had seven months to go until the elections. He wasn't discouraged by the double-digit lead of his opponent. He would shift the public's thinking. The vaccine was the key.

He was at Trasium, the partially constructed casino and condominium towers in Las Vegas. He'd arrived via the helicopter onto the roof helipad. Before mengalvirus had hit, Trasium had been one of his bigger political accomplishments. It'd been the Strip's most expensive project to date, promising thousands of construction and casino jobs. Of course, the promise had never fully materialized. Instead, the virus had materialized. Nonetheless, he'd made lemonade out of lemons, as he was apt to do. Through a maze of LLCs, he'd secured a sizable equity stake in the towers for pennies on the dollar. When menglavirus faded —and it would fade under his presidency—he would be able to realize a huge financial gain on the towers. These days, he had two residences in Nevada, a house in Henderson for himself and his fiancé, and a block of Trasium condominiums in the casino for his use. For the past two years, Naomi had been using one of the condos.

But he wondered what he was truly doing with her. At times, he thought he loved her. At other times, he wondered if he only loved her because she was dependent on him. Still at other times, he thought he didn't love her at all, not really. Rather he was infatuated. Maybe even a little obsessed. Because if he did love her, he would've left his fiancé already.

Frank, the senior security team member for the casino, stopped him as he walked towards the rooftop stairway with his personal security team. Frank waved Scott aside and the senator understood. He held up his hand to his security contractors to hold up and went with Frank. They huddled together at a communications tower.

"I want to talk to you about your friend, senator," said Frank.

"Go ahead."

"She left yesterday."

"Left the casino?"

"Yes."

"Where'd she go?"

"She went to the provisions facility."

"On the strip?"

"Yes, senator."

"And?"

Frank hesitated.

"And?" the senator said again. "Spill it."

"She bought pregnancy tests."

The senator made sure not to express any emotion. He didn't want to seem surprised. In actuality, he wasn't really. He figured at some point, she would've gotten pregnant. They'd been intimate for long enough for it to be a legitimate possibility, even if he hadn't necessarily expected today's news. "Is there video footage?" he said.

"Yes, senator."

"Delete it. Keep the news off the grid. Away from the rest of casino security. I won't be happy if I read about this online."

"Of course, senator."

Scott and Frank dispersed. Scott waved at his contractors, who rejoined him, and they descended the stairs from the roof to the service elevator one floor below. One of his contractors was still carrying the cooler. Scott had intended to use one of the vaccines for himself and one for—well, he wasn't sure anymore. He'd intended it for Naomi, probably. Even though just five minutes ago he hadn't been sure if he loved Naomi, he'd been thinking about vaccinating her. Five minutes ago, he'd seen the White House in his future, despite what the doctor had said, because he knew he had all the leverage he needed—the doctor's wife and daughter—to get the doctor to comply. Now, he saw the White House slipping away because of the pregnancy. America already didn't like him. The polls were evidence. They liked his fiancé, though. He'd planned on making sure America loved him as much as they loved his fiancé by securing a menglavirus vaccine, but he wasn't sure that America was going to love him when they found out he'd been keeping a twenty-year-old in Trasium Towers for two years and knocked her up to boot. He was forty-five years old, young for US president, but too old to be with a twenty-year-old whom he'd more or less packed away in a Las Vegas condominium. His fiancé, though, was perfect in age and disposition, exactly the same age as he and also committed to politics. He didn't need his campaign managers to tell him what he knew to be true. At times, he was disappointed in himself, but then he reminded himself that life was too short to be disappointed. As he and the contractors got into the service elevator, he considered life without Naomi. Again, he thought he loved her.

Part of the way down to the sixty-first floor, he pulled the emergency stop on the elevator. "I'm taking the stairs the rest of the way," he said to the contractors. "You guys take the elevator." He stepped out of the elevator, walked down the hallway of the partially completed, vacant sixty-eighth floor, and entered the stairwell at the far end. He took the stairs down the rest of the way to Naomi. He wanted a moment to collect his thoughts and formulate a plan about her. His bottom line was that he couldn't get distracted from the vaccine. He couldn't lose sight of the White House. He couldn't let today's news get in the way. He needed to find a solution.

Harrison was finally back in San Diego. The senator's security contractor was still with him, buttressing his viewpoint that the contractor was less a bodyguard and more a prison guard. After arriving back in San Diego, they hadn't gone to Riogenrix to pick up his Accord. The Escalade they'd used to get to the airport with the senator yesterday was the same one they used to leave the airport now. As the contractor drove him home, Harrison wondered if security contractors ever slept. Despite his fatigue and attempt on the plane, Harrison hadn't. He wasn't feeling horrible yet, but knew he would soon. In residency, he'd never acclimated to the thirty-six hour shifts that characterized being on-call. If he hadn't enjoyed medicine so much, he didn't think he would've able to stay awake for a day and a half-, every four days for three years. Even so, he'd been happier in the physician-scientist space rather than the physician-only space, because with research, he never noticed the time, whereas when he'd been on call, he'd always been acutely aware of the clock's vise. Either way, he was glad to be back in San Diego. He was glad to be going home.

As they pulled into Harrison's neighborhood in Mira Mesa, he felt anxious. It was early morning, around the time he would be leaving the house to go to Riogenrix on a normal day—if normal days existed anymore. Nonetheless, he was finally home, after a day away. He didn't feel relaxed, though. He wondered if perhaps he was anxious because he wasn't at Riogenrix and he had a lot of work to do after all. He dismissed the thought. No, his uncertainty wasn't related to Riogenrix, at least not in this moment. Rather, he felt as if he'd been away from home for too long this time. This time—in the day he'd been away—he had the feeling life had irrevocably changed. Vaccine development was intense but steady, a predictable routine most of the time. Now, he felt as if his marriage had changed, his relationship with Sofia was changing, and his career was about to change. He'd been able to be diligent during the past five years of V-202 development— and the five years before during BOOSTers work—because he'd been able to rely on a stable routine. He was a person of routine but now he didn't know what his routine was going to be going forward.

Yet, he couldn't chalk up of all of his hesitation to a change in his routine. He felt—maybe even knew—there was a more sinister change in his life awaiting him. He felt—yes, he knew, he *did* know—the last couple of days didn't add up, from the V-202 denial to the senator showing up at Riogenrix to being whisked away to Nevada. As the senator's security contractor pulled the Escalade in front of the house, Harrison's dread intensified. He didn't need to shake the feeling that Jasmine and Sofia weren't all right because now he knew. The front door to the house was open.

He didn't wait for the SUV to come to a stop. He pulled the door handle and got out. He cut across the half-dead grass to the front entrance. He stood at the door, saw the damaged frame, and called out the names of his wife and daughter. They didn't answer. He called out to them again. He felt fear but tried to advance past it. He pushed through the door, stood in the modest foyer, and scanned the first floor. He saw the living room, undisturbed. He yelled their names and again heard no answer. He glanced towards the kitchen, saw nothing there, and went upstairs.

As he climbed the steps, he remembered how he'd found Sofia at the window twice. He wondered for how long she'd been waiting up for him, if it'd only been those two times or if it'd been other times as well. He tried to remember what day or night that had been, but couldn't get the days or nights of this week to straighten out in his head. She'd said something to him.

Be safe, Daddy.

When he arrived upstairs he heard the quiet and had no doubt. They were gone. They weren't at the park like they were yesterday or the day before or whenever Jasmine had said they'd gone—he knew they weren't, especially so early in the morning. They'd been home and something horrible had happened to them overnight. He went to Sofia's room first and saw nothing but an unmade bed. He went to the window, looked out of it, and saw what he had never noticed before, the way that it angled towards the street.

And now he remembered what she'd said.

Waiting for you, Daddy. I need to talk about astronauts.

He hadn't talked to her nor given what she'd said much thought but now he knew what she'd meant. She'd been at the window because she'd been watching astronauts on the street.

People in biosafety suits.

He didn't know how many there'd been, but he knew they'd been there. She'd told him, and he hadn't listened. He hadn't protected her. He'd never been home enough to protect her.

He left Sofia's room and went to the main bedroom. He felt as if he couldn't breathe when he saw the blankets strewn across the ground. He smelled foul sweat, the odor of people who'd never been here before. He went to the adjoining bathroom, checked it, saw nothing, and went to the closet, and saw his pants piled on the floor. He glanced upwards to where Jasmine kept her pistol safety box. It wasn't there. He looked around the closet, and saw the box on the floor. It was open. The pistol was gone.

He returned to the bedroom. The security contractor was there, standing on top of the blankets, blocking him. The contractor was dangling a phone in his hand. He held it out to Harrison. "The senator wants to speak to you," he said. He tossed the phone. Harrison caught it and held it to his ear.

"We need the vaccine, doctor," the senator said. "We don't need your wife. We don't need your daughter. We don't even need you. We need the developmental notes and protocols. We need to know how to produce your vaccine, step-by-step. We need to know monitoring concerns. We need it now."

"What did you do to my wife and daughter?"

"We didn't do anything. Nothing yet."

"Bring me my family."

"We will, doctor. But first you need to bring us the vaccine."

"I don't care about the vaccine. Bring me my wife and daughter."

"Glad you understand, doctor. We'll make it happen today. As good as done."

The senator hung up. At first, Harrison had no doubt about what he was going to do next—he would deliver all of his notes and developmental techniques to the senator to get his wife and daughter back. He would deliver *everything*. He would even allow them to take *him* as well so long as Jasmine and Sofia were returned to him safely. He didn't understand the senator's intentions but had no desire to dwell on what they might be. Not now, not with Jasmine and Sofia having been abducted. He only needed to get them back.

But then he saw the contractor pointing a gun at him. As Harrison stood in the raided bedroom, he understood the stakes at play with his menglavirus vaccine.

The senator had assigned a security contractor—a mercenary, by the old name—to keep tabs on him, make sure he didn't leave the senator's reach.

He remembered how the colonel had been surprised V-202 had been rejected by the FDA, as if he hadn't known.

He thought about the menglavirus deaths of his lead researcher and head of security—too big a coincidence for him to believe they weren't unrelated.

The stakes for V-202 were bigger than menglavirus, even if he didn't know what they were yet. He had no doubt he would turn over V-202 in full to the senator to get Jasmine and Sofia back, but he didn't know if the senator was really going to give them back, because the senator's abduction reeked of a desperation and violence so deep Harrison didn't think there was any way he could trust him. In fact, the senator had already acted with horrible dishonesty. He wondered how much he should go along with the senator's demands versus how much he should carve his own path to get his family back.

He saw Jasmine's pistol on the ground near the bed, almost underneath it. He still had the phone in his hand. He dropped it. He knew now he needed to carve his own path. He couldn't trust the senator. He needed to trust himself.

He lifted his palms in front of him, conveying to the contractor that he was ready to go peacefully with him. The contractor kept the pistol in hand but Harrison saw the shift as the contractor stepped towards him. The contractor angled the gun slightly towards the ground. The tiny amount of relaxation on the part of the contractor was all Harrison needed. He didn't hesitate. He knew what he needed to do. He dove at the contractor's legs and connected with the kneecaps. The contractor stumbled but managed to stay upright. Harrison rolled along the floor until he got to the bed. He reached beneath it. He grabbed

Jasmine's pistol. He didn't have to think about what to do next. Nor did he hesitate. He planted himself on his knee, and fired the pistol at the contractor's chest.

Thunderous sound swallowed the bedroom. The contractor fell backwards. Harrison had aimed for the torso and hit his mark. Harrison didn't think he'd killed or even permanently hurt the contractor, because the contractor was wearing armor, but he'd incapacitated him enough to get away from him. He stood up and stepped on the contractor's chest, applying as much pressure as he could to make sure the contractor stayed down while he moved past him towards the bedroom door.

He left the room with Jasmine's pistol and ran downstairs. He sped through the house to the garage to get Jasmine's car before the contractor could recover. He opened the garage door and got into her Volvo wagon. He gunned the engine and reversed out of the garage onto the street. He put the car into drive and floored the accelerator. He didn't know what to do next, so he did what came naturally to him—he drove to Riogenrix.

When Gregory arrived at the Riogenrix campus, he planned on going mainframe to mainframe to physically remove each single computer server by hand. Tedious but definite. Old-fashioned but riskless. He started in such a way, entering Building Jenner and grabbing one of the servers in the west wing of the administrative offices, when a better way materialized. As he walked out of Jenner with a frame in his hands to the lot where he'd parked his van, he saw Riogenrix's chief administrative officer. She was pulling onto campus. He'd studied her, of course, when he'd first zeroed in on Riogenrix. He recognized her Jeep. He waited to see if she would notice him too. But she was at a distance still, only just getting onto campus, only now driving past the main gate. She didn't see him and didn't turn the Wrangler around.

He moved off of the walkway onto a stretch of grass. He

placed the frame on the ground and crouched behind a concrete wall that ran around part of the parking lot. He waited. The woman pulled into the parking lot. He heard her idle the engine and finally turn it off. He heard her Jeep door open and close and then he heard silence. He figured by now she'd noticed his gray van. By now, she'd realized it didn't belong in the Riogenrix parking lot. So he stepped from behind the wall.

"Hi, Selene Torres. You don't know me, but I know you."

He stepped towards her.

Naomi was full of worries. She'd been worried about telling the senator about the pregnancy but now she was worried about her mother as well. She was in the living room on the condo. The senator was in the main bathroom. She heard the senator —Senator Scott, as he'd told her to refer to him the first time they'd met—come out of the shower. She had her phone on her lap. She'd been calling her mother for the entirety of the senator's shower. Her mother hadn't answered at all. Naomi knew— couldn't shake the feeling—something bad had happened.

When the senator returned to the living room, he was dressed in slacks. His hair was wet and newly slicked. He had the cooler in his hand, the same one he'd had when he'd entered the condo earlier. He hadn't let go of it since he'd arrived, even taking it with him into the bathroom. Naomi knew the cooler was important. When she'd asked him about it, he'd only smiled and let the question slide off of him.

Now, he took the cooler with him to the bar nook. He poured himself a tumbler of whisky and returned to the living room, with the drink in one hand and cooler in the other. He sat in the lounger. He placed the cooler at his feet and raised his glass.

"So, tell me, Naomi, how have you been?"

He didn't need to say or ask anything else for her to know that *he* knew she was pregnant. By now, the casino security would've had enough time to pull footage from the provisions facility. Either way, she hadn't told him yet, and with each minute that passed, she wanted to tell him even less. She didn't have a good feeling about telling him. While she'd been intent on telling him about the pregnancy last night, now she felt hesitant. She didn't like the way he was confronting her. She knew he had something on his mind. She wished there were a way out, but she didn't even know how she got *in*.

"I'm not sure," she said. "You tell me."

"A lot is new in the world." He used the tumbler to point to the cooler on the ground. "I have a present for us."

"Do you?"

"I do. But I think you should talk first, Naomi. Then I'll talk. So tell me, what's new?"

She didn't care about what was in the cooler. She knew by his tone that whatever was in the cooler really wasn't a present. She also knew she had to tell him about the pregnancy sometime and she knew he was making sure the *sometime* was now. She could imagine the other questions he would levy at her if she didn't tell him now.

Where did you go yesterday?

What did you buy?

She wondered if she *seemed* any different, whether pregnancy had changed her demeanor at all. Again, she told herself she didn't look any different. She'd thought all morning about the consequences of her being pregnant. For a few minutes, she'd almost panicked thinking about him not wanting her in his life anymore, but the panic had passed. In its place, she'd come to the realization she didn't mind being alone. She preferred it, had become accustomed to it as a kid when she'd quickly learned she didn't want to be around her mother when she was drinking, which was almost all of the time. She liked living in the condo, being on her own, even if she knew she wasn't *really* subsisting on her own, because she was always under his thumb, living at his place, and taking advantage of the security he provided. But when he wasn't here, she felt as if the space was her own. After all, she was the one who lived here, spending day after day inside by herself while the whole world turned around her, or at least however much it turned during menglavirus.

"I'm pregnant," she said, coming out with it.

He didn't seem fazed. "How long?"

"Four or five weeks."

"Brand new. Are you happy?"

"I think I am."

"Good. Pregnancy is a big deal. Raising a child is a big deal. Challenging. Of course, you know about the challenges of raising a child from your own experiences. Are you nervous?"

"I'm fine."

"Excellent. Myself? I would be nervous if I were pregnant. It's a strange world out there. Well, what are we going to do?"

She noted the *I* and then the *we*. She said what she'd been thinking but been afraid to verbalize, even to herself.

"I'll begin prenatal care."

He continued to sip from the tumbler. Seconds passed in silence. Finally, he placed the tumbler on the coffee table. He picked up the cooler and placed it in his lap.

"I have a menglavirus vaccine for you, Naomi. It comes out of San Diego, your part of the woods. It is a legitimate vaccine, the only real vaccine that exists in the world. Of course, I hadn't known that you were pregnant when I received the vaccine. I don't know if the vaccine is safe during pregnancy."

She wondered if the senator truly did have a vaccine. She didn't completely discount the possibility. After all, he was on a congressional committee related to menglavirus. It made sense that he would have access to whatever the latest vaccines were. But in the two years she'd been with him, or at least since she'd been in his condo—she'd never really been sure that she was *truly* with him, never really sure she'd ever really meant anything to him—he'd never purported to have a vaccine. She was inclined to believe him. If he had a vaccine for her, she also was inclined to believe he loved her after all.

"How many?" she said.

"Two."

She knew the implications. "Only two?"

"Yes, only two."

"For us?" she said.

"Yes."

She felt herself softening.

"What else is bothering you, Naomi?"

For two years, she'd trusted him, and she decided she needed to trust him now as well. If he betrayed her trust, she would leave him. She'd never intended to be dependent on anyone but menglavirus had changed her plans.

"I think something is wrong with my mother."

"What's wrong with her?"

"I don't know. She usually calls me every Tuesday night but she didn't call me yesterday. So I called her today. Four times. I left two voicemails. She hasn't called back. I don't know if she is okay."

He reached for the tumbler, drank from it again, and placed it back on the table. "I have a trip to San Diego on the books for to-night. Vaccine related, of course. Why don't you fly out with me? It's been too long since you've gotten out of Las Vegas. I can take you to your mother's house before my meeting, and we'll return to Las Vegas the same night. Of course, I'll ask the scientists dur-ing my meeting if the vaccine is safe for a pregnant woman. I'm *mostly* sure they'll say yes, but it's best to be *completely* sure."

She hadn't left Las Vegas in the two years since she'd left her mother's house. She was anxious about seeing her mother again, but she couldn't help but feel her mother needed her help. Again, she told herself that on the outside, she looked no different, but on the inside, she knew she was changing. She wanted to see her mother, which was new to her.

He put the cooler back on the ground. He opened it and pulled out a syringe. He held the syringe out to her with one hand while pulling up his sleeve with the other. While the cooler was open, Naomi looked inside. She saw dry ice packs and a second syringe.

"What do you say?" the senator said. "You can inject me now with my vaccine. And I can inject you tonight with your dose.

Once I confirm it's safe for pregnancy."

Despite her hesitation, she went to him.

As Harrison pulled Jasmine's Volvo onto Riogenrix Way, he saw the gate was open. He sped up, not caring about what other messes were awaiting him. But as he approached Building Jenner, he did care, because he saw Selene from a distance standing only a few feet away from a man without a mask. Harrison floored the accelerator. He couldn't figure out exactly who the person was, but he looked vaguely familiar. Selene was backing away from him. Harrison had Jasmine's pistol on the passenger seat. He reached for it as he pulled up next to the walkway, the screeching tires hitting the curb. He rushed out of the wagon with the pistol and pointed it at the man. The man didn't flinch, almost didn't react.

"It's a pleasure to see you again, Harrison Boyd," the man said, as if they knew each other.

But Harrison didn't know who this man was. He didn't know if he was with the senator or acting on his own. He'd come to grips with the fact that anyone—senators, governments, companies, kidnappers, contractors, and combinations thereof—could be after the vaccine. He knew the man was threatening Selene. He kept the gun trained on the man. "Selene, let's go," he said.

She didn't move or acknowledge him, as if she was frozen into place.

"Selene," he said again. "Let's go."

She turned towards him this time. He saw the uncertainty on her face and then the relief. He didn't have to tell her again. She ran towards him and the Volvo. Harrison kept the pistol pointed at the man without a mask as she got into the passenger seat of the wagon.

"Who are you?" Harrison said to the man, keeping the gun steady.

"You offend me, Harrison."

"Do you work for the senator?"

"Don't we all, in some way or another?"

Harrison noticed the man without a mask had a thigh holster. The man hadn't reached for it yet but Harrison knew it'd only be a matter of time before he did. Harrison didn't delude himself—he wasn't a gunman. He'd handled a firearm from time to time in medical school because his roommate had taken him to a shooting range but he knew nothing about them other than you pointed and fired. He didn't want to get stuck out here. If the man knew the senator, he wasn't going to acknowledge it without coaxing, but Harrison wasn't in the best position to coax.

He kept the pistol pointed at the man as he too stepped into the wagon. For now, the man without a mask didn't budge. "Are you okay?" he said to Selene. He reversed the car under full acceleration. He didn't remove his foot from the accelerator until he'd pulled the wagon all the way back to the Riogenrix entrance. The man without a mask didn't follow them—for now.

"I'm okay," Selene said. "Who was he?"

"I don't know. I was about to ask you the same."

When they got through the gates, he swung the car around until the wagon was pointed away from campus. He put the car into drive, punched the accelerator again, and they left Riogenrix for what he knew would be the last time.

The neighborhood felt depleted. She and Sofia were in a bedroom in a worn-down house someplace in Chula Vista with a single queen bed and an attached bathroom. The one window in the bedroom had bars on it. So did the smaller window in the bathroom. They hadn't been blindfolded when they'd been brought here yesterday. The man without a mask hadn't seemed to care, which worried her even more. They'd driven through a partially burned neighborhood until they'd come to a boarded-up house on a cul-de-sac. She knew the neighborhood had once been desirable but now was left to fend for itself. Thankfully, Sofia had finally fallen asleep this morning. She was sleeping now on the bed while Jasmine sat next to her. Jasmine was watching the bedroom door. She hadn't slept, of course. As Sofia's mother, she was supposed to keep her daughter safe, but she'd failed. She'd been thinking all night about how to get out of this room, out of this house, out of this neighborhood that wasn't their own. She'd come up with nothing.

The man without a mask had told them when he'd locked them into the bedroom that they wouldn't be here long. They would be leaving soon. Jasmine didn't know what *soon* meant. For her, *soon* meant never having been here in the first place. She also didn't know what *long* meant, because even a single second in this situation was too long. There were no clocks in the room but she got a general sense of the time because of the light coming in through the window. On a regular day, now would be the time when their lessons would be hitting the first roadblock, when Jasmine would have to decide whether to keep pushing ahead on the math and reading or call it quits. Again, she was thankful Sofia was sleeping. She wished that Sofia would sleep for the entirety of the day and night. She didn't want Sofia to wake up to the nightmare that was their life right now. She never should've gone to the park. She never should've left the house.

Except, she knew they would've come for her and Sofia no matter what Jasmine had or hadn't done. Harrison had a vaccine, and the vaccine worked, and the man without a mask and the other two men with biosafety suits were after the vaccine. She understood the stakes. She didn't know how Harrison couldn't have. If he'd had a vaccine, he should've known people would be after it. More than money was at stake. The future was at stake.

She waited to hear a door open at the front of the house indicating the man without a mask was back. For now, she heard nothing. She needed to save her mental and physical energies for getting Sofia out of this situation. To a certain degree, she knew she had leverage—or to be more accurate she *was* the leverage.

Jasmine knew the man wanted the vaccine but she could also tell he didn't have it yet. She didn't know what Harrison's plan was or what he'd found out, but she hoped she could trust him to do right by his family for the first in a long time.

She put her hand on Sofia's shoulder while Sofia slept. She would make sure they got out of here.

Richard was in his personal biosafety laboratory. He was using his workstation to model Harrison's notes from the mirror, seeing if he could get to the same point Harrison had achieved. He hadn't been successful thus far. He'd been working on the modeling for hours, breaking only to take gulps of water from a flask he continually filled from the filtered faucet at the back of the lab. The first few hours had been okay, even good— much better than last night when he'd had partial mirrors only —as he'd delved into the research that Harrison had put together over the past five years. He'd seen the roadmap Harrison had followed. But as he'd moved further into the work, he'd understood less, and now he was understanding very little at all. The constant work reminded him of his younger days, when he'd subsisted on research alone, from sunup to sundown, day after day, week after week, content to work and work until breakthroughs materialized. Today, he didn't have week after week or day after day or even sunup to sundown to crack Harrison's vaccine work. He was working on borrowed time. It'd been several hours now since he'd left the first two messages with Jason Carr's assistant. He didn't have cell reception in the laboratory, but he'd provided the number for the landline. It hadn't rung yet. He'd been waiting minute by minute, steeling himself to let Jason know he had a menglavirus vaccine but also that he didn't understand anything about it. Even so, he knew the real reason for his unease wasn't because Jason would know he had had nothing do with the vaccine's development, but because the more time passed, the less confident he became that Jason was going to call back at all. He kept thinking Riogenrix was going to need to have a go at the vaccine themselves. Specifically, Richard was going to need to have a go himself. And he clearly wasn't ready to have a go at it.

He decided he needed a break, maybe eat a sandwich or drink a cup of coffee. He left the biosafety lab and went upstairs to the main floor. Cellular reception returned and he called Jason Carr again. He left another message with his assistant, the same one from the morning, again saying his phone call was urgent. He tried to get the assistant to patch him through or at least provide him with Jason's current cell phone number, but the assistant kept saying that Dr. Carr was busy.

Richard had nothing else to do other than trudge onwards. He decided against the sandwich but took a cup of coffee with him back downstairs. Before he punched in his access code to enter the laboratory—before his cell reception faded again—he decided to call Mostafa. He couldn't remember exactly when he'd spoken to his old friend, whether it was yesterday or the day before, because the days were already running together. He didn't know if he expected Mostafa to pick up. Of course, Mostafa didn't. The call went straight to voicemail. Richard didn't leave a message, knowing—without trying to think about the reason why—there was no point. He figured he'd called simply to hear his friend's voice, even if it'd been on a voicemail prompt. He pocketed the cell phone, entered his access code, and reentered the biosafety laboratory.

Harrison was anxious, more so than he'd ever been. It was mid-afternoon and he and Selene were in her house. He hadn't wanted to come here because of the cell phone tracking, but she'd waived off his concerns, telling him she was part of the process as well. She had a small but airy three-bedroom house in Point Loma, on the peninsula, only four blocks from the beach. He'd never been in her house before. He'd always viewed their relationship as professional but now understood it'd been more distant than professional. He hadn't focused as much on people as he'd focused on his computer models and pipettes. She'd placed the vaccines on the top shelf of her refrigerator next to several bottles of mineral water and now they were sitting on opposite ends of her dining table. He found himself not knowing what to do with himself. From where he sat, he saw two pictures of her late husband on the sideboard—one of them by himself at a campsite, the other one with her at Seattle's Pike Place Fish Market. He tried to remember how he'd died, but couldn't. Selene had come to Riogenrix as a widow, her life already laid out—or so Harrison had arrogantly thought.

He looked away from the sideboard and stared at the cell phone on the table. It was the phone the contractor had given him on the plane as a replacement for his own. He felt icky with it in his possession, as if the senator were by his side right now. But he couldn't get rid of it because otherwise he didn't know how the senator—or the man without a mask, if he was working with the senator, and Harrison was pretty sure he was—would contact him. He figured the senator would find a way to contact him even without the cell phone, but he couldn't take the risk of a delay. He needed to get Jasmine and Sofia back.

The senator hadn't contacted him though. It was as if the senator were waiting him out, making him desperate enough to make sure Harrison wasn't going to avoid what he needed to do. But Harrison wasn't going to avoid anything. He didn't care about V-202, wasn't thinking about menglavirus anymore. Vaccines and viruses were luxuries at this point.

He picked up the cell phone to make sure it had reception. As he did, it rang. He was startled by the ringtone. The caller ID said unknown. Now that the phone had rung, he almost didn't want to pick it up, fearing whatever he might hear. But, of course, he picked up. The man without a mask spoke.

"What do you have for me, Harrison?"

"I have whatever you want," Harrison said. "Whatever you need."

"I need all of the processes and procedures to manufacture the menglavirus vaccine."

"You have it already. You have me."

"I want your processes."

"You already have the processes. You took the mainframes."

"You're not the best at documentation, are you?"

"The processes are in in my head."

"I want to know, step-by-step, how to produce your vaccine."

"I can give it to you."

"I know you can. And I know you will. I'll give you the rest of the day, Harrison."

"And then what?"

"Then we meet."

"Where? When?"

"Do your work first, Harrison. We'll talk again when you're finished."

"What about my wife and daughter?"

"What about them, Harrison? They're fine. I'm not in the murder business. Get your work done."

The man without a mask hung up.

Harrison said to Selene, "He wants me to recreate the vaccine on paper."

"What about our mainframes? He took them."

"The mainframes still need to be interpreted. The blanks need to be filled in. It could take weeks or months to fill in all the blanks for someone who doesn't know the specifics of the mRNA techniques Richard and I developed."

"Can you recreate the vaccine on paper?"

"A lot is in my head, but, yes, I can. Do you have a computer?"

She brought him a laptop from the kitchen counter.

"How long do you need?" she said.

"A few hours, at least."

"We'll get Jasmine and Sofia back, Harrison."

Harrison was quiet. "Thank you, Selene," he said.

"For what?"

"For remembering the names of my wife and daughter."

"Why wouldn't I remember?"

Harrison hesitated. He couldn't remember her late husband's name. He'd only heard about him in passing, mostly from Richard. But she remembered his wife's and daughter's names, even though she'd spoken to them only in passing. Harrison wasn't one to express his feelings, especially regarding his work. He didn't think feelings really mattered regarding Riogenrix. But he knew his reality had changed over the past few days. Work wasn't just work. Riogenrix always had been his existence. But it'd been the existence for so many other people as well. Selene was as instrumental in Riogenrix's daily subsistence as he or Richard, if not more. She kept the company running, through whatever personal tribulations she might've faced. He'd worked with her for ten years but had done so little to get to know her. He understood his failings with his family extended to Riogenrix. The past couple of days were proof Riogenrix wasn't just a small vaccine development company. It was a company with big ideas and bigger people to make those ideas come to fruition. Selene was Riogenrix too.

"I can't remember your husband's name," he said.

"Bobby."

"Bobby. That's right. I'm sorry, Selene. I never really tried to get to know you better. I never really tried to nourish our relationship away from logistics. We've worked together for ten years but I haven't put in the effort. I'm sorry for being so distant."

"Get this done, Harrison," Selene said. "And we'll have another ten years—or twenty or thirty—to get to know each other."

Harrison nodded, appreciative of Selene's words. He opened the laptop and started filling in the blanks of his life.

Col. Burt Johnson had been up since 0530 the prior day. Now, it was early afternoon. He was pushing two days awake, a stretch of time not foreign to him but not exactly typical anymore. After a morning of telemeetings with the Department of Defense, he was at his workstation in his office, digging through BERTA, USAMRIID-West's proprietary systems network, trying to catch up on the entirety of the work done at West since its classified inception. He was running through the list of projects in which West was involved, deep diving when he could. He'd found the supporting documentation for several prophylactic and therapeutic projects related to nMAQ25 but still couldn't gain access to a highly classified collection of studies referred to as Project Fountain and Project Soda Can. Additionally, he still didn't have keycard access to parts of Building Delta. He'd been patient thus far, but couldn't be patient anymore. The interaction overnight with the senator had been odd, even odder than usual. Dr. Harrison Boyd had mentioned the FDA had denied his vaccine application. But Col. Burt Johnson had seen the data on the vaccine from the NIH. He didn't understand why the FDA would be shutting down the doctor's vaccine if it worked. Furthermore, he didn't understand why the senator would've brought the doctor by West in the first place—presumably to finalize V-202 for widespread testing, manufacture, and distribution—if the vaccine was already DOA. Maryland didn't support losers and he was pretty sure West wasn't supposed to either.

Burt left the office. He walked to the south wing of Building Charlie to Command and Control Systems, where there was an onsite technician in charge of maintaining security permissions for BERTA. Over the two weeks Burt had gotten to know the systems technician, he'd come to appreciate the kid as being smart and studious, although impressionable and overwhelmed at times. He was skinny and tall but hunched a lot. Burt stood in the doorway and waited for the technician to stand up. When he did, Burt said, "I'm still waiting on full access to BERTA."

"I'm waiting too, sir," the technician said. "I'm still waiting on D.C. to provide me with clearance codes to update your system permissions."

He'd never asked before, assuming for the past two weeks D.C. had meant the Department of Defense. Now knowing D.C.

probably didn't mean what he had assumed, Burt asked, "DoD or someone else?"

"Congressional Committee on Menglavirus, sir," said the technician.

He wasn't surprised by the answer. Burt said, "Congress doesn't work at the same speed with which the US Army does. Just grant it."

"Grant what, sir?"

"My access."

"I can't."

"Why not?"

"I have to wait for the clearance codes."

Burt remained standing at the doorway. He was purposefully quiet. He'd noted over his career, both in battle and military medicine, that a sustained seriousness of intent worked wonders.

"Don't I?" the technician said, clearly unnerved by the colonel's silence.

"I am the commander here."

"That's true, sir."

"I do have the clearance, because I am the commander. I'm supposed to be running this place. But I can't run this place if some congressional committee continues with its glacial pace."

"So, grant it, sir?"

"Yes."

"I will work on it, sir. I have to find a workaround. I almost have to hack the system."

The technician looked at Burt for a response. Again, Burt employed silence.

"I will get it done, sir," the technician said.

"How long before I have the clearance I need to do the work I need to do around here?"

"Ninety minutes, sir."

Burt went back to his office in the north wing of Building Charlie. He sat at his desk and emailed Dr. Mostafa Abdou at the NIH again about the V-202 data they'd briefly discussed last week. He'd sent one email already since the senator had left, but still hadn't heard back. Although he'd never spoken to Dr. Abdou in person, he had the doctor's contact information at the NIH via the doctor's email signature. He called Dr. Abdou at his work number, but got a systems voicemail. He left a message, thanking the doctor for his correspondences from the prior week, and he asked the doctor if he would have time to speak to him today about V-202. He called the cell phone next, leaving the same message. As he hung up, he told himself if he didn't hear back from Dr. Abdou by the end of the morning, he would follow up directly with the director of the NIH. He had the feeling that Dr. Mostafa Abdou wasn't the kind of person to let voicemails and unreturned phone calls linger for long.

After the calls, he went back to digging through BERTA. As he pulled up the projects for which he did have clearance, he thought there was irony in having all of this security clearance within the US Army yet access always came down to some technician pushing a bunch of buttons.

Senator Scott Spaulding watched an empty afternoon sky from the balcony of his high-rise condominium on the Las Vegas Strip. He had his cell phone in his hand, waiting for the phone call from China's Ministry of State Security. Naomi was sleeping in the second bedroom, like she'd been doing for two years now, ever since he'd taken her under his wing and allowed her to stay here, but right now she was taking a nap, something she usually didn't do. He understood her needs were already changing with her pregnancy. He didn't have a lot of time, not with the vaccine or the elections or Naomi.

He didn't mind having a child—a political heir, so to say. He just didn't want to have one in this manner. He'd worked hard to secure his party's presidential nomination, but, even so, he was trailing in the polls. Having a child would probably help him, allow him to become more humanized, but having a twenty-year-old whom he'd kept from the world as the mother of the child wasn't going to help. He had a fiancé who fit the bill of what a first lady should be—established, reserved, and, importantly, his age—but he wouldn't have a fiancé anymore if she found out about Naomi. In the polling, his fiancé was an asset, one of the factors that made him more *likable*. He promised himself he would do what he'd been delaying and marry his fiancé in one of the weekends to come in a simple civil ceremony. This would provide a boost to the campaign. But he understood marrying his fiancé meant removing Naomi from his life.

Of course, the main boost was getting rid of the doctor's V-202, brokering the deal to bring the vaccine to the US from China, not only putting an end to the country's menglavirus disaster but also ending the country's coldest of wars. He would convince the Chinese to distribute the menglavirus vaccine to Americans, making him the candidate to bring a cure home. Meanwhile, China would make sure he won the elections by hook or crook.

After tonight, he wouldn't need the doctor anymore—or that strange consultant. The consultant would've secured the developmental data from Riogenrix. In turn, Scott would turn it over to China's Ministry of State Security. China had physician-scientists as well. They could figure out the gaps and still get the vaccine ready for him in advance of the November elections. He would be happy to be done with the consultant. The guy creeped him out. The always-on white lab coat was more than odd.

For now, he was pretending to be happy with Naomi's news. He wanted her to think he was on board with her having a baby. But, tonight, after they returned from San Diego, he would apply the pressure. He didn't know much about her mother, but thought her mother's radio silence was a good guise for getting her to go with him. He was concerned Naomi wasn't going to play along. Despite the fact she'd been living in his condo for two years, he knew she'd always been particularly hesitant about their arrangement, but not sure enough about what to do next to leave. But now she would form a plan, one constructed from pregnancy. If he showed he didn't want the child, she would use his feelings as her motivation. In this regard, he knew her. He was already concerned that if he left for San Diego without her, she wouldn't be here in the condo when he got back. Of course, he could assign security to her while she was here, but such an escalation of tensions so quickly between them would undoubtedly lessen his chances of convincing her to get rid of the pregnancy on her own. He had little doubt she would dig in. His goal was to remain neutral and try to be friendly until the deed was done.

Scott supposed he only had himself to blame. Of course, Naomi was going to get pregnant at some point, because that was how biology worked. He didn't need to be an MD to know. Nonetheless, he was angry. He wasn't used to getting pushback. He hadn't foreseen today's complications.

Finally, the unknown phone number for which he'd been waiting appeared on the caller ID of his cell phone. He closed the sliding glass door of the balcony for privacy. He picked up. "Ni-hao," he said. He'd been practicing.

Gregory was in the rundown Chula Vista house, working on the frames. Evening was nearing. Over the few hours since he'd assembled them, he'd gleaned both a lot and very little. The reassembled frames took up the entirety of the living room. As he reviewed the frames, he found himself remembering how much he loved medicine. For the thousandth time in his life, he wondered if he'd made the right decision in leaving medical school six weeks before graduation or whether he should've continued on with the residency with which he'd matched. For the last nine hundred and ninety-nine times, he'd gone back and forth on the issue. Today, though, he didn't. He was sure he'd made the right decision. He didn't like being the biggest weirdo in a field full of weirdos, but that was what others had made of him.

For the first time in over a decade, he felt his world opening up. The entirety of his life had been about finding inroads before people kicked him off. He'd never taken a handout, never relied on anybody other than himself. But now he saw the fork and knew where he would be taking it. He was a biomedical espionage consultant, the best there was in a shadowy industry, but he'd never been completely satisfied with his work. The pull of medicine—real medicine, particularly life as a Johns Hopkins educated physician-scientist—had always been present. Now, after hours of rifting through Riogenrix's V-202 developmental data from the mainframe, he felt a familiar urgency to get into the game. He enjoyed the complexity of medicine in ways he couldn't describe. He needed to have his own biomedical company, something to show himself he'd succeeded after all.

He texted Harrison from his encrypted phone. He sent him a message of when and where they were going to meet. As he waited for the notification to show that Harrison had reviewed the message, he left the house, walking through the front door to the chill outside. Except for him and a couple of vagrants, the streets were empty. He walked the two blocks to the second Chula Vista house he'd acquired a few weeks ago, the one where he was keeping the wife and daughter. The wind picked up as he walked and the air became heavier. He buttoned his lab coat. He briefly wondered if the weather was going to take a turn for the worse overnight but didn't dwell because he wasn't planning on being in San Diego for much longer. He reached the end of the street where the second house was located. He let himself in through the front door. By now, he'd received the read receipt notification on the message to Harrison.

He stood in the darkened living room, motivating himself through action. He'd affixed large trash bags to the window panes to block light and prying eyes from outside. He went to the room where he was storing the wife and daughter. He undid the deadbolt on the outside of the door. The wife was on the bed, sitting with her knees folded into her chest. The daughter was sleeping beside her and the wife had her palm resting on her daughter's back as if she were comforting her. She glared at Gregory as he entered; he could feel the snarl in her gaze. He pushed any hesitation out of his mind. If the medical community thought he was a freak, he would become a freak.

He took a picture of the woman and daughter with the encrypted cell phone. He left the room and bolted the door behind him. He sent the photo to Harrison. He went back to the darkened living room and removed a canister from his lab coat. The canister didn't contain the senator's modified menglavirus, the one that had become so useful to him. It contained the so-called native virus, the same strain that was everywhere else in the world. He needed the wife and daughter alive for a while longer, but eventually he wasn't going to want them alive at all. When he took the wife and daughter out of the house later tonight, they would get the appropriate exposure. For him, the wife and daughter were loose ends. As he waited for the notification showing Harrison had received the photo, he opened the canister in the living room. Harrison wouldn't be able to reply to the picture, but Gregory was sure that Harrison would have plenty to say later tonight.

By late evening, the technician had come through. He'd taken longer than the ninety minutes he'd said he'd needed, but he'd provided Burt the full clearance for BERTA. Burt spent a half-hour reviewing Operation Fountain. He found nothing unusual in the joint DIA-CIA intelligence files as related to the origins of nMAQ25. The files noted that nMAQ25 was a gain of function virus gone wrong, having originated from China's Army virology laboratory. It'd escaped unintentionally from the lab because of faulty biosafety containment procedures. While reading the case files for Operation Fountain, Burt learned nothing new, at least not to him. The US Defense Intelligence Agency hadn't released information on the true origin of the virus to the public, but he'd known the truth for some time now.

Operation Soda Can was more of the same, nothing particularly new. It confirmed that in addition to nMAQ25—referred to as "native" menglavirus within the documents—China had created several other sub-strains using gain of function, including a faster-acting form of the virus, referred to as nMAQ61, or simply, "modified" menglavirus. It infected human respiratory cells in the same manner in which native nMAQ25 did but exhibited over one thousand times more affinity for the lungs' angiotensin converting enzyme receptors. The modified strain acted more quickly, cutting disease progression from a couple of weeks to no more than one or two days. People died more quickly and horribly. Again, there was nothing new here, at least not for Col. Burt Johnson. Again, the public wasn't aware of the modified menglavirus, but the colonel had been aware for some time. After all, USAMRIID conducted the same kinds of GOF studies on hundreds of viruses every year in order to understand pathogenicity and virulence. China's problem—and consequently the world's problem—had been in the containment of menglavirus rather than in the gain of function studies themselves. He was about to close the files when he noticed the last line:

> The CIA and DIA believe modified nMAQ61 is being actively produced by the People's Liberation Army of China in multiple doses for release in select international locations—including the United States—after widespread domestic vaccination in China for native MAQ25 itself.

The tidbit of information was concerning, truly upsetting, but again nothing new. He knew China—along with dozens of other countries, particularly Russia—had robust microbiological warfare and terrorism capabilities. But conventional wisdom was that China wasn't foolish or proud enough—take your pick—to employ them.

Burt had read dozens of similar reports over the past decade. The goal of US intelligence agencies was to find the loosely possible along with the more probable, while the goal of the White House, US diplomats, and US politicians was to make sure the loosely possible never became broadly probable. He was about to close the file and move onto the next one when he noticed a certain Senator Scott Spaulding, Chairperson of the Congressional Committee on Menglavirus Vaccines and Therapeutics, had ordered the "eyes only" classification of the report—and no other eyes were listed.

Again, the senator was smackdab in the middle of menglavirus.

Burt's feeling that the senator had ulterior motives far more nefarious than the current menglavirus situation returned more strongly. He didn't know exactly what the senator was planning, but he knew the senator was aiming to do something hugely out of bounds. He closed the files and went back to Command and Control Systems in Building Delta to ask the technician to get a hold of Dr. Harrison Boyd for him.

Maybe, he thought, the doctor had some much needed insight.

The photo made the horrendousness of today hit home again. Harrison was desperate to get Jasmine and Sofia back but he also couldn't shake a gut feeling that the senator wasn't genuine in his intent. He couldn't imagine the senator would simply allow him to walk away with his wife and daughter without repercussion, not when there was an election coming up. He couldn't shake the feeling he wasn't actually going to see Jasmine and Sofia again.

Even so, he'd spent the last several hours reconstructing V-202, filling in whatever blanks might've been on the mainframe. Because of the doubt he had regarding the senator—and the man without a mask—he'd made two different sets of files on two different external hard drives. Then, he'd copied each hard drive onto another. All sets had his complete notes on V-202. They were step-by-step guides to producing the vaccine. However, the first two hard drives—which he'd labeled A1 and

A2—were intended for a vaccine developer who *hadn't* used the mRNA techniques he and Richard had pioneered. They pieced together the mRNA processes upon which V-202 was based. The second set of hard drives—labeled B1 and B2—had the same information as the first set of drives as related to V-202 but weren't pieced together as a step-by-step guide on mRNA techniques. Instead, the second set of drives assumed the vaccine developer already had an expert knowledge in Riogenrix's mRNA techniques. The A drives would allow even the most unsophisticated vaccine developers to get V-202 up and running within days or weeks whereas the B drives would still require months of work as the vaccine developer acquired knowledge of the mRNA processes underlying V-202. The B drives would seem like typical notes of a physician-scientist who'd spent the entirety of his career dealing with mRNA; they would seem like an oversight. In reality, the omissions were intentional. The senator's vaccine team—whoever and wherever they were, because he couldn't believe the colonel was going to be the end user—would take a few days to realize the detailed step-by-step mRNA techniques were absent on the B drive. If he'd felt reassured that the senator was truly going to return Jasmine and Sofia to him without harm, he would've only made the A drives. But by keeping some details of mRNA processes out of the B drives, he maintained leverage in case Jasmine and Sofia weren't in fact returned to him tonight.

Selene was standing in the kitchen, away from the dining table, and had been standing there since the two messages appeared on the cell phone. She was fiddling with a glass of water while she waited.

"Have we reached Richard?" he asked her.

"Not yet. Nothing overnight, nothing this morning. He must be in his biosafety lab. There's a landline in there, but I can't recall the number. I've never called it. I have the number at the office, of course, but I'm not sure we should be going back there. If the senator is after the vaccine, others will be after it as well."

"Are you confident Richard will strike a deal with Steptech to manufacture and distribute the vaccine?"

"I have no doubt. And Steptech—Jason Carr—will able to provide security as well."

"Then I have no doubt either." He handed her the A drives. "Richard will be able to get V-202 to Steptech and Steptech will get the vaccine out to the public with the information on these drives."

"And the other drives you made?"

Harrison knew Selene was waiting for him to tell her about the two text messages he'd received. "I'm meeting the man without a mask at the old golf course in La Jolla in two hours. Those drives are for him."

"The old golf course meaning Torrey Pines?"

"Yes."

She didn't ask him to clarify anything else about the B drives. He knew she knew.

"I'm sorry Riogenrix is over," he said to Selene. He'd been thinking about what he was going to say to her and he said it now. "I'm sorry I couldn't succeed. I'm sorry I let you and the company down." He knew Selene's life was tied into Riogenrix as much as his. He tried to take solace knowing that on the open market Selene would find a good job with one of the larger vaccine companies but found no real comfort in the realization. She'd founded Riogenrix as much as Richard had. Nonetheless, if she was hurting, she wasn't letting her hurt show.

"I know and it doesn't matter," she said.

"You'll be highly sought after by industry."

"Again, it doesn't matter."

"Nothing matters to me except getting Jasmine and Sofia back."

"Nothing matters to me except the same."

"Good. Because we have three doses of V-202 in the cooler. And one is for you."

She stopped fiddling with the glass of water. She folded her arms across her chest. "No, it isn't. I've already had this exact discussion with Richard. None are for me. I'll wait like everyone else."

"There might not ever be a vaccine after we hand over the work to the senator. We don't know his end game. We are relying on Steptech to go toe-to-toe with the senator, but what happens if the senator becomes the White House? Will Steptech be able to go toe-to-toe with the next US *president*?"

"If there's no vaccine ever, I'm okay. I've survived five years already without one."

Harrison wanted to make sure he verbalized himself correctly. He wasn't trying to be nice in telling Selene to use one of the three vaccines on herself. He was being straightforward. He was looking towards the future, one in which menglavirus might be here to stay forever. She was part of the future. Jasmine and Sofia were part of the future. He didn't see himself as part of it. He knew Richard was in the same position as he.

"I don't think I'm going to survive whatever the senator is planning. I'm okay with not surviving so long as Jasmine and Sofia survive, so long as we get them back, so long as we can get them into a real life again, so long as they prosper. I've kept them away from living for five years. Even when we get them back from the senator, I need to get them living a true existence. There are three vaccines. One is for you. The other two are for them. Take one for yourself first. Then you give Jasmine and Sofia the remaining two vaccines. Please. Take care of them, if you can, and I can't. But first take care of yourself."

She unfolded her arms. "You'll be okay, Harrison."

"I don't think that either of us truly believes I'm going to be given free rein to talk about how the man who might be the future president of the United States abducted my wife and daughter. The senator isn't going to let me float around."

"If he doesn't let you float around, what makes you think he'll let me?" She trailed off. Harrison knew what she was thinking. She didn't continue verbalizing the thought they both were having: *Or them—Jasmine and Sofia?*

Harrison couldn't think about not getting Jasmine and Sofia back, because not getting them back wasn't conceivable, so he said what he hoped was true. He also noted how easily death was delivered these days, so innocuous in appearance—expose to nMAQ25, wait two weeks, and refresh. He thought about the two nMAQ25 deaths at Riogenrix and couldn't shake the feeling they hadn't truly been community-based cases.

"They're not involved," Harrison said. "They don't know anything about the senator, so presumably, they'll be allowed to walk free. So long as I give the senator what he wants, Jasmine and Sofia will be okay. And I will give the senator exactly what he wants—once I know they are safe with you."

Harrison and Selene watched each other. "Bring a vaccine dose, Selene. Please. I'll inject you."

Selene didn't budge from the kitchen.

"Please keep an eye on Jasmine and Sofia if I'm not around to keep an eye out for them. Please take care of Sofia if something happens to Jasmine."

He waited. He'd said to Selene what he'd been needing—trying—to say while also not saying what he knew she refused to hear, which was, yes, he did think Selene deserved to be vaccinated with one of the three doses of V-202. He had no more pretenses of needing to be objective to see if V-202 worked. It worked. Even without the Phase 3, he knew it worked. The senator knew as well, which was why Jasmine and Sofia had been dragged into this mess in the first place.

Finally, she went to the fridge. She removed a prefilled syringe from it. She returned to the kitchen table and set the syringe down.

"Are you okay?" Harrison said. She nodded, and Harrison reached for the syringe.

Not unexpectedly, Dr. Boyd didn't answer any of his phone calls. Col. Burt Johnson told the technician to locate the doctor's phone. The technician didn't need long to track it.

"It's here, sir."

"Where?"

"The phone is along the perimeter of West. It's in the vehicle depot."

"Which parking depot is that?"

"Golf, sir. Along the southwest part of the installation."

"Let's go."

Burt led the technician out of Control and Commands in Building Charlie to the transport lot, where a Humvee was on standby. Burt summoned the Humvee over and they rode it to the perimeter. At the vehicle depot, they got down and Burt told the private first class driving the Humvee to come with them.

The technician led both of them to a black Cadillac Escalade with exempt plates. He said, "The doctor's phone is in the SUV, sir."

"Open it."

The technician pulled on the driver-side doors and then walked to the passenger-side and did the same. He pulled on the liftgate as well. The vehicle was locked.

"Break it," Burt Johnson said to the private first class.

"Sir?" the private first class said. He'd been standing back from the colonel and technician.

"Break the vehicle's window, private first class," Burt said.

The soldier stepped forward and removed his service pistol. He used the butt to crack the driver's window. The safety glass didn't shatter, so the private first class used the butt twice more to smash a hole into the window. Finally, he used the butt to widen the opening. The soldier reached in, unlocked the vehicle, and opened the driver's door. The alarm sounded and the horn blared.

The technician went to the vehicle and searched inside. He pulled out a cellphone and said, "It was in the glove compartment, sir. Turn it on?"

Burt nodded.

"The battery is almost dead, sir."

"Have you figured out the passcode?"

"Yes, sir."

Burt took the phone from the technician. He thought about

the senator's arrogance in leaving the doctor's phone at West, as if the senator were invincible, as if the presidency already were his. There were several unread voicemails and text messages, all within the past twenty-four hours. He went through them.

He listened to the voicemails from a Richard Hahn.

He read the text messages from the same Richard Hahn.

He listened to the voicemails from the doctor's wife.

He read the text messages from the doctor's wife.

As he stood in the rapidly chilling Nevada night with the doctor's phone, he understood he'd been right to mistrust the senator.

He was about to send a text message back to the Richard Hahn who'd left the voicemails and sent the text messages when the phone died. He handed the phone to the technician instead. "Charge this," he said, and turned to the private first class. "Take us to Building Delta." He was done waiting for clearances. He needed to see what was happening under his own nose.

Scott found himself reaching out to Naomi. It was 10 p.m. and they were inside of her mother's house in Mira Loma. He was as shocked as she. When he'd convinced Naomi to come with him to San Diego by telling her he would take her to her mother's house, he hadn't expected her mother would be dead. But she *was* dead, completely rigid and cold, totally unmoving and unresponsive. He wasn't an expert on times or causes of death, but the security contractor who'd come inside the house with them had an inkling she'd been dead for one or two days already. He couldn't disagree.

He brought Naomi into his arms. She wasn't crying, but she was stiff, clearly as blindsided as he was at seeing her mother laid out on the floor with a half-empty tumbler and a bottle of gin on the folding snack table.

"Let's go," he said, wanting to get out of the house immediately. The security team figured Naomi's mother had suffered a heart attack, but they weren't medical examiners. Scott had to consider the possibility she'd died of menglavirus. Although he'd been vaccinated, it'd only been a few hours back. He couldn't be sure the vaccine had taken so quickly. In the data Riogenrix had submitted to the FDA regarding Phase 2 trials, the company had noted 'significant' immune responses within hours but Scott Spaulding didn't know what *significant* meant. He did know, though, that Riogenrix's Phase 3 application had noted full immunity in twenty-four to forty-eight hours. Scott Spaulding didn't have full immunity yet. Sure, he had a fitted FN99 mask on, but if Naomi's mother had died of menglavirus, he didn't want to be around her body in any way.

Naomi let Scott embrace her before pulling away from him. She walked to the folding table and picked up the gin bottle. She ran her fingers along the rim before returning it to the table. She crouched beside her mother and ran the same fingers along her mother's face.

"Let's go," he said again to her. He was becoming increasingly irritated—disturbed, even—the longer he stayed in this god-damned house. Naomi wasn't vaccinated and had no immunity at all. Nonetheless, she was potentially exposing herself—and consequently him. "Wash your hands and let's go."

"Go without me," she said.

"We came here together and we'll leave together."

"What about my mother's body?"

"We'll bury it. I'll have the team take care of her. We'll ship her back to Las Vegas and bury her in Henderson. She'll be close to you."

Naomi didn't respond. She was separating her mother's strands of hair, arranging them so her mother's forehead showed.

"Stop touching her," Scott said.

"She's dead. What is she going to give me?"

"Doesn't matter. Leave her alone. Wash your hands. Now."

She left the body and walked towards the back of the house. When she was out of sight, he turned to the contractor. "She sits in the third row of seats on the opposite side of the vehicle," he said. "Away from me." If Naomi hadn't been pregnant, he would've left her now, right here in San Diego at her dead mother's house. In that moment, he understood the love he'd thought he'd had for her—or whatever other feelings he'd had of infatuation or pride or whatever else—were gone. She'd become a set of problems.

He heard water running. As he waited for her to return, he had a second thought. He wouldn't mind after all if she came down with a case of menglavirus—so long as she contracted it in a *controlled* environment. In fact, he would be very *happy* if she got menglavirus. He thought about the canisters he'd provided to the consultant. Scott had deliberately stayed away from the canisters of modified menglavirus after taking them from Building D of USAMRIID-West, but in a day or so, he would have full immunity. A sealed canister in his possession wouldn't be a bad thing. If Naomi didn't decide on termination in a day or so, he would decide on termination for her.

Ever since she'd married Harrison, Jasmine had thought about family. She thought about what family meant, how to be a family, and how to maintain one. She thought about how friends became extended family. She thought about how friends had a role within the family that wasn't easily replaceable, if at all. Then menglavirus had hit and she'd stopped thinking about anyone other than mother and child, her and Sofia. Everyone else had fallen by the wayside.

She was in a cargo van with Sofia. The van had four rows of seats and cargo space. They were in the cargo space in the back of the van, separated from the rows of seats in front of them by a perforated steel partition. The man without a mask was in a captain chair in the third row and he still was wearing a white lab coat. One other man was in the front row. He was wearing a biosafety suit. Sofia was huddled close to Jasmine and

Jasmine kept rubbing Sofia's shoulders and running her fingers over Sofia's hair. When Sofia had been an infant, she'd liked the rubs, but when she'd started to crawl at seven months, she'd stopped caring about them, so Jasmine had stopped giving them. She realized now how much she missed the nurturing she'd once given Sofia, the kind Sofia had seemed to grow out of, but in reality hadn't.

They were on the road in La Jolla, headed towards Torrey Pines. She knew the route. She used to come to Torrey Pines often when she'd first moved to San Diego with Harrison. This was before she'd had Sofia, when she'd been working, when she'd needed time to herself. She used to walk the easier trails that meandered around the golf course. She used to regularly think about the family she expected to come with Harrison. He had already been putting in long hours, even back then, but so had she, so they hadn't been butting heads. When she got pregnant with Sofia, she stopped the treks to Torrey Pines. She felt sick too much of the time, and when she wasn't feeling sick, she was too busy preparing for the family life that was coming. She hadn't been back to Torrey Pines in years.

"We'll be safe here," she said to Sofia, whispering in her ear as she massaged her shoulders. She was trying to keep Sofia calm. "I used to come here a lot before you were born."

"Is Daddy coming?" Sofia said.

"Yes. He will." Despite their marital issues, she couldn't imagine he wouldn't come. No, he would participate. She knew he would.

"Are we leaving with him?"

"Yes."

"Do you promise?"

Jasmine didn't answer. She didn't want to promise anything she couldn't guarantee. Harrison would come, but Jasmine didn't know what would happen thereafter. Sofia didn't seem to expect an answer either.

When they reached the outskirts of Torrey Pines, the van pulled over to the side of the road and parked next to a Ford truck. The man without a mask got out of the van and went to the truck and Jasmine craned her neck to see to whom he was talking but couldn't make out anyone or anything. The few functioning streetlights were flickering. Jasmine wondered how many men in total the man without the mask had on his payroll. Finally, the man without a mask got back in the van and they continued driving into Torrey Pines. She kept her hand on Sofia's shoulders. She kept massaging her, telling Sofia with her hands that everything would be okay.

Harrison left Selene's house in Point Loma by himself under the darkness of night. He drove to Torrey Pines in Jasmine's wagon. He had the cooler in the backseat. He planned to administer V-202 to Jasmine and Sofia the minute he had them back. He had every intention of leaving La Jolla with them. He had a canvas grocery bag on the passenger seat that contained the external hard drives B1 and B2. Meanwhile, he'd given the A drives to Selene. Beside the bag with the B drives, he had Jasmine's gun. Harrison had developed V-202 with the goal of distributing it to everyone in the world. He'd wanted to save lives. He'd never intended the vaccine for menglavirus to be a death sentence for large parts of the world's population, but if the senator had his way, V-202 would go from being one of modern medicine's most beneficial accomplishments to one of its most wasted.

The golf course at Torrey Pines had seen better days. No one truly played golf anymore. The course used to be full of manicured grass but now was overgrown with weeds that would become fuel for brush fires in the hot summers. In fact, large parts of the resort had already burned down, the result of fires which no one had cared to focus on when they'd happened. Now, the golf course was known for its desolation and the unpredictability of those who chose to frequent it for their own purposes. Harrison had played golf very briefly in medical school when he'd taken the research year with Richard at Salk. A lot of students who'd rotated through Salk had. After all, Salk abutted Torrey Pines. Harrison had bought a set of used clubs and played a few times with some of the other students, but he'd never been good. The golf bug hadn't bitten him the way it had some of his other classmates, the ones who would plan their schedules around how many times a week they would be able to get in nine or eighteen holes. Midway through his research year, he'd given up on golf completely. He hadn't been able to carve out the time golf necessitated, both in terms of bettering his game and playing it. By the time he'd reached the halfway point of his research year, he knew to what he would devote his spare time, which was mRNA. He'd given his already used clubs away to another student who'd been rotating through.

He drove north into the southern part of the resort, along the cliffs. He was headed to where the man without a mask had noted in a text message he and Harrison would meet—a parking area near what used to be a hang-gliding port. As they drove, Harrison thought about Richard, who was a rocky two-and-a-half-mile trek through the cliffs and canyons, further south, in a more isolated, out of the way part of La Jolla. Harrison hoped he would see his mentor, friend, and business partner again, but didn't know. Harrison wasn't ready for life to end, but he knew he would willingly die for Jasmine and Sofia if that was what getting them away from the senator's grasp required.

When he arrived at the glider-port, Harrison understood why the man without the mask had chosen this location within Torrey Pines. The glider-port was a forgotten part of San Diego, a stretch of emptiness only a few forced steps away from the rocky waters of the Pacific below. He wondered why he'd never been here before and if he'd missed out on too much life by being so cooped up on the Riogenrix campus all of the time. He thought about how it would've been nice to have brought Jasmine and Sofia here in the pre-menglavirus days, if not to hang glide, at least to enjoy the grassy flats, feel the ocean air, and watch the beauty of gliders in flight.

He parked in an empty lot and waited in the car. A few

minutes later, a van approached the parking lot on the opposite side of the glider-port, almost a hundred yards away. As soon as Harrison saw the van, he knew Jasmine and Sofia were in it—he had no choice but to believe they were. He cinched Jasmine's gun into his waistband, grabbed the canvas bag, and got out of the car. He was ready to use the gun if needed.

Harrison advanced towards the van across the barren glider-port, each step getting longer and the stride brisker. He felt Jasmine's gun pushing against his waist with each step and the bag with the hard drives banging against the outside of his knee. He focused his gaze on the van, keeping an eye out for Jasmine and Sofia. He couldn't see them, but he felt them, maybe even saw a flicker of movement from within the van's cargo space.

The driver's door opened and the man without a mask stepped out. He held a cylindrical canister in one hand. He held up his other hand, indicating to Harrison he should stop where he was. Harrison didn't stop. He couldn't stop even if he tried. He found himself incapable of thinking about what he was doing for the first time in a long time. He was all reflex, little thought.

He went towards the van. He went towards Jasmine and Sofia. He went towards the man without a mask.

Dr. Jason Carr's day was finally ending, or at least the office part of it was. He was set to go from the office to the airport in order to fly out tonight via one of Steptech's corporate jets to Raleigh-Durham in North Carolina to tour Steptech's newest vaccine manufacturing facilities. He was reviewing financial projections on his desktop while he waited. He had thirty minutes until his security team was going to take him to the airport. Even though Steptech hadn't yet gained Phase 3 approval for their newest attempt at a menglavirus vaccine, they were prepared to manufacture it the minute the FDA gave them the green light. He was forcedly hopeful about Steptech's latest entry. He had to be. They had nothing else in the pipeline. In the race to finding a preventive vaccine for menglavirus, capacity was just as important as development. The new facility in Raleigh-Durham was going to expand their capacity even further.

But he couldn't focus. Over the course of the day, he'd received two more messages from his assistants telling him Richard Hahn had called. He didn't think Richard would be calling him so insistently only to discuss Steptech's acquisition offer. He couldn't shake the feeling Richard was undergoing a hard time. In some way or another, Richard needed his help. They weren't friends anymore but they remained colleagues in the vaccine space. They always would.

Finally, after delaying for the entire day, he picked up the office phone. He called Richard's cell phone. The call went straight to voicemail. He left a message. Then he went back to the financial projections, but again had difficulty concentrating. Now that he'd decided to call Richard, he found himself truly worried. He didn't like not knowing. He entered the second phone number provided by his assistant into a reverse number engine to which Steptech subscribed. Curiously, the phone number tied back to La Jolla. Specifically, the landline fed into Richard's house on the cliffs. He racked his brain, wondering what was going on. Now, he remembered about the home lab that Richard once had mentioned he'd set up. Jason was more curious —and concerned—than ever. He called Richard again, this time to the alternate number. The phone rang and Richard picked up.

"What's wrong, Richard?" he said. "How is your health? Has the sarcoidosis flared again?"

"No, thankfully, no. I'm fine."

"Jesus, Richard. What the hell? All of this hounding just to discuss my acquisition offer?"

"What acquisition offer?"

"Don't play games, Richard."

"I don't know about any acquisition offer. But I have a working vaccine."

"A vaccine? For what?"

"Menglavirus."

"What do you mean?"

"I mean that I have a way to stop menglavirus."

Jason wondered if the old guy was losing touch with reality. He began to think calling Richard back had been a mistake. "Do you? Well, what effectiveness do you have?" he said, humoring his old partner. He expected to hear sub-ten percent, the same as DK2, which was why the FDA had rejected Richard's vaccine earlier this week.

"Over ninety-nine percent in Phase 2."

Jason wasn't sure he'd heard correctly. "What'd you say, Richard?"

"Ninety-nine percent. *Over* ninety-nine percent."

"Ninety-nine percent? Are you sure you're okay?"

"Very sure. And I need to give it you. I need Steptech to take over our vaccine project and I need Steptech to take it over right now."

"Is this the same vaccine the FDA rejected for Phase 3?"

"Yes."

"Why would the FDA reject a vaccine that's ninety-nine percent effective?"

"Exactly. Which is why I need to give it to you."

"Okay, I'm confused but interested. Tell me more, Richard."

Richard proceeded to discuss the work with messenger RNA proteins his protégé at Riogenrix—Harrison Boyd—had conducted over the past five years. A few minutes into the discussion, Jason stopped him. He remained incredulous. He wanted to *see* the data rather than only hear about it. "Are you near a workstation?" he said.

"Yes."

"Send me the Phase 2 data. If you have the same email address, I'll send you a secure email now. Reply back."

"I have the same email."

"Good."

Jason fired off a quick email with no subject to Richard. As he waited for the reply, he didn't interrogate Richard any further. There was no point. Only the data mattered. Two minutes later, a secure reply email with several attached files entered his inbox. He opened the email and reviewed the attachments. He didn't have to look at more than the first several pages of data to know Richard had been telling the truth—Riogenrix had a legitimate menglavirus vaccine.

Now, he was worried, but for a different reason. He recognized the anxiety in Richard's voice. He knew the extreme importance a menglavirus vaccine had, not only in the medical sphere, but in the political realm as well. He knew from experience how other companies and even state actors did everything they could to get their hands on what others had innovated. At Steptech, they'd dealt with their fair share of espionage. They'd engaged in their fair share as well.

"Are you safe, Richard?"

"Yes."

"Tell me what you need from me."

As Richard did, Jason kept an eye on the time. He knew he was going to have to reschedule his flight to Raleigh-Durham. He would be headed to San Diego instead.

Selene left Point Loma with two copies of the A drive. As she drove, she called Richard again on his cell phone, like she'd been doing all day. This time—finally–he picked up.

"Where have you been, Richard? I've been calling you all day."

"I've been here. I've been in the lab. I'm upstairs now."

"Any progress?"

"I've had some progress on Harrison's vaccine, but not a lot. But I've had a lot of progress on getting Jason Carr to step in on the last leg of vaccine development. Steptech will get the Phase 3 trials underway, get emergency use authorization from the FDA, and manufacture and distribute the vaccine worldwide. They'll distribute it at cost. It won't be a financial success for Steptech, but they'll receive credit on developing the vaccine. They'll also get a lot of public goodwill, which they need, considering the backlash because of the markups on their therapeutics. Overall, Jason will be more than happy with the results for his company. Either way, by next year, there will be no more menglavirus."

She felt a strange mix of emotions. She was happy V-202 would get out to the public. She had no doubt in Jason Carr's ability at Steptech to muscle the Riogenrix vaccine through the barriers established by the senator over the past few days. He surely had enough money and political pull to get it done. But she also felt saddened. Riogenrix truly was no more. She had no doubt she would reinvent herself, get another career going at another biotechnology company, but she knew her next career wouldn't be her own anymore. Nor would it be with Richard. She understood that the last several years had changed his future. Due to health and age, he wasn't going to be able to get back into vaccine development as anything other than an emeritus.

"When are you meeting with Jason?" she asked.

"He is flying here tonight. He'll come directly to La Jolla and he'll bring a full-fledged security team with him. How are Jasmine and Sofia? How is Harrison?"

"Harrison should be conducting the exchange now. I'm worried the senator isn't going to play by the rules."

"Yes, I'm worried, too. If the exchange doesn't go as planned, Jason has pledged his security resources to getting them back. We'll get them back, Selene. We'll get everybody back. We'll make sure everybody is safe and stays safe." He paused, cleared his throat, and paused again. "I'm sorry, Selene. I should've been on top of our security needs for all of us from the get-go. Jason never would've let what has happened at Riogenrix happen at Steptech."

"I don't think any of us could've foreseen the last few days," she said, not wanting to delve into *could've* and *should've*. They'd all made mistakes. She certainly had. "I have all of Harrison's notes on a hard drive. I'll see you soon, Richard. Jason Carr will be a very happy person."

She hung up. She felt sadness, but told herself not to wallow —doing so wasn't her personality. So she sped up. The streets were empty. She drove as fast as she could. She needed to get to Richard's house in La Jolla.

Col. Burt Johnson didn't find any gain of function experiments being done on menglavirus in Building Delta, at least not as conducted by the US Army. He found worse. Specifically, he found China's modified super-virus, in genuine physical form. He found dozens of pressurized cylindrical canisters lined up in carbon steel storage cabinets. The canisters had project numbers stamped on them, the same identifying markers noted in the Operation Soda Can files. Room 500 in Building Delta contained Chinese-made canisters containing nMAQ61, the GOF version of menglavirus that went from exposure to infection to death within the span of twenty-four to forty-eight hours.

Burt was concerned. He didn't think he could be more concerned. But then he stepped out of Building Delta and saw the technician waiting for him in the courtyard. He went from being concerned to very worried. Burt had ordered the technician to track down Dr. Boyd in order to get a fuller picture of the senator's intentions. The technician told him what he'd found.

The doctor's house in San Diego had internet-connected security cameras that stored five days of video on a commercial server. The technician had located video showing three men—two in biosafety suits and a third who was wearing a lab coat instead—forcing their way into the doctor's house. They'd abducted the doctor's family. Burt had a strong feeling that the man in the lab coat whom the technician was referencing was the same man the senator had brought to West.

Back in Control and Command, Burt watched the video with incredulity. He saw the invasion and abduction with his own eyes and was ashamed such an act against humanity was happening in his own country. Unfortunately, he'd become used to seeing kidnappings and killings overseas, where unending sectional strife and war had become the norm, but wasn't accustomed to seeing it in places like suburban San Diego. He was genuinely shocked with the brazenness of the abduction. The technician pulled up another video and Burt watched the doctor come home several hours later to the raided house. He entered the house with one of the senator's security contractors but left alone in a rush via a Volvo wagon in the garage. Burt didn't need to see any additional video in order to know that the senator had been behind the abduction. Sure enough, the man in the white lab coat was the same.

Burt called the senator now. He didn't waste time with niceties.

"I don't know exactly what your intentions are," Burt said, "but I know your actions are illegal, unethical, and antithetical to everything for which our country stands."

At first, the senator was silent. When he did answer, he spoke with a growl. "Watch yourself, colonel. Don't lecture me."

"What did you do with his family?"

"Whose family?"

"The doctor's. Harrison Boyd's."

"I don't know what you're talking about."

"I saw the videos from the doctor's house."

"That doesn't clarify anything for me."

"They were abducted by your guy. Where is the doctor? Where is his family?"

"I'd like to know the same."

Burt reined himself in. He prided himself on his ability to process information step-by-step and think actions through to the end before proceeding down a given path. He plotted his way through the senator's motivations now. He went to where the senator's end game went.

"Why did the FDA deny the doctor's vaccine?"

"I don't work for the FDA, colonel. I'm a Congressman, not a researcher."

"Why are you working with China's MSS?"

Another silence, another growl. "Those are strong accusations, colonel. Be careful of what you say next."

He kept digging, went for the essence of what he deemed the senator was angling. "Why are you trying to turn the doctor's vaccine over to MSS?"

"You're on the administrative side now, colonel. Your job is to keep my labs at West in shape. I pushed for those labs. I secured the funding. I spearheaded the formation. Your job isn't to question me. You're not boots anymore, colonel. You're a pencil pusher. So stop wasting my time and get back to pushing pencils —*my* pencils—around."

The senator hung up. Burt hadn't needed the senator to answer all of his questions to understand. Burt knew enough to act.

Except, the senator had been right—he was a pencil pusher now. He was no longer a boot, hadn't been in years. He found no sadness in the realization, because he'd done good work on the US Army's military medicine missions, work that was hugely satisfying. But now—right now—he was a pencil pusher, doing no good work, other than falsely administering the senator's private projects in an off-the-grid US Army microbiology laboratory. He had the opportunity now to be the *right* kind of administrator, one that made a difference. He had no doubt in himself and who he was. He was an army man and military physician who had a distinct impression as to how the US should be positioned in the global arena. The US was a leader, here to help those countries who requested her help. The US Army's spearheading of the Ebola vaccination project in West Africa had been the perfect fulfillment of a worldview he fully endorsed. He was here for America, and America was here for those who needed her.

Right now, the doctor needed his help. The doctor's wife and daughter needed his help. And the world needed the doctor's help.

He'd been using army-issued, encrypted satellite phones ever since he'd arrived at West. He knew every one of his phone calls was logged, ready for monitoring if desired. If the senator became president, Burt had no doubt he would be tried for treason. But Burt was going to make sure the senator didn't destroy the country—and the world—by becoming US president. He called Camel, a man with whom he'd served in Iraq during what seemed like a lifetime ago. They'd been close then and had stayed close. While Burt had stayed on with the US military after his tours in Iraq, committing himself to military medicine through the Uniformed Services University of the Health Sciences before completing residency in surgery at Walter Reed Medical Center, Camel had branched off into lucrative contracted private security, similar in nature to the senator's own contracted security team. Over the years, Camel had amassed a small team of ex-military men. They were men who'd made their pre-virus living protecting political leaders and diplomats overseas but now with the War on Terror usurped by menglavirus, they were operating domestically, mostly protecting corporate executives by offering the protections budget-strained law enforcement could no longer ensure. Unlike the senator's contractors, he knew Camel maintained a code of ethics, one they both shared.

He called Camel.

"What's up, doc?" Camel said, using the same expression he'd been using on Burt since he'd become a physician.

"Where are you these days, Camel?"

"Atlanta."

"Get a man or two and get yourselves on a plane. You're coming to get me. And then we're going to San Diego."

"Sounds fun, doc."

"It isn't. But it's necessary. I'll brief you when you get here."

"I'll see you doc."

Burt hung up. He latched the satellite phone to his belt. He knew his military days would be over after tonight but he would rather his career be done than have the whole world be done instead.

Harrison felt Jasmine's gun rubbing against the back of his waist. He moved his right hand—he was holding the bag with the B drives in it with the left—behind his back to grab the handle. But the man without a mask pulled out his own pistol first and pointed it at Harrison.

"Stay chill, brother."

The wind was picking up. Harrison could barely hear him. He wondered how much of a chance he stood in a firefight with the man without a mask—particularly in the wind. Harrison wasn't a sharpshooter. He knew what he was—he was a physician and scientist. He needed to outthink the man without a mask in order to secure the safety of his wife and daughter. He pulled his hand away from his back, leaving the pistol where it was.

"Slow down and walk towards me with your hands held out in front of you."

He raised both of his hands in front of his body, lifting the bag in front of him. It thudded against his chest as he moved forward. He walked towards the man without a mask and the man without a mask walked towards him. They closed the gap between them from twenty-five feet to twenty and then fifteen. Harrison told himself not to mess up.

When he and the man without a mask were only several feet away from each other, the man without a mask held up his hand, and said, "Stop."

Harrison stopped. The wind gusted again and the ocean waves roiled the rocky cliffs below them. He looked towards the parking lot again, saw the van, and this time he saw a flicker in the back window. He glimpsed Jasmine's face.

"What did you bring me, Harrison?"

Harrison saw both age and youth in the man, both discipline and recklessness. He trusted him and didn't. Again, he felt as if he knew the man without a mask, as if they'd crossed paths before.

"I have complete vaccine notes on the hard drives in this bag."

"Two copies?"

"Yes."

"Hand them over."

"I need my wife and daughter."

197

"They're in the van."

"You can let them go now."

"Oh, can I? Just like that?"

"Yes."

The man without a mask chuckled. "Tell me, Harrison. Do you remember me?"

"I feel as if we've met before, but I don't think I know you."

"So you don't remember me?"

"No."

"You do know me, Harrison. Or knew me. We were at Hopkins together. For a short period of time, we were in the same medical school class."

Harrison studied the face of the man without a mask. At first, he still couldn't place him. His medical school class had contained only one hundred and twenty people and he'd known all of his classmates. Then he knew why the man without a mask had said *for a short period of time*. Harrison had taken a research year with Richard at the Salk Institute between his third and fourth years of medical school. When he'd returned to medical school for his fourth year, he'd joined the class behind him. Whereas the first two years of medical school were academic, focused on classroom learning, the third and fourth years were clinical. During the clinical years of medical school, students were dispersed amongst dozens of required and elective clinical rotations within many different hospitals and departments. When he'd returned to medical school for his fourth year, he'd known almost none of his new classmates. But he'd shared a fourth-year internal medicine rotation with the man without a mask.

"Gregory Miller," Harrison said.

"So you do remember, Harrison."

"What happened to you, Gregory?"

"You tell me."

Harrison remembered back to the fourth year of medical school. He vaguely remembered that Gregory hadn't graduated, although he couldn't recall the circumstances. "You left medical school only a few weeks before graduation."

"Yes, I did."

"Why?"

"Wouldn't you?"

More details were coming to him. "You had problems with the Match."

"I didn't have problems with the Match. I got screwed by the Match. I should've matched with Hopkins for residency. I didn't."

"The Match is a crapshoot."

"For me, it wasn't even a crapshoot. The Match was already rigged against me. Tell me, Harrison, did I know any less than you?"

Harrison recalled their few weeks together on fourth-year internal medicine. No, Gregory hadn't known any less than he. In fact, Gregory had been an excellent diagnostician. However, he'd also been arrogant, particularly in relation to the resident and attending physicians who evaluated them. Medicine was full of people who were egotistical—Harrison knew he, himself, could be arrogant at times—but Gregory's bigheadedness had made him completely dismissive of others. Harrison remembered how Gregory had berated the nurses more than once when they'd called him for abnormal lab values that were scarier on paper than they were clinically. He'd always wanted to show his superiority at the expense of other students, mocking other students' answers to questions posed to them by the residents and attendings. He'd mocked many a resident as well. He'd even ridiculed attendings. Harrison remembered how Gregory had been assigned a presentation on beta-blockers in congestive heart failure, but had used that presentation as a method to mock an attending physician's own research, pointing out that the already established carvedilol was the gold standard in neuroendocrine blockade, but fedivolol—the attending's own research focus—was an utter failure.

Gregory had had his class' top academic ranking during his first and second years. Harrison didn't know exactly how well

Gregory had done in the clinical years, but imagined he hadn't done too well, if fourth year internal medicine was any indication. Again, Gregory had been an excellent diagnostician, always well-read and knowledgeable, able to answer all of the clinical questions thrown at him by the resident and attending physicians, but he'd been dismissive at the same time, quick to squash the other students and even attending physicians who hadn't been as sharp. In medicine, there was a fine line between a little bit of healthy arrogance and full-out dismissiveness

"You were an excellent diagnostician," Harrison said, "but you're angry now. You were angry then too."

"I am angry. I deserved to match at Hopkins, just like you."

"Maybe you did, Gregory. But how is whatever you're doing now making anything better? You could've gone to where you matched and worked yourself to where you wanted to get. The school and hospital don't make us who we are. We still need to fight our way through."

"Exactly. Now, I'm fighting my way through. Isn't it curious how the independence I always had and that the residents and attendings always criticized me for is serving me well now? At the end, we're by ourselves. We have to push for ourselves. There are no mentors wiping our asses."

Harrison knew Gregory was prodding him. He wasn't interested in fighting back. But he did want to know one thing. There could only be one reason why Gregory was the man without a mask. He'd gained immunity. "How did you get your hands on V-202?"

Gregory smiled, clearly willing to talk as much now as he had back then, so long as the talking was about himself. "For as good of a physician-scientist you are, you are a poor administrator. Once you had a legitimate menglavirus vaccine, you needed to have beefed up security, both from outside and within. Your lead biomarker research associate was easily influenced."

"Did you kill her?"

"Her? No. She got menglavirus the old-fashioned way. She contracted it through her lover."

As Gregory spoke, he shifted the metal canister from one hand to the other. Harrison began to understand more, especially in relation to what he'd learned yesterday—or was it today?—at USAMRIID-West. He didn't know exactly what non-native GOF strain of menglavirus was contained in the canister, but he knew that it was extremely dangerous.

"What about my head of security?"

"The old man? Yes, I guess that was me. You didn't protect your team."

Again, Harrison felt Gregory baiting him. He fought the impulse to lash out in return. He reminded himself of his goal: Get Jasmine and Sofia back. Now, he knew for sure he didn't trust the senator, because he didn't trust Gregory Miller. He couldn't shake the feeling that tonight wasn't the end. Jasmine and Sofia weren't going to simply walk out the van and return to him as if nothing ever had happened. Again, Harrison looked towards the parking lot where the van was. He didn't see Jasmine in the window this time, but knew she was inside, doing everything she could to keep their daughter safe. He needed to do everything he could too.

As Harrison looked towards the van, another vehicle, a black Cadillac Escalade, pulled into the lot. It idled several spaces away from the van. It had exempt plates. Harrison didn't have to see inside the Escalade to know the senator had arrived.

Gregory had his hand out. He was waiting for the bag.

"First, I need to see my wife and daughter," Harrison said.

Gregory chuckled again. "Of course, you do. You were always a stickler for details." He held the canister in the air and made a circle with it. A man in a biosafety suit got out of the driver's side of the van and went to the cargo door at the rear. The astronaut opened it. He pulled out Jasmine and Sofia.

Harrison felt relief. Jasmine and Sofia were alive. They seemed okay. They weren't wearing any filtering masks, but they were fine. He held up his own hand to show them that he was here. "Everything will be okay," he said, shouting into the wind, hoping that his voice would carry.

Just as quickly as Jasmine and Sofia had appeared, they disappeared again. The man in the biosafety suit pushed them back inside the van and closed the door. Harrison again became angry, a feeling he wasn't accustomed to feeling, but which he'd been experiencing for the bulk of two to three days now. He was angry at everyone: the man in the biosafety suit, the senator, and now Gregory Miller. And he was angry at himself for allowing his wife and daughter to be placed into the situation they were in now. He tried to rein in his anger to let his mind process the scene. He knew it was time to end this nightmare. He handed over the bag with the B drives to Gregory.

But as Gregory reached out to take the bag from him, Harrison heard shouting from the parking lot. Harrison looked towards the lot and saw a woman running across it. He didn't recognize her. She was probably in her early twenties. For a moment, he thought she was an illusion. He wasn't sure, but he thought she'd come out of the senator's Escalade. Sure enough, the SUV's lift-gate was open. And a security contractor—one of the contractors from Harrison's trip with the senator to Nevada—had gotten out of the passenger side. The contractor was sprinting after the woman.

Harrison didn't know who the woman was or why she'd been in the senator's Escalade or why she'd left it, but it appeared as if she were trying to get away.

Gregory turned to look at the commotion. As soon as he did, Harrison dropped the bag and lunged forward. He deliberately aimed for Gregory's legs and toppled him. As soon as Gregory hit the ground, Harrison righted himself, and darted towards the van, brushing past his one-time classmate. Harrison didn't understand what was happening in the parking lot but knew that whatever was happening wasn't supposed to be. He knew he needed to act now to get Jasmine and Sofia back.

From behind him, he heard Gregory cursing. As Harrison ran across the glider-port, he watched the woman running across the parking lot. She was closing the distance to the van and pointing what looked to be a gun at the man in the biosafety suit. She fired the gun and the man in the biosafety suit fell backwards. The woman reached the van and stepped over the fallen astronaut. She opened the cargo door and reached in. She seemed to be pulling Jasmine and Sofia out. Sure enough, Harrison saw Sofia first and then Jasmine.

As Harrison reached the edge of the glider-port, Jasmine and Sofia stood outside of the van, only fifty yards away. The woman stood at their side and the man in the biosafety suit lay on the ground.

"I'm coming," Harrison yelled, still running.

He was getting closer to them but knew he wasn't going to reach them before the senator's contractor reached them first. The woman with the gun must've known the same. She said something to Jasmine and Sofia. Then she turned towards the contractor and pointed the gun at him. She fired at the senator's contractor and he went down.

For a moment, Jasmine and Sofia were free. As Harrison ran towards them, he and Jasmine made eye contact. In that moment, he felt the entirety of his life pour through him. He felt like a husband and father, scientist and physician, all at once. He felt hope and dashed dreams, old and new. He felt the weight of his family life against the weight of his work. He felt the love he'd always had for Jasmine and Sofia overwhelm him anew.

Jasmine broke eye contact first and she pulled on Sofia's arm. They started running. They ran away from the parking lot, away from the van, away from the contractors and men in biosafety suits. They ran away from Harrison. They ran towards the cliffs.

Harrison stopped running as the distance between them grew again. He understood. He stood at the northern edge of the parking lot and watched as his daughter ran towards the southern edge. He was mesmerized by her stride. He hadn't seen her run in years, at least not like this, outdoors and uninhibited by the rules of being inside. She ran fast, as if she'd been waiting for five years to stretch her legs. He understood now more than ever the harshness of the last five years. He watched his eight-year-old daughter run away from him. And he watched Jasmine run beside her. They both had the same elegant, methodical running form, even though Jasmine was running more slowly than she was capable, keeping her speed down for Sofia. They reached the southern end of the parking lot and hit the singed grass south of the glider-port and continued onwards until they disappeared into the downward curve of the hill.

He watched them until they were gone, knowing he needed to buy them as much time as he could. He looked back towards the van. He saw the second contractor from the senator's Escalade headed towards the woman. The contractor had his gun trained on her. Harrison wanted to help her, whoever she was and however he could, but heard footsteps behind him. He knew they belonged to Gregory. He turned to meet his one-time classmate head-on. Gregory was upon him. Now, Gregory was the one who lunged forward. Harrison braced for impact.

They became intertwined and fell. They scuffled for several seconds on the ground, neither seeming to gain a clear edge. Again, Harrison felt anger course through him. It was anger not only towards Gregory and the senator but anger at himself as well for not letting his wife and daughter prosper over the past five years. As the anger percolated, he felt the strength that came from being a husband and father rise within him. He felt himself gaining the upper hand. He pinned Gregory to the grass and reached for Jasmine's pistol in his waistband.

Before he could pull out the gun, he felt his breath leave him. He fell forward and hit his head against the dirt. He felt hands on him. He saw a contractor in a mask standing over him. The contractor turned him over and kicked him. Harrison tried to raise Jasmine's pistol, but the contractor swung the butt of his own gun at Harrison. Pain ricocheted through his head. He looked towards the southern edge of the glider-port to see if he could still locate Jasmine and Sofia, but they were gone into the cliffs.

He held on for as long as he could and then he passed out.

PART 4

R*un.*
Run fast.
Run like we used to.

Jasmine took only one glance at the glider-port where Harrison and the man without a mask were located before knowing what she and Sofia needed to do. She thought about Harrison and what she could do for him but pushed the thought aside and instead thought about Sofia and what she could do for her daughter.

Run.

She pushed Sofia forward, and as her daughter ran across the parking lot, Jasmine ran with her. She strode at her daughter's side, keeping her pace even with Sofia's, urging on her daughter, knowing Sofia could run faster, wanted to run faster, would run faster.

Run fast.

As she ran, she wasn't thinking about the man without a mask who'd abducted them or the woman who'd come to the van to open it or Harrison who was still at the glider-port. She was thinking about Sofia, her daughter, her charge, her responsibility through love and obligation. She felt unending love for her daughter, and in this moment, she felt again the love for Harrison that had been eluding her for the past few months.

Run like before.

They reached the cliffs, running together, away from everyone.

Naomi didn't know what kind of meeting happened at a run-down golf course and barren glider-port in the dark of a windy night but knew it wasn't something she wanted to be a part of. She'd especially known this after she'd seen the van and the woman and girl inside. She'd known what to do for her own self —and the woman, and the girl, and her own child yet to be born. She had her mother's pistol. She'd taken it from her mother's house when she'd gone into the back to wash her hands and had hidden it in the side of her pants. She knew how to use it. Naomi hadn't known who the woman or the girl in the van had been, but she'd known they hadn't belonged where they were.

Now, she was back in the SUV, although not by her own choice. Eventually, the senator's security team had regrouped. They'd surrounded her, forcing her to lay down her mother's pistol. She hoped the woman and girl would get away. They'd run to the cliffs. If they knew where to go, they could fade away.

The senator was outside of the SUV, talking to a man without a mask who was wearing a long, grass-stained lab coat. She was watching them through the side mirror while they had an animated discussion. Finally, the man without a mask handed a canvas bag to the senator. He handed over a canister as well. After another verbal exchange between them she couldn't hear, the senator returned to the Escalade. He sat beside her. She wasn't in the third row this time. She was in the second row, the same as he. He had her mother's pistol. He didn't look adept at using it, but it wasn't hard to point a pistol at a person and shoot. He pointed it at her now with his right hand and held the canister in his left.

"I let you live because I thought you deserved a chance," he said. "But with life comes responsibility. In this canister, I have a highly lethal, modified version of menglavirus. Tomorrow morning, you're getting a termination. I've already arranged the procedure in Henderson. If you decide you don't want to get the termination, or if you pull any of the goddamned tricks you pulled today, I'm going to open this canister. Remember, I'm on my way to immunity." He put his hand on her wrist and squeezed. She flinched, making him squeeze tighter. "Do not mess around with the future President of the United states of America."

The senator tapped the seat in front of him with the pistol. Both of the contractors were back in the Escalade. She'd incapacitated the first one for a couple of minutes when she'd shot him in the chest, but hadn't killed him. He'd been wearing body armor. The Escalade pulled out of the parking lot.

She had nothing to say to the senator in return. She pulled her wrist away and rubbed it. Her mother was dead. However inexplicable the idea was, her mother wasn't coming back, would never see her pregnant, would never see Naomi's child. Neither would Naomi and her mother ever reconcile. She'd died alone and estranged. She wished she'd picked up any of the hundred phone calls from her mother over the past two years. As they drove back to San Diego Airport, Naomi knew she—just like the woman and girl from the van—needed to get away.

Gregory returned to the glider-port. One of the contractors from his hired team was dead. He wondered if he'd imagined what had just happened. As he walked back to the glider-port, he saw Harrison on the ground, and knew he hadn't. He stood over Harrison.

His work for the senator was done, despite whatever the senator had said. Now, Gregory was only working for himself. During the commotion with the woman with the gun—he had no idea who she was, but took her sudden appearance from the senator's SUV as proof the senator was in over his head—he'd placed the second hard drive in the canvas bag in the van. He'd handed over only one drive to the senator. Now, he needed to decide if was going to follow the senator's orders to kill Harrison. He'd given the senator a canister but he had several more in his possession. He wasn't happy the wife and daughter had escaped.

He called one of his hired contractors who'd been stationed at the perimeter. "Search Torrey Pines for the mother and girl. They went south from the glider-port. Start there. Call me when you find them."

He reached down and removed Harrison's fitted HN99 mask. He put his hand on Harrison's neck, felt for the carotid pulse, and put his palm over Harrison's mouth to feel his breath. Harrison was breathing and his pulse was regular. He was alive. Unconscious, but alive.

He had two options: infect him or leave him alone.

He weighed the options, particularly in regard to the senator. The senator had been clear—infect him. But if Gregory was going to sell the vaccine to the Russians, a little help in running interference on the senator wouldn't hurt. If Harrison survived, perhaps he could create a bit of havoc for Scott Spaulding, finger him for the serious crimes he'd orchestrated. A man like the senator couldn't just disappear like Gregory could, nor would the senator want to. Gregory had what he needed, his own copy of the vaccine notes on the hard drive, which in combination with the mainframe, would give him a distinct advantage in getting V-202 to the Russians before the senator got it to the Chinese. A little messiness for the senator and his presidential bid could help Gregory. It could raise the value of his services.

Gregory had a new canister in his hand. He didn't pop it. Yes, a living Harrison could be useful. He put away his pistol and checked his watch. Midnight was nearing. He didn't have time to waste. He left Harrison where he was and headed back towards the van in the parking lot to delve into the hard drive.

They walked by the wan light of the moon across the rocky, narrow trails through La Jolla's cliffs, well south of the glider-port. They'd run until they couldn't run anymore, several minutes at Sofia's full-out speed, until the man without the mask and the other men with him had faded from earshot, until the grass and weeds of Torrey Pines had become chalky cliffs. Now, they were on another narrow trail, cutting through the canyon. They'd been hiking for a half-hour. Jasmine knew they needed to maintain speed, be faster even, not only to keep distance from the man without a mask, but to stay ahead of the night. The wind was picking up and the air was becoming moist. She knew rain was on its way and didn't want them to be carving the narrow trails of the canyon when they became slick.

The winds cut through the canyons, creating howls. Jasmine kept waiting for Sofia to tire, maybe even ask Jasmine to carry her or tell Jasmine she was cold, but even as Sofia clearly became tired and the night became colder and damper, she didn't ask. It was as if Sofia knew she and her mother weren't just daughter and mommy now, but partners. Nor did Sofia ask Jasmine about Harrison. Sofia was trudging forward, being incredibly strong. As Jasmine led Sofia, she wondered if so much of her daughter's difficulties over the past two years with her lessons had been less because of Sofia's lack of effort and more about Jasmine's lack of motivation. Jasmine understood now that Sofia had always fed off of Jasmine and Jasmine's own dreariness had fed into Sofia's.

Sofia didn't ask as they walked and hiked, but Jasmine told her what she herself believed. "Daddy will be all right," she said and this time, she didn't lie.

She didn't promise they would see him again, because she didn't know if they would. She hoped they would, but she didn't want to focus her hopes on Harrison, whom she couldn't help right now. She wanted—needed—to stay focused on Sofia.

Over the next half-hour, they took one trail southwest, toward the ocean, to another trail that ran parallel to it. As they came to another trailhead, Jasmine slowed down, and Sofia slowed down as well. The trailhead opened up into two different directions along two different trails, one trail snaking westwards, back towards the ocean, and the other heading directly east, dumping into the residences that lined the cliff. Jasmine needed to make a decision, whether to find another trail to continue cutting zigzags through the canyon or head towards one of the paved roads that dotted the residences. She thought about where they could go, to where they were ultimately headed, and didn't know.

"Uncle Richard lives here."

"What, honey?" Jasmine said.

"Uncle Richard has a house on these cliffs."

Jasmine surveyed the trail leading to the residential road, and said, "How do you remember, honey? You haven't been to Uncle Richard's house in years."

"I remember. I have the pictures."

Sofia was right. Richard Hahn lived on these cliffs. She wasn't exactly sure how far away from him they were, but she knew that they were decently close, because his house was one of the mansions south of them along Farm Road.

"You're right, honey," Jasmine said. "Let's go see Uncle Richard. Do you think you can run again?"

"Yes."

"Let's run to his house."

Sofia started running in the direction of the street and Jasmine followed, matching her daughter's stride.

Selene was rounding the curve of Farm Road in her Wrangler when she saw two people running in tandem along the side of the street. At first, she thought they were two women, but then she saw only one of them was a woman and the other was a girl. Neither of them had masks on. When the woman noticed the Jeep, she took her daughter by the hand and they turned ninety degrees and ran off of the road, into the front yard of the house adjacent, disappearing into the shrubbery. Selene slowed down the Wrangler. She recognized them now; she pieced together the past couple of days and knew who they were. Of course, she did.

The woman was Harrison's wife.

The girl was Harrison's daughter.

Jasmine and Sofia.

She pulled the Jeep over to the curb, outside of a large, imposing house with a yard that sloped back into the hills. Jasmine and Sofia had run into the yard and Selene thought about what was on the other side of the shrubbery and figured it was the canyon and hoped they hadn't reached it yet. She didn't know why Jasmine and Sofia were running along Farm Road but was glad they were because it meant the man without a mask no longer had them. She wondered why they weren't with Harrison but pushed the thought out of her mind. Thinking about Harrison right now would do no one any good.

She got out and called out to them. She used their names. She used her own name.

"I'm Selene. I work with Harrison Boyd and Richard Hahn. Do you remember who I am?" she said.

She hoped Jasmine and Sofia would. She also hoped that if they did remember her, they would know she wasn't one of the horrible people who'd made their lives hell for the past two days. She hoped they knew she was here to help them however she could. Selene waded into the thicket and shouted their names again. She couldn't help but wonder if the man without a mask was close by, whether all of them were going to be waylaid.

Jasmine stepped out of the shrubbery with Sofia. They were holding hands.

"Do you remember me, Jasmine?" Selene said.

"Of course, I remember you, Selene."

"Come with me."

"We're coming."

Jasmine and Sofia stepped out of the brush and Selene led them at a fast jog back to the street.

Sofia didn't know the woman who worked with Daddy. She

had no pictures of her, didn't remember her, didn't know if she'd ever met her before. But she knew that sometimes her memories were only because of the pictures she had on her tablet, so she thought maybe she really did know the woman who worked with Daddy. Maybe she really did know the woman Mommy had called Selene.

They were in the woman's Jeep. Sofia was in the back with no booster seat and Mommy was in the front. Sofia was tired and her legs hurt and her skin was cold and she was thirsty but she told herself not to complain. The roof was closed but she felt chilly. They were going to go to Uncle Richard's house. And then all of them together—Mommy and the woman who worked with Daddy and Uncle Richard and her—were going to wait for Daddy. Sofia had no doubt her daddy was okay. She knew he would join them soon.

She turned around as they pulled away from the trail, trying to remember where they'd been in case she needed to know later on. As she turned around, she saw an astronaut. He was watching them.

Today, she didn't wait to tell anyone. She didn't wait for Daddy to come home. Today, she wasn't home and Daddy wasn't coming home. So she told everyone.

"Mommy, look. Selene, look."

They looked.

And the person with whom Daddy worked, Selene, slammed on the gas and they took off down the street.

Col. Burt Johnson had brought the technician with him. The technician had been uncertain at first about leaving West but then had become excited when they'd actually gotten on Camel's plane. The technician had spent the entirety of his brief army career in buildings sitting in front of workstations. Now, he was actually going to be working from the field.

Of course, the technician wasn't on a sanctioned US mission.

Neither was Burt, of course. Camel had touched down with his team of two additional operators in a private airstrip sixty miles south of USAMRIID-West in an executive jet, where Burt and the technician had met them. Camel was wearing black tactical pants, a black T-shirt, and black tactical boots. He wore wrap-around Oakley sunglasses with reflective lenses even though they were in the plane. Burt knew the reason why—Camel had a zigzag scar along his right eye, an old wound from the War on Terror days. In whole, he looked as ready for the part as he was. They were circling San Diego Airport, waiting to land. The airport was layered with fog and slicked with rain. Flight control was waiting for the fog to disperse, which control had been telling them for the last ten minutes would be any minute now.

Burt had never been on an executive jet before. He'd flown transport military and transport planes his entire career. "Moving up, Camel," he said. "How'd you get a hold of this anyway?"

"The domestic security business has been good, brother. For us, the virus has been a boon. You would do very well running your own security operation."

"I'm an army lifer, Camel."

"I know it, brother. I couldn't do it, but I respect you for it."

Burt turned to the technician. He'd been waiting for the technician to update him since they'd started circling the airport. "Progress?" he said. "Anything yet on Dr. Boyd?"

"I think I found the doctor, sir. I filtered all of the cellular location data over the past fourteen hours that travelled within the triangle that is San Diego Airport, the Riogenrix campus, and the doctor's house. I found a cell phone that went from the airport to the house and then Riogenrix. Let's call it phone X. From Riogenrix, another cell phone joins phone X. Let's call the other one Y. The two phones were together for the next several hours. First, they were stationary in Point Loma, San Diego. Then the two phones split up. Phone X went to Torrey Pines in La Jolla. An hour later, phone Y went to a residential neighborhood, also in La Jolla, before being shut off. X remains at Torrey Pines. There's been no change in location. Y belongs to Selene Torres, the chief administrative officer of Riogenrix. X must be the doctor on an unmarked cell phone."

"Torrey Pines? As in the golf course?"

"Yes, sir."

"How long has the doctor been stationary?"

"An hour."

"Have you called the cell phone?"

"I'm awaiting your guidance, sir."

"Call it."

"Yes, sir."

Burt shifted forward in his seat as the technician used a laptop with a satellite connection to call the phone. The doctor didn't pick up.

"Is there any other cellular traffic near the doctor?"

"Nothing now, sir."

"How far from the airport to Torrey Pines?"

"Fifteen miles north, sir."

Burt turned back to Camel. "What do you think?"

"I think we're going golfing, but don't expect any hole in ones."

Burt got up and went to the front of the plane. The plane had two pilots, one of them a former military man. The other was a civilian. "How long before we land, gentlemen?"

"We're still waiting for permission," the civilian pilot said.

Burt employed the silence he'd always found to be successful.

Sure enough, after a few seconds, the former military pilot spoke up. "How long do you want, sir?"

"I need now."

The former military pilot glanced at the civilian. The civilian nodded. "Of course, sir."

Burt returned to his seat. As he buckled in, the pilot announced over the intercom a manned runway had become free and the jet would be landing. Burt shifted back into his chair and nodded at Camel. He didn't like how phone X had been stationary for an hour. He hoped the doctor was still alive.

Gregory was parked outside of the Salk Institute in La Jolla. The concrete walls of the institute rose around him, buffering the quickening night wind and developing light rain. He had a laptop on the center console of the van and the external hard drive provided by Harrison plugged into the laptop. He was reviewing the research and development steps Harrison had taken to get V-202 from theoretical possibility to legitimate vaccine. He was following much of the work Harrison had transcribed but also found himself perpetually stuck. For every one step forward, he took an equal step back. The hard drive was missing key information over and over again, the essentials of the mRNA techniques themselves. For example, Boyd had documented the gopher technique as it related to mRNA washing but didn't actually delineate how to perform it. The more Gregory reviewed the hard drive, the more he understood what Harrison had done. Harrison had played a game with him, given him the developmental steps for the menglavirus vaccine while withholding the essential mRNA techniques upon which those steps were based. In the hands of a full-blown vaccine company, the hard drive would surely be sufficient to reconstruct the vaccine over the course of a couple of months, because they had hundreds of researchers who could pull all of the literature on the mRNA techniques employed, but even so, the reconstruction would be painstaking. He was flying solo. He needed more.

Gregory had always prided himself on his acumen, the way he'd been able to study hard and smart in medical school to achieve the highest academic grades in his class. Ever since he'd obtained notification from that woman who worked as a senior researcher for Riogenrix that Harrison had achieved what thus far had been unachievable, he'd been preparing for today, reviewing Harrison's published works on mRNA vaccination techniques and protocols. He'd expected to understand more than he was now.

He didn't know how much of his incomprehension was because Harrison had left out key steps in the vaccine's development versus his own greenness. He thought back to first year lectures in medical school, particularly the two pathologists who'd not only taught the course but written the books. They were foremost experts on pathology, the tree of medicine from which all other branches of medicine originated. Despite their world-class expertise, they'd been horrible instructors, unable to explain the basics before delving into the complex. For the first four weeks, he'd been lost, as had everyone else in the class. But he'd buckled down, bought and read all of their books and not just those related to the course, gone to their office hours, and filled in the gaps the professors had left open. After the fact, he'd realized the professors had been more than just assholes— they'd been intentional. They'd wanted their students to seek them out, because once he'd filled in the gaps and gotten down the basics, the rest of the course had been easy. He'd gotten the class' highest scores in pathology and from there he'd coasted through the rest of the academics, securing the class' top ranking for the first two years.

Now he was at that stage again. He needed to fill in the gaps Harrison had left out. Once he got the gaps, he would excel, just like he had before. He wasn't disappointed in himself for not understanding a hundred percent right now, because he'd anticipated something along these lines. He'd intended to hold onto the wife and daughter for a couple more days for this reason, to keep the doctor on as a consultant, per se. Of course, the senator had messed up those plans. He didn't know who the woman with the gun had been, but he'd known she hadn't belonged at the data exchange.

Either way, he wasn't going to be able to be involved in the vaccine with what he had now. Maybe in a few weeks, he would be able to fill in the blanks, but he didn't have a few weeks. The senator would turn over the doctor's notes to the Chinese within days, and they would have a small army of scientists dig through the server to match them up with Harrison's documentation.

Via brute force, they would fill in the blanks before he could.

He was about to close the laptop when he got a phone call from one of the contractors roaming the area.

"We saw the wife and daughter."

"Where are they?"

"We couldn't follow them. We were on foot. They were in a Jeep. They were with Selene Torres, the Riogenrix administrator. But they were in La Jolla, not too far from Torrey Pines. They were on a residential road called Farm Road. It's where all of the cliff-side mansions are located."

"Keep looking. Locate them."

The bottom line for Gregory was that he didn't understand Harrison's gibberish. He had two choices. He could be content he'd finished his work with the senator, forget about his own involvement in the vaccine, and unwind his life into a quiet existence. Or, he could go back to Harrison, grab him for good to fill in these blanks, and become the lead. Even so, he wasn't confident Boyd would offer up any more information unless the wife and daughter were at play. He didn't need more than a second to decide. He'd decided already, weeks ago. He was tired of being a consultant. He needed to be the physician-scientist he deserved to be. Russia would make him one.

He pulled up a map of the area on his laptop. The contractor had noted the wife and daughter had been on Farm Road, where the mansions were. He scrolled the area and checked the satellite imagery. The road led to nowhere, more cliffs and the ocean beyond. Either they were going someplace specific on Farm Road or they were passing through to get someplace else. If they were headed someplace else, they were probably gone from his grasp forever, in which case he was stuck with the first choice, turn over the notes and disappear.

He kept scrolling the street, checking each house on Farm Road. Finally, he came across 1150 and recognized the address. The house belonged to Harrison's partner at Riogenrix, the old man who'd founded the company and pioneered most of the techniques upon which Harrison's mRNA vaccine was based, the man who'd accepted Hopkins students into his lab at Salk but hadn't accepted Gregory because he hadn't been able to get the sycophantic letters of recommendation the old man had required.

Gregory wasn't a man who believed in luck or coincidence. He favored preparation, correlation, and causation. The wife, the daughter, and the administrative officer were headed to the old man's house.

He started up the van. He wasn't far off from understanding the intricacies of Harrison's mRNA vaccine. He only needed a little guidance, a push in the right direction. As he pulled out of the Salk Institute, he called his lead contractor. Now the second option had a part A and B. He could get back the daughter and wife and finish off his education by reapplying pressure to Harrison or he could just get after the old man. The old man had invented mRNA vaccines. He would be able to provide enough technique to get Gregory started. He chose option two, parts A *and* B.

Senator Scott Spaulding watched Naomi. She'd been his lover for the past two years, a woman he'd allowed to live in one of his condos in exchange for what he'd always perceived as safe companionship. He'd kept her isolated from menglavirus not only for his benefit but hers. She'd survived, even prospered, in Vegas because of his vigilance. In turn, he'd prospered as well, because he'd been able to avoid unnecessary menglavirus risks presented to men like he, men who were sought after by others. He had a fiancé but he wasn't the kind of man to not take advantage of his station in life. Naomi had been a reward for his hard work. But now she'd put a damper on his prosperity, completely messed up his well-plotted plans in the span of less than twenty-four hours. She'd not only tried to go from down-low companion to mother of a child he didn't want, but she'd also placed him in legal danger by pulling off those shenanigans back in San Diego. He hadn't intended for the wife and daughter to go free. If he hadn't secured what he'd set out to obtain—the doctor's complete notes on a vaccine that was going to catapult him into the White House—he would've deemed the entirety of his efforts a failure.

They were back on the jet, each of them quiet as the plane waited for clearance to take off. Dense fog and rain had settled into the airport before they'd boarded. They were sitting opposite each other in the jet's captain chairs, a small table separating them. She was looking out the window, even though there was nothing at which to look, just night and tarmac. She had her hand on her belly. He wanted to tell her to take her goddamned hand off her belly, because there was nothing there yet to feel, and there would never *be* anything there to feel. But he kept his thoughts to himself. His newest goal in relation to Naomi was to keep her quiet and subdued long enough to finish his work with China. He still had the remaining vaccine, which he now figured would go to his fiancé, if it went to anyone at all. He was inclined to dump it.

The feelings he'd had for Naomi earlier in the night were now conflicted, such that he doubted what feelings he'd had for her anyway. He didn't want to keep her as-is but also didn't want to let her go. He wanted to turn the clock back, get back to the simple existence the two of them had had when there'd been no pregnancy. He wanted her to terminate and then stay on with him but knew he was being wishful.

Either way, he wasn't going to let her leave.

The plane moved forward. They were finally taking off. He had a contractor watching them, making sure Naomi didn't do anything rash again. Letting the wife and daughter out of the van had been damaging enough. He wasn't going to let her cause any more trouble. He finally had what he needed to get himself elected as the next President of the United States. He would call China when he arrived back at the condo. He would deal with Naomi as well—all of her. Right now, he would rest, indulge himself by envisioning the future. He closed his eyes and saw the White House.

A man was standing over Harrison. The man was thin and sinewy. He had on running shoes and was using the shoes to nudge Harrison in the side. He wore a baseball cap. He also wore a mask.

"Are you all right, man?"

Harrison didn't know. "I think so."

"Thank, God. I was worried you were dead. I saw you on the ground. I didn't want to get too close to you, though, in case...you know..."

Harrison knew. "In case I have menglavirus?"

"Yes."

"Thanks."

"Do you?"

"What?"

"Have menglavirus?"

Harrison felt damp grass and wet dirt beneath him and light rain on his head. It was foggy. He brought his hand to his face. He wasn't wearing a mask. He wasn't sure exactly where he was or why a man in running shoes was hovering over him. He knew he always wore an FN99 in public but didn't know why he wasn't wearing one now. "I don't know. If I have it, I'm prodromal."

The runner took several steps backward. Harrison wasn't offended. He would've done the same. As Harrison tried to push himself into a seated position, he saw an approaching shadow. The shadow walked with a deliberate pace, intentional and assertive. He looked around, saw cliffs and canyons. He couldn't fully put together where he was and why.

The shadow neared and he saw a man in military uniform. The man was lean and well-built. The runner turned around to look in the same direction as Harrison. The runner had been retreating from Harrison but now he retreated from the approaching shadow as well.

Harrison now knew the man approaching them was Col. Burt

Johnson. He remembered why he was on a grassy clearing at night.

Jasmine and Sofia.

Torrey Pines.

The man without the mask and the senator.

Gregory Miller.

The colonel reached them and Harrison tried to push himself from seated to standing but felt dizzy, as if he were going to faint. He remained seated and waited for the feeling to pass.

The runner raised his palms in front of him. "I'm sorry," he said to the colonel. "I know I'm not supposed to be here, but please don't—" The runner had trailed off as he'd realized the man in front of them wasn't police but military and then finished his thought anyway by saying, "—arrest me?"

"Who are you, sir?" the colonel said to the runner.

"I was running by when I saw this man on the ground. I always run through Torrey Pines at night when there's no one around. I know I'm not supposed to be here. I know the reserve is closed, but I find running maintains my sanity. I wanted to get in a final run before the storm really kicks in. I didn't mean to break any laws."

The colonel cut him off. "Keep on running by, sir."

The runner didn't have to be told twice. He turned and darted away. After placing a quick distance of twenty yards between him and the colonel, he turned around, saw Harrison and the colonel still watching him, and ran faster still.

"Need a hand, Dr. Boyd?" the colonel said, extending his palm. "I'm here to help find your wife and daughter and keep your vaccine."

Harrison had no idea where Jasmine and Sofia where or if they were even safe. He knew Gregory and the senator were still out there. He took the colonel's hand. He let the colonel help him to his wobbly feet.

After the last forty-eight hours, Jasmine didn't think she could be any more surprised than she'd already been, but here she was, surprised again. Thankfully, though, the surprise was better than any of the other horrible ones that had enveloped her and Sofia's life over the past two days. The surprise was that Sofia was still drawn to Uncle Richard, as she called him, as if they'd spent every day together for the past five years rather than having spent none. They were at Richard's house in La Jolla, finally. They were safe, hopefully. Richard had received them several minutes ago.

"Do you remember me, Sofia?" Richard had said to her when he'd let them into his house. "I'm your godfather."

"Yes. I missed you so much, Uncle Richard."

Sofia had gone to him, embraced him while he embraced her. Sofia and Jasmine weren't wearing masks and Richard's mask was old, frayed, and poorly fitted. Jasmine startled when Sofia went to him, an old man who'd deliberately kept himself safe. Jasmine called to Sofia to come back to her, but Richard raised his hand as if to say that there was no need, he was okay, they would all be okay. He told them that Dr. Jason Carr, his old partner at Steptech, was flying in with two executive security teams now. They would go off of the grid until he arrived.

Now, Sofia was sitting on the couch with Richard, playing games with him that Jasmine never had known Sofia to play—charades and Simon Says—as if she'd been playing these games all of her life. Jasmine had never played these games with Sofia, but Sofia knew them anyway, presumably by watching videos on her tablet. Or maybe Sofia had played these games before, but just not with Jasmine, maybe with Richard in an existence so forgotten now it was as if it'd never existed—at least for Jasmine, because it clearly had existed for Sofia. Jasmine knew Sofia looked at the photos on her tablet, but hadn't known the true effect they'd had on her. Her daughter had been missing the life she'd once had, one filled with people who loved her, people who weren't Mommy or Daddy. At least for now, Sofia had regained her life.

Jasmine watched them from the kitchen, where she stood with Selene, mesmerized by the interactions of an eight-year-old girl and seventy-eight-year-old man who hadn't seen each other in years. She was saddened as well, despondent again as she thought about all that Sofia had missed over the past five years and would continue to miss if Harrison's vaccine didn't see the light of day. Like everything else in the house, the kitchen was massive, and Jasmine felt herself wanting to get lost, float away for all of the mistakes she'd made over the past five years— and not just hers but Harrison's—but she knew she couldn't and wouldn't because of what she saw in the living room. Life wasn't over yet, menglavirus be dammed.

As of now, they were *almost* okay, because not all of them were here. Harrison wasn't here. Selene reassured them—he was coming, it was part of the plan. When they'd arrived at Richard's house, Selene had called Harrison on a phone that he'd received from Senator Scott Spaulding. He hadn't picked up— Jasmine tried not to think of the reason why—but she'd let him know in two voicemails and two text messages that Jasmine and Sofia were all right, and they were with her, and they all were with Richard. Selene didn't explain to Jasmine why Harrison had a phone from the guy on television and Jasmine didn't ask. But Harrison hadn't arrived yet. After seeing the mayhem at the glider-port, Jasmine wasn't sure he would. Yet, she tried to remain confident. As she watched Sofia now, she thought about Harrison. He was her daughter's father and her husband still. He'd come for them at the glider-port, given up his life's work in exchange for them—or at least tried, because the man without a mask hadn't intended to let them go. She didn't know who the woman was who'd opened the van, but knew the woman had probably saved their lives. Regarding Harrison, she wasn't delusional—she didn't think she and he would ever reconcile to their old relationship, the one they'd had in the very beginning, because she knew who Harrison was, and she knew what drove him. Nonetheless, she wanted the best for him, and she wanted him here.

And she hoped he got here soon.

Because she was tired and getting wearier by the minute. She was trying not to think about her fatigue, though. Or the aches of her body. She didn't want to consider the possibility that the fatigue was due to anything other than the tribulations of the last forty-eight hours. She didn't want to consider the possibility she'd been exposed.

She watched Sofia and Richard, who were still playing charades, and felt as if the rest of their lives were finally going to begin, so long as they could hold on for a couple of more hours.

Gregory was on the street several houses down from Richard's house on 1150 Farm Road. He was with his team of hired contractors—minus two. One contractor had died at the gliderport. Another man was at San Diego Airport, preparing a jet for their departure. The contractor at the airport had been the one who'd notified Gregory he would soon have visitors, the one who'd seen the colonel arrive from USAMRIID-West with his own team of contractors just as the senator had left.

"Get outfitted," he said to his team, and they were doing just that, standing outside of their vehicles. Gregory knew what was coming in relation to the menglavirus vaccine, which was one final race to the end. He made sure each man was outfitted in combat biosafety suits, which were infection control suits specifically geared towards chemical warfare. They were easier to maneuver in than the traditional laboratory suits—and far harder to obtain. Gregory wasn't worried about the raid. His team of contractors was professional. They would get the job done. But he didn't want to leave a huge trace. He was off the reservation, acting on his own now. He wasn't going to be able to depend on the senator's protection. In fact, he was sure the senator was going to come after him at some point as well. The senator wouldn't want a mess, no investigations, no law enforcement actions that somehow became national security interests. 1150 Farm Road was thirty minutes away from the airport. Gregory and his team had enough time.

Gregory had met the colonel once, a few years back, when Gregory had gone to an industry conference at which the colonel had spoken about the US Army's Ebola work in West Africa. This had been before menglavirus. He'd spoken to the colonel briefly, trying to gain insight on real world efficacy rates for the Ebola vaccines for a client that was developing their own. He'd disliked the colonel. The colonel had been dismissive when Gregory had discussed the for-profit Ebola endeavors. The colonel had been even worse than the usual self-righteous doctors with whom he'd usually dealt, because the colonel was not only a self-righteous doctor but a self-righteous military man. Gregory preferred men like those in his security team who understood their worth and acted out of straightforward motivations.

Gregory adjusted his lab coat, particularly the side pockets. He didn't put on a biosafety combat suit, because, of course, he had no need. After he and his men were properly outfitted, they left their vehicles, walked the block to 1150, and reached the old man's house. They approached the gate.

One of his team members planted a small charge along the gate. The charge went off. The gate, being more decorative than functional, buckled. As the gate crumbled, he thought, *Let's see who gets here first, colonel. You or me.*

Gregory led his team up the long driveway. He had canisters of nMAQ61, the super-modified virus, tucked into the side pockets of his lab coat. The canisters were his choice of weapon, but just in case, he also carried a submachine gun in his hands.

By the time the colonel arrived in La Jolla, Gregory intended to be gone.

Selene felt herself reverting to what she knew. She began to work. Staying occupied was something she'd done more of after her husband had died. She knew in their industry, there was no such thing as too much work. Harrison worked, Richard *had* worked, and she'd worked as well, as much as each of them. She felt better when she worked, less apt to consider the aspects of her life that bothered her.

She was bothered now. Despite the relative tranquility of the past thirty minutes, she knew serious threats remained for all of them. She was worried about Jasmine and Sofia, knew they were sick, could see it in the clamminess of their skin. She was worried about Richard, who didn't seem to have it, but certainly would have it soon enough. He was adamant about sticking to his old, disintegrating mask. She was worried about Harrison, who'd been left behind and still wasn't here. She was worried about the men who'd come after all of them for a vaccine. She was worried about how the men were still out there, the senator was still out there, the virus was still out there. She had a feeling —more than a feeling, an unsettling knowledge born of always working—that the strangeness of this week wasn't over yet.

She dismissed herself, snuck away downstairs two floors to the basement. She walked by the biosafety lab Richard had built into the bottom floor with almost vain aspirations at the end of the Steptech days and then had modernized at the outset of menglavirus. She walked to the house's panic room, trying to control her pace but quickening her steps anyway, needing to get to the cameras, needing to work in the way she knew. Once inside the panic room, she surveyed the security system. It was similar to the one at Riogenrix, dependent on video cameras. She stood and watched the cameras.

She didn't need long to see she had been right to be concerned. A flash of light soaked one of the monitors and the front gate to the house collapsed. She noted five men ascending the driveway. She enlarged the images, trying to determine if Harrison had arrived, but knew she was being wishful. She watched the enlarged images, saw four men in odd biosafety suits and one in a white laboratory coat. The suits were thin, not the type they used at Riogenrix, some kind of military version. The combat suits made the four men in them gray blobs on the screen. The fifth man was harder to spot, but Selene recognized him, nonetheless. He wasn't wearing a combat suit. Rather, he was wearing only a white lab coat, the same one he'd been wearing when he'd confronted her in the parking lot at Riogenrix. He was the man without a mask.

The astronauts were here, as Sofia would say. And they'd changed into their work clothes.

Selene didn't wonder how the astronauts had found them. It probably hadn't been hard. Richard's house was one of the more notable ones on the cliffs. It wasn't hard to put two and two together.

She surveyed the panic room. She'd come downstairs to the basement for a reason. She'd had a hunch. Now, she noted two handsets in chargers next to the server for the security cameras. They had similar handsets at work that the security team had used in what now seemed like a different existence. They were two-way radiofrequency handsets with access to the 800 MHz spectrum. They served as panic communication devices during the old days when cellular connection had been spotty. She grabbed both headsets, thinking that for once the old technology was going to come in useful.

She left the panic room with the two handsets and rushed upstairs to the top floor.

Richard knew bad events would come eventually, because the stakes for Harrison's vaccine were too high for everyone who'd been involved in stealing it to simply slink away into the night. Already, the deception employed by others in order to obtain Harrison's vaccine had been relentless. He had no reason to think the pursuit of V-202 would end until the vaccine was in the hands of an entity such as Steptech, who had the systems and resources to safeguard it. If he'd been asked one week ago about whether Riogenrix had been such an entity as well, he would've said *yes*. He couldn't have imagined there would be people impeding the widespread distribution of the only legitimate vaccine for menglavirus to the global population. He would've been even less inclined to imagine the person doing so would've been a US senator. He would've thought the world would've been lining up to help Riogenrix.

But, so far, tonight had been good, better than he could've conceived of even a few hours ago. At least for now, Selene was safe, Jasmine and Sofia were safe, and the vaccine would soon be safe. He only needed Harrison to be safe too. Earlier this morning, he never would've imagined he would see his goddaughter again. But he had and he was happy. He wasn't surprised they still had a bond. He knew the night wasn't over yet and the happiness could still be threatened, but for now, he was good.

"Do you remember me, Sofia?" he'd asked when he'd first seen her.

"Of course, I do. I missed you a lot, Uncle Richard," she'd said.

He'd missed her too, more than he'd allowed himself to feel. She had always been the grandchild he would never actually have and the goddaughter he actually did. Now, she was motivation again for him to push the vaccine through the obstacles imposed by the senator. He had no qualms about working with Jason anymore, no ego to quash. He wanted the vaccine distributed. He didn't care anymore that he wouldn't be able to offer his former partner at Steptech any insight on the vaccine. He only wanted Sofia to be able to live a good life.

He saw Selene return. She'd gone downstairs several minutes ago. He hadn't asked her where she'd been heading when she'd left, but he'd suspected she'd gone to the security room. He'd felt her unease when she'd left, as if she also knew the night wasn't over. Now, she was back. She positioned herself in the living room with her back to the windows, facing him as the rain pelted the glass. Sofia had tired and was sleeping on the couch and Jasmine had placed the throw over Sofia and was sitting beside her. Richard looked up at Selene, waited for the happiness he'd been feeling for the past hour to fade again.

"The man without the mask is here," Selene said. "He has four other men in biosafety suits with him."

Richard didn't need additional explanation. The biosafety suits were clear signs of what was to come. The night hadn't been over, after all.

"Let's go to the bottom floor," he said, trying to keep his voice upbeat and calm. "Let's get everyone to the lab." He stood up and went to Jasmine and a sleeping Sofia. "I'll carry Sofia. I still have some strength in me for an old man."

He saw the doubt in Jasmine's face. He understood the doubt —he himself would have doubt about a seventy-eight-year-old man with sarcoidosis who'd been holed up in his house for the past five years carrying an eight-year-old girl down two stories of steps. But he also saw the fatigue in Jasmine's face and knew she had the virus and her body was succumbing to it. He knew Sofia's body would eventually succumb too but didn't want to think about it.

"I promise," he said.

"I'll be right behind you, Richard," Jasmine said. "If you need a break, just turn around and hand Sofia to me."

He leaned over and scooped up Sofia. She felt both lighter and heavier than he imagined—lighter because he was a seventy-eight-year-old man who'd been home for five years and heavier because he'd last carried her when she was three years old. He didn't let his body betray him, though. He cradled her in his arms as he walked across the living room, Selene in the lead and Jasmine behind them. At the stairs, he twisted his body to keep an eye on the steps below him, making sure he didn't misplace his foot. He never had before, but he found himself doubting all aspects of his life that he'd never doubted before. He descended the steps with purpose, and as they reached the last switchback,

Sofia stirred, partly asleep and partly awake.

"Where are we going?" she said.

"We're going downstairs," Richard said. "I have a safety lab on the bottom floor. You'll be excited to see the lab."

"Is Daddy here?"

"Soon. He'll be coming soon."

She closed her eyes and fell asleep again. As he descended the final stairs to the bottom of the house, he thought about how he'd certainly missed being around his people, people who were important to him, people he loved in one way or another, such as Selene, who was a friend and colleague, and Sofia, who was his goddaughter and buddy and de facto granddaughter. No matter what happened to him tonight, he would treasure the sixty minutes that had come prior to now, when life had been excellent.

Jasmine didn't know if Richard was going to make it all the way down the two flights of switchback stairs to the bottom floor, but he seemed determined. He advanced with good speed and agility, as if he'd saved himself for one last push. Selene was in front of them, confident and definitive in step and path. When they reached the bottom, Richard caught his breath, and then he led them to the laboratory.

Jasmine couldn't remember if the laboratory was new or not. She had probably been to the bottom floor no more than once. It was carved into the cliffs—there weren't any floor to ceiling windows down here. She noticed two metal doors marking the two exits outside of the lab on each side of the floor. She wondered where the doors led and figured they existed in case of emergencies, which in this house, probably meant a biosafety leak rather than something mundane like a fire. She couldn't picture the doors leading to anything other than jagged cliffs, but figured any exit was better than none at all.

From where she stood just outside of the lab, she could see

it was made up of three separate parts. The main door leading into the biosafety lab had a camera above it and a keypad fixed beside it and had windows with tempered glass edged up against it. It led into the first part of the lab, which looked to be a dressing room. Lockers lined the walls and a large hamper like the kind found in hospitals was near the lockers. She knew from her marriage to Harrison that the first part of the biosafety lab was a preparation room. It was where a person would change out of their clothes into lab attire.

A second door at the far end of the prep room led to a similarly sized space with another door and another set of fixed windows. In this second space, coiled tubing hung from the ceiling. Again, she knew from her marriage with Harrison that the tubing contained disinfectant spray. She saw a glimpse of an open shower in the corner. She couldn't see the floors but knew they would contain drains. The second room was a decontamination unit. She knew a decon room in a commercial laboratory would contain biosafety suits but saw none in Richard's lab. She figured Richard hadn't done enough work to maintain the suits previously stored in it. The decontamination room had another door buttressed by yet another pair of tempered glass windows. From there, she couldn't see much further inside, but knew the actual workspaces were beyond the last door, in the third and final part of the biosafety laboratory.

Richard handed Sofia back to her so he could access and open the main door. Sofia stirred, but didn't wake. She felt warm, too warm, and Jasmine wondered if Richard had noticed. She hoped she was imagining the warmth because she knew what it meant. Again, Jasmine thought back over the past few days to the park and abduction and all of the possible exposures in between. In addition to noticing Sofia's warmth, she noted her own struggle carrying her. Her hands were shaking and she hoped the shake wasn't coming from Sofia but from her herself. She told herself it was just another sign of fatigue and nothing else. She wanted to chalk it up to the past two days, not wanting to consider other causes.

Richard waited for the facial recognition camera outside of the lab to recognize him before entering an access code on the keypad. The main door leading into the first part of the lab clicked. He pulled the door open and waited for Jasmine to enter. She went inside the first part of the lab—the prep room—and straight towards the next door that led into the decon unit, still carrying Sofia. She waited for Selene and Richard to join her. But neither Selene nor Richard followed her, at least not yet. Richard was holding the door open for Selene, but she wasn't passing through. Instead, she was speaking to Richard. The two of them were still outside of the lab, still on the other side of the prep room. Selene was keeping her voice low and Jasmine was too fatigued and now too far away to pay attention to what they might be saying. She heard a jumble of words but couldn't focus on listening. Selene had two devices in her hands and she gave one of them to Richard. She turned and walked away and Richard was left standing at the main door.

Finally, Richard went through the main door and entered the prep room. He went directly to the second door where Jasmine was. "Selene is going to get us help," he said. There was no keypad attached to the second door, no access code to enter. Instead, there was a large square button to the side of the door. Richard pressed it, there was another click, and he opened the second door leading into the decon unit.

Jasmine was too tired to ask where Selene was going and what kind of help she was getting so she didn't. She moved forward. Once inside, she saw the drains on the floor she'd known would be there. She looked up and saw the sprinkler heads lining the ceiling. She hoped Richard would be quick. The fatigue was taking hold more. She was feeling cold. She didn't have the strength to hold Sofia much longer. Sofia was stirring again—she was awake now—and Jasmine said to her in a rushed, hushed voice, "You're going to walk now, honey." She put Sofia down, guiding Sofia to stand on her own. Jasmine felt less relief than she thought she should've and she knew her body was succumbing.

Richard went to the final door and pushed another button. There was another buzz. Richard held the final door open for them. Jasmine touched Sofia's shoulder, urging her forward. Sofia walked past Richard into the workspace of the biosafety laboratory. Jasmine followed close behind. When they were both inside, she took her daughter's hand. Once inside, Jasmine turned and they waited for Richard to enter after them, but he didn't. He said, "I can slow them down. Riogenrix is my company. They'll be happy to talk to me. I can buy you time."

As he spoke, the old mask he'd been wearing gave up. The straps broke and the mask slipped from his face and fell to his chin. He didn't try to fix it. He pushed it aside and let it fall to the ground. Even though Jasmine was struggling to pay attention, she'd heard what he'd said: buy *you* time. Not, buy *us* time.

She saw three camera monitors above the door leading into the workspace. Each monitor showed a preceding part of the lab: one monitor for the camera outside of the main entrance showing the ground floor, one monitor for the camera in the prep room, and one monitor for the camera in the decon unit. She couldn't see Selene anymore on any of the monitors. Wherever she'd gone, she was out of sight. Jasmine looked away from the monitors and watched Richard. When Jasmine had first seen him tonight, she'd seen an aged man. When he'd played with Sofia, the aged man had disappeared and a younger man had taken his place. She saw the aged man again as he started to close the door.

Sofia spoke up. "Uncle Richard, where are you going?"

Jasmine could feel the alarm in Sofia's voice. Sofia didn't want Richard to leave, not now, not after finally having seen him again for the first time in five years.

"I'm still here, Sofia. I'll be upstairs. You stay down here. Sleep and rest and I'll see you in the morning."

"No. Stay with us, Uncle Richard."

He didn't move. He didn't enter the workspace. Sofia walked towards him. But as she was two arm's lengths away from him, she bent over and coughed. She took another step and coughed again, this time in a fit. She didn't take any more steps towards Richard. Instead, she looked up at him with tears in her eyes. She understood. She'd grown up around the virus, knew what the virus did, knew what the cough meant, both for her and those around her. She wanted to go to him but knew she shouldn't because to go to him now would mean to infect him.

Sofia was still.

Again, Jasmine thought about the park two days in a row, the abduction, the derelict house, the two days without masks, but mostly she thought about Sofia, a single cough followed by a fit of coughing, and hoped there would not be another cough because she hoped Sofia wasn't sick. But she knew better. Sofia was sick and would only get sicker. She saw the fear on Sofia's face, even saw shame, and knew Sofia was thinking the same thing Jasmine had thought when they'd entered the house: They didn't want to expose Richard in case they had something. She moved towards her daughter to hold and comfort her. *You have nothing to be ashamed about, honey*, she thought as she went to her.

Sofia coughed again.

Instead of closing the door, Richard left it open. He stepped into the workspace. He smiled at Sofia and gently held up his hand to Jasmine. Jasmine knew what he meant. She stopped going to her daughter and watched as Richard went to her daughter instead. He crouched in front of Sofia. He hugged her. Sofia clutched him and he stayed with her in an embrace. She didn't let go and he didn't pull back. After several seconds, he spoke something into Sofia's ear. Jasmine couldn't hear what he said but Sofia nodded. She let go of Richard and slowly returned to Jasmine. He waited until Sofia was back at Jasmine's side before returning to the door. He walked back through it, left the workspace, and reentered the decon unit. He turned and waved goodbye. Finally, Richard closed the door.

Jasmine brought her daughter close to her. She knew no matter what might happen next to Sofia and her here in the lab, they were safer in here than Richard was out there. He had decided, and he'd decided on Sofia. He'd decided on them.

Gregory's hired guns had no difficulties breaching the house. Along the perimeter of the property, a basic security system had triggered panic locks for the doors and windows, but the security system had been designed to keep out everyday burglars, not ex-military security contractors. His team used another explosive to get the oversized pivot door at the entrance to the house to fall. They entered the foyer in the house's top floor.

Even from the top floor foyer, he could see glimpses of the churning ocean beyond. At this time of night, there wasn't much of a view, but he knew in daytime, it was a different story. It was a view for a man who'd spared no expense on carving a house of concrete out of a cliff. Even so, he knew the founder of Riogenrix hadn't earned the house based on his work at Riogenrix but had become wealthy because of Steptech. Not being profit-oriented with Riogenrix had been a mistake by all involved. If Riogenrix had been more profit-oriented, they would've been able to build out the types of infrastructure large, extremely profitable corporations had. They would've had security, both at the company's campus and for their key executives. But Gregory had found no security at the founder's house. Entry had been easy.

"Find the old man. Find the woman. Find the wife and daughter. Bring them back here. All of them."

He knew from his records search that the house was eleven thousand square feet spread out along three levels. He thought finding everyone in the house might be harder than gaining access to the house had been but he still didn't foresee any difficulties. He estimated he had twenty-five minutes before the colonel showed up. He was getting close to being in a time crunch. Nonetheless, he foresaw success. After all, the colonel wasn't coming with the US Army in tow.

Even if twenty-five minutes weren't enough time, Gregory had an advantage. He had canisters in the side pockets of his lab coat. The contractors had canisters too. *Let the colonel come*, he thought. He had everything he needed to handle him.

72070.

July 20th, 1970.

Selene thought about her birthdate as she progressed along the rain-soaked cliff. However, she wasn't thinking about her birthdate because she was thinking of herself. Rather, she was thinking about Richard. He'd given her the five digit access code into the biosafety lab, the emergency code used to override the facial recognition cameras and lockout mechanisms of the emergency exits buried into the cliff. The code was 72070—her birthday. He hadn't had to explain why he'd chosen her birthdate as the access code. She knew as well as he. They were friends who'd worked side-by-side for the better part of three decades. Without either of them ever having to verbalize as such, they knew they were each other's most trusted friends. Each of them had always been there through good times and the worst of times for each other.

Now was the worst of times. But Selene had a chance to change that.

She was on the cliff. She'd left via one of the emergency exits flanking the biosafety laboratory on the bottom floor. The exit opened to a flat landing and then a trail of fifty feet carved into the rocks. But after fifty feet, the carved-out trail ended. Now, she was on her own, trying to scale the cliffs and return to Farm Road before the winds and rains swept her away.

She'd told Richard she wasn't going to get into the laboratory. Rather, she was going to take her chances on the cliff, try to reach Farm Road to get help. She believed Harrison would arrive. And she believed he would arrive with help.

Keep Jasmine and Sofia safe in there, she'd said. *I'll get to Harrison.*

He'd given her the emergency access code and she'd left.

The going on the cliffs was slow and methodical. The night

was dark and the rain was constant. The rocks were getting slicker by the minute. She figured that soon these cliffs would be completely untraversable. Already a single misstep would send her falling down the rocks into the violent night tide below. A heavier rain would guarantee such a misstep.

But she wasn't going to be on these cliffs when the rain picked up. She would make sure she was on Farm Road. She was a hiker. She knew what to do, how to advance. She'd been hiking ever since she'd met Bobby. These cliffs weren't part of a usual trail, but they'd been traversed before by others, just like everything else in San Diego, and she would traverse them now. She didn't care if no one had crossed them in the dark of night with rain falling because she told herself there always was a first. Riogenrix was full of firsts and tonight would be another one for the company.

She hadn't been hiking—if that was what this was right now —since her husband had died. She'd purposefully avoided any hikes but now she wasn't avoiding them any longer. She didn't believe in heaven or the afterlife, but she believed Bobby was here with her. He was guiding her because he would always be a part of her. She wasn't going to fall.

She gripped the cliffs with her hands and slid her feet along the paths, slowly working her way north and upwards. She moved one step at a time. Over the years, she'd heard people say not to look down when a trail changed from wide to narrow. The advice was dispensed usually by people who were afraid to keep going or by those who were guiding those who were afraid to keep going. Bobby had never told her not to look down. She had no problem looking down. She understood the implications. The rocks and water were waiting for her. But she wasn't waiting for them.

She moved onwards, like she'd been doing since Bobby died.

Harrison's worldview shifted again. The cause this time was

having the blanks on the past few days filled in by the colonel as they drove with the entire team—three contractors in tactical clothes and a young military man in uniform—in two Toyota Tundras to La Jolla. The colonel told Harrison more about the senator than Harrison ever had wanted to know, including what the colonel had learned about Operation Soda Can. Harrison had one overwhelming thought as he listened—he needed to vaccinate Jasmine and Sofia. After finding him strewn on the ground at Torrey Pines, the colonel had escorted him to Jasmine's car, parked north of the glider-port. Harrison had been afraid the cooler was going to be gone, but to his relief it'd still been there.

Harrison and the colonel were outside of Richard's La Jolla house. He had the cooler in his hand. The rain had intensified and the winds were picking up. He'd known the circumstances had shifted for the worse even before they'd arrived at the house because he'd called Richard and Selene multiple times over the past several minutes but each time no one had picked up. Now that they were outside of the house, there was no doubt. The demolished gate leading to the driveway was proof enough. Harrison didn't have to be a military expert to know there'd been an assault on the house. Nor did the colonel sugarcoat what needed to happen. Gregory Miller was here.

"We can't wait," the colonel said. "I need to go in."

"I'll go with you," Harrison said again, still trying to convince the colonel.

"No offense, doctor, but this isn't your forte. You did an amazing job with developing V-202, but your work with the menglavirus vaccine isn't done yet. You have to oversee the Phase 3 trials for emergency use authorization, modify dosing schedules, and ensure production adheres to the standards you set, so the vaccine remains as efficacious throughout the global supply chain as it was at Riogenrix. If—or when—the senator's modified version of the menglavirus becomes widely prevalent, your work will take on an additional urgency. You stay here. I have men who will go in with me. We have to operate in combat biosafety masks. We both know what might be coming."

Harrison didn't pretend he was a military man. He barely knew how to use Jasmine's pistol. But his work with V-202 wasn't worth doing if he didn't have Jasmine and Sofia in his life. He'd provided Selene with his complete notes on V-202 via the A drives. His vaccine for menglavirus would survive, be passed along to Steptech, and finished with the expediency and scale needed to bring it to the entire world. V-202 didn't need him anymore. His family did. He needed to take the two vaccine doses from the cooler to them. He needed to provide them with the protection he'd been remiss in providing previously.

"I have to go with you, colonel. Even without a combat mask. I have to vaccinate my wife and daughter. After everything you've told me about the senator and his modified version of menglavirus, I can't take the chance they'll die from it. I have my wife's pistol. I'll hold my own."

The colonel sighed. He took Jasmine's pistol from Harrison, inspected it, and handed it back. "Stay well behind us—" he said. He abruptly stopped speaking. He crouched and told Harrison to do the same. The colonel kneeled behind the Tundra truck. He lifted his rifle toward the north, back towards the street. Harrison followed the colonel's lead and got down as well. A person was approaching them.

Right away, Harrison recognized the person. She was Selene.

"I know her," Harrison said. "She's Selene Torres. She works with me as our chief administrator."

The colonel lowered the rifle. Harrison stood up and ran into the street. Selene came towards them. She was rain-soaked and her hands were bloody. She didn't waste time in telling him what he needed to know.

"Jasmine and Sofia are safe. They're in Richard's biosafety lab." She eyed the men behind Harrison. "Who'd you bring?"

Harrison introduced the colonel and he stepped forward. "What do we need to know, Ms. Torres?" the colonel said to Selene.

"I saw five men on the security cameras," Selene said. "I don't know if there are more."

"Was Gregory Miller one of them?"

Selene clearly didn't recognize the name, so Harrison clarified: "The man without a mask."

"Yes."

"What about Richard?" Harrison said, preparing to ask the question for which he thought he probably already knew the answer. "Is he in the biosafety lab as well?"

"No."

"What is he doing?"

"Buying time."

He is waiting for Gregory Miller, Harrison thought.

"Did you bring the vaccines?" Selene said.

"Yes."

"Give them to me. I'll take them back along the cliff and get back into the lab."

"No, Selene. Thank you. But no. I'll take the vaccines to them."

"I'm better qualified, Harrison. I'm a hiker and I know those cliffs already because I've already gone through them once. It's raining and those cliffs are only going to get harder to pass."

The colonel agreed. "The cliffs are a good option, doctor," he said. "If your wife and daughter are accessible via the cliffs, Ms. Torres can hike to them. She can vaccinate your wife and daughter. You stay here, doctor. Your vaccine needs you."

Harrison knew Selene was right—she knew those cliffs and knew how to navigate them having already traversed them once. Still, there was one reason that overruled all others and he said it now.

"I want to see my family," Harrison said to Selene, and the colonel, and to himself.

Harrison could tell Selene wanted to convince him she was the best person for getting back into the biosafety, but he knew she wouldn't. He knew she understood.

Sure enough, she said, "You need the emergency access code to the lab. It overrides the facial recognition cameras. The same code allows entry back in through the two emergency exits feeding into the cliff."

"I'm ready," Harrison said, "whenever you are." Emergency exits of course didn't require access codes for egress as leaving in a hurry was the goal. But having restricted access for entering through emergency exits was the norm, particularly when related to biosafety research facilities.

"72070," Selene said.

He repeated it. "Did you use any pneumonic to remember it?"

"It's my birthday. July 7, 1970."

Harrison felt embarrassed. He had no idea July 20, 1970 was Selene's birthday. Every year, a couple of weeks after the Fourth of July, she took a few additional days off of work, but he'd never thought anything of it other than assuming she was maximizing the summer. Come to think of it, he'd never celebrated her birthday or anybody else's while he'd been at Riogenrix. Now he knew.

"I'm sorry," he started to say, but Selene cut him off.

She handed him a two-way radio. It was one of the house's internal handsets.

"Who has the other one?" he said, although he already had an inkling.

"Richard."

Harrison took the two-way radio. He turned to the colonel. "I won't keep you any longer, colonel," he said. "Thank you for helping me and my family. I'll see you on the inside."

"Yes, I'll see you on the inside, doctor," the colonel said. "I'll see you at the ground floor lab." He turned towards his men who were waiting on the curb and made a gesture in the air. The three contractors headed towards the house as the colonel fell into step behind them. Harrison watched them before turning back towards Selene.

He had the two-way radio in his hand. He hadn't spoken to Richard in days. He didn't know how much time he had but knew he needed to say thank you. He pressed the connect button on the radio. Richard picked up.

"Are you safe?" Harrison said.

"I am," Richard said. His voice was distant but firm, confident as always. "So are Jasmine and Sofia. And so is the vaccine. I brokered a deal with Jason Carr of Steptech. He's ready to receive the world into his arms. He promised me he'll do the right thing. He'll get the vaccine out to the world."

"You made the right choice with V-202," Harrison said.

"*You* made the right choices, Harrison. Every day you worked on the vaccine, you made choices, and you made the right choices, because the vaccine works, and the vaccine will save hundreds of millions of lives and bring seven billion people back into the world."

Harrison paused. He knew what he wanted to say and wanted to make sure he said it all. He thought of the two decades they'd spent working together, first as a student and teacher and then as partners, not exactly a father-son relationship, but a relationship just as important—a student who had learned from a teacher who had wanted to teach him, a bond not even menglavirus could break. "Thank you, Richard. I can't express how important your guidance and confidence in me has been over the years. You took me in as a student and treated me as a colleague from day one."

"I did what every good mentor does. I believed in people who could advance the field."

"How have you been feeling, Richard?"

"Better than ever."

But Harrison could hear the breathlessness as Richard spoke.

"Use the nonrebreather, Richard. We'll be there soon for you."

They disconnected and Harrison pocketed the handset. He didn't know if he would ever see Richard again but he knew Richard Hahn would live on not only in his work but in the people whose lives he'd touched, as a mentor, partner, and friend.

"Ready?" Selene said. "If you're leaving, you need to leave now."

Harrison nodded and opened the cooler. He removed the two prefilled syringes with needles and packed them into his pants pocket while Selene reviewed the route with him.

He glanced towards the house once more. The night was windy and rainy, so different than it'd been earlier in the week. Soon he would see Jasmine and Sofia. He would be clear in expressing his love to them. As he turned back around, he saw a flash of light and heard an explosion.

"Time to get going," Selene said.

"I would like to celebrate your birthday this year, Selene. I'll plan the party."

Selene nodded but looked wistful, as if she wasn't sure the celebration was going to happen. He reached out his hand and she took it and they shook hands as two people who'd worked together for a decade but hadn't gotten to know each other until only recently. He felt the warmth of her personality in that shake. When they let go, he turned, and headed up Farm Road to the trailhead that would start him on the path around the cliff and to the biosafety laboratory on the bottom floor of Richard's house.

Jasmine and Sofia, he thought, *I'll see you soon.*

Richard Hahn wasn't hard to find. He was on the top floor, tucked away in his bedroom. He wasn't hiding, but instead was sitting in a chair beside an end table with a portable tank of oxygen at his side and a nonrebreather mask on his face. He had a handset in one hand and in the other he was holding the mask to his face as if every oxygenated breath was a godsend. Gregory stood inside the large bedroom and surveyed it. It was set up against the cliffs to take advantage of the views. The bedroom was simply appointed. A king-sized bed occupied one corner of the room while the reading chair and end table occupied the other. The room felt empty, though, as sterile as any operating room he'd been in as a student. And it was about to feel even emptier.

Gregory eyed the end table but saw nothing on it but a few books and journals. He could tell the bedroom wasn't a place where the old man got any work done. He approached Richard, walking around the end table, and took the handset from him. The Riogenrix founder offered up resistance, but it didn't amount to much. Clearly, Richard Hahn was frail and getting weaker. Gregory examined the handset and recognized it as an in-house walkie-talkie intended for panic situations. It was older technology but clearly relevant right now.

"How many of these do you have and where are the other ones?" he said.

Richard didn't answer. Gregory didn't really care about the answer itself but did care that the old man thought he didn't need to answer in the first place.

"Let's move on, Hahn. Where is the doctor's wife? Where is his daughter?"

Again, Richard didn't answer, but unlike with the handsets, Gregory *did* care about the answer. The house was big and would take time to search, even with his four-man team. He pressed the button labeled CONNECT to figure out how many people were on the other handsets and who they were. There was silence. Nobody immediately responded. He waited. Sure enough, a man's voice came through.

"Are you okay, Richard?"

Gregory smiled. He recognized the voice. Harrison had the other handset. Gregory wasn't sure how Harrison had managed to get it but didn't waste time on the matter. He kind of liked he had his former classmate on the other line.

"Don't respond, Harrison," Richard Hahn said. "I don't have the handset. The man without the mask has it."

Gregory's smile widened. *The man without the mask.* He liked the way it sounded, like a new form of the Lone Ranger but with a twist. Still, he liked the way 'doctor' sounded better. He'd spent the entirety of his career in biomedical espionage being careful to distinguish between having gone to medical school and having graduated with a doctorate in medicine. Part of his allure as a trusted resource for obtaining biomedical information was because clients assumed he *was* a doctor. After all, he wore the white coat. But he'd always been careful not to *call* himself a doctor. He supposed the reluctance was own insecurity. Today, though, he thought about recognizing himself for what he was. He *was* a doctor, goddammit. He'd done everything he'd needed except for six weeks and one walk. When the Russians picked up V-202 from him, they would recognize him as he deserved to be recognized. In their eyes, he was a doctor. They'd been calling him as such during his negotiations with them—and he hadn't stopped them from doing so.

"Although I appreciate the nickname the old man has given me, you can call me Dr. Miller. You can also tell me if you're coming my way, Harrison."

"You're not a doctor, Gregory," Harrison said. "Not because I care about a few weeks of medical school. I don't. You know enough to be a doctor. In fact, you know more than enough. But you're not fit to be a doctor. You're not upholding the values of medicine. But you can change. Let my wife and daughter go. You can have me instead."

"I feel like we already went down that route, Harrison."

Harrison started saying something else, but Gregory turned off the handset, and tossed it across the room. He had no use for it. He was done talking to Harrison. The old man, however, was another story. He sat down on the bed across from him.

"I applied to your lab at Salk as a student," Gregory said to Richard, letting himself sink into the mattress. "Gregory Miller. Third-year at Hopkins. I guess you didn't like my recommendations, though. I guess *I* didn't like them either."

"I don't know what you mean. I don't remember your application."

"I was a student at Hopkins. One year behind Harrison Boyd to start, same year as Harrison Boyd to end."

"Student rotations at Salk were always competitive. I'm sorry if we didn't accept you, Gregory."

"I"m 'Dr. Miller' now. Forget the past, old man. Tell me what you know about V-202. Maybe you and I can work together now and I won't need your partner's wife and daughter after all. Shall we head to your computer?"

Gregory stood up. Richard didn't, so he pulled him to his feet. He would drag the old man if need be. Even though he knew Richard Hahn was deteriorating, Gregory was feeling great, better by the minute.

Richard was struggling. Harrison had been right to tell him to use the nonrebreather. He had been feeing increasingly short of breath since he'd first left the house and the shortness of breath had worsened after the walk down the stairs to the bottom floor with Sofia in his arms. He knew his health had caught up to him. He also knew this time there would be no preventing his body from failing. There would be no immunotherapy, no months of steroids, no escalating doses of methotrexate. He'd arrived at the last part of his life. He'd spoken the truth when he'd whispered in Sofia's ear about today and tomorrow and the year and decades to come.

Gregory Miller—he refused to call him a doctor because to call him one was to give in to the man's madness—hadn't allowed him to bring the oxygen with him. He didn't care about himself right now. As Gregory forced him through the house, Gregory removed a metal canister from his lab coat. He kept rubbing his fingers over it. Richard had a good idea what the canister contained. He had one goal—stall. He needed to buy time for Harrison and whatever Harrison had figured out. The longer he kept Gregory looking for the developmental details related to the vaccine, the longer that Harrison had to organize a response from the outside.

Gregory dragged him through the double doors that led into his home office. His office was also on the top floor of the house, but set against the street rather than the ocean. He'd always considered a view an unnecessary accoutrement for serious work. The office was divided into two halves. The first was an area for sitting. Here he had a couch along one wall, two oversized arm chairs along the wall adjacent, a coffee table placed in between them, and a bar with an undercounter fridge. When he'd still been a working man, this part of the office had been where he would sit with guests who also were part of the industry. It was where they would discuss business and medicine and the unrelenting march of science, where they would have a tumbler of whisky and discuss the scientific loves of their lives. When he was alone, it was where he sat to catch up on research journals and review studies. The other part of the office was where he did light work. He had a desk with a workstation, filing cabinets, and built-in bookcases.

He avoided the half of the office where the workstation was and instead sat on the couch. He was legitimately worn out now. Beyond worn out. He glanced at the wall. On it, he'd hung a genuine Ray Robertson painting he'd bought on a whim in his early days after exiting from Steptech. He'd bought it at an auction in Melbourne when he'd traveled the world for two months, taking the break he'd told himself he needed and deserved.

At the time, he'd known nothing about Robertson—and still knew very little—but had liked the clean lines, color, and abstract cityscapes of the painting, and so he'd bought it for seven hundred and fifty thousand dollars without hesitation. Of course, the gravity of what he'd done had set in afterwards, when he'd actually received the painting via chartered courier service a month later in his new La Jolla house. The feeling hadn't been about the painting itself or even about the huge sum of money he'd spent, but it'd been about the implications. He'd been in his late fifties at the time and should've been in the prime of his research career, but instead was becoming a man who collected art while knowing nothing about it. Two days after the purchase, he'd reached out to the Salk Institute to formalize a research position there. From then on, he'd admired the painting as a reminder of what he was—a physician-scientist— and what he wasn't—an art collector and everything else.

"Wrong place, old man."

"I'm fatigued. I can barely breathe."

"Get to your computer, old man."

"We can talk here."

"Oh, can we?"

Gregory went to the desk himself. He sat down in the high-back executive chair. He moved the mouse and glanced at the computer monitor before moving onto the drawers. "One question, one answer," he said, as he shuffled within. "Let's see what you really know, whether you're worthwhile to me after all. How did Harrison allow for exact cytosome delivery while also providing for interactions with endosomal RNA receptors? How did he achieve what has always been a failing of mRNA vaccines? The lack of immunostimulations induced by cytosome delivery? We'll start there, old man."

Richard actually did know the answer. He'd developed the technique a decade ago with Harrison as they'd worked on the BOOSTers. It was a complex process requiring significant technical know-how. If Richard could share this information with the man in enough detail, he could keep him here for several more minutes. They could even repeat this process with several other questions. Harrison would certainly have enough time to get whatever he was working on well underway and executed.

"It's a complex problem," Richard started to say, planning to go into minute detail to buy time. But as soon as he started to explain, he stopped, because Gregory had located the hard drives labeled A1 and A2 in the bottom drawer of the desk. He held them up. He turned them over, inspecting them. He plugged one and then the other into the computer workstation. Richard again tried to broach the topic of immunostimulations, again hoping to delay him, but the crazy man held up his hand.

"Shut up, old man. I'll take these. The A drives, huh? They're much better than the B drives I got. They're a hell more complete, that's for sure." Gregory picked the canister off of the desk and stood up. He walked towards Richard. "Which leaves us with only one more question— where are the mother and daughter?"

Richard felt the shortness of breath worsening but told himself to push through. He wasn't going to tell Gregory anything about Jasmine and Sofia but still needed get him talking to continue to stall. Even a minute would help.

"What do you have in the canister?" Richard said.

"Something I don't think you're going to need, old man. Where are they?"

"They're not here."

"One more chance, old man."

Richard didn't answer.

Gregory removed a pistol from the side of his leg and pointed it at Richard. As the pistol was raised to his face, Richard looked at the painting again. He didn't want to look at Gregory. He knew what was coming and was okay with it if it allowed Harrison the time he needed to get to Jasmine and Sophia. As he looked at the painting, he realized he'd been wrong about its relevance to him. He'd always admired the painting as a reminder of what he was and what he wasn't, but now he realized he'd made a faulty conclusion. He was a physician-scientist, but he was also a friend, godfather, and mentor.

Before he died at the hands of the crazy man without a mask, he understood he was much more than he'd allowed himself to believe during the last five years of his life.

Much more.

She didn't know if he believed her, but she'd placated him at least. Naomi had finally told the senator what he'd wanted to hear, which was that she wanted to terminate the pregnancy. She told him the pregnancy was an accident. It wasn't what she wanted with her future in front of her. She told him she loved him and she would do what he advised.

Naomi was back in the condo with Senator Scott. She was pacing the bedroom, trying to figure out her future. The senator was in the living room. Naomi finally was acknowledging what she'd always known, which was that she'd never had a legitimate relationship with the senator. At times, she'd thought she had. She'd thought he'd cared about her. Most of the time, she'd even considered herself fortunate to have him in her life. But their relationship had been one of convenience. She'd wanted to get away from her mother and so she'd gone to Las Vegas when menglavirus had choked San Diego, but Las Vegas had decayed as well. After a couple of months trying to subsist amongst the wreckage of the virus, she'd gone to him. He'd accepted her by putting her up in these towers. Now, her mother was gone. She had no disillusionments over the strained relationship they'd had but knew that what she had with the senator was worse than what she'd had with her mother. Her way forward in life was with herself and her baby. There was no more mother with whom she could reconcile and there was no relationship here with the senator in which she could prosper. She knew she and her baby were living on borrowed time so long as the senator was still around.

She didn't know all of the details, but she knew enough to makes sense of what was happening. The senator had a vaccine to menglavirus. Somehow, he was going to use the virus to catapult himself into the presidency. She also knew he wasn't bringing her along on his trip to the White House. Of course, he wasn't bringing the baby along either.

For him, there was no baby. For her, there was. She didn't know how she would be able to raise a baby in a world of menglavirus, but she knew she needed to believe in herself. She'd never considered having a child before. She wasn't even confident she wanted to have a child—the termination sounded right at times —but she felt a pull towards creating an existence that was better than the one she'd had. The pull had only intensified since she'd seen her mother dead. She wanted to be better to her child than her mother had been to her.

She left the bedroom and went to the living room. She would have only once chance.

She knew what she had to do.

Col. Burt Johnson was having a flashback. He pictured a beaten down town in the Iraqi desert with sandstorms and choking heat. He remembered flaring violence getting worse by the week. He remembered mothers, fathers, and children caught in between too many sides to separate, all of them losing lives, loved ones, and subsistence. He thought of the men and women with whom he'd served, men and women who were honorable in intent, wanting to serve their country while serving the people whose towns and homes they were supposed to protect. Despite the way all aspects of policy and circumstance had been stacked against him, he'd done good work, kept up his ethics, maintained comfort for those who'd needed it, which had been everyone in those decimated towns. When he left battle for military medicine after five years, he hadn't been disillusioned. Instead, he'd wanted to double down on saving the mothers, fathers, and children over whom he had charge. Trauma and vascular surgery had been the right decision for him.

But Burt wasn't in Iraq anymore and hadn't been in almost two decades. He was in La Jolla, involved in a raid on a domicile to rescue a mother and daughter and whomever else were inside the large house, in what should've been sunny San Diego, but instead was a rainy, windy battle zone. He signaled to Camel he was ready to proceed onwards and they entered the house through the imploded front door. Camel and his men were the lead on the rescue operation and he was the assist. He was less concerned about the bullets and bombs that would fly and more concerned about the virus that would leak. He had no delusions. He knew the target—Gregory Miller—would release the modified version of menglavirus, the super-GOF'ed version, if he hadn't already.

He didn't know if the doctor would be successful in navigating the cliffs, but he would bet on him. He'd seen the determination in the doctor's personality the first time they'd met at

West. The doctor's vaccine, V-202, had been as much a consequence of the doctor's unwavering persistence as his brilliance. Burt's goal was to deal with the men occupying the house so the doctor could reach his wife and daughter with the vaccines. Burt had never thought in terms of suicide missions before. The US Army wasn't one to make its soldiers expendable. *Suicide mission* wasn't part of his lexicon. He fully intended to leave La Jolla at some point with Camel and his men. He didn't know in what shape they would be, but he knew they would be alive. He didn't get the same sense about the doctor.

Although the doctor had a chance getting into the house via the cliffs, he wasn't a military person. If the doctor got involved in a standoff or firefight that Camel, he, or the team couldn't dissolve, the doctor wouldn't be leaving La Jolla, regardless of what happened with the GOF menglavirus. Burt knew that to honor the doctor, he needed to not only get the wife and daughter out, but also get the doctor's vaccine out to the public.

Camel gave the team the signal to move forward. All of them had their biosafety combat masks on. They didn't have full biochemical warfare suits, but they had the best available equipment for them right now in this moment. Burt checked his rifle, patted the pistol at his thigh, and followed the team through the massive house on the cliff.

Gregory didn't allow himself to feel poorly. He had goals. The old man had placed himself between Gregory and his goals. Gregory knew he'd had to kill the old man. He'd given Richard Hahn a choice and Richard Hahn had chosen to die. Gregory wasn't a person who spoke false promises. He'd established his own self-ethics in medical school when he'd walked away from matriculation after getting screwed over by the residency programs. He'd lived every day of his life since expressing no regret over his decision. He wasn't about to express regret now. He hadn't wanted to waste a canister on the old man. A bullet was better.

He had the portable hard drives labeled A1 and A2 in the side pockets of his lab coat. Even so, he would need time, at least a couple of days, to delve into its contents. Now, he just needed to get out of San Diego. He knew the colonel was headed inside the house—if he hadn't already made it. The wife and daughter would act as leverage for him. He planned to walk out the front door, get on a private plane at San Diego Airport, and start his new life. He didn't intend to be felled in a firefight.

He left the office, closing the double doors behind him. One of his hired guns was approaching him with a quickened stride from the living room. Gregory understood what the urgency meant. He was right—the colonel was on the premises.

"How many men?" Gregory said.

"We count four, which includes the colonel."

"Military?"

"Ex-military, most likely."

"Contractors?"

"Yes, seems like it."

"So they're just like you guys. Not a problem, right?" He patted his lab coat where he'd placed the A drives. "Besides, your payday just went up. It'll go up again if you find the wife and daughter."

"They're on the bottom floor. They're in some kind of biosafety lab."

"Get them."

"The lab has reinforced steel doors. It has glazed windows It has security access."

"So? Use the explosives."

The contractor shook his head and Gregory understood. He'd made a miscalculation, hadn't figured out ahead of time what he realized now. The biosafety lab was built with pylons onto the bedrock. An explosion in a part of the house directly embedded in the cliff and buttressed by the pylons would transfer the explosive forces to the biosafety lab itself, thereby causing the lab, and the house above it, to implode. If Gregory wanted to secure the wife and daughter, or even walk out the front door rather than wading through crumbled concrete, he wouldn't be able to blast his way into the biosafety lab.

"We have advantages," Gregory said. "The first is location. We already occupy the space. We can hold them off. We *should* hold them off. The other advantage is science. We have the better science." He held up the canisters. "Stave them off, keep your masks and suits on, and in a few hours, we'll walk right out of here as the last men standing. Get the HVAC system on full blast. Let's get the air circulating through here to make sure we aerosolize the entire facility. We release a canister on every floor."

"Do you still want the woman and girl?"

"How much time do you need to crack the access code to the lab?"

"Ten minutes if I can find a control room."

"Get started."

The contractor nodded and turned back towards the living room.

"One more thing," Gregory said. "Give them FN99 masks."

The contractor nodded again and left.

Gregory wanted to walk out with the wife and daughter but knew doing so would be a luxury. Once he opened the canister, he wasn't going to be walking out with them. Besides himself, no one not in a full biosafety respiratory suit was going to walk out of the house. While the native menglavirus had an incubation period of days, the modified version nMAQ61 had an incubation period of only minutes. No more than one hour after exposure to nMAQ61, the infected person felt the typical prodromal symptoms of fatigue and body aches. No more than two hours after exposure, the infected person's symptoms manifested with cough and shortness of breath. No more than three hours after exposure, the person experienced a full cytokine storm whereby walking even a few steps would be unexpected and herculean.

He only needed to hold out for two or three hours. He palmed one of the canisters. He was getting closer to where he needed to be. He had every intention of walking out of here.

Harrison felt the urgency in every small step he took along the rocky cliffs, knowing each second that passed represented another possibility of harm. He needed to get to them. Selene was right. Of course, she was right. He hadn't doubted her when she'd said he would struggle to gain access to the house from the cliff, but he didn't have any other options.

As he inched his way around a narrow bend in the darkness, he felt his foot slipping. He grabbed onto the face of the cliffs with his hands and knew he was tearing them open but held on the best he could. The more it rained, the colder it got. The rain pelted him. He felt his ankle twisting, slipping away from him. He knew if his ankle dipped below the cliff the rest of him would follow. He gripped the cliff more tightly and felt wetness from the blood breaking through the skin but held on. The two syringes were in his side pocket and he hoped he hadn't crushed them as he'd tried to pull himself into the rocks.

For a moment, the wind gusted in the opposite direction, fortuitously pinning him against the cliff rather than ripping him from the ledge. He used the gust to pull himself back up. He brought his ankle up and felt his foot gain stability on the path below. With both of his feet on the path again, he went forward, knowing each step brought him closer to his family.

Now that he had the A drives, Gregory felt redemption. He had what should have been his, if not in actuality, then in process. He had been the top medical student at Johns Hopkins for his class during the first two academic years and he should have excelled in the clinical years as well but the hierarchical nature of medicine had held him back. If he had one regret about working with the Russians, it was that he would never gain the recognition he deserved here in the US. He would never have the medical degree from Johns Hopkins.

As he walked towards the stairs leading to the two floors below, he raised a canister. He brought it out in front of him, disengaged the safety mechanism, and opened the release valve.

Here comes the cytokine storm, he thought.

As a viral load in the millions escaped from the canister, he knew that if he had to do the project all over again, he would've separated himself from the senator at an earlier stage. He probably wouldn't have taken the wife and daughter. They were only pieces to be moved, not the pieces that mattered. He would've nabbed the research on V-202 before it hit clinical trials, learned how to fill in the gaps himself, and taken it to market himself, here in the US. He had no doubt that he would've had billions in capital lining up to help him out. He might even have spoken to Johns Hopkins about those six weeks of medical school he hadn't completed. He was sure that with a menglavirus vaccine in his repertoire, the stiffs at the medical school would've been happy to complete his degree, make official his doctorate in medicine.

If he would've kept an eye on Harrison at a much earlier stage, before Phase 2 data, he would've had a chance at being what he knew deep down he wanted to be. He could've really been a doctor, a true physician-scientist from Johns Hopkins, where the best of physician-scientists originated.

Now that novel menglavirus strain 61 with gain of function was spreading in the house, he went down the stairs.

Naomi McGraw was waiting. Watching the senator and waiting. Waiting for him to get another phone call. She was sitting across from him in the living room, listening to him talk about the presidency. She had difficulty believing that even two days ago she'd been fascinated by him. Now, he just sounded desperate, like a man who thought he deserved what he didn't. She was nodding, playing along, hearing but not listening. Biding her time. Waiting for the right moment.

Finally, his phone rang. He glanced at it, smiled, and went

outside to the balcony to take the call.

Yes, she'd been waiting for this moment. She got up and went to the sliding glass door he'd closed behind him. She watched him. He eyed her through the glass but didn't stop speaking or pacing the balcony. She couldn't hear what he was saying through the panes but didn't care. She wasn't focused on his life. His battle wasn't hers. Her battle wasn't the White House. Her battle was turning the corner on her own life, moving forward, and starting anew with her baby. She found herself wanting to touch her belly. She couldn't explain the concern she had for the little baby growing inside of her. Nor could she understand the unease she felt about letting her baby down. But she had these feelings. They were new but real.

She waited, patiently. As he would expect her to wait. While he talked on the phone on the balcony. She waited on the other side of the glass slider. She made sure to wait long enough. Until just the right moment. Until he was too focused on his phone call to wonder about her.

She opened the slider.

He saw it coming, but she was fast, and he wasn't able to stop her. She charged into him, pushing him towards the unfinished edge of the balcony. He stumbled and tried to collect his balance but she crouched and pushed forward.

He teetered at the edge of the railing.

She knew what to do. She continued doing it. She knelt, grabbed his leg, and stood back up, using the entirety of her force to carry him over the balcony. He went over the railing. He reached at her but she kept pushing, kept putting her weight and strength into the lift until she'd thrown him over the balcony.

She watched him as he fell from the sixty-first floor.

She stood by herself on the balcony, just her and her baby.

As Harrison neared the last bend of the cliff, he saw only a straight line separating him from the house. From here on in, he had a legitimate trail to follow. He wanted to run but stopped himself, knowing his forte had always been steadiness. The rain was violent and the wind seemed to shake the ground. If he ran now, he risked the chance of falling from the rain-slicked cliffs into the turbulent, rocky waters below. He checked the two vaccine syringes in his pocket, felt that both were still intact, and thought he and the colonel were going to pull off the rescue after all. He told himself not to mess up now. He maintained a constant speed, deliberate and measured, until he reached the emergency exit door along the side of the biosafety lab. He knew there was another emergency exit door within the biosafety lab itself but to reach it would require one more stretch of hazard that would take several more minutes to traverse.

He went for the nearest exit, inputting the access code Selene had given to him. Again, he thought about the decade he'd spent working with her but not getting to know her. When he'd been a resident at Hopkins, staff birthdays for the nurses, technicians, and support staff were always causes of celebration. Attending physicians bought meals, nurses brought food, and residents celebrated with hungry stomachs and worn-out bodies the birthdays of those hospital staff members who were as much a part of their educations as were the patients and journals. Harrison remembered those quick hospital parties jammed into break rooms. He'd been fond of them back then, excited to commemorate with those whom he worked. He wondered what had happened to him over the past several years. He'd immersed himself in his mRNA vaccine work at Riogenrix while ignoring everything and everyone else around him.

He entered the access code. For a second, nothing happened. He waited for the click at the emergency exit to sound, signifying the door was now unlocked. The click didn't happen. He took a deep breath and reentered the number, wondering now if he'd entered the right number in the first place.

July 20, 1970.

He entered 72070 again.

Again, there was silence, but after a second of nothingness, he heard the click. He figured he simply hadn't heard it the first time because of the wind. He pulled on the door and entered Richard's house, knowing the modified version of menglavirus and the rapid sickness to which it led awaited him, but also knowing Jasmine and Sofia were awaiting him as well. He wondered if the colonel was thinking the same thing. He wondered if the colonel had contacted anyone for additional backup, maybe the San Diego SWAT team or even just a few regular police officers, anyone to help in the rescue operation. Or he wondered, if instead, the colonel had decided taking the house by themselves was the only option because of the modified menglavirus Gregory possessed.

He wondered only for an instant. He knew the answer. The colonel thought the same as he. They were on their own. Harrison took a deep breath of the outside air, a mix of cold saltwater spray and rain. He breathed as much of the air as he could because he knew every step he took inside the house was going to push Gregory Miller's modified GOF mengalvirus deeper into his system.

For several minutes, Selene stood on the street, facing the famous Paulson House that Richard owned and occupied. She looked for signals that Harrison and the colonel were progressing or had even achieved success. The rain intensified and she became soaked through, but she stood and watched. The house was set below the street, causing her view to be obstructed. The rain only made the sightline worse. Finally, she withdrew from the street and stood under a scraggly tree.

She found herself praying, something she hadn't done in a long time, at least since when she had met Bill in her early thirties and married him without hesitation. She wasn't a religious person, didn't hold onto a sense of faith. She'd become a person of science during the decades she'd worked in the mRNA space. Since her roles had always been administrative and operational—first with Steptech, then with the Salk Institute, and finally with Riogenrix—she'd become methodical. The faith she'd once had hadn't exactly vanished, but it'd definitely gone underground. It'd become something about which she thought little, because she'd spent the bulk of her life thinking about the details of keeping research labs and institutions running.

She prayed now, though. She remembered her husband and the way he'd had faith. It'd been a foolish faith, but it'd been a faith nonetheless, believing he would never fall so long as God looked over him. She felt good praying, as if praying were a way to remember Bobby and the life they'd led. She'd done her best to continue her life after his death. Now, fifteen years later, she'd lived a life she was proud of. She'd been lonely at times but hadn't felt alone until the past couple of years when mengla-virus had gone from being something the government had promised would be gone in an instant, to something the medical community had promised was here to stay.

She didn't know to whom she was praying or whether she was even praying at all or simply putting together her thoughts, but she reviewed the life she'd had thus far, one full of various, changing types of love, friendship, and independence. She knew that even though the details of those involved in her life would change again, she would still have love, friendship, and independence at the end.

After praying, she felt better, but the relief was brief, because a few seconds after collecting her thoughts, the anxiety of watching and waiting returned, as if she hadn't prayed at all.

When they moved past the foyer, the gunfire began. Camel signaled positions to the team and they took them. Burt knew the tactics they were employing were as basic as could be. They were going to take fire, fire back, advance, reestablish positions, and do it all again. Camel and the team would handle the bulk of the engagement while Burt made his way down two stories to the biosafety lab, where he hoped he would encounter the doctor's wife and daughter alive. Even if the doctor succeeded in gaining access to the biosafety lab, he didn't think any of the three of them stood a chance of navigating the cliffs back up to the road. The rain had gone from intermittent showers to a steady drizzle to a downright downpour. The rocky trail of the cliff would be impassable, if it wasn't already.

Take fire.

Give fire.

Incapacitate the targets and move forward.

The way through the house was straightforward. He fired back at the targets and waited for Camel's signal to move forward. He knew the doctor and the doctor's wife and daughter depended on him. He knew he wasn't going to let them down.

Harrison heard the noises coming from upstairs. He understood the colonel had entered the house. If Harrison had been any later, he would've been too late to get to his wife and daughter. He walked quickly along the bottom floor of the Paulson House, slowing at corners to make sure Gregory or his men weren't waiting for him. Even so, he never stopped walking, because he knew hesitation would end them all. His goal was to enter the biosafety lab to vaccinate Jasmine and Sofia. Thereafter, he would guard the lab from outside by hunkering down and providing the last line of defense until the colonel arrived. He knew Jasmine and Sofia needed to be in the lab until they achieved full immunity, at least twenty-four hours. He knew the time for walking out the front door had passed. He didn't consider what he would need to do if the colonel didn't arrive. He knew failure was not an option and the colonel knew as well.

He finally reached the biosafety laboratory carved into the bottom floor. There were two polycarbonate windows on each side of the entry door. He peered inside but didn't see Jasmine or Sofia in the prep room. The prep room had another two windows looking into the decon unit. He tried to see through the second set of windows but didn't see much. He certainly couldn't see clearly into the workspace. The room had fluorescent lights running continually whether there was someone in the lab or not, but right now the lights were running on the minimum setting. He hoped Jasmine and Sofia were there.

He returned to the door, ignored the facial recognition camera, and entered the emergency override code, having no doubt about what it was anymore: 72070. He would never forget. The door clicked and he pulled it open, walked through the prep room, and directly to the next door leading into the decontamination area. Once inside the decon space, he went to the final door. He pushed another button. The final door opened and he walked into the workspace of the clinical lab.

He didn't see Jasmine or Sofia at first but didn't have to see them to know they were there. He felt them, the same way he'd felt their presence every single night he'd spent in the house with them. Even when he'd come home late, he'd felt their presence, their energy in the house, something that made the house seem alive. He felt the same way now.

"Jasmine," he said. "Sofia," he said. "I'm here." He hesitated, wondering if he needed to say anything else—*It's Harrison* or *It's Dad*—but then he heard movement and finally saw them.

Jasmine appeared first, coming out from one of the airlock stations. He saw the expression on her face he'd seen a few days ago, the same expression she'd had when she'd told him she'd gone to the park, an expression that was a mix of determination and weariness. In that moment, he felt his own weariness and understood no matter what happened now, even if they all escaped unscathed, there was no way to undo the hurt he'd caused her over the years.

A split second later, Sofia appeared. In that moment, as he saw Jasmine and Sofia standing together, he shook off his weariness. Life could never feel better than it did right now.

He withdrew the two vaccine syringes, held them up, and went towards his family.

Sofia knew she was sick. She knew she'd gotten the virus that had kept them inside for so long, the virus they'd been avoiding. She felt tired and had a headache and her body hurt. Since she was sick, she knew she shouldn't go to Daddy. But she couldn't stop herself. He was coming to her and she wanted to go to him as well. She started towards him, but felt her mommy pulling her back. At first, she resisted. Then she saw the astronaut entering Uncle Richard's lab. She saw the astronaut passing through the room that Mommy had said was for cleaning away infections. She understood why Mommy was pulling her back.

Sofia stopped going forward. As she let Mommy pull her back, she saw the astronaut gain access to where they were, where Daddy now was, the part of the lab where Uncle Richard did his work. She knew the astronaut was here to get her father. The astronaut was here to get them all.

She'd spent a lot of nights waiting up for Daddy to tell him about the astronauts, but hadn't been able to stay up late enough. Now, she would make sure that Daddy knew about the astronauts. She raised her hand, pointed at the astronaut, and screamed.

Daddy turned around.

As she screamed, she thought, *I finally told Daddy.*

He finally knew.

Naomi stood in the kitchen with the cooler on the counter. She withdrew the syringe. She stared at it as she rotated it, wondering if it was real, whether menglavirus really would be a thing of the past for her. She decided that soon she would find out. She tapped the syringe to get rid of the air bubbles, just like she remembered from her own shots, back when she'd been a kid, back when she used to get childhood immunizations, back when her mother hadn't yet succumbed in full to the bottle. She injected herself in the arm and placed the used syringe back in the cooler and left the cooler on the kitchen counter.

She had no bags or luggage but she had a mask and she put it on. She would use the mask for the next few days—and maybe even a week, just to be sure—until immunity kicked in. She knew the senator's contractors would come to the condo but she had no intention of being here when they did.

She left the condo through the front door and walked to the emergency staircase at the end of the hallway. As she passed the fire alarm, she pulled on it. She waited for the alarm to sound. Sure enough, it did. She figured the confusion of the alarm coupled with the senator's smashed body on the concrete would create enough havoc for her to walk out of the casino forever. She patted her belly, felt her baby, and started down the first of sixty-one flights of stairs to the rest of her life.

For a moment, Harrison felt joy. He had never felt such happiness as when he saw Jasmine and Sofia again. Now the joy was gone. He felt terror. He knew even before he turned around that Gregory's men had found them. He saw Jasmine's expression change to one of alarm and heard Sofia scream. He wondered if he'd somehow led them right to his family. He envisioned them being ripped from him.

As he turned around, he felt a boot against his calf. His balance wavered and he felt the fall as it was happening. He foresaw himself crushing the two syringes of V-202 and knew he had to get them to Jasmine. As he hit the floor, he shifted the syringes to avoid compressing them against his body. He had made sure not to brace himself with his hands and instead absorbed the shock with his right shoulder. The fall hurt, sending numbness and pain along the entire right side of his upper body. He didn't know if he'd held on to the vaccines or protected them. As the man in the biosafety combat suit approached him, he turned his hand palm side up, saw the two syringes still clenched in his hand, and felt a moment of relief.

"What do you have there, man? Shots? For me?"

The man in the biosafety suit was standing over him. As the man reached down, Harrison summoned all the strength he had in his hand and flung the syringes towards Jasmine. He watched the syringes leave his fingers and arc in the air. They landed on the vinyl floor and rolled in Jasmine's direction. The man in the biosafety suit left Harrison and went after the vaccines.

Harrison felt pressure against the outside of his thigh where Jasmine's pistol was. He pulled it out from the holster the colonel had set up for him and held it in the air. He pointed the pistol at the man in the biosafety suit. He swept his thumb over the safety and flipped it into the off position. His hand was numb, so as he manipulated the pistol, he watched his hand to make sure it was doing what his brain was telling it to do. He aimed at the man in the biosafety suit, once again consciously directing his body. He didn't know if V-202 would provide enough immunity in such a short period of time against the modified GOF menglavirus Gregory had but he knew V-202 was better than nothing at all. He hoped it gave Jasmine and Sofia a chance and he knew they needed the vaccines now.

He fired twice.

His hand listened. The man didn't immediately fall, but stumbled forward several feet, giving Jasmine time to run towards the syringes.

Jasmine crouched in a sprinter's position.

She ran.

He kept the pistol trained on the man without a mask and waited for Jasmine to reach the syringes.

Jasmine saw Harrison had thrown something to her. As it landed on the floor, she saw exactly what it was. He'd rolled two syringes with attached needles towards her. She didn't need more than a moment to know what the syringes contained. Neither did she need to tell Sofia to stay where she was. Sofia knew. Of course, she knew.

She saw the man whom Sofia called an astronaut going after the vaccines and she saw Harrison raise the pistol at him and saw and heard and felt him fire it. As the astronaut stumbled, Jasmine moved, darting towards the syringes with whatever speed she could muster. She felt drained, worse now than even five minutes prior. She wondered how much longer she could hold out before feeling completely incapacitated. She went to the vaccine.

She saw the next few seconds happening before they happened. She saw the way the astronaut was losing his balance. She saw the syringes still rolling in her direction but losing velocity. She saw the astronaut still reaching for the syringes as Jasmine neared them. She saw him stumble. She saw the vaccines slide along his path. And she saw him trying to smash his feet on the syringes, as if he were thinking that if he can't have them, no one can.

She was at the syringes now. She was able to grab only one of them before the astronaut managed to bring his foot down on the other. She looked up at him, saw the angry eyes beyond the visor of his biosafety suit. She shoved him. He fell backwards and finally fell to the floor. She looked towards Harrison. They made eye contact and she knew he would do whatever he could to protect her and Sofia. As Jasmine looked backwards towards Harrison, she glanced at the monitors above the laboratory door and saw another astronaut approaching the main entrance of the biosafety lab. The man without a mask was standing behind the latest astronaut.

Harrison noted her gaze. She and Harrison didn't need to say anything to each other about what was happening. Despite their tribulations, they'd been married for fourteen years. She knew in this moment that Harrison could read her. He didn't have to turn around to look at the monitors to know.

She scooped up the second syringe as well. The astronaut had severely damaged it but she held out hope that it was still functional. She ran towards her daughter with the two syringes, the intact one and the damaged one. She knew she should rub alcohol along her daughter's arm before injecting the vaccine but also knew that wasn't going to happen.

"Lift your sleeve, honey," she said. Sofia was staring at the carnage in the lab, watching her father and the astronaut on the ground and the new astronaut gaining access to the biosafety lab. Jasmine touched her elbow. "Sofia, pay attention to me, honey. Lift up your shirt. Your daddy has a shot for you."

Sofia turned towards Jasmine as if she were surprised to see her there.

"Now, baby," Jasmine said.

Sofia broke out of her trance and pulled up her shirt. Jasmine uncapped the undamaged syringe and plunged the needle into the upper arm of her daughter. Sofia didn't flinch. "Good job, baby."

Jasmine inspected the second syringe, the damaged one, the one the astronaut had deliberately stepped on. The needle was twisted and the syringe itself was mostly crushed. While the syringe she'd used to inject Sofia had had a full half-a-milliliter of vaccine, the damaged syringe had less than half that amount. She glanced back towards the workspace entrance, saw the motionless astronaut on the floor, and saw the new astronaut swinging the main door open to the prep room. Again, she saw the man without a mask, also at the main door, waiting for the astronaut to clear the space in front of him. She looked at Harrison and they made eye contact again. He nodded. She returned her focus to the syringe. She straightened the needle, pulled her sleeve above her shoulder, and plunged the needle into her arm. She injected what remained of Harrison's vaccine into her own body.

When she looked back up towards Harrison again, the astronaut had entered the prep room and the man without a mask was right behind him.

Sofia didn't feel the injection. She remembered how Daddy used to tell her the best way she could help him out was by working with Mommy. He'd said this to her when she'd started home school, when she hadn't wanted to have Mommy as her teacher. She was working with Mommy now, though. She found herself doing what Mommy told her, even if she didn't know what she herself could do to help out Daddy.

She wanted to go to her daddy. She didn't like seeing Daddy on the ground. She knew he needed help. She knew that she couldn't give him the kind of help he needed but she could listen to Mommy.

She stood up, found herself stepping towards him. She felt Mommy pulling her back and now Sofia felt herself trying to run to him but Mommy held onto her. Sofia resisted the urge to break free. She needed to work with Mommy. She let Mommy bring her back and hold her.

"I love you, Daddy," she said. She found it hard to speak but knew he heard her. She was only saying everything he already knew.

She felt her mommy wrapping her arms around her, pinning her to her body. Sofia felt warm. She knew the warmth was from her own self but from Mommy too.

"Thank you, Daddy," she said, and let herself sink into her mommy's arms.

Jasmine heard her daughter.

Thank you, Daddy.

Harrison had failed in so many aspects of his marriage and family life. Right now, he was doing his best to succeed. Jasmine understood—Sofia understood as well—Harrison would sacrifice everything, including himself, for them. He was doing so now.

Harrison was getting up from the floor. Once on his feet, he mouthed *stay here* to Jasmine, before turning around and heading back towards the entrance of the lab. He exited through the same door from which he'd entered a few minutes prior, entering the decon unit. Jasmine watched on the monitor above the doorway as he sped through the decon unit to the door leading into the prep room, reversing the course he'd taken—they'd all taken—to get into the workspace of the biosafety laboratory.

At the same time Harrison reached the door leading back into the prep room, the second astronaut reached it from the other side.

While Camel and his team dealt with targets on the middle floor of the house, weaving themselves through hallways and bedrooms, Burt descended the stairs to the bottom floor. Each step of the way, Camel protected him, laying down fire. Camel's team had been exchanging gunfire with the targets for several minutes now, holding positions and advancing at deliberate paces, but Burt couldn't wait any longer. He knew he was working on a constricted time schedule.

When he reached the bottom floor, he understood why Harrison had gone radio silent. Gregory was downstairs with one of his own contractors, a man in a full-blown biochemical combat suit. The contractor had entered the first part of the lab, presumably a prep space. Gregory was at the main door. He was about to enter the space as well. He was going after the doctor's wife and daughter—again. From the bottom of the stairs, Burt aimed his rifle at the targets.

"Turn around, Gregory," he said, just as Gregory put his left foot into the lab.

Gregory turned around, but the colonel didn't feel any relief. He knew more targets were floating around the house. He didn't have a great idea as to where they were. Nonetheless, he knew he needed to focus on Gregory right now. He approached Gregory with his rifle aimed.

Sure enough, as the colonel neared Gregory, he saw a flicker from the corner of his eye. Had he been younger and still in the game as a solider, he would've had enough time to turn and fire at the flicker, thereby neutralizing the threat that existed, and then turn back around to the initial target, all before the initial target turned on him. But he wasn't younger, and he wasn't a man who lived as a solider anymore. By the time he turned towards the flicker to fire and neutralize the target, Gregory had fired at him. He felt the jolt in his shoulder as a bullet thudded through him. He couldn't maintain the positioning with the rifle. He stumbled and tried to prop himself against the concrete wall.

Gregory came towards him, his own gun raised. Burt told himself not to fail now. He was an army man, trained to survive. He would survive and he would finish the mission of rescuing the doctor's wife and daughter. Yet, he couldn't help but feel his mind slipping for a moment to his own past existence, as if he knew he was nearing the end of his own life. He'd had a good life, an honorable life, as a military man. He'd struggled as a family man while fulfilling his military life, but he'd certainly tried to keep the family together the best he could. He wished he had been present for his ex-wife and son more than he had, but he knew that for certain types of men and women, only narrow paths existed. He was one of those types. He'd chosen the path of his work. He didn't regret the decisions he'd made and today was the reason why he had no regrets. He was a trained military man and he would complete his self-declared mission.

As Gregory approached, Burt was able to secure his rifle. He fired shots in the direction of the target. The shots caused Gregory to stop advancing. Burt knew he'd bought himself no more than a second of time but he was determined to make the best of it. He cradled his rifle, ignored the pain in his shoulder, and advanced forward.

Harrison was in the decon unit. The door to the clinical work-space—the door leading to Jasmine and Sofia—was shut behind him. He noticed he didn't have Jasmine's pistol in his hand any-more and he figured he'd neglected to pick it up from the floor in the workspace when he'd fallen. He noted the heaviness in his arm and knew it wasn't totally due to the fall he'd taken a couple of minutes ago. He felt heaviness in his neck and legs as well. He felt warm. He had no doubt Gregory had released the modi-fied strain of GOF menglavirus. He knew infection had set in. He fought through the fatigue, but knew at some point, he would be unable to so do. He intended to hold on until Jasmine and Sofia were safe.

He glanced at the monitors in the decon unit and saw Greg-ory had moved away from the lab. Instead, he was advancing to-wards the colonel on the ground floor. Harrison knew he needed to deal with the threat in front of him, the astronaut, before he could hope to deal with Gregory. He went to the door leading into the prep room to apply pressure to it, trying to prevent the contractor's entrance into the decon unit, but he was too weak to keep the man out. The door swung open and Harrison was thrown against the floor.

He looked up and saw the contractor standing above him. The contractor was pointing a gun at him. Harrison waited for the shot. He knew he'd failed Jasmine and Sofia again.

He heard the gunshot. He felt the decon unit shake. He waited to feel pain tear through his body or maybe feel nothing at all as he simply sank into death. The pain didn't come. Neither did the nothingness. Instead, the contractor standing over him flailed backwards. He heard another shot and the contractor was thrust backwards again. Blood sprayed Harrison, and he heard the hissing of air being released from the positive pressure suit. Harrison didn't understand what had happened. He looked at his hand again, wondering if he had the pistol after all, thinking maybe he'd fired the shot. But he saw nothing in his leaden hand. He wiped at the blood on his face with his other hand, wondering where he'd been shot, but didn't find a wound on himself.

"Come inside, Harrison," someone said.

He looked up and saw Jasmine. Now he understood. She had the pistol in her hand and she'd been the one to fire at the man in the biosafety suit. She must've taken it from the ground in the workspace. She had her other hand outstretched and was waiting for him to take it.

He wanted to take it but knew he couldn't. He was infected with whatever modified menglavirus the senator had released in the house. He shook his head at her and forced himself to stay right where he was.

"Go back inside the workspace, Jasmine," he said. "I have menglavirus. I can feel it. It's a modified strain. Stay away from me. Please go back inside."

"I have it, too," Jasmine said. "Come inside the workspace, Harrison."

"How much of the vaccine were you able to administer?"

"All of it to Sofia. Some of it to me."

"The vaccine is boosted. Both of you will be okay. The induced antibody response to the virus will kick in within hours and you'll have full immunity within a day. Please go back inside."

"Come with me."

She still had her hand outstretched and now she reached down and grabbed his. He tried to let go, but she wouldn't let him. He allowed himself to get pulled up, back to his wobbly feet. But he didn't allow himself to go inside the biosafety workspace with her.

"I can't go with you right now," he said. "You and I cannot take the risk that I spread the modified menglavirus to Sofia."

"I'm already here. I'm already near you. I have it. She has it too."

"I have a different version. It's hundreds of times more virulent than what you and she might have. I know the vaccine will work against the typical menglavirus, but I don't know if it'll work for the version I have, the version that is floating through the house now." He closed his eyes and thought about V-202. He knew it would work for Sofia if she had the original strain. But with every second Jasmine stood exposed to the modified version *he* had was another second *she* was exposed. "A US Army colonel is in the house. He's going to get you and Sofia to safety. But I need to help him."

Before he could turn away from her, Jasmine embraced him. He felt her arms around his back and her head against his chest. He knew he should push her away but couldn't. He felt all of the love of fourteen years of marriage washing over him, the good and the bad that he'd put her through, the hopes and dashed dreams with which she'd had to deal. He wanted to hold onto her forever in order to make life right between them but he knew he couldn't. So he let go of her. He stepped back and she let him. They stood in silence in the decon unit, neither of them sure what to say next to the other. Finally, he reached past her and pressed the button next to the door leading into the workspace. The door clicked and he pulled it open for her.

"I'm sorry, Jasmine," Harrison said.

"I know," Jasmine said.

"Go," he said, and he touched Jasmine's lower back to urge her forward. She handed him the pistol. Then she went forward, returning to the workspace as Harrison stayed in the decon unit. He glimpsed Sofia again as Jasmine walked through the open door. He waved at her—he wanted to go to her but didn't—before making sure to close the door again.

Embracing Jasmine and seeing Sofia gave him one final burst of energy. He turned to finish the work he'd started. He hit the red emergency lock button on the adjacent wall of the decon unit. It was intended to stop the spread of a pathogen from the workspace to any other part of the house in the event of a breakdown of the lab's safety systems. After he hit the containment button for the laboratory, the door to the workspace clicked, a sign that it was now locked until the diagnostics system ran a full systems check. The diagnostics would take two hours. Jasmine and Sofia would be safe inside the workspace during that time. No one would gain access. There were emergency provisions in the workspace and he was certain Jasmine would find them.

The opposite wall—adjacent to the door leading into the prep room—had a similar red button. It sealed the entrance into the decon unit as well. He didn't press the second button. Instead, he pushed the door open into the containment unit and hurried next to the main door of the biosafety lab. He ignored the button on that wall as well as it would lock him inside the prep room. He pushed through the main door and stepped into the basement.

Immediately, he saw Gregory and the colonel. Gregory was advancing towards the colonel with his rifle raised. The colonel had already been shot once and he was struggling to aim his rifle. The colonel fired at Gregory but failed to connect. Gregory regrouped and advanced towards the colonel again. Harrison knew what he had to do. He couldn't feel his right arm, but he looked down, and saw he had Jasmine's pistol in his hand again. He raised the pistol, leveled it, and fired at Gregory. He missed with the first shot, and fired again, and again missed. But he got Gregory's attention. Gregory stopped advancing towards the colonel and turned towards Harrison instead.

Gregory looked haggard and angry. Harrison knew Gregory would always be angry. He would always feel as if he'd been shortchanged in medical school. Maybe he had. Harrison knew many brilliant physicians who'd struggled to make names for themselves. He knew circumstance and plain old luck were as important as the strictest diligence in obtaining success. Harrison had had good circumstances; he'd been lucky over his career as a physician-scientist. He'd stumbled into Richard's Salk Institute lab as a student and was taken under his mentorship. He'd gotten the breaks he'd needed.

For a moment, Harrison felt sorry for the man in front of him. But then he thought about the hundreds of millions of people who would die if the modified menglavirus spread from this house in La Jolla to the rest of San Diego and the rest of the country and world thereafter. Harrison tried to fire Jasmine's pistol again but couldn't muster the strength. The virus had taken complete control of his body. The pistol dropped from his hand. He thought that now was going to be the moment of his death. He felt his body slumping. He closed his eyes and waited for a gunshot to sound and a bullet from Gregory's rifle to pierce through his chest. He collapsed on the ground.

A gunshot sounded but a bullet didn't pierce through him. He opened his eyes. The colonel was standing again, struggling to maintain his stance, but keeping himself on his feet. He'd fired at Gregory. Gregory turned back around to return the fire. The colonel steadied himself and fired again. Harrison could see the years of training in the colonel's technique. The colonel connected, shooting Gregory in the face. Gregory staggered. The colonel fired twice more, hitting Gregory in the face again each time. Gregory fell to the ground as a bloody, deformed mess, only a couple of feet away from Harrison.

Harrison took one look. Gregory wasn't breathing.

Then he looked away and closed his eyes.

The raid was over.

"Hold up," Jason Carr said to his driver, although he didn't really need to say anything at all. The driver was a security contractor, just like the rest of his four-man team. They were in two armored Lincoln Navigators. Jason was in the rear of the first Navigator. Something—everything—was amiss at Richard's La Jolla home. The place resembled an overseas warzone. The front gate had been blasted and a fire was burning at the front of the house. He was suddenly thankful that the SUV was plated with bulletproof glass and outfitted with a bioweapon air filtration system.

"Looks like we aren't the only ones here, boss," Jason Carr's head of security, a multi-tour Afghanistan war veteran, said from the passenger seat.

"Definitely not," Jason said.

"What should we do, boss?"

On the way over, Jason had called the landline on which he'd spoken to Richard earlier. No one had answered. He'd called the cell multiple times as well. Again, no one had answered. He didn't need to see anything more to know why.

"We're here," Jason said to the security team. "And we have an objective. Are you guys up to it?"

"You hired the best, boss," the head of security said. "We'll be all right."

The driver parked the Navigator on the driveway, past the blown-in gates, and the second Navigator pulled in behind them. One by one, the teams got out of the vehicles. Each man had a combat biosafety respirator, rifle, and body armor. But as they started up the driveway, a young man in an army uniform approached them. The head of security lifted his rifle at the man and walked cautiously to him. They spoke for several seconds. Finally, the contractor radioed him. "He says there are four friendlies and five hostiles. Nothing we can't handle."

"Keep me updated on the radio," Jason said, and the security head gave him a thumbs-up.

Jason watched his team walk up the driveway. The soldier in the army uniform went with them. If there were circumstances to control in the house, his team would control them. He didn't know what—or who—his security team was going to find inside, but he knew they weren't going to find Richard alive. Richard had called him for a reason. He'd known his time had been limited. If Jason's security team found the hard drives Richard had promised, he would make sure to keep his word. He would do the Phase 3 trials, get emergency use authorization, and manufacture and distribute the vaccine globally at cost. He would make sure whatever had happened here tonight in La Jolla wasn't going to happen anywhere else. Richard had prepared for the end of the menglavirus era by prepping a vaccine and Jason would make sure that the vaccine happened.

Jason sat in the back of the armored Navigator and waited for

his team to bring him the vaccine that would end the menglavirus era.

Jasmine had watched on the monitors. She'd tried not to
watch but couldn't pretend she wasn't involved. Sofia hadn't
watched, though. Jasmine hadn't needed to tell Sofia not to
watch. She was too tired and feverish to muster the energy to
watch what she already knew she shouldn't.

Jasmine had watched Harrison advance towards the man
without a mask. She'd watched the man without a mask turn
around and advance towards Harrison as well. She'd watched
a wounded man in military fatigues advance towards both of
them. She'd watched until the man without a mask was dead.
Then she'd closed her eyes, taken a breath, and held Sofia.

She felt so tired. Now, when she opened her eyes again, she
didn't have to watch on the monitors anymore. She saw Harrison through the tempered windows.

Harrison was pushing through the main door. He staggered
into the prep room then pushed through the second door and entered the decon unit. He didn't push through the third door into
the workspace, though. Instead, he held his hand to the last window separating them.

Sofia seemed to sense her father was nearby. She looked up,
saw him at the glass, and wriggled out of Jasmine's embrace. She
went to the door, stumbling along the way, but was determined
to stay on her feet. She didn't look at the dead astronaut on the
ground as she went. When she reached the door, she pulled on
it, but it didn't open. Jasmine figured Harrison had activated a
safety system. He pointed to a small, white button near the door.
Sofia pressed it. Jasmine heard Harrison's voice. The button was
for an intercom.

"I love you, baby girl," he said.

"I love you, too, Daddy."

"You're going to be okay."

"Because of the shot?"

"Yes, because of the shot."

"Because of your shot?"

"It wasn't just my shot, baby girl. A lot of people—people you've met, like Uncle Richard and Selene, and even more people you haven't met—put together the shot. It wasn't just me. Not at all."

"Will *you* be okay, Daddy?"

"I'll be okay if you are. I'll be okay if Mommy is okay."

Jasmine got up from the floor and joined Sofia at the window. They kept the intercom on and Harrison and the two of them stood across from each other—Harrison on one side of the window and Jasmine and Sofia on the other—and after a few minutes when none of them could stand any longer, they sat with each other. They were separated by concrete and glass and connected only through an intercom but they sat together as a family for the first time in years.

EPILOGUE—14 YEARS LATER

The gloom of June had lifted two days ago, just in time for graduation. The skies were clear and the sun was strong and getting stronger by the hour. Sofia was on the University of California San Diego campus. She was sitting on the dais with her department classmates. She texted Selene to see if she'd found seating yet. Today was Sofia's college graduation.

Sofia had gone to college on a scholarship from Richard's foundation, which Selene had helped set up after his death. She was the forty-fifth student thus far to go through UCSD on a Richard Hahn, MD, Scholarship for Academic Excellence, but she hadn't received it simply because of Selene. She'd worked for it and knew she deserved not only the scholarship but the recognition she had gained during her undergraduate career. She was headed to Johns Hopkins Medical School in August, also on scholarship, where she planned to become a physician and scientist. Most people figured she was following in the footsteps of her father but they were only partly correct.

She'd survived menglavirus. Or at least, she'd survived the original strain. There'd been a modified strain released in Richard's house that rainy, violent night fourteen years ago. She still had some breathing problems for which she needed to use daily inhalers but she was able to hike and jog most of the time without issue. She knew the inhalers were permanent. Her pulmonologist had told her the MRILD she had—menglavirus-related interstitial lung disease—would only worsen over time, but for now she felt okay. She also knew medicine was a rapidly changing field. New treatments for MRILD were on the horizon. She was optimistic about the future.

Jason Carr, Richard's one-time business partner, had gotten her father's vaccine out to the public. Steptech, which once had been known mostly for its ruthlessness in the biomedical space, had utilized its global reach to manufacture billions of doses around the world while the US Army had spearheaded its distribution not only within the US but to every country that needed it, which, of course, meant every country in the world. Nowadays, the elderly Dr. Carr was long since retired, enjoying not only his wealth but the philanthropic recognition that had come with getting a menglavirus vaccine out to the public. In most circles, he was a hero.

Of course, Sofia knew who had actually developed the vaccine. She'd survived menglavirus because her mother had administered her father's vaccine to her. Her mother had self-administered the vaccine as well, but she hadn't survived. She'd lived several months before she'd finally succumbed to the chronic respiratory failure that had set in after her own menglavirus exposure. For a long time, Sofia didn't understand why she had survived but her mother hadn't, but when Sofia had turned eighteen, she'd finally gotten a copy of her mother's medical records, and found out her mother hadn't received a full vaccination dose. She had given the full dose to Sofia instead.

She missed her mother. She also respected her more than she imagined she would ever respect anybody else. She'd excelled academically to honor her mother and she understood that every time she studied or cracked a book or took an exam, she was honoring her. She remembered being home-schooled during menglavirus and the difficulties she'd given her mother during this time. She'd made sure to excel in her academics to tell her mother thank you in the only way that mattered. She wondered at times if her mother had known Sofia would turn around her academics. She couldn't help but think that her mother always had known.

Her father had died more quickly than her mother. He'd succumbed within hours. She remembered sitting next to him, separated by the glass and concrete of Richard's biosafety lab, while he struggled to breathe. Eventually, her mother had wanted to turn off the intercom, but Sofia hadn't allowed her. She'd sat with her father until he'd died.

Of course, she knew her interest in medicine came from him. She knew she was like him in so many ways and she tried to pick the best parts of him to emulate. Even as a graduating senior in college, she knew the pull of work when a person was passionate about it, the way it consumed a person, and she promised herself she would maintain perspective, but also knew everyone promised the same. She had an inkling she could end up being like her father, focused on work over all else, if she didn't deliberately try to be different.

She missed her father every day.

She also missed Richard—who always would be Uncle Richard to her—more than anyone could understand. He'd always been her friend and not just her godfather. She still had her tablet. It was old and slow but it worked. She looked at the photos of them still. She found herself talking to him in her head whenever she did. She remembered everything about their last embrace, every word he'd spoken to her fourteen years ago in the lab.

Thank you for visiting me, Sofia. Seeing you tonight has been the best surprise I ever could've had. I know you will become the exact person you want to become.

All of them—her mother, father, and Uncle Richard—had sacrificed themselves for her, not just on that horrible day fourteen years ago, but every day in their lives that led back to her. Others had sacrificed themselves as well, not just for her, but for everyone like her, everyone who'd grown up during menglavirus, everyone who'd known nothing other than the bleakness of that era. She spoke to the colonel from time to time. The army had stripped him of his command for his off-the-book mission, but he'd settled into a humanitarian career in the nonprofit sector. She'd last spoken to him at the start of the academic year when he'd been leading a measles vaccination project in Iraq. She would call him again this afternoon. He would be happy to hear she'd graduated today and she would be happy to hear about his latest inoculation effort.

Selene texted back, telling her she'd found a seat in the middle of the reception. From her own seat on the dais, Sofia looked out at the modest crowd. In the morning, the entire department had walked with the rest of the college at the athletic center. Now the microbiology department was having its own ceremony in the shaded quad outside of the student labs. It didn't take Sofia long to spot Selene. She was waving.

Selene had taken Sofia in after her mother had died. Selene had given her all of the love and order she'd needed to prosper. Selene had never tried to be her mother nor had Sofia looked to replace her mother but Selene had provided the guidance and support she'd needed and would always need. Sofia knew she would always be privileged to have Selene in her life.

She waved back at Selene. She waited on the stage for the satellite ceremony to commence. She knew today was the start of the rest of her life. Even though her mother, father, and Uncle Richard weren't physically here to see her, she knew they manifested in her daily actions. They were still here because *she* was still here. Parts of them were in her. As the satellite ceremony started, she smiled to herself. She was excited about what life was going to bring.

While Sofia Boyd graduated in San Diego, Pyotr Bobrov was in Koltsovo, Russia. He looked at the alarm notification on the control system workstation. The notification read F141. He didn't know what notification F141 meant other than the F related to the filovirus lab. He was new at the Russian State Centre for Research on Virology and Biotechnology. He was still trying to adjust not only to life in Siberia, but also his secluded life in a government biosafety level four laboratory. He'd gotten the position as a nighttime junior technician two weeks ago because his uncle was a top-level administrator within the Kremlin. Despite the nocturnal hours, the position was supposed to be a good one as it paid well and promised promotion. He wasn't very academic. He was nineteen and had only done two years at university in Moscow before flunking out. He preferred partying to studying. His uncle had made sure he would party no more, though, by shipping him to the lab in Siberia.

He was in a large monitoring room. Dozens of workstations lined the desk he was facing. He waited for notification F141 to pass. It didn't pass, so he typed the override code into the control system. Finally, the control system quieted. The notification alarm turned off.

He looked around the monitoring room. It was 0115 and he was manning the lab by himself. He knew he needed to figure out what notification F141 meant, but he didn't want to call the senior technician. The senior technician was home, asleep with his wife. The senior technician already disliked him. He had been skeptical of Pyotr from day one, warning Pyotr that mistakes were not tolerated in his labs. Pytor was supposed to know all of the nine hundred and seventeen alarm notifications generated by the control system. He didn't know more than five of them, though. He decided to keep quiet. He didn't want to wake the senior technician. He didn't call. He needed this position.

Worse, he feared his uncle. He didn't want to get on the wrong side of that man again. He knew his uncle wasn't going to give him another chance. His uncle would send him to Siberia's agriculture system next if he messed up again.

Yes, he would keep quiet.

When he got off of work, he would delve into the systems handbook. He would study and memorize the nine hundred and seventeen alarm codes, even if it took him months, so the next time there was a notification, he would know what it meant and what to do.

For now, though, he was pretty sure everything was all right.

ACKNOWLEDGEMENTS

Nicole Valdez, Erin Lynn Alstrom Cook, Jae Kim, Corey Kruisheer, James Jordan, Ellen Marker, and Keith Klein...thank you for your guidance and insight throughout.

ABOUT THE AUTHOR

Hassan Riaz

 Hassan Riaz is a writer and physician. His fiction has appeared in ANTIOCH REVIEW, SLICE MAGAZINE, FICTION ON THE WEB, and a dozen other publications. He has a primary care practice in the Los Angeles area. THE VACCINE is his first novel. You can find him at hassanriaz.com.